SEARCHING
FOR
SOLOMON HENRIQUES

A novel by Harry A. Ezratty

Read Street Publishing
Baltimore Maryland

www.readstreetpublishing.com

Searching for Solomon Henriques

By Harry A. Ezratty
ISBN: 978-0-942929-52-2
Copyright © March 2022

This is a work of fiction. Some of the characters portrayed in this novel were actual persons. Most historical events did take place, although conversations have been imagined.

Read Street Publishing
133 West Read Street, Baltimore, MD 21201
www.readstreetpublishing.com
editor@readstreetpublishing.com

Layout/Design: Richard Gottesman, Sutileza Graphics
Cover Design: Richard Gottesman, Sutileza Graphics
Front Cover Painting: Danijel Frka
Back Cover: A page from the Tables of Zacuto depicted behind the Rock of Gibraltar

BOOKS BY HARRY EZRATTY

Non-Fiction

How to Qualify for Multi-Bar Practice

The Seaman's Handbook of Rights

How to Collect and Protect Works of Art

Jews in the New World Trilogy
>*Vol. 1: 500 Years in the Jewish Caribbean:*
>>*The Spanish and Portuguese Jews in the West Indies*
>*Vol. 2: They Led the Way: The Creators of Jewish America*
>*Vol. 3: The Builders: Jews and the Growth of America*

Baltimore, A City Divided: the Pratt Street Riot

Fiction

Searching for Solomon Henriques

The Dan Nikolas Esq., series:
>*Flags of Convenience*
>*False Passage*

The Noah Pardo Series:
>*The Bureau of Military Information*
>*The 20-Cent Quarters (in preparation)*

DEDICATION

To Loren, who followed the road back.

1

BARCELONA, SPAIN
SEPTEMBER 1941

Lieutenant Jg. USN James Ennis awoke with a soft cry. Sitting up, he wiped a film of sweat from his forehead with the back of his hand and saw that his room was still dark except for a narrow sliver of daylight where heavy red drapes failed to lay tight against the room's only window.

He felt an unfamiliar pressure across his chest; as if a belt had been tightly wrapped around it. Was it fear? He moved his hand to the left, feeling for the soft, silky skin of Lucy's arm. She wasn't there. Why?

Disorientation ebbed as he began thinking. *Where the hell am I? Oh yes, not home. Barcelona, on my way to Gibraltar. The boat taking me there gets here tomorrow morning.*

He rubbed his eyes with his fists, hoping to clear away sleep's sticky haze. *What a dream that was. A real nightmare! So real. So frightening.*

The feeling in his chest was slowly disappearing. He could breathe now without the pain. But he still had the metallic taste of fear in his mouth.

Where was I in that nightmare? It was like a dungeon, very old. Thick stone walls surrounded it; only a few windows high off the ground. Yes, definitely a dungeon. Someone was being beaten! Me? I don't know; I remember men in rags lying on filthy sheets, trying to ignore the screams surrounding them. There was candlelight. And it was noisy, accented by a babel of languages from the prisoners – slaves? But it was so long ago. Never mind; I've got to get up and moving.

Rising from his bed, Ennis tried remembering the essence of his dream, but it was already disappearing, like wind-blown clouds scudding across the horizon. Only small fragments of it remained. Other parts, the ones that never make sense in such dreams, as when classmates, relatives and friends you haven't seen in decades play important parts, escaped him. He marveled at how and why these people were dragged up from his memory after all these years. Were they symbols of some sort? Yes, they're symbols. But symbolic or not, something in that dream had really frightened him.

Ennis stared again at the sliver of light on the wall by the drapes. It told him it was no longer night. The glow of the numbers on his wristwatch said 6:35 a.m.

Ennis had experienced such uncanny events before, but they were never accompanied by fear, nor the discomfort of pain. The first one he remembered was when he was a student at the Naval Academy. He had been reading in his room one night and a popular tune began running around in his brain. He turned the radio on and there was the same tune and at the same place it was playing in his head.

Another time, he was thinking about a friend and the phone rang. There was that same friend on the other end of the line. It happened too often to be coincidental. The incident that made him think he might have some special insight was when he was shopping at an outdoor farmer's market on a cold November weekend, near his home in New London, Connecticut. Some nights before, he dreamt he had met an old high school friend from his Springfield, Massachusetts days. In the dream, it was cold and his friend was wearing a dark blue overcoat with a long red scarf, the ends of which spilled down the front of his chest. He also wore a matching red knit cap pulled down over his ears. There, on the next weekend, was his friend warmly clad exactly as he had appeared in the dream. It finally motivated Ennis to visit a friend who was a psychologist.

"It's what we call precognition," his friend told him. "It's also called ESP, extra-sensory perception. That may be what you're experiencing. It's some sort of forethought, or clairvoyance if you will. We're only just beginning to get a handle on this. Some of my colleagues and professors are experimenting with it. There's a professor at Duke University; S.B. Rhine. He gets people to try and tell him what hidden symbols are on the reverse of playing cards. Some are good at it; most of us aren't. Rhine calls it parapsychology."

That conversation was seven years ago. The science of psychology in the 1930s knew that it occurred among a small element of the general population. Ennis had many of these experiences since that time, but none of the type he had just experienced. What made it very real was that for the first time, it had been accompanied with fear and pain. What psychologists had advanced was the theory of *déjà vu*, the concept that one experiences an event that occurred in the past as if it were occurring anew.

Get going, man! Forget the dream, get showered and dressed. Have breakfast, start the day. I have a little time to discover Barcelona, a city I've never been to. And this is the perfect September day to stroll along the city's streets.

He stumbled across the unfamiliar dark room, feeling his way to the bathroom. Turning on the overhead light, he squinted into the mirror, his eyes adjusting to the strong light as he prepared to brush his teeth and shave. At 28, there were no age lines on his face; nor grey threads in his dark brown hair. Not yet. No glasses either, for his green eyes. A silly thought, yet there were fellow cadets of his class at the Academy who did have grey in their hair already, and not just a few who had receding hairlines and used glasses for reading.

Ennis unbuttoned his pajama top and patted his stomach, verifying that it was still flat. He wondered what he would look like with a beard and a mustache. *Shave every day when you are in the Navy, Ennis. Your face must be as smooth as a baby's bottom, otherwise, you go on Report.*

༄ ༄

Dressed in civilian clothes, James Ennis strolled from his hotel to the nearby street called Las Ramblas, one of Barcelona's main thoroughfares. Once, before the Spanish Civil War of the late 1930s, this street had been lined with fine hotels, shops and merchant's stalls leading downhill to the City's port. The War had ended just over a year and a half earlier, and Ennis could see the lingering signs of battle. The outsides of buildings were pocked by shrapnel; many shops were empty and citizens of Barcelona were walking about wearing clothes that seemed too worn for this attractive city. Even at breakfast in his hotel, butter was sparingly offered and his waiter apologetically told him that milk was limited to one glass per person.

He put all that aside to enjoy this pleasant Fall day. A strong morning breeze blew around him. The yellow and red Spanish flag on a nearby flagpole snapped sharply in the wind. He could see the tall and slender monument to Christopher Columbus, or *Mirador de Colóm*, as it is known in Catalan. It was here in Barcelona that Columbus related to King Ferdinand and Queen Isabella the events of his historic voyage, offering a Caribbean native, brilliantly colored parrots and exotic fruits as solid proof of his exploits. Of course, in those days, he wasn't known as Columbus. He was Cristobal Colón…Cristavao Colóm as the Catalonians still insist on calling him. His discoveries would earn him the titles Don Cristobal Colón, making him a Spanish noble and, more important for him, the title he ached for: Admiral of the Ocean Sea, that vast body of water that would later be called the Atlantic Ocean.

Fluent in Spanish, Ennis knew from reading reports, that the citizens of Barcelona preferred to call themselves Catalonians instead of Spaniards, prompting the etched name Colóm, not Columbus, on the monument. Columbus was all things to all men. He was variously known as Genoese, Catalan, Majorcan and Spanish. Even, as some fools were claiming, Scandinavian.

Whenever possible, the people of Catalonia spoke a dialect called Catalan, instead of Spanish. Try as he might, Ennis was unable to make any sense of the signs he saw posted throughout the city in that language. Announcements in Catalan over radio stations were also a puzzle to him. But he knew that he was good – actually

4

talented - in languages and if he had the time, he could soon be fluent in Catalan. He already spoke Spanish, which he had studied and won honors in at Annapolis, and German and French, which he pursued on his own time. He knew that Catalan would not be difficult. He also liked to study the history of each country whose language he spoke, but the U.S. Navy's business always had priority on his time.

As he walked toward the harbor, he saw a furniture store, with the name Henriques as proprietor. He thought about how he would like to have the time to find out more about the beginnings of the Ennis family. It was a distinguished one. The first Ennis had changed his name from Henriques. Where had those Henriques people come from? When? And why had they changed their name? That was a family puzzle, which no one as yet had sought to solve. The first Ennis had fought and died in the Revolutionary War in the retreat from the Battle of Brooklyn in 1776. At the close of the 19th Century, after losing a prosperous business and the family fortune, the Ennis' entered politics. James' father became a Councilman, a Massachusetts State Senator and finally, a long-term Congressman from Springfield, Massachusetts. He used his influence to get his son James into the United States Naval Academy.

His great-great-grandmother was Miriam Mendoza: another Spanish name that intrigued him but left no clue as to the origins of the Ennis family. His father once told him, in a moment of confidential reflection, that Grandma Miriam had been quietly buried in the cemetery belonging to the Jewish community. His father left it without any further explanation. James had never thought to seek out her grave. *I'll check it out first chance I get,* he promised himself as he came closer to the water.

A 1937 graduate of the U.S. Naval Academy, Ennis earned a degree in Marine Engineering. After four years, he was now a Lt. Jg., assigned to the Electric Boat Company at Groton, Connecticut, builders of America's submarines. He was using his engineering skills as the Navy's representative to help in the manufacture of America's undersea boats. The United States was not at war, but President Franklin Delano Roosevelt had been casting a keen eye on conflicts in Europe and the Far East. He was beginning to

5

understand that Americans should start arming themselves. The Navy had sent Ennis to Gibraltar, Britain's naval base on the Mediterranean coast, to learn everything he could about England's submarines. America was now committed to mass producing submarines that were designated as the Gato Class.

When Ennis asked why he didn't fly directly to Gibraltar, the Commander in charge of vessel construction said, "It's important that you present yourself with the image of a businessman who is also taking some time out to sightsee. England and Malta have submarine bases that are under daily air raid attacks. In Gibraltar, you won't be disturbed or subject to such dangers. A fishing boat will pick you up in Barcelona and take you down the Spanish coast to Gibraltar."

Today, at the foot of Las Ramblas which ran to the city's old seaport, Ennis planned to explore what the experts believed to be a faithful reconstruction of the *Santa Maria*. It was permanently docked at a pier for tourists and scholars to explore. This was the largest of the three boats that included the *Niña* and the *Pinta*. The *Santa Maria* was the flagship Christopher Columbus commanded on his voyage to the Caribbean.

When Ennis learned he would be in Barcelona, he read about the city and made a list of things he wanted to see during his short time there. The *Santa Maria* and the Maritime Museum topped his list. Now, as he neared the pier on this fine September day, Ennis could see her: the *Santa Maria* had three masts etched against the sky, with sails tightly furled. He boarded the boat, mounting a wooden gangplank. As he moved through the *Santa Maria* his respect for Columbus rose several notches. The great mariner had always been one of his naval heroes.

Less than 68 feet long, the *Santa Maria* was the largest of the three ships and was constructed entirely of wood. She was fitted with just one small cabin aft. She had a crew of about 39, some of them not even professional seamen. One represented the Crown's financial and political interests, another was an interpreter, and there were also medical personnel aboard. Strangely, although Colón always made a point that one of his chief aims of discovery was to convert non-Christians to Christ, no priest sailed on this 1st trip. They would accompany Colón to the New World on his second and third voyages, which were colonizing ventures. His last trip, exploratory as was the first, again carried no priest.

Colón sailed his *Santa Maria* across 3,000 miles of unknown sea using a minimum of astronomical tools to help guide his way. As Ennis ambled through the boat, he marveled at the cramped holds and narrow deck spaces. This boat was little more than one third the size of the submarines America was building. Like the *Santa Maria*, submarines were acknowledged to be cramped and uncomfortable vessels. Walking across the decks, he had a sense of familiarity with her hatches and her planked decks, yet he had never been aboard such a boat before. He ascribed his familiarity to the deck plans and the many photographs and descriptions of the *Santa Maria* he had seen and read over the years.

However, when he entered the ship's only cabin, Colón's home, Ennis had a definite feeling of having been in this place before. Here was the captain's small desk and his sleeping bunk, its spare wooden frame crammed against a bulkhead. Somehow, he felt he had seen all this before. And it was while Colón sat at his desk.

In addition to their Captain, three crew members would crowd this cramped room. Yes, he had been here before, standing in front of Captain Colón, absorbing his charismatic presence. The briny smell of ocean-soaked tarred wood, and thick mooring ropes; the familiar feel of the deck beneath his feet; the sense of standing uncomfortably in this small space; having to crouch as he entered Colón's cabin, was not new. Was there also a feeling of humid air filling the cabin? The thick moist air of the tropics? He smelled salt air, but that could have been because the boat lay in Barcelona's harbor. Then he saw the cross on the bulkhead behind the desk and he had an acute sense of discomfort. He tried, unsuccessfully, to put the feeling aside. As Ennis left, he edged sideways past a line of tourists waiting to enter the cabin. Were these thoughts part of the feelings his psychologist friend had spoken about? A remembrance of past events?

The next morning, Ennis waited at a designated pier, luggage in hand. An 85-foot steel-hulled fishing boat chugged alongside him, its engine idling noisily. The boat's name was *Lolita*, the name

7

he had been told to look for. The operator poked his head out from the cabin's doors, calling out to him loudly in Spanish. "Señor Ennis, welcome aboard."

The fishing boat's wooden deck was slick with a thin film of early morning dampness. A crewmember took the bag Ennis passed across the gunwale. Noting the way he handled himself while boarding, the sailor realized that though his passenger was dressed in fine civilian clothes, he was no landlubber. His passenger safely on deck, the operator returned to his steering cabin and gunned the boat's idling engine. A blue-grey plume of smoke rose from the exhaust at the stern and *Lolita* jumped forward, proceeding south along Spain's Costa Brava.

The crewman, who had introduced himself as González, sat beside Ennis on a bench on the open deck. The autumn sun was warm and pleasant. The glare of the sun's light rose up from the Mediterranean Sea into the fishing boat like shards of broken glass. Passing along the Coast, and speaking in Spanish, González pointed out the country's main Mediterranean cities which lay to starboard: Valéncia, Alicánte, Cartagéna, Almeria and Málaga. Ennis observed busy maritime traffic outside all these cities. Spain's maritime life was bustling despite recovering from the ravages of her Civil War. Enjoying the warmth of the sun on his face, he thought his home in Connecticut was as pleasant as Spain's, this time of year.

Although Spain was calm and serene, across the northern Pyrenes Mountains, the natural barrier separating Spain from the rest of Europe, was a continent occupied by the German army. After swiftly defeating the surrounding European countries, Germany humiliated France by slicing it in two. France was occupied by the German Army in the north and by a friendly, puppet Vichy government in the South. Northern France was the base for daily air raids across the English Channel to a vulnerable England. Far to the east, the German Army had defeated a heroic Polish Army in just a few weeks. Germany divided Poland with its Russian ally. Today, in peaceful Spain, not a cannon nor a rifle associated with War could be heard.

Ennis could see North Africa. Spanish Morocco was to his left, just a few tantalizing miles away. He marveled at how close the

African continent nestled into Europe. He remembered its history; how, in the year 711, thousands of Moslem Berbers crossed this Strait of Gibraltar, the narrow gap between Africa and Europe. They invaded and finally conquered Spain.

Now he saw a highway snaking along the Moroccan coast. The sailor silently offered Ennis his binoculars. He made out a large truck, bright red Arabic writing on its side, speeding behind a yellow, open-topped sports car. There were some small buildings along the road and people were standing beside them, *perhaps drinking their morning coffee*, he thought.

After it passed Malaga, the fishing boat turned to starboard and pulled into the protected Bay of Gibraltar, trolling past a long pier and smoothly settling at a dock. Cutting his engine, the operator left his position at the helm, walked over to Ennis, shook his hand and in a perfect English accent, said, "Welcome to his Majesty's Dockyard on The Rock, Lieutenant. Keep walking straight ahead. Commander Ian McDonald is waiting for you."

9

2

GIBRALTAR
SEPTEMBER 1941

His Majesty's Docks was a busy place and, as one could see, on a war-time footing. It was bursting with representations of the Royal Navy's might; still undisputedly the world's largest and most powerful. Docked here were British and Canadian Corvettes, the swift escort-protectors of ocean convoys and dedicated pursuers of Germany's deadly U-Boats. They were commanded to destroy the German undersea predators with their depth charges, known familiarly as 'ash cans.' There were other larger ships of war here as well; Cruisers and Destroyers were jammed into all the available space inside the sheltered Bay of Gibraltar. Ennis could make out the flags of New Zealand and Australia on some of the warships lined up at piers or anchored in the waterway. Merchant vessels were also anchored here. Most had fled from their countries before they and their crews could be snapped up by the Germans. The ships were now dedicated to carrying the supplies and personnel necessary to defeat the Fascists.

This British Crown colony, with its imposing naval force, guarded the narrow Strait by which all ships had to pass between the Atlantic and the Mediterranean. This was England's strategic hold over her lifeline to the Suez Canal and access to her important Asian Colonies of Hong Kong, Singapore, Malaysia, Burma and India – and to the rich oil fields of the Middle East. No ships could pass through the 7.7 nautical miles at the Strait of Gibraltar without England's permission.

Gibraltar became a British colony in 1713, when Spain ceded the territory in perpetuity by treaty after the War of the Spanish Secession. Over 200 years later, General Francisco Franco, Spain's dictator, had other ideas about what the definition of perpetuity meant. The Fascist-leaning Franco would have been pleased to have England return the colony: then he would allow German and Italian warships to pass through the Strait. It would have demonstrated his attachment to and appreciation for the two dictators, Hitler and Mussolini, who had materially assisted him in his great victory over Spain's Republicans in the recent Civil War. For now, however, he was forced to be neutral, merely annoying and harassing the English. Having just won a debilitating Civil War, Franco's first priority was to rebuild a war-weary country. He was also dedicated to making life inconvenient for his British neighbors whenever he could. One way was to act as the eyes and ears of his German and Italian friends, as to Britain's activities in Gibraltar.

As Ennis arrived at this base located at the southernmost point of the Iberian Peninsula, the British were evacuating civilians to London and other parts of their Empire. Had a referendum been held today as to whether Gibraltar's citizens wished to return to Spain or remain British, its citizens would have overwhelmingly voted for the latter. The political situation regarding this small swatch of land, 1500 feet high, almost three miles across and nine miles wide, was the source of anguish for Spain and her political and diplomatic relations with the British Empire.

As the operator had said, Lt. Commander Ian McDonald was waiting tor Ennis. McDonald did not salute, as his American guest was not in uniform. A strong handshake and a wide smile substituted.

"Welcome to the Docks. We'll see to your gear, have some lunch and then get on to the business of your visit. I'm Lt. Commander Ian McDonald. Since we'll be working closely, you needn't call me Commander except in the presence of others. When we're alone, Ian will do."

"And I'm Jim, or Jimmy if you prefer," Ennis said.

McDonald was a cheery 30-year-old and like Ennis, a professional sailor. Tall, thin, with a board-flat stomach and bright blue eyes, McDonald had a shock of sandy blonde hair he could not tame. He was a contrast to Ennis, who was just under six feet, with brown hair and green eyes. McDonald nodded to a nearby sailor, who had accompanied him. The sailor snapped up Ennis' luggage and asked him to please follow him to his billet. After a wash-up and still in his civilian clothes, Ennis was escorted by McDonald to Gibraltar's Officer's Mess.

"I want to introduce you to my officers," the Commander explained. "There are only four of us on our boat, with a crew of 29 enlisted ranks. We're quite compact, you know. And when we're at sea, we are very informal in all ways, including our dress. Well, you'll see once you get aboard and we're out to sea. I have orders to take you out for a week, clear of the War zone. They sent you here to be free of air raids. Malta and the home ports in England get visited daily by the Hun's bombers. They want you out of harm's way, I suppose."

As they approached the dining room table, three submarine officers rose from their seats, announced their names, and shook hands with Ennis. They looked as if they were barely out of high school. After more than two years at war, England was calling up every qualified male it could muster, in this desperate fight for its life. The proof was here at this table.

That they had been at sea for almost two months also showed: most of the time submariners work indoors in tightly enclosed areas, even while the boat is on the surface. They had the familiar greyish pallor that Ennis had often seen on submariners at the Electric Boat Company. It was peculiar to all submariners just off patrol or sea trials.

McDonald explained Ennis' presence to his officers. "Lt. Ennis has come to us from America to learn all about how our submarines work. It seems that the American Navy is mass- producing submarines and they would like to learn whatever they can from us. And we are certainly pleased to oblige our cousins from across the sea. Any questions the Lieutenant may have, feel free to respond. Nothing is off limits to him. For all the time he is here, he is one of us. He has free access to our boat and to all of you, for that matter."

13

The three young officers smiled at Ennis. The one who looked to be the youngest, an Ensign, said, "Welcome to Gibraltar, sir."

McDonald continued. "You Yanks are not in the War yet, but this is a good step forward to your entry." It was said with genuine friendship as McDonald, holding a glass of Scotch whisky, aimed it toward Ennis and toasted him, saying "To the United States of America and her future role as our ally."

The young officers responded with "Hear, hear." With their whiskey glasses extended toward their guest, they clinked glasses and quickly downed the contents.

America was already involved, supplying England with ships of war, tanks, planes, weapons and ammunition. They were just short of standing beside her on the battlefields. Everyone in Washington and London knew that one delicate incident could bring America into the War.

Ennis sipped his own whisky, and then said, "Here's to England. May you defeat all your enemies."

Everyone smiled at this good will Ennis had spread. The four Englishmen understood that this was a sympathetic Yank dining with them. They also knew about America's unsympathetic Ambassador to England, Joseph Kennedy. He was a shamefully open admirer of Hitler and Mussolini. More than once, Kennedy had said publicly that the English could not defeat her enemies and would lose the War. He wanted all Americans to understand this and to urge President Roosevelt to discontinue the expensive – and to him – futile act of arming the English in a War his country should not enter.

Ennis noticed waiters bringing heaps of fresh vegetables, small tubs of butter, two pitchers of milk and a crusty bread to the table. "We're catching up on our fresh food after a long time at sea eating out of boxes and cans," McDonald explained. "We're barely a day back from 47 days at sea, so the crew is still being debriefed. Tomorrow, our boat starts a clean-up, some minor repairs, torpedo and weapon rearmament. We'll be in port a week or two, on leave. You came at a good time. We are the *Undaunted*. All submarines of the U class have names starting with the letter U. On this last patrol, we bagged an Italian troop ship and a small fuel tanker. We caught them as they were on their way to North Africa to beef up their army. We can start working tomorrow as the debriefing should be completed by then. Feel free to call on us for anything you need. Even though we are on leave, I'll get the crew to go out for a day or two so you can see how we operate."

"I thought I might walk around and see 'The Rock' for myself, as long as I'm free."

"Good idea. Dinner is at eight and we dress for it in military. See you then."

After lunch Ennis, now on his own, dressed in his uniform. Since the colony was being stripped of its civilians, he thought it best; it seemed everyone else was dressed in military. In the dining room and now on the street, there were many interesting-looking uniforms from different countries. Mostly from the British Empire, he guessed. There were also the Free Fighters who had managed to escape from their defeated countries, such as France, Poland and Holland. They joined England in the common struggle against Fascism. He strolled into the town, glanced into empty shop windows, and walked to a spot where he could look across into Spain. There, shading his eyes from the bright Spanish sun, he could see far into the country and toward the lush green plains of Andalusia. Five-hundred years ago, this was Islam's last remaining stronghold on the Iberian Peninsula. Far off, the bright green surrendered to a greyish-green and then into a hazy mist.

Despite the civilian evacuation, he noted a gift shop that was still open; most shops he had passed were shuttered. The sign on the shop's window read *La Casa de los Regalos*, the House of Gifts. It would be a good thing to bring something back for Lucy from this place. As he entered from the sunlit street into the cool, shadowy shop, a young lady perhaps 25 years old, rose from a chair on which she had been seated behind a counter. Her straight, jet-black hair was draped over her shoulders, and she had deep black eyes and long lashes that were as dark as her hair. She peered at Ennis in an almost embarrassing way.

"Welcome back," she said in a firm voice that betrayed an English accent overlain with another one unfamiliar to Ennis.

"I'm sorry. I've never been here before," Ennis replied.

The young lady looked carefully at Ennis before saying, "Excuse me. I must have mistaken you for someone else." But she was obviously not satisfied with his comment and continued to stare at him. It was almost rude, and Ennis felt uncomfortable. He broke her stare by saying, "I thought all the colony's civilians were being evacuated from Gibraltar."

"My family insists on staying behind. We won't leave here. Can I help you with something?" With a sweep of her hand, she called his attention to the amply stocked shelves around them.

"I'd like to get something for my wife. For the kitchen, I guess."

"Might she like this?" She held up an interesting-looking hand-carved and brightly painted trivet. She told Ennis it was made by Spanish Gypsies and informed him as to its price. "It's unusual," she explained. "Most trivets will hold only one pot. This one will hold three. It's very handy."

Ennis smiled. She was a first-class saleslady. "That looks fine. I'm sure she'll like it. Can you wrap it up?"

"Certainly."

After putting the trivet in a box, she covered it in multi-colored wrapping paper, a precious War-time commodity in short supply. The woman looked closely at Ennis again, carefully thinking about what she was going to say. She paused, then gathered the courage to go on.

"My name is Esther. Esther Alhadeff. The Alhadeffs came here to Gibraltar many years ago, from Morocco." She pointed in the direction of Africa. "I was not even born when they came here. We are Jews. The English have treated us well in Gibraltar. More than a quarter of us living here are Jewish. That's why I will never leave this place, no matter what the Germans and Italians do. Gibraltar is my home. No one can chase me away. Until now, it's been quiet. There have been no air raids like those experienced in England and Malta. I expect it will stay that way. We are so close to Spain, and we are so small that any bombs dropped here would almost certainly end up in neutral Spain."

As she spoke, Esther Alhadeff was fussing at a shelf beneath the counter. Finally, she located what she was looking for: a scrapbook bound in soft white leather. She carefully laid it on the counter.

Across the cover, hand-printed in bright red ink, were the words MEETING OF EUROPEAN JEWISH LEADERS. GIBRALTAR, 1938. She opened the book, which contained photographs and many printed agendas for the meeting, pasted on stiff sheets of black paper. She stopped turning the pages and swiveled the book around, so Ennis could see it. She pointed to a glossy black and white photo and to one man among several, all of whom were sitting around a table. They were all smiling, drinking coffee and wine and smoking cigarettes. Esther was seated among them, smiling and holding a cup of coffee.

"Do you know this man?" she asked. "He looks very much like you. He is who I thought you were."

Ennis was startled. "He does look like me!"

"Yes. That's who I thought you were when you came in. He was one of the participants to the meeting we held here in 1938," Esther said, while pointing to the words on the book's cover.

"Who is he? Where is he from?"

"As I said, he was one of the delegates. He is from Amsterdam. You are Jewish?

"No. Do you know this man's name?" Ennis persisted.

"Yes. He is Aarnald Henriques."

When Ennis left the shop, at Esther's advice he walked to the border between Spain and 'The Rock.' It was closely guarded on both sides. A barren causeway of hard-packed, ochre-colored earth ran from Gibraltar into Spain. It looked like a deserted no-man's land. Nothing was growing there. Ennis imagined innocent men being gunned down for violating the neutrality of this insignificant patch of land. He walked over to an English military policeman at the border post. After receiving a crisp salute, which he returned, Ennis asked, "How do I get into Spain, Sergeant?

"I'm afraid it's a bit dicey, Sir. The Spaniards ain't too happy to see people entering from here. From Gibraltar, I mean. They don't recognize our right to be here, you see. They make up excuses for creating long delays and they figure out all kinds of ways to keep people from entering from this side. They want Gibraltar back, Sir, and so they can make life uncomfortable for us, they do. If we gave it back, we'd have Mussolini and his nibs Mr. Adolf Hitler here in a flash. Is this your first visit here, Sir?"

"It is, Sergeant."

"Then if you don't mind a suggestion, Sir, you might get out of your uniform and into civvies and sign up for one of those tours like some innocent tourist." The sergeant pointed to a group of boxy-designed automobiles, all black and of 1930s vintage, lined up nearby. "You being an American and all, not sounding like an Englishman, you could get across easily with a tour."

"Thank you, Sergeant. I might do that."

James Ennis looked out across the roadway from Gibraltar leading into the vast expanse of Spain toward Cordoba and Seville, and said to himself with an uneasy sense of alarm; *I might have been here before.*

3

THE PORT OF PALOS, SPAIN
JUNE 25, 1492

Hundreds of families, mostly Jews, a few Moslems sprinkled among them, were jammed along the beach at the Spanish port of Palos, south of Seville. They were preparing to set out on the sad and depressing exile from their ancient Iberian homeland. Some were heading west for nearby Portugal; others would be sailing further east to the Ottoman Empire on ships sent to fetch them by the Great Sultan of the Empire, Bayazid II. These people were being evicted from Spain because of their religion. Some were lying on the ground, awaiting their turn to board the anchored vessels.

One of the waiting Jewish passengers this dreary day was Abraham Zacuto, a one-time advisor to Queen Isabella and King Ferdinand on the important matters of the world's geography and its trade routes. He also explained the mysteries of the heavens to them. A true Renaissance man, he taught Mathematics at the University of Salamanca where Jews were prevented from teaching. But a Catholic Bishop, impressed with his genius, had personally sponsored him. Zacuto was also a Rabbi, a philosopher, the creator of navigational instruments, nautical maps and author of the legendary "Tables of Zacuto," used by the great seafaring explorers, Cristobal Colón, Ferdinand Magellan and Vasco de Gama. The Tables accurately predicted the movement of the sun, moon and the then-known planets, as they made their way around the sun. During Zacuto's lifetime, all serious mariners who sailed the seas consulted his books and plotted their positions using his upgraded instruments. He had even advised and personally encouraged

Cristobal Colón, who would soon be leaving on his own voyage for the New World, in his efforts to obtain backing for this venture. "You will succeed after much difficulty," he had predicted. Today, Zacuto was bound for Portugal, where one of his university students, Josef Vecinho, an advisor to the Portuguese King, had arranged a position for him at Lisbon's Royal Court.

But today, on this June day, Zacuto had written in his memoirs, *"On Monday, the 25th of June of the year 1492, I left at noon, never to return, because the king, Don Fernando, and the Queen, Doña Isabela, annihilated be their names and memory, banished all the Jews who lived under their rule..."* Doubtless, Zacuto's fellow exiles at Palos waiting on the beach to be taken away, felt the same.

José Pereira and his family, among those many unfortunates at Palos, sat at a crowded, overflowing café on a hill overlooking the Harbor with their cousin and close friend, Felipe Henriques. The exiles were not permitted to take anything of value with them; they had been forced to sell their homes and businesses for much less than real value.

Felipe Henriques, a descendant of a Jewish family that had been forcibly converted a half-century earlier, would remain in Castile as a Catholic. His family had served Castile's Royal House for almost one-hundred years. Originally settled in Cordoba, the Henriques family moved to Seville to better serve their masters. Their cousins, the Pereiras, had never converted, choosing exile instead. They had worked out a plan to salvage their assets and José was explaining the necessary financial requirements to Felipe.

"Felipe, I finally received all the documents for a sale. Here are the deeds to both my house and shop and their keys. I already sold all the stock from my leather business. Everything's been deeded to you for ten percent of its real value. That's what most Jewish properties have been selling for. Everyone knows we must sell our property by Royal order. Might as well just give it away. It's all legal, the sale I mean. Paco Moreno, the Notary, made sure it was a proper and legal transaction." José slid a packet of papers and a ring of keys across the table to Felipe.

"Good," Felipe Henriques said. "As soon as you are settled in Portugal, let me know how to reach you. I will sell the property for its real value and send the money on to you."

Felipe had already spent hours trying to convince José to convert, so that he could remain in his homeland and continue life there as the Henriques family had done 50 years ago. He finally stopped trying, convinced it was useless. The two men, friends and cousins, embraced, each wiping tears from his face. Felipe kissed José's wife and their two children, finished the last few drops of his wine, paid the café bill and watched José and his family head down the hill to the pier and exile.

This was the end of the *Conveniencia,* that golden era in Spanish history when Jews, Christians and Muslims respected each other and worked together to make Spain a special place. Felipe remembered his father telling him proudly that Spain was not like the rest of Europe. Many of its citizens could read and write; there were great institutions of learning here, libraries, and marvelous cities with wonderful architecture, lit at night with torches so that one could enjoy the city during the evening, unlike other European cities. And there was respect for the followers of all faiths.

"Remember, Felipe," his father would say, "how all religions were once respected in Spain. In the city of Seville is the stone tomb of the great King Alfonso *el Sabio,* Alfonso the Wise. On the base of that tomb there are carved inscriptions extolling him in Spanish, Latin, Arabic and Hebrew, for everyone to see; proof of the Jew's importance and his special place in Spanish society."

As Felipe watched the backs of his cousins receding toward the pier, he felt something was wrong: it shouldn't have been a perfect summer's day, cooled by a mild sea breeze. There shouldn't be a bright azure sky with puffy clouds and hawks silently circling the beach seeking to capture morsels of food for their meals. This was a day that should have been dark and depressing, with clouds concealing the sun, perhaps even accompanied by a cold drizzle of penetrating rain. Such dismal weather would have been more appropriate and in keeping with the terrible events occurring this day.

Felipe left the café, walking in the opposite direction from his cousins, wondering whether he would ever see them again. Then he pushed the rest of the way up the hill to where Pedro Alvarez, the Henriques family overseer, was waiting for him. The two of them would together make the tedious trip back to Seville. As he reached the crest of the hill and walked toward Pedro, he thought, *What kind of rulers do we have that throw so many thousands of good citizens out of the country? This is their home; they have lived here for centuries. They wanted to make this place great and famous for its revival of ancient Greek and Arabic sciences, literature and philosophy. Why didn't José stay? We Henriques, and other families, still remember and honor our Old Faith in secret. We do so in peril, but we don't forget our ancestors. True, it is dangerous. Even close advisors of the King and Queen have been arrested and made to do humiliating penance for their heresy. After I retired, the women of my family told me of the secret; that they were praying in the Old Faith. Of course, I always knew what they were doing; I wish they hadn't told me. Now I am formally burdened with this information which I had long suspected.*

Felipe's thoughts were interrupted by Pedro Alvarez, who handed him the reins of his mule. He said, "You said a tearful goodbye to the Pereiras, Don Felipe?"

"Yes, Pedro, it was very sad."

"They are good people, sir, Don José and his family. They do not deserve what is happening to them. I am a good Christian, Don Felipe, but I cannot understand what is going on. Why do we do this to them?"

"Nor I. It is a political matter."

"You must be careful now, Sir. Now they are looking for anyone who practices the Hebrew rites secretly. The Inquisition has its many ways of finding out who such people are."

"All of us could be in trouble regardless of who we are," Felipe said. "All of Castile is wary of every relative, friend and neighbor. Jealousy, competitors for a woman's love, business rivals, even just dislike of a person are reasons for denunciation, even where there is no heresy."

"The Henriques family have been advisors for a long time to the Royal family of Castile. Surely, the Queen will keep your family safe. And your son Jaime will be sailing with Captain Colón as the Queen's representative. What an honor, Don Felipe. Hopefully, these are shields for your family's safety."

"Pedro, no one is safe from the Inquisitors. They have arrested priests, Monsignors, Bishops and even personal advisors to the King and Queen. Even though we have been overseers to the Queen's royal household, as you are to ours, why should the Henriques family feel it has a special immunity?"

Pedro was quiet for a long while, as the mules picked their way across the stone-filled highway to Seville. Finally, he said, "When Doña Flora closes the dining room and draws the drapes; I know she is in prayer. I stand outside the door to make certain no one interrupts her. No one will ever know what she is doing, certainly not from me."

The two men rode along, mostly in silence. It was a perfect summer month, not yet oppressively hot. Birds were soaring above them and a fresh breeze off the Mediterranean cooled the travelers. Felipe Henriques finally said, "You are a good man, Pedro. Perhaps, for your own safety, you should look to serve another family with less danger at its doorstep."

"And where would I find another family that treats me as one of their own? That has me sit with them at their meals? That shares their secrets with me? I have no wife or child, only my sister. You are my family. No, Don Felipe, I stay with you and the Henriques family, unless you force me to leave."

The two men rode on. No more words passed between them until they returned home, where Flora Henriques greeted them at the door with obvious fear in her voice. "The Cardonas, two houses from us, were arrested by the Inquisition while you were gone. They found religious candles in their basement and a menorah. We must expect that they will eventually name us as secretly praying in the Old Faith. I have often prayed with Maria Cardona."

Without being told, Pedro Alvarez began gathering up all the religious items used by Doña Flora. He placed them in a sack and stowed them in the back of a closet in a woodshed in the Henriques garden. Then he placed several sacks of mulch over them. As soon as it was dark and everyone was asleep, he quietly dug a large hole and placed the sack within it, covering it with soil and mulch.

Felipe Henriques sold José Pereira's property within the week. A heavy feeling of doom lay over him since he heard of the Cardona arrest, and he wished to complete this transaction as soon as possible. Two months later, he received a letter from José. It read:

> *Dear Cousin and friend Felipe,*
>
> *We are all well and are now living in Braganca in Portugal, on the other side of the border. I can be reached through Martin Ordones, a merchant in Braganca. He is aware of all my transactions and can be trusted. He is my new business partner. Matters may be sent to his attention.*
>
> *Your cousin and friend, José*

Felipe sent a gold note for the sales amount, drawn on the banking house of Delgado de Granada, in favor of Martin Ordones in Braganca, Portugal. A month later, Inquisition guards knocked on the door of the Henriques home to take Felipe and Flora away. The Cardonas had caved in under torture. The Henriques children, Manuel and Alicia, left their home the day after their parents were arrested. No one in the neighborhood could help the guards as to the children's' location, as no one knew where they were. The house was locked, and neighbors told the guards that the overseer, Pedro Alvarez, had not been seen since the Henriques were arrested.

Some of the neighbors said that before he disappeared, Alvarez was seen rummaging through the Henriques' home. "Probably looting the place," one neighbor suggested. "He knows where all the valuables are."

Pedro was indeed collecting all the valuables he could find: gold and silver chains, bracelets, coins and rings. They would be needed to care for Felipe and Flora's surviving children. Especially if they were forced to flee Spain to save their lives.

A month later, a message arrived at the empty Henriques house. It was seized by inquisitional guards. It came from Portugal, from José Pereira, thanking Felipe for his help and with heartfelt love from all the Pereiras. Then José wrote, "May the Pereiras have the opportunity to repay the Henriques' good deeds of love and loyalty."

This letter was used by the Inquisition as primary proof of Henriques' heresy and illegally assisting Jews. Before receipt of the letter, the Inquisition had treated Felipe and Flora with some respect. They suffered only interrogations and minor inconveniences. After the letter, they were subject to painful tortures and were finally condemned as unrepentant heretics. For their stubborn refusal to name others complicit in their sins, as punishment they were consigned to the dungeon where experts at questioning recalcitrant heretics worked to loosen tongues.

ɘ ɘ

To be arrested by the Inquisition was an act of terror. It was a physical and mental ordeal, which it was carefully crafted to be. Inquisitors, according to Church or Canon Law, were not permitted to draw blood, nor to kill a party while in their custody or under investigation. As a result, some highly sophisticated torture procedures and machinery were devised to comply with this rule. Pouring water through a cloth into a suspect's mouth, replicating the sensation of drowning, or the agonizing pressing of a thumb screw were only two of the favored procedures. If a person was eventually condemned to death, the Inquisitors turned him or her over to the civil authorities to handle the matter of the heretic's demise.

When Felipe and flora Henriques appeared before the Inquisitors, they were permitted no counsel for representation. If, on some rare occasions counsel was permitted, he was selected by the Inquisitors and could not examine a witness. An accuser, his or her face completely covered to maintain anonymity, faced the accused while a litany of heretical acts was presented, all intended to accuse the condemned with the sins he was alleged to have performed. No questions by the accused were permitted of the accuser.

The process began with mere inquiries, especially for honored persons as Felipe and Flora. An accused appeared before a panel, usually of three priests. The accused were urged to confess to his or her heresy by pinch-faced, thin-lipped Inquisitors who never revealed what the actual heresy was. Thus, the accused couple had to guess at what their crimes were. They were the ones the Cardonas had accused them of. But how could Felipe and Flora know what they were?

Often under torture, an unfortunate might confess to a made-up heresy to relieve himself of the constant, ongoing pain. Then he would be told that was not the heresy of which the Inquisitors were aware; the one of which he was being accused. Felipe and Flora were finally accused of Judaizing, a serious heretical act and were told to reveal the names of those who were associated with their heresies. This, Felipe and Flora refused to do. When Felipe was shown the letter indicating he had sold property on behalf of a Jew to avoid the law, he said, "That is not a crime of heresy. It is at best a civil or criminal concern that should be tried by a Civil Court, not a Church Tribunal."

The head Inquisitor smiled; his lips as colorless as his voice. "Ah, but it is, Don Felipe, if we can show that one Jew was helping another. I suspect that in this case, that will not be too difficult."

"Then I demand a lawyer who will petition the Civil Court for the right to argue my case there."

"You shall have no access to lawyers. We shall decide your guilt or innocence here." With that said, the Inquisitor slammed his desk with an open palm, accenting the finality of the decision. It sealed the couple's fate. Their refusals to confess to any heresy finally condemned them to the Inquisitorial dungeon.

Their first sight of the place where torture was applied as a method of extracting confessions was chilling. As they descended the stairs into the large space, the sight of the activities below them struck fear in their hearts. At the foot of the steps, a man was laying on a wooden table, his bare feet exposed. He was receiving blows to his feet with an iron bar. His tormentors were obviously at it for a while, because the recipient of this treatment was almost unconscious, his reddened feet swollen to proportions Flora could never have imagined. A large, hot fire was burning in a nearby hearth and there were several branding irons set into the burning coals. Their shafts were glowing red hot. The heat covered this corner of the dungeon like a suffocating blanket.

At the far corner of the room, a man with his hand stretched out on a table, was howling as a sweating, un-shirted brute was turning a vise-like device which clamped his fingers under great pressure. A wall rack lay unused for the present. Nearby, two men were hanging by their arms which were tied behind their backs. A man and a woman lay unconscious on the floor. Felipe concluded that they had been tortured close to death, as he knew Inquisitors were not permitted to kill or draw blood during these torture sessions. A foolish concept at best. Who knew which man or woman's delicate physical condition would give out during torture and result in an unwanted death?

They started with Flora, removing the top part of her garments, exposing her breasts. All the men stopped their work for a moment to gaze at her nakedness. They tied her hands behind her back, inserted a cloth deep into her mouth and poured water over it. Gagging, she felt she was drowning. Felipe had to watch his beloved wife at death's door, not knowing if it would be an instant too long before the cloth was removed, a mistake that could result in her death.

They hung Felipe off the floor, his arms tied behind his back. Later, water was also poured down his throat. Frequent beatings were carefully applied to prevent the drawing of blood. They stretched Flora's body on a rack, placing her fingers in a vise and beat the soles of her feet until they were so swollen she was unable to walk, put on stockings or slip her feet into shoes. She had to be carried back to her cell after the day's sadistic work. Felipe was stretched on the rack and hung again; left for two days dangling without food or drink, soiling himself as he swung in mid-air.

Flora and Felipe Henriques, brutalized and half conscious, were adamant. They would not reveal any names. The frustrated Inquisitors finally turned them over to the local civil authorities to arrange for their death, which had been ordered by the Church. They were to be burned upon a pyre of dry twigs. Should they repent at the last minute, they would be garroted before the twigs were torched, to avoid the pain of a fiery death. Their ordeal would be witnessed by a festive crowd of thousands; for Felipe and Flora were not alone that day. Others were burned alongside them.

Those facing lesser crimes and punishment marched before the crowd in a parade of shame, wearing a special yellow mocking garment called the *sanbenito*. It was painted with a representation of the devil holding a pitchfork, while rising up from the flames of hell. Later, the garment would be nailed to a wall of the church the family attended. Often the cloak would hang there for centuries. With their names emblazoned on the *sanbenito*, the family would forever be associated with Judaic heresy. Spain and the Church would never forgive these religious criminals.

Flora and Felipe refused the garrote. They went to their death in the month of December 1492, accompanied by the cheers of many laughing spectators as well as the hawkers of cakes and wine, who hoped to make sales from the applauding spectators.

Human ashes rose to the sky, dimming the sun over Seville.

4

THE ISLAND OF CUBA
JANUARY 1493

On a warm winter day, Jaime Henriques, ignorant of what his parents had undergone in Seville, stood before his Captain, Cristobal Colón, who was seated on a low wooden stool in a quiet corner of the deck of his new flagship, the *Nina*. Jaime was clad in a filmy cotton shirt and cotton breeches. All clothing protocol had been cast aside ever since the first day the crew came ashore on the island of San Salvador. Colón, and those who were expected to act as soldiers, including Jaime, had donned steel body armor and helmets. The hot sun beating down on them caused the explorers to feel as if they were trapped inside an oven. From that time on, armor was used only in battle or when enforcing the law.

Colón was scratching entries into the ship's log, using a long goose quill. His former flagship, the *Santa Maria*, no longer existed. She had been stripped of all her useable gear after having struck a reef on Christmas day. A careless crew member, charged with the watch, fell asleep. During his slumber, the boat slipped from her moorings and moved onto a reef. The reef's rapier-sharp rocks knifed long gashes into her hull. Her holds rapidly flooded with seawater, until the *Santa Maria* lay useless.

She would be converted into a land fort, constructed out of her salvaged timbers and gear: cannon, tackle, sails, water kegs, wires, etc. Thirty-nine of the flotilla's crew volunteered to remain in Cuba, since the smaller boats, *Nina* and *Pinta*, were unable to accommodate three full crews. Colón would return, he promised, as soon as he could to relieve the men who stayed behind. The makeshift fort, the first European community in the newly discovered Caribbean, was called *La Navidad* after the holy Christmas season and the day the *Santa Maria* died on a Cuban reef. The *Nina* had no cabin, so Captain Colón had to work wherever he could find space: in the corners of the *Nina's* holds, along the mid-ship bulkhead, at her stern, sometimes even on the safety net strung out to the bowsprit on the boat's forepeak. No mind. He truly preferred standing at the helm of the livelier and easier-handling *Nina*, which he looked forward to commanding on the long return trip to Castile. She sailed much better than the aggravatingly sluggish *Santa Maria*. He had to give up his privacy though, but that was only for this one voyage. He would sleep beside his crew, but he was still their captain, no questioning that.

Colón was making all the necessary preparations for the trip back to Castile. He was anxious to return to the royal court of Ferdinand and Isabella to relate the tales, first-hand, of his adventures and to enjoy his rewards, financial, social and political. He would become famous and vindicated. His discovery would bring him all the honors he had sought. This had already been agreed to by Colón and Ferdinand and Isabella in *Los Capitulaciones de Santa Fe*, the contract between himself and the Crown. Colón's magnificent efforts would seal forever the mouths of his many doubters and detractors. And more, he was now a Don, a nobleman, and he had earned that other title, Admiral of the Ocean Sea. Cristobal Colón and his heirs would enjoy these titles forever.

"Yes, what is it, Henriques?" Colón asked, while looking up at the young man standing before him, who was blocking the sun's rays on the document he was writing.

"I have the loading report you requested, sir, regarding such food, drink and other necessaries we'll be needing for our return trip to Castile. I need your permission to begin loading the boats. I took it on myself to ready the cargo before you saw the final loading plan. It awaits your approval."

"Ah yes, Henriques. Let me see what you've prepared."

Colón's piercing blue eyes scanned the report and at the same time he was also taking measure of this young crew member, just a few years out of his teens. He had dark brown hair, soft, pleasing grey eyes and was tan and lean after having worked for many months at sea and in the newly discovered islands. While Colón was well over six feet, very tall for these times and towering over all his crew, young Henriques was only an inch or two shorter than his Captain, whom he adored. Colón had early during the voyage noted that this young man spoke with the precision of someone born into quality, not with the rough accents of the street. Nor did he use the bawdy language of those who made their way at sea. He looked at the loading plan.

"Well prepared, Henriques, and very thorough, too. I know you're not a seaman by profession. Nevertheless, you seem to have taken well to the sea."

"I have come to love the sea, sir."

"We've had little chance to speak at length during our voyage, but the Queen chose well when she appointed you to act as her representative overseeing her interests." Colón held up the plan as proof of his statement. "Your family has been close to her Majesty, I've been told."

"We have served the royal family of Castile for over a century, Captain. I was raised with the duty to serve the Crown in all its wishes, which I have tried to do."

Henriques felt awkward hovering above his Captain, forcing him to look up at one of his crew. The young man bent low so that he sat on the heels of his feet while talking to Colón at the same eye level. He saw that Colón appreciated the gesture, because he smiled. The Captain could be a martinet. Henriques had observed that more than once during the long and difficult voyage across the Ocean Sea. Seeing him smile now, Henriques was aware he was pleasing his Captain, who was unexpectedly revealing a softer side to his personality.

"And from what I have seen, you have been doing an admirable job of it. When we return to Castile, I will be assuming the title, Admiral of the Ocean Sea. I'll be sailing again, and I'll need bright young men to serve with me. Have you thought of what you'll do after we return to Castile?"

"I have not, Captain. My family owns many properties. They have always assumed I'd take charge of them to insure they produce a good income for us."

"Well, think about serving with me on future voyages I will be making. You would stand to earn a great deal of money from your position. For now, I want you to continue to assist in loading all these necessaries aboard. We don't have the same space we had on the larger *Santa Maria*. You might also consider using water casks as ballast."

"Yes, sir. I have already started. And I have thought of water casks as ballast. See it here, sir?" The young man pointed to a line in the boarding plan. "May I begin loading, sir?"

"Yes, Henriques." Colón nodded approvingly as he returned the loading plan.

Henriques took the plan and rose, feeling a cramped stiffness in his legs. He stretched them out to banish the pain. He saluted his Captain and walked toward the bow. Boxes and packages of cargo lay piled up on the ground alongside the boat, waiting to be loaded. In the tropical sun, half-naked, sweating seamen were laboring with the cargo. They began loading using a boom, lifting ship's stores that were collected in a swaying cargo net. He saw the ship's interpreter, Luis de Torres, on deck marking off the stores as they came aboard. He was using another copy of the list Jaime had made for the Captain.

Henriques enjoyed spending time with de Torres during their long voyage. He discovered that the other man spoke many languages. While Henriques spoke only Spanish, Portuguese and Latin, he planned to add more to his array. De Torres was no rough sailor. He spoke, read and wrote well; he was cultured and learned, too. While at sea, both men made efforts to learn the seaman's special language. They came to call each other Luis and Jaime, as friends would. Early into the voyage, de Torres felt comfortable enough to confide to Jaime that he had been the Chief Secretary to the Governor of the Catalonian province of Valencia. Because he was a Jew, he had been forced from his position shortly after January of 1492, when the Edict of Expulsion was issued by Queen

Isabella and King Ferdinand. By August, all who refused to convert to Christianity were forced to leave Spain on pain of death.

"Where did you learn your Hebrew, Luis?" Jaime asked, after Torres mentioned that he spoke that language as well.

"At home. My Hebrew name is *Yusef ben Levi ha Ivri*: Joseph, son of Levi the Hebrew. Captain Colón wanted me on the voyage because he knew I speak many languages. But I couldn't sail as a Jew; only if I converted. So the night before we left, the Captain arranged for a priest to come to the dock to convert me.

Luis looked silently past Jaime with glazed eyes. Jaime thought it was wrong that a man so accomplished had to give up everything in his life, simply because of his religion. Yet Jaime, whose family were retainers to royalty, felt his King and Queen had good reasons for what they did. It was not his place to question the Crown, only to serve it as the Henriques family had always done... and faithfully, he knew.

After several conversations with Luis, Jaime felt secure enough to tell his new friend, "You know, Luis, my family were forced converts in 1432. My grandfather used to tell me there was a raid on the town where he lived as a young boy. It resulted in the conversion of many of its Jews. We have been Christians since then."

"Anusim," Luis said.

"What's that?"

"It's Hebrew. It means Jews who were forcibly converted."

"I never heard that term before. Sometimes they call us New Christians, as if it were a plague. Then, there's that ugly term *Marranos*, swine. I suppose Their Majesties think they'll resolve the problem of Jews and Moslems in Spain by forcing them all out."

"No, it won't. There are many who still are Jews in their heart and secretly practice their old religion."

"That's true, Luis. It even happens among trusted advisors to the Crown, like the Sanchez, Santangel and de la Cabelleria families. We should be careful and not talk too much about this. There are those among the crew who might think we are heretics and denounce us." Jaime silently added to his advice with a finger to his lips. Fear even followed those who were thousands of miles away from Castile, isolated at sea or on strange islands where the Church had no representatives but men willing to inform on their colleagues for coins of gold or silver. On occasion, while at sea, when Luis stripped naked to wash himself with seawater drawn from the ocean, Jaime saw Luis' circumcision. *Luis will never be able to wipe away the stain of his Jewishness.*

On the 15th of January, Jaime Henriques readied himself for the return trip to Castile, unaware of what he and his fellow crewmembers would be facing on the voyage home. Fierce, life-threatening storms lasted for weeks without respite. Often, the crew sincerely believed they would never return to their homes. In addition to a lack of food and drink, which ran low because of unexpected weather delays, their boats were swamped with waves, causing them to sail much of the way with their decks awash, level with the rampaging sea. Their sails shredded into tattered rags. Fearful that their masts might splinter, the frightened crew slept as best they could, often in water inches deep. They used up most of the fresh water stored in the casks which had been used as ballast.

Sailing the *Niña* became more difficult. Colón ordered the empty casks filled with sea water. Heavy weather continued for weeks. The crew thought each day was to be their last. They all prayed to God, offering up many supplications. The crew selected members delegated to make pilgrimages to the shrine of the Holy Mother in return for they safety, should they survive these merciless storms. When they could find a dry space, they lit votive candles to the Blessed Virgin. Prayers were offered in hopes they would be spared violent deaths at sea. Only through Colón's remarkably skilled seamanship, were they able to outlast the sea and its unusually long period of storms. Colón upheld his reputation as one of the age's finest navigators.

After reaching safety on a deserted island in the Canaries, where there was neither food nor potable water, they sailed further on. Reaching a Portuguese island, they filled their casks with fresh water and obtained food from the inhabitants. From there, they set course for Lisbon, where Portugal's King Manoel entertained Colón and permitted him to refit and resupply the ravaged *Nina*. No doubt the King lamented his refusal to authorize a flotilla of ships, as had been requested by Colón almost a decade earlier.

The crew finally arrived safely at Castile, on March 15, 1493.

Jaime Henriques was unaware he would soon be facing something even more terrible than his struggles with the stormy Ocean Sea.

5

BARCELONA, THE KINGDOM OF ARAGON
MARCH 15, 1493

Martin Alonso Pinzon had the important task of acting as second-in-command to his chief, fleet Captain Cristobal Colón. Despite his role, Pinzon was always a discipline problem, even before the flotilla sailed. It began with the early days at Palos de la Frontera, where he first met Colón. Professing his commitment to sail with Colón as a sign of his loyalty, he nevertheless tried unsuccessfully to wrest command of the fleet. His churlish conduct continued during the voyage to the New World, when he broke away from the flotilla in mid-ocean, unsuccessfully hoping to find land on his own.

Once reaching the Caribbean, Pinzon sailed on future gold-seeking adventures without Colón's permission. It would not be disregarding the time-honored maritime codes of conduct in any way, to say that at times his actions bordered on outright mutiny. At best, they were certainly those of an insubordinate and surly second-in-command.

Revered by the natives of his hometown of Palos, many sincerely believed that Martin Alonso Pinzon was the discoverer of the New World; not "that lying foreign upstart, the phony Admiral of the Ocean Sea, Cristobal Colón." Colón had no choice but to use Pinzon, as he held the loyalties of the City's seafarers in his hand and knew where to get the best boats for Colón's enterprise.

During those stormy days at sea on their way back to Castile, Pinzon again broke away from Colón's command. A first-rate and talented mariner, Pinzon was to survive the ferocious storms which daily threatened to destroy them on the Ocean Sea. He then beat the *Nina* back to Barcelona because Colón stopped at the Canaries and Portugal for a refitting and re-provisioning of his spent vessels. Appearing alone before the Royals, as Captain of the *Pinta*, Alonso Pinzon told Isabella and Ferdinand that it was he who was responsible for discovering the new lands.

The Royals wisely rejected him, ordering him back to Cadiz. The King and Queen had already been advised of Colón's safe landing at Lisbon and his return to the Castilian port of Cadiz. The Royals now awaited his presence in Barcelona.

Pinzon died not long after his ordered return to Cadiz, leaving his family to fight a lengthy, bitter and losing legal battle against Colón and his heirs regarding the issue of who was the real discoverer of the West Indies. It has been said that the court battles involved with Colón's discoveries were history's longest lawsuits: they went on for almost three centuries.

The refreshed crew of the *Nina* sailed into Barcelona on the last days of winter. They had thankfully left the terrible memories of their stormy return behind them. Handsomely dressed and well-fed, the crew found only a small and curious crowd to greet them. As Jaime Henriques descended from the *Nina* to the pier, he saw a familiar face among the onlookers: it was Pedro Alvarez, the overseer of his family's estates.

"Pedro. How good to see you. Are you alone? I don't see anyone else."

Jaime understood by the scowl on Pedro's face that whatever news he had; it was not good.

"Don Jaime, I have some serious news. Prepare for a shock." The overseer paused and swallowed hard before continuing. "Your parents are dead, and your brother and sister are in hiding."

Jaime turned ashen. "I don't understand, Pedro. Why? How?"

Of course Jaime could not understand. His parents had been secret Judaizers, practitioners of the Old Faith and had not planned to tell all their male children of it until the time was ripe. Among Spain's hidden Jewish community, a family's real religion was a secret usually kept by the women and passed down to women, because they had less daily contact with the public than their husbands and so were less apt to reveal the secrets.

Legally, after 1492 Spain was to be free of Jews. Yet a stubborn group remained, secretly practicing their rites. The Catholic Church's Office of the Inquisition was dedicated to finding and eradicating them. It was a dangerous game which secret Jews, once denounced, rarely won. Women lit candles on Friday nights as an affirmation of their Judaism. They continued the use of a few incomprehensible words of Hebrew, as a link to a religion whose rituals and their meanings were fast fading, as untutored generations passed. As each new generation arose, it became less knowledgeable of Judaism's religious practices than the previous one had been. But the women ensured their families ate little or no pork, fasted on certain days during the year and, in the Fall on special days, fed the rivers and streams with breadcrumbs as a symbol of an expiation of their sins. It was acts such as these that were the slim connections to their ancestral faith and to which they still held a fascinating and abiding loyalty. It was these things that had trapped Jaime's parents, unknown to him, when he was thousands of miles away.

"You have to come with me, Don Jaime; our lives are in danger if we stay here. You must leave now," Alvarez implored. He looked around to insure himself that no one could hear him. "The Inquisition, the Hermandad," he whispered, so low that Jaime had to ask him to repeat.

"But I have these financial accounts that must be presented to Her Majesty. I can't just disappear; it's the Queen. What is this all about?" With the word Inquisition, Jaime had become jittery. Just the mention of that organization was guaranteed to send waves of fear throughout most of Spain's citizens.

"Can someone else deliver them? I'll explain everything later," Pedro asked nervously, looking around for any suspicious characters, fearing someone might be monitoring him. "We must leave as soon as possible."

After a moment, Jaime said, "I'll ask Captain Colón if he can present the report on my behalf."

Jaime walked over to Cristobal Colón, who was talking with some guards as he waited to be admitted to the Royal presence. Taking him aside, Jaime said in a low voice, "Captain, do you see that gentleman with the blue cloak standing beside the gangplank?"

"Yes, I do."

"He is Pedro Alvarez, my family's overseer. He has been our trusted servant for over 20 years. He has just told me my mother and father are dead and my younger brother and sister are in hiding. And that they and I are in great danger. He begs me to leave with him now. I would ask you to give this account of the Queen's expenses and profits from this voyage to Her Majesty on my behalf. It is quite detailed. I doubt she would have any questions. I would ask you to give it to her with my excuses for not attending in person."

Colón asked no questions. He was aware, even though the word Inquisition was not spoken, that these facts indicated the Holy Order was on the trail of the Henriques family. Colón was no respecter of the Inquisition. He would do what little he could, short of putting himself in danger, to help the young man of whom he was fond. But he was on the edge of the greatest moments of his life. He would not jeopardize that in any way. He took the papers handed to him and said, "The Queen won't be pleased, Jaime. But let us pray she will understand. Go. I'll do what I can. But I can't guarantee you anything, you understand."

Jaime nodded in assent.

When the rest of the crew appeared inside the royal castle, Colón began explaining his voyage to his King and Queen in detail. He observed Queen Isabella dressed in yellow, green and red silks. Her shiny auburn hair bordered on red, just as that of Colón's. Her eyes were also replicas of Colón's, a bright blue. She was tall, too, like the Captain. They were of the same age, born only months apart, and could easily have passed for brother and sister.

Isabella was obviously pleased to see the return of her successful explorer. Throughout the presentation, King Ferdinand remained silent. Colón's voyage was exclusively an enterprise for the Kingdom of Castile, of which Isabella was Queen. Ferdinand's kingdom, Aragon, was to have nothing to do with the New World.

In fact, Isabella decreed that only Castilians could travel to her newly discovered lands. Anyone else required her permission.

Isabella maintained tight control over her realm, Castile-Leon, separate and apart from Ferdinand's Aragon. That had solemnly been agreed to in their marriage contract.

The Queen leaned forward in her chair and smiled broadly at Colón. Everyone at Court had known for years that Captain Cristobal Colón was one of her favorites. Some vicious gossips even intimated, without any good or real proof, that Colón was very much more than just her favorite.

Interrupting Colón, she asked, "And where is my personal representative, Don Jaime Henriques? He is one of my favorites. I am not pleased with his absence."

Colón straightened up. "He begs the Queens's pardon, but he is greatly distraught. He has just learned his parents are dead and his young brother and sister need attending to. He begs that you receive his report, which he entrusted to me to deliver to you, while he cares for them. He is now the children's only family."

Colón held up the report for Isabella to see. She sat back in her chair, a displeased look on her face. She pointed to a Bailiff, who instinctively knew he was to take the report from Colón and place it in her hands.

"How did Don Jaime comport himself during the voyage?" she demanded to know as she opened the scroll, preparing to read it.

"In the finest manner, Your Majesty. He was always concerned with the shares you should be receiving in Your Highness' participation of the enterprise. I have even asked him to consider joining my retinue on my future voyages, so well did he learn the ways of the sea."

"I am aware of his parent's heresy. It troubled me deeply. His family has for long looked after our interests with great diligence and loyalty. But heresy, from wherever it stems and by whomever, may not be countenanced. I knew nothing of his siblings." The Queen pointed to the Captain of her guards. "Go quickly. Fetch Don Jaime Henriques. Tell him not to fear. The Queen guarantees his safety."

After issuing orders to her guards, Isabella gave each crewman a cash gift. To Colón, she gave two cash prizes: one for being the crewmember who first sighted land and another for his work as Captain of the successful enterprise. Then she gifted him a mansion in Seville, once belonging to a now forgotten, exiled Jew.

Three hours later, Jaime and a trembling and fearful Pedro Alvarez appeared before the Queen. They had been tracked down by Isabella's efficient guards as they were on their way out of the city. Her business with Colón and his crew concluded; the grand hall was closed. She met Jaime in her private chambers, a great room filled with a large desk where the Queen worked, an ornate but comfortable chaise lounge, and several high-backed chairs. One was higher and more magnificent than all the others. When the Queen was not at her desk, this was the chair in which she sat. A half-dozen young Ladies in Waiting stifled giggles as they stood watching the handsome Jaime enter the room.

The Queen waived Jaime's report before him, remarking, "We have read your report, Don Jaime. Don Cristobal was right: it is a fine piece of work. We have no questions about it. We are pleased to see that you have carefully looked after our interests and returned to Castile safely. Admiral Colón has told us of the terrible storms you sailed through to return home. You have a great future in my Court.

"We are aware of your parents' death. I was upset about it because of the close relations between our families. You must know, Don Jaime, the Crown and the Church are dedicated to cleansing all Iberia of Islam and Judaism. There can be no exceptions. We regret your parents. The Henriques family has been loyal to mine for many years. There is no reason you cannot continue in that tradition, including your brother and sister. I believe none of you knew anything of what your parents were doing. I am ordering an investigation and if it reveals what I expect, that you three children were unaware and innocent of your parents' lapses, then we may continue as before."

The Queen looked to Pedro Alvarez. "You, I understand, are the family's overseer?"

"I am, your Majesty." Alvarez looked nervously at the two guards who stood silently at the door.

"Don't be afraid. Everyone is under my protection, including you, Señor Alvarez. And the children, of course. You need not fear for their safety. You will have my two guards with you to prove my word. Should anyone attempt to harm you, Don Jaime, or the children, they will pay a heavy penalty. I can guarantee that. Now, Señor Alvarez, do you know where the children are?"

"I do, Your Majesty."

"Then find them and bring them here to me. I will have the Inquisitors ready to determine their innocence and that will be the end of this unfortunate affair. How long will it take you to bring them here?

"Over five weeks, My Queen. They are in the west country, in *Zamora*, almost at the border with Portugal."

"Why are they so far away?" the Queen demanded to know, with petulance in her tone.

"It was the only safe place I could find for them in haste. They are with a relative, Your Majesty." Pedro was not too anxious to name his sister and get her mixed up in this situation, which was quickly becoming complicated.

"Good, then. We expect to see everyone here after five weeks. Now go."

The two guards placed themselves alongside Jaime and Pedro. For the next days, while the four men rode on the long trip to the town of Zamora to fetch the children, the guards were never out of sight. They protected their charges as if they were two chests full of the Queen's jewels and gold coins.

6

GIBRALTAR
OCTOBER 1941

In the early morning darkness, James Ennis rose from his bed, dressed in his uniform and made his way to the dimly lit passageway leading to the *Undaunted*'s submarine pen. Two armed guards, previously alerted to the American's presence, saluted and greeted him saying, "Good morning, Sir." One of them pointed to the steel ramp leading to the submarine and turned on the boat's outside lights. The cleaning crew had yet to arrive. The *Undaunted*, docked before him, was shaped like a huge steel cigar, its conning tower rising high from the only outside deck like a large canister.

Undaunted was blessed with three eyes: the periscope, which stealthily poked up from beneath the sea while the vessel sailed hidden beneath the surface; the outside conning tower, its cramped space open to the elements, exposing the Captain and one or two officers as well as a pair of lookouts. While sailing on the surface, they all scanned the ocean constantly with binoculars for likely prey or for their enemies. The boat's last set of eyes were a combination of radar and sonar. They had radiant electronic screens glowing green, revealing the proximity of vessels, friendly or enemy, on the surface or below. That the *Undaunted* could locate vessels even as she lay fathoms below the surface of the ocean was the result of modern scientific invention. *Undaunted*'s eyes were most important to her safety and mission.

Unlike sailors on surface vessels, submariners had few opportunities to enjoy the sun's warmth or the moon's light. The boat had only one outside deck, which was not designed for recreational activities or leisure. The crew had little opportunity to enjoy the surface of the sea.

Ennis climbed up the straight, 90-degree ladder to the open conning tower. Once on its deck, he descended into the boat through the manhole-like entry, down into the tight confines of the *Undaunted*. He was instantly struck by a submarine's familiar aura: a cloudy haze filled with a combination of disagreeable stenches: diesel oil, sea water, unwashed bodies, an improperly flushed toilet, the greasy smell of kitchen cooking, and stale tobacco. It was, of course, the curse of all submarines, which was why they were called "pig boats." He noted how small the *Undaunted* was; only about 200 feet long, with barely enough room for the basic comforts for its crew of 33. There was only one head, as bathrooms are called aboard vessels. The British also called it the 'loo.'

As he proceeded through the boat, ducking beneath low overheads and lifting his legs over foot-high watertight doors, Ennis used his fountain pen to scratch notes as to his findings onto blue lined paper in his small notebook. At dinner last night, one of the young officers confided to Ennis that they neither showered nor washed clothes while on patrol. That would not do on an American submarine, which would be longer than the *Undaunted* with a larger crew. Besides being a matter of esthetics, it was also a matter of health. At the Electric Boat Company, executives told Ennis they were designing a boat that could patrol for as long as 75 days, almost twice the length of *Undaunted*'s cruising capacity. The American crew would be much larger than that of the British submarine. America's submariners would have to shower at least every 10 days and wash their clothes, too, he noted, No less than three heads with showers are needed, otherwise serious health issues would arise. He underlined these observations as he entered them into his notebook.

American submarines built at the Electric Boat Company were designed to be at least 100 feet longer than the *Undaunted*. They needed to carry a water supply necessary for cleaning, cooking and accommodating 30 crew members more than the *Undaunted*'s 33. Ennis would also be recommending the instillation of the new system of air conditioning and a heavy-duty refrigeration unit to store food. Fresh fruits and vegetables disappeared quickly on long patrols. Refrigeration would extend their life at least a bit longer. It helped alleviate a problem that old-time sailing ships had going back to Columbus, of constantly running out of fresh water and food, often resulting in scurvy with its deadly fever, the loss of teeth and bleeding gums. Toward the end of his epic voyage, Columbus' crew was drinking brackish water out of wooden kegs, cut with rations of wine to make it drinkable. And they were down to eating a daily diet of stale, stone-hard, maggot-ridden hard tack, softened with olive oil and wine to make it palatable.

Later, when he returned to Connecticut, Ennis would have to take out his slide rule to determine how much space could be allotted to 63 men for living and stowing their gear, equipment and supplies on a boat only 300 feet long. Then there was the issue of the stowage of enough food for a 75-day voyage: most of it packed into canned and cardboard packages. He'd figure that out, too. On the *Undaunted*, they stored food everywhere there was available space. He knew instinctively that some of the American crews, maybe as many as a dozen men, would have to sleep in the torpedo room, even atop the dynamite-packed torpedoes. It couldn't be helped. Canned and boxed food would have to be stored in every space on the ship, beneath beds, in closets and even in the heads.

Submarine crews often worked in shorts and tee shirts. Ennis didn't know if batteries could be used to power an air conditioner. Probably not. It would have to be checked out, in any event. Even if it was possible, the noise of an operating air conditioner beneath the sea would give the submarine's location away to a searching enemy. That was another problem to be solved.

Ennis was sitting at a table in the boat's small Officer's Wardroom, putting all this information into his notebook, when Ian McDonald walked in.

"Good morning, Jimmy. Made an early start, I see."

"Good morning, Ian. Yes, I thought I'd get here before the cleaning crew to be out of everyone's way."

"Good idea. Have you had any breakfast?"

"No. I'll be finished in a moment, let's have some."

The two men left the sub and walked to the Officer's Mess. Dawn was rising. Only a few officers, dressed in whites down to their shoes, were seated. They were beating the breakfast rush that would occur within the next hour. The clinking of silverware on porcelain dishes was accentuated by the emptiness of the dining room. There was a feeling of quiet sleepiness, the few persons present speaking in hushed tones like the patrons in the diner at Groton, which Ennis sometimes frequented early in the morning when he didn't want to make breakfast.

"Can you stay with us for another month, Jimmy?" McDonald asked.

"I suppose so, if it's beneficial to my mission here."

"Good. I can guarantee you that it will be. I received word this morning that my layover will be cut to less than a week. The Jerries are stepping up their supply lines to North Africa. General Rommel, one of their best tacticians, is now heading the German army in Africa. Admiralty wants every available submarine out hunting for enemy tankers and troop ships. I'd like you to come along as an observer. You don't have to be with us for the whole patrol. I'll be stopping at our submarine base at Malta for a refuel and more torpedoes. They could only give me six here. I'll need more for my work. After two weeks, we could let you off, so you could return to Gibraltar from there. We've been giving the Italians a good licking. With the Jerrys entering North Africa to assist their Italian allies, who are losing the War, it will get very sticky. Admiralty wants us to keep them off balance."

"I'll have to get permission. I'd be a neutral sailing on an English ship of war. I'll call home after we finish eating. I'll get someone on nighttime duty." Ennis looked at his wristwatch. "At home, most of the decision-makers are still asleep. I can get the night watch ready to discuss this when they start working. Let's see what the boys upstairs say. Our President has his hands tied when it comes to the War, you understand. Politically, America doesn't want to get into another big one, especially if it's in Europe."

"I understand. If you come, you'll certainly get some good insight into what we're doing here."

"I'll remind my people of that when I speak to them."

"Where do you live in the States, Jimmy? Is that how they call it, The States?"

"Yes. I live in Groton, Connecticut, where I work as the Navy's representative at the Electric Boat Company. I have a marine engineering degree, so that's why I'm here; to see what you folks do and how you do it. Hopefully, we can learn some things from you."

"Where did your family come from? Before America, I mean. I hope I'm not too inquisitive."

"No, that's all right, Ian. Family legend says we first came to Holland from Spain or Portugal. Why, I don't know. We were known as Henriques at the time. That was our family name. I've been told that by my father and grandfather. From Holland, we went to England. I guess we were merchants who left Amsterdam for better business opportunities in London. So, Ennis was not our original name. Since they say we were Henriques back then, I suppose it shows we were originally Spanish or maybe Portuguese early on. I don't know too much about it. One ancestor, Solomon Ennis, came to America just in time to get into the fight against your King George. He was killed in the American Revolution. He had a son named James. Like me."

James Ennis smiled. "Now we are practically allies waiting for something to happen to throw us together in a War we all know we must eventually fight together against Germany and Italy."

"Yes," McDonald agreed. "History is strange. We've all been hoping you Yanks would have joined us by now. I don't know how much longer we'll be able to stand alone."

သ ઝ

Three days later, during the second week of October, Ennis informed McDonald that he had received permission to sail as a neutral observer on the next patrol. McDonald was pleased. There would be an extra man, meaning more food, and they would be a little more cramped, but he'd work that out. It would only be for two weeks.

"You can't wear your uniform," McDonald said. "I'll get an engineer's khaki jump suit for you, buttons up the front with no insignia. Very neutral. I'll have someone find some weatherproof oilcloth to wrap up your uniform and other changes of clothes. I can guarantee you that when we get to Malta, you'll be a soaking, smelly mess."

As scheduled, before the end of the week the *Undaunted* was cleaned, loaded with food, water, and equipment, as well as the few armaments that were stingily allotted to her. She slipped from her pen like a silent otter sleekly slicing its way in pursuit of underwater dinnertime prey. Once in the Mediterranean, *Undaunted* made a maximum speed of 13 knots on the surface and 11 submerged: something Ennis would urge the builders at Groton to exceed. Ian McDonald would navigate along the surface until his lookouts or radar noted the presence of enemy vessels steaming nearby. Ennis was impressed with the radar operators' ability to precisely locate enemy ships and even detail their distance from the *Undaunted*. While Ennis was having tea in the Officer's Wardroom, McDonald, looking very grave, squeezed in alongside him.

"It seems the Germans have sent out a group of ships to help their Italian allies on convoy. I can expect some excitement on this patrol. Just got confirmation of that over the wireless. Looks is if the game is getting a little dicey."

"So we can expect some heavy encounters?"

"Yes. I'm afraid so. Sorry. You may see some real combat. I'm still scheduled to stop at Malta in two weeks."

"I'm a military professional. I was taught at the Academy that you can't expect to avoid conflict. Eventually, I'll be facing an enemy dedicated to killing me," Ennis explained, as he changed into his jump suit. He hurriedly transferred whatever was in his pockets to the jump suit, then he continued, "Don't concern yourself about my safety. We both knew I was taking risks when I agreed to sail with you. I'll surely learn something that will save some Americans sailors in the future."

7

MEDITERRANEAN SEA
OCTOBER 1941

After three frustrating hours stalking his prey, which had been using a zig-zag course to confound enemy submarines, Lt. Commander Ian McDonald finally had the former Italian cruise liner, *La Gloria*, in his sights. She had recently been converted into a troop ship. Closely tracking her course for several minutes, he was now able to set her up for an attack, firing two lethal torpedoes into her port side. The first torpedo struck the bow. The second was a direct hit mid-ships, where ammunition must have been stored. After the second strike, there was a huge explosion, lifting *La Gloria* out of the water. Fire and black smoke obscured any decent view of her.

McDonald and Ennis were outside on the conning tower, torpedoes having been fired while *Undaunted* was on the surface, her decks awash, making for a more accurate attack. Ennis looked at the sinking ship through binoculars. She was still wrapped in a cloak of fire and black smoke. He could see men leaping through the smoke out of the ship into the water, some of them aflame as they plunged into the ocean. He turned away, thinking, *I don't suppose I can ever get used to this; men dying like that. No chance to save themselves.* He looked again for lifeboats but could see none, as the smoke was now being blown away by the wind. He hoped there might be some being loaded from the other side of the ship.

McDonald fired two more torpedoes at a tanker but there was no explosion. Defective torpedoes: not unusual at this early stage of the War. Another point for Ennis to make at Groton when he returned.

Steaming straight at them now was a Cruiser, preparing to attack the *Undaunted*. It was almost certainly loaded with deadly depth charges. The enemy had located the *Undaunted* and was about to make life difficult for her and her crew.

"Clear the tower," McDonald roared. "Dive, dive, dive! Take her down, fast."

Two lookouts, McDonald, Ennis and one other officer scrambled down the narrow hatch one by one. The last lookout into the hatch dogged the cover down after his entry.

"Cover secured, sir," he called out. It was routine procedure.

"Rig for depth charges," McDonald ordered the seaman at the helm. "Take her down to 150."

"Down to one-five-oh, sir," the helmsman repeated, as the *Undaunted* began her descent to 150 feet. Ennis could feel the angle of the boat heading downward. He held on to the chart table to maintain his balance. He looked around and saw that the crew seemed to have their favorite places to hold on to. They had been through this before. Ennis had sailed on submarines many times, but never in combat. It was always a shakedown cruise or a test; never like this, waiting for an attack that could sink the boat and drown the crew. He remembered what one of the crew had told him when they started their voyage, "If we get hit with depth charges, sir, stay clear of the bulkhead. Otherwise, you'll get an awfully bloody and unpleasant bang-up when the boat starts rocking." It was good advice.

"How far down will she go?" Ennis asked McDonald.

"She's certified at 250 feet. The hull is not supposed to withstand pressure beyond that. I've never had her past 250. I'd like to see her do 300. That would give me better escape options."

Ennis made another mental note to have the engineers at Groton strengthen hulls to enable American boats to drop to 300 feet. Now he heard the cavitating sounds of a large ship's propellers churning somewhere on the surface above them. The enemy was searching for *Undaunted*. Luckily, most of the older Italian ships had yet to be equipped with sonar. He hoped this ship was one of them.

Or could she be German? If so, they would almost certainly have sonar and depth charges, too. Then he heard something strike the hull sharply at the stern. It was like a sledgehammer striking a steel door. It was followed by a scraping sound, as if someone was dragging a heavy metal container along the boat's hull. It disappeared and several seconds later, an explosion rocked the sub's interior, moving everything from side to side and causing everyone to sway.

Ennis followed the advice to stand away from the bulkhead, finding a spot by the chart table which was secured to the deck. It moved with a frightening and creaking sound, straining with the twisting of the boat. Ennis held on tightly, keeping his body from slamming into the table. The boat's lights flickered and went out, but then came on again after several frightening seconds. The feeling he had a few weeks ago after his nightmare, returned: tightness around his chest and that metallic taste of fear on his tongue. He looked around him at the crew. *They're frightened, too*, he noticed. *They've all been through this before, yet how could anyone ever get used to this?*

McDonald sidled over to the chart table while holding on to pipes and red-painted valve wheels protruding from the bulkhead for support as he slowly moved toward the table. The boat was still rolling and pitching. It swayed again as two more depth charges exploded nearby, one immediately after the other. McDonald, now at the chart table, consulted a map, putting his finger where his boat was located.

"Take her down to one-eighty," he ordered.

"Down to one-eight-oh, sir," the helmsman repeated.

McDonald looked at Ennis. "That's the bottom," he explained.

Ennis felt the boat straighten out, then descend and finally touch the sea's bottom with a cradle-rocking bump on the ocean floor. Although they had touched bottom, the boat settled at an angle making walking difficult, as if one were in the fun house at a county fair. He noticed for the first time that he had been tightly gripping the edges of the chart table and his knuckles were white with tension. He released his grip. The men around him were also beginning to ease up. He swiped a hand across his face, the sweat of fear had dampened his forehead.

"Most depth charges are rigged to explode at about 150 feet. At 180 we should still feel the explosions, but we'll be safe from any real damage," McDonald explained.

After an hour, noise from the charges stopped. McDonald waited 15 minutes and ordered the boat up to periscope level. He peered through the sub's scope, then folded the scope's handles. "They're gone. Let's get up to the surface."

Once on the open sea, the crew scrambled out of the deck hatches, seeking fresh air. It was one of the few times during a patrol that they could come out on deck. They directed their faces towards the breeze. Some of the men removed their tee-shirts, flapping them in the wind, hoping to dry accumulated sweat.

The blowers were activated to clear out the stale air below. Batteries were set for recharging. Lookouts were posted. *Undaunted* was in a war zone and at any time enemy planes could spot them, revealing their position to nearby vessels. That would subject them to another attack from the air or the sea.

It was nighttime now and the crew could see blood-red flashes of cannon fire and burning ships on the horizon, as enemies clashed with each other many miles away. After getting some air, Ennis went below, trying to sleep in the tiny cabin he shared with two officers.

With dawn breaking, one of the lookouts shouted. "Enemy planes. At two o'clock. I see two, Sir." He was pointing to the boat's starboard bow.

McDonald, who was on watch, turned. "Yes, I see them. Looks like Stukas. Everyone below. Dive, dive, dive!"

Everyone scampered down the hatch. Before they were all below, two gull-winged Stuka dive bombers were preparing a bombing run. The first plane dropped with a shrieking, fearsome sound, a siren purposely built into the outside of the plane sounding its infamous eerie and frightening whine, activated as it dove on its target. The sound usually stopped the hearts of those below, knowing that they were targets for the deadly bombers.

A bomb was let loose on its target just as the cover to the conning tower was secured. It landed about 200 yards away, rocking the partly submerged boat. As the *Undaunted* was descending to below 150 feet, two more blasts were felt. The shock waves rolled the boat to the port side. Books, maps, pencils, loose coffee cups, anything that wasn't secured flew about the cabin. *Undaunted* straightened up. No one bothered to pick anything up. That would come later.

Ennis, almost thrown from his bed, rushed to the boat's navigation area. Two more bombs dropped ineffectually. Nevertheless, they frightened the crew and rocked the *Undaunted*. The radar operator pushed his headphone closer for a clearer sound. Blips on his screen verified what he was hearing. Turning in his seat, he looked at McDonald.

"A ship, sir. Sounds like a Cruiser. She's looking for us."

"How far from us?"

"About 3,000 yards. And Sir, I would say from the sound of her engines, she's not Italian."

McDonald snatched the headset from the operator's head and jammed one earphone to his right ear. "You're right, Blaine. She's German. Where are we now, helmsman?"

"One-two-zero descending to one-five-zero as ordered, Sir."

"Take her down to one-seven-oh and let's get out of here."

"Descending to one-seven-oh, Sir."

Just then two more explosions rocked the *Undaunted*. Bombs from a Stuka, and close. A valve at the bulkhead opposite Ennis, who was now standing by the chart table, popped open and a powerful stream of sea water shot across the room, drenching him. Now the Cruiser was overhead and dropping depth charges. Another valve cracked, more water pouring into the boat about 20 feet from Ennis. Then two more. Men raced around the cabin armed with spanners, ready to seal off the leaks. They sloshed through water and Ennis noted he was now standing in seawater that was rising. The lights in the cabin went out. In all the confusion, someone shouted, "Turn on the emergency lights, for God's sake."

The *Undaunted* was flooding fast. Blasts from depth charges had popped five valves on the conning tower, causing sea water to shoot across the command post, soaking the crew who were working at that level. Light bulbs and glass covers on the clocks and meters, exploded. Men used flashlights to illuminate the darkened interior and control panels until someone located a pair of heavy-duty lanterns. More importantly, several crewmen were frantically working on the valves to stem the flow of sea water which, if it continued, could prevent the *Undaunted*'s ability to rise to the surface. Working in front of the valves, men were ignoring the blasts of high-pressure sea water while struggling to turn large wheels by hand or working with spanners to shut down the smaller valves. Each explosion created new crises: loss of light, flooding, frightening noises from secured joints separating, exploding glass and light bulbs. By the flashlights settling on sailor's faces, Ennis saw that fear was evident. After one blast, a seaman fell, surfing across the flooded deck, crashing into the bulkhead with a bone-cracking sound. Only God knows what the situation was like on the decks below, in the engine and torpedo rooms.

So, this is what I volunteered for, Ennis thought, as he wiped his face after being hit by another shower of sea water. He was completely soaked, his feet chilled after standing for a time in ankle-deep water. It was obvious that the crew was trained to deal with a depth charge attack; they knew exactly what to do to keep the *Undaunted* afloat and in fighting condition.

Below, in the engine room, engineers were scrambling frantically to maintain the power plant and keep it from dying. Water-tight doors had already been slammed shut and dogged down to prevent flooding from one compartment of the boat to another, which would have dangerously altered the vessel's balance. Slowly and with great effort, all valves were shut off, but the navigating deck remained ankle-deep in water now mixed with oil. The smell of brine permeated the area.

On the deck below, oil was oozing from leaking and damaged tanks. McDonald ordered the boat taken up to 100 feet. The crew sighed with relief; the ballast tanks were operating and the *Undaunted* could safely rise. Accumulated water and leaking oil would have to be pumped out through the bilges. McDonald called down to the engine room for a damage report.

"Most of the batteries have suffered some damage, Sir," the Chief Engineer informed McDonald. It would soon be necessary to surface, as they were losing their charges fast. The *Undaunted* would have to sail on the surface the rest of the way to Malta, a 60-mile trip, during which they would not be able to dive to avoid the enemy. Luckily, they saw no enemy vessels during the laborious, eight-hour return to Malta.

8

MALTA
NOVEMBER 1941

Malta, like Gibraltar, was an English colony and the Union Jack flew high over the island. *Undaunted* limped into the docks at Grand Harbour in Valletta, Malta's port and the island's main city. Standing on the open conning tower as the boat neared the docks, Ennis was looking through binoculars at a city devastated by air raids. At every street corner, rubble had been swept into large piles. A combination of 30 German and Italian bombers had just dropped their deadly cargos on the city and its harbor facilities. Since Germany began funneling its soldiers to North Africa to beef up its Italian allies, Valletta became the object of daily and brutal air raids.

Malta was strategically located between the island of Sicily and North Africa, perfectly placed to cut off the enemy's supply line of men and materiel from Italy to the North African desert war. The enemy's strategy, on the other hand, was to starve the island: it kept it from receiving desperately needed supplies. They would stop food, fuel, planes, military personnel and ammunition from reaching Malta. If successful, there would be no fuel, no ammunition, nor any personnel to man Malta's fighters, bombers or its submarines. It was the 20th Century's version of the medieval city-siege. Instead of surrounding a city or a castle with soldiers as in the past, the siege of Malta was powered by daily air raids and enemy warships sinking merchant vessels attempting to reach it. Time and again, Allied convoys were prevented from reaching Malta. Targeted for these attacks were not only the military, but the civilian population as well.

From the conning tower, as Ennis watched smoke and flames rising from the city, he could hear the sound of the all-clear siren. He watched the creators of this devastation, now specks far away in the sky, a deadly flock of silver birds heading north as they returned to their nests to load up and come back to inflict more destruction. The bombing of Valletta and the rest of Malta was Ennis' introduction to modern warfare: deadly assaults from the sky on helpless civilians and their cities. He understood why he was sent to Gibraltar to study submarines: in England or Malta, with their daily raids such as these, he would be subject to danger which would interfere with the work he was sent to do.

Still damp from the flooding of the navigating deck and streaked with lubricating oil, his face covered with a two-week growth of beard, Ennis could not wait to shower, shave and change into the uniform he had brought with him. Fortunately, it had not been soaked with water, packed as it was between several layers of thick oil cloth. As he cleaned up, he noted the fledgling beard and thought, *It might look good if it had another week or so to fill in*. But soon, he was clean-shaven again. After cleaning up, he located the Military Travel Officer, who notified him that he would have to wait two days before he could return to Gibraltar.

"Several of our civilian planes were damaged during the last air raid, Lieutenant. And our active military who are heading for the war zone have priority for travel, as you may imagine," he explained. "We should be able to get you out of here headed for Gibraltar in two or three days. Malta is an interesting place, Sir. It goes back a long time and has a fascinating history. I might suggest you take advantage of the inconvenience to poke about a bit."

That he would do, Ennis decided. He located a tourist guide, a man named Marco, who walked him about the city, pointing out significant structures and their history as they picked their way across the bombed-out ruins and accumulated mounds of rubble resulting from the many air raids. Marco explained the island's connection with the famed Knights Templar, the Knights of Malta, and Arab pirates. For 200 years, they had enjoyed a lucrative trade, kidnapping travelers off sailing ships and holding them for ransom. While waiting for their release, these unfortunates who were held as slaves lived in slave quarters, dungeons or in the homes of persons who paid to have the captives working for them. Some of the favored slaves even ran their own businesses in town. Those who did not fall into these groups were brutally treated because their ransom was slow in coming or seemed never to come at all. The pirates saw no redemption for this group which they had to feed and care for, so they used them in the most terrible fashion as working slaves.

"Non-Muslims and Jews were a large part of the slave community," Marco explained. "If you came to Malta by ship, Lieutenant, then you either passed through the old entrance we call the "Jew's Sally Port" or another nearby entrance. Close by was the slaves' quarters. It's still there, badly damaged by air raids. I recently read in the newspaper that the government is planning to raze it. After being used as slaves' quarters, it was converted into a hospital and then, a school. I attended grade-school classes there. There it is."

Marco pointed to a nearby three-story stone building. Its exterior was pockmarked from the many shrapnel holes it had suffered. On one side of the building, a second story wall had been partially blasted away, leaving a gaping, almost square opening which allowed the interior walls to become visible. The roof had also been shattered, the result of having been raked by bombs. The sky peeked through ragged openings. Ennis had that odd feeling when looking at it.

"Can we go in?"

"I don't know, sir. It's been empty for a long while. If our government has it scheduled to be razed, it probably means it's dangerous to go inside. As you can see, it's been badly damaged with all the bombings. It's over 300 years old, you know. I would imagine it's quite fragile from age and all the bombings." He looked at Ennis and considered his options. Thinking there might be an extra fee to inspect this building not on his normal rounds, he smiled and said, "Follow me, sir."

Marco carefully walked around the building, kicking away the dusty debris in his path. He found a recently constructed and makeshift gate, a wooden entry. He yanked at it, turned back to Ennis, and said, "Give me a hand here, sir, if you please."

The two men pulled at the makeshift door several times until there was a gap large enough for them to squeeze through. They entered the darkened building, smelling its damp walls and the accumulation of ancient dust. Thin shafts of light came in from bombed-out holes in the walls that were crisscrossing the room.

"Is there a basement"? Ennis asked, at the same time wondering why he was interested in the basement of an old slave quarter. But interested he was, and he knew that strange sense of his was at work once again.

"When I went to school here years ago," Marco said, "I recall there was one. Old-timers used to say that it was where the slaves used to live. I never went down into it though; I was always afraid to do that, you know."

"Let's see if you can find it."

Marco reluctantly dug into his khaki-colored kit bag, which all Maltese wore slung around their shoulders since the onset of the daily air raids. It contained a gas mask, bandages, gauze and other emergency items, and a flashlight – which he called a torch. Marco switched it on and swept the room with it as they walked around the ground floor. He stopped at a dilapidated and heavy wooden door. There were still some old and peeling posters on the wall next to the door. Marco said he remembered them from when he was a young boy at this school. The door did not open easily.

"I remember now. That's the entrance to the old slave quarters. It was next to the posters!" Marco was almost shouting, pleased that he was able to locate it so swiftly.

The two of them pulled at the old door using all their strength. After a frightening scraping sound, a shower of dust, small pieces of rock, and loose plaster rained on their heads and shoulders. They brushed themselves clean and tried the door again. It finally yielded to their strength, accompanied by another louder and more frightening noise.

They carefully descended several large and smooth stone steps, depressed in the center from centuries of use, to a huge, high-ceilinged but airless space. Weak rays of light shone through several dingy windows located high off the floor. They were all curtained by years of accumulated grimy dust. As they passed through, they could see a few dim shafts of light.

Continuing forward, they disturbed piles of dust which kicked up from the floor and swirled about them in an airy ballet within the weak light. Proceeding through the room, Marco illuminated the way with his torch, and they heard the claws of rodents scraping across the stone floor as they scurried past them, disturbed by the light and the unusual sound of humans invading their realm.

Several yards past the base of the steps and below a window, Ennis slowed down. His right hand gently touched the clammy wall. He was feeling for something he instinctively knew was there. Suddenly, he knew. He had been here before. These were the large stone walls he had seen in his dream a few weeks ago.

As the beam of the torch swept across the room, Ennis recognized the places in his dream where men sat on sheets and blankets, their hopes for freedom fading. He was looking at inscriptions carved into the walls by prisoners, centuries ago. After walking halfway across the basement, he stopped, his fingers making circles, cleaning layers of dust away from the surface for a better look.

"Marco, put the light here," Ennis said in a voice full of excitement. "There!" He grabbed Marcos' elbow, aiming the torch at the wall. Now he could see it plainly.

> *Aaron Haim Henriques I mi ijo, Jaime, de doze anyos.*
> *Somos esklavos I prizyoneros*
> *En la Kweva de los esklavos, el anyo 5492*

Ennis read the legend, chills running along the nape of his neck. Slowly, he translated the inscription:

> *Aaron Haim Henriques and my son Jaime, twelve years old*
> *We are slaves and prisoners in the Cave of the*
> *Slaves, since the year 5492*

Who were these people with the same name as my ancestors? How did they come to be here? And what kind of Spanish is this? So odd, the spelling. And what about the date?

                   ℬ ℛ

Not all members of the Henriques family had chosen to seek asylum in Portugal in 1492. Several members of the family opted for the Ottoman Empire. It was an easy and sensible choice: the Empire was on its way to becoming Europe's most powerful and the Sultan, Bayazid II, publicly encouraged Spain's exiled Jews to move east, to his realm. He eagerly awaited their arrival, even sending his own ships to Spain to bring them to his cities of Constantinople, Izmir and Salonica, the Empire's seaports. He could not understand how the foolish Isabella and Ferdinand could banish some of their most useful and productive citizens.

In Salonica, the exiles took a sleepy backwater and converted it into a major Ottoman seaport, destined to become one of the largest and most important Jewish cities in the Mediterranean. Religious seminaries flourished, attracting students from Egypt, Italy, Syria and other Mediterranean venues and it was a place where rabbis came to study the intricate mysteries of the elusive Kabbalah.

The Ottomans were pleased: they were neither merchants nor traders. They were fierce and successful warriors. The Sultan would take this important opportunity to benefit from the well-known commercial acumen of his new citizens. He could leave business matters to the newcomers. Turkey would become a major trading nation, her seaports bursting with ships arriving from the world over. In addition to the armies of the Ottoman Empire, its civilian communities would also prosper.

Using their regular commercial networks, the newcomers ran overseas enterprises like the tendrils of an ivy plant, reaching from the Empire to Western Europe, Africa and even the New World. The Henriques family and others like them, now in the Ottoman Empire for almost two and a half centuries, benefitted from this prosperity.

In 1732, Aaron Henriques, an Ottoman citizen and a trader in wine, wood and manufactured leather products, was aboard the

Pasha Osman, a three-masted sailing ship out of the port city of Salonica in northern Macedonia, where many Jews lived. The ship was bound for Alexandria, Egypt, where Aaron would display his array of goods at a Mart owned by a fellow Jew, Isaac Ben Ezra. Accompanying Aaron was his 12-year-old son Jaime. It was time for Jaime to learn the secrets of business and how to turn profits from the sales of wine, wood and leather. From now on, having reached the age of 12, he would remain at his father's side during every transaction, learning how to become a successful businessman.

On their second day at sea, Aaron and Jaime were on the ship's main deck. After a while, a sailor high in the crow's nest, called out, "Sails to the port bow."

Seamen and passengers rushed to the ship's bow. The sailor called out again, pointing to the distant vessel, "She flies a black flag with Arabic writing across it."

"She's a Barbary, a pirate ship!" a sailor next to Aaron Henriques at the ship's railing cried out, fear rising from his throat. There was a commotion among the passengers, some of whom were not acquainted with pirate kidnapping on the high seas. When fellow passengers informed them of what was about to happen, their faces paled with fear and horror.

The Captain called for his crew to arm themselves in defense. It was a useless order. The pirates, sailing aboard a swift ship, quickly overcame the *Pasha Osman*. They were adept at boarding and overwhelming commercial vessels, which were always slow-moving, burdened as they usually were with passengers and trade goods. The pirates had arrested such ships many times. Within a half-hour, the Captain of the *Pasha Oman* surrendered to avoid bloodshed. The pirates quickly and with great efficiency began sorting out their booty: cargo, arms, ammunition, food and the human loot, men and women to be held for ransom. They would be herded like cattle on to the pirate ship and sent west to the island of Malta. There, they were to be held as slaves until their ransom was paid. The pirates were delighted to see so many Jews among the passengers, for even if Jews had no family or money to meet the Pirate's ransom demands, they were still ransomed.

"Those stupid Jews," the marauders would say. That was because Jews had a charitable organization which paid the ransom for poor and needy Jews. Holding them for ransom was good business for the pirates, so long as the fools insisted on ransoming every Jew, whether or not they could afford it. No matter, the kidnappers thought; it was to their benefit.

"You will go to Malta, and you will be contacted by the representative of the organization that redeems Jews," the pirate Captain told his two dozen Jewish passengers that had been sorted out. "You are to cooperate with him. That will ensure your swift release, which I am certain you are anxious to affect." The pirate chief advised his hostages in perfect French.

"Our Captain was a French Christian who was himself captured by the Barbaries. He converted to Islam. Today he is one of the greatest pirates on the sea," one of the sailors told Aaron as the prisoners were moved to the pirate ship.

The trip to Malta was miserable. Only some brackish water and putrid food were afforded, most of which the captives refused to eat because it was not kosher: ritually clean for consumption. When they finally reached Malta they were driven with whips and clubs past an entrance called "The Jew's Sally Port." From there, they were dumped into a large dungeon with stone walls, which would be their home until they were ransomed.

The men were separated from the women. They were searched once again to make sure the pirates at sea hadn't missed anything of value. The dungeon was filled with half-naked men stretched out on filthy sheets and blankets. Others wandered about aimlessly. Some of these poor creatures had been driven mad, speaking or mumbling only to themselves. One man who was sitting in a corner, was howling as if he were a wolf baying at the moon. The noise was a cacophonous babel of many languages: French, German, English, Spanish, Portuguese, Arabic, Greek and Turkish. Aaron noted there was even a group of Chinese men shouting amongst themselves. The noise was constant: it continued even at night.

The Maltese agent of The Jewish Society for the Redemption of Captives, Gabriel Matarazzo, came to seek out his new charges after they'd endured a week of this difficult life. He was a small thin man, about 50 years of age, with a dark head of thinning hair and black eyes. He carried a large satchel from which he always managed to pull something to help relieve the pains of captivity. He had complete and unmolested access to the slave quarters, as the captors knew he was the main source of obtaining their ransom demands. From time to time, under special circumstances, he was even able to assist non-Jews. Matarazzo was always a welcome visitor to the Barbary slave quarters: he was a very important person to both slave and captor.

"I'm here to help you get out of this place," he said to Aaron and Jaime in Ladino, the language used by descendants of Spanish and Portuguese Jews. It was Spanish peppered with words from the Mediterranean countries. "Give me the names and addresses of your closest relatives who I can contact to help raise the ransom for you and your son."

"How long must we remain in this horrible place?" Aaron asked.

"I can't say, *hermano*. It depends on how much your family can raise to redeem you. Can your family pay the ransom?"

"I don't know. How much is being asked by these animals?"

"They haven't told me yet. Most times I can make a combination of family money and the rest from our organization. It takes time, making inquiries back and forth between countries. You could be here for two years, maybe more."

"No! I don't think we can stand this for two years." Aaron turned his face toward his son Jaime as he said this.

Matarazzo was used to this conversation and the pain it caused the new prisoners. "All the captives say that, but they all endure this place as you will, because you know the Society will eventually get you out. Those other unfortunates you see," he was pointing to men wandering aimlessly about, "have no money or any hope for ransom, nor do their poor families. I will see you from time to time and bring you news and some comforts." Matarazzo reached into his satchel and pulled out two oranges and two apples. "Make sure you hide them. Such things are quickly stolen in this evil place."

It was the first real food Aaron and Jaime could eat since their captivity, since the fruit was not impure. They devoured them with relish. Only the stem of the apples would survive their hunger, and the oranges were eaten completely, pits and rinds included. Jewish law requires its adherents to stay alive at all costs, even if it means violating the laws of Moses, even to eating parts of the vile pig.

Matarazzo went back to rummaging through his satchel, finally pulling out a small Hebrew prayer book. "To keep you close to God," he said as he disappeared. Aaron looked after him in disbelief.

౭ ఞ

Aaron and Jaime did finally accommodate themselves, as Matarazzo had predicted. They had no choice. They found a group of Jews who gathered to hold religious services whenever they could. Father and son found solace in their prayers and knowing that Matarazzo was really trying to help.

Jaime reached the age of 13 while in captivity. Still, he performed the rites of Bar Mitzvah, the passage of a Jewish child into manhood, according to religious law. One of the captives was a Rabbi and he helped Jaime prepare his Hebrew so he could lead his fellow slaves in the religious service. Now, Jaime was considered a man by his co-religionists. Fellow captives celebrated this significant day with him, shaking his hand, patting him on the back and wishing him luck. It was an event that brightened up another miserable day. Some managed to bring things for the celebration: a saved cupful of wine, pieces of stale bread, even a slab of cheese. No one asked how anyone was able to come by such things. It was an occasion that was spoken about for weeks.

Over time, Aaron and Jaime saw the older members of their prayer group disappear. "Their ransom was paid," they would be told. But sometimes the release came through death, resulting from beatings or the lack of strength to continue on in this hard life. Hope would always soar when a member of the group was liberated. Matarazzo's visits would be greeted with, "When will I be freed?" There was never a satisfactory answer. Meanwhile, the prayer group was being replenished with a fresh contingent of unhappy slaves. After a while, Aaron and Jaime were among the older veterans among the group and knew their way around with the guards and how to manage life to make things easier in this world of captivity.

On regular occasions Muslim Imams would visit the slaves and advise, "All you need to do to leave this life of misery is to convert to Islam and accept Allah." It was tempting. Many slaves would do anything to escape this difficult life of captivity. Some Christians embraced Islam as a passport out of slavery. The pirate Captain who had kidnapped them was a good example. If a slave converted, he would be released and was qualified to join the Sultan's army. If talented, he could rise to the heights in the military. He might even join the Sultan's court as an advisor. Few Jews succumbed to this temptation, holding tight to their faith, often with the help and encouragement of fellow Jewish slaves.

One night after many months of hard labor lifting heavy stones to build a sea wall, Aaron went to sleep despite the noise. Father and son were now able to ignore the din, exhausted as they were. Sleep was always welcomed. Aaron was awakened by a sharp pain at his back. He rose from the floor.

"What is it, papa?" Jaime asked.

"Something sharp is digging into my back."

Jaime reached beneath Aaron's sheet. "Here it is, a stone."

Aaron looked at the stone. It was triangular, and sharp at its point. He reached into the pouch that was securely tied around his waist, never leaving his side. He drew out a precious candle and a match given to him during one of Matarazzo's visits. He lit the candle and used the stone to write on the wall.

"I'm scratching this into the wall so the world will not forget us," he said to his son. "We are among the many slaves who have endured the worst of hells in this place, simply because we are Jews."

જી ન્ઠ

Ennis was re-reading the words on the wall. As a Spanish-speaker, he was intrigued by the spelling. He had never seen anything like it, even when reading old Renaissance classics at the

Academy. He put it down to the well-known fact that writers at this time in history were not too fussy about their spelling.

He committed the words to memory, since his notebook was back in his billet. Aaron Henriques, or whoever it was who'd etched these words into the wall for someone to find 200 years later, was obviously literate, but a poor speller. He was, however, able to communicate his thoughts clearly. *But the year 5492? What was that about?*

"Are you Jewish?" Marco asked.

"No."

"I thought not, sir. They are a fussy lot, the Jews I mean. I don't care for them too much. Never did. They are forever getting in people's way. Are you a professor when you are not in your Navy?"

"Yes." Ennis was not about to explain to Marco that Aaron and Jaime may have been among his ancestors. Nor that he recognized this place of agony from a recent dream. He felt that Marco's Jewish slur was directed at him. He couldn't explain why, but he knew he would have to get rid of this man as soon as possible.

"I want to do a rubbing of this inscription," Ennis said in a stern voice. "Is there a church or other place nearby where I can get the special paper they use for rubbings?"

"Yes, Lieutenant. There is a church close by. It's next to an old cemetery and many of my tourists like to make rubbings of the tombstones in the graveyard. You'll be able to buy the kind of paper you want. We can walk there, it's not far."

When they arrived at the Church, Ennis paid Marco and thanked him for the tour, even though it was cut short. Ennis was relieved; he felt he couldn't spend another moment with Marco.

At the church's shop, Ennis asked the clerk if he knew anything about the year 5492. The clerk did not, but a priest standing nearby turned to Ennis, saying, "Excuse me, I hope I'm not being rude. I couldn't help overhearing your question about the calendar date and I believe I can help you." The Priest was in his early 50s, and wore a dark black suit. The starched white collar surrounding his neck, together with the black dicky, placed him as Roman Catholic. He spoke with a Midlands English accent.

"No, sir, you are not rude at all," Ennis said with a smile "Any help you can give me would be appreciated." He went on to explain what he had seen on the dungeon wall.

"But that's wonderful," the Priest said as he finished filling his pipe with tobacco, tamping in the leaves with his thumb quickly so he could continue this conversation.

"I believe I can help. That's a date from the Hebrew calendar. The Jews count from a time in their history which goes back much before our own modern calendar, you know. It's a fascinating and complex system."

Ennis thanked the Priest and then asked, "Do you know what year that corresponds to in our time?"

"I can't give you an exact date right now, but if you come with me to my office here at the church, we should be able to figure it out. I'm Father Richard, by the way, originally from Manchester, England. Pleased to know you. I'm one of the priests here who teach Latin and French at the Church school. An American, aren't you? I can see from your uniform you're American."

"Yes. I'm a Lieutenant in the Navy."

"Sometimes I mistake you Yanks for Canadians." Father Richard extended his hand.

"I am a Yank, as you say. You can call me Jim."

"I should have known. You Americans are friendly from the first. Let's go to my office."

They walked out of the shop into a pleasant, quiet quadrangle filled with freshly-mown grass, flowering bushes and stone statues of what Ennis believed to be Saints of the Church. It was one of the few places in Valletta as yet untouched by the bombings; an oasis of peace in a city filled with rubble and destruction. Ennis wondered how long this little plot of land would remain this way. The enemy's bombs were sure to eventually find their way into this corner of Valletta.

Entering Father Richard's office, Ennis could see he was in the presence of a scholar. This medium-sized office was filled with shelves loaded with an army of books neatly and carefully divided into brigades of Latin, English, Spanish, German, French and even Hebrew.

"Do you speak all these languages, Father?" Ennis asked as he waved at the books.

"Well, I would say I have a better reading ability with some of them than a speaking ability, but I do have much more than the basic knowledge of them all. I speak Spanish and French fluently. And, of course, Latin."

"Even Hebrew?"

"Oh, yes., I studied Hebrew at the Seminary as a student. I'm quite good at it, I must say. Only in reading, that is. How can you understand the Old Testament if you can't read it in its original language? It's a mistake some of our seminarians make, depending on some of those spotty translations, I mean. A bad translation can throw you off, you know. Do you speak other languages?"

"I'm fluent in Spanish. And I speak French and German."

"Then you must know what I mean." The Priest dropped into the seat behind his desk, which was piled high with books. Multi-colored pieces of paper acting as bookmarks peeked out of the many volumes, manuscripts, newspapers and letters. He signaled Ennis to take a seat, accompanying the gesture by saying, "Please make yourself comfortable, Jim." He moved some of the books on his desk to a different site for an unobstructed view of his guest.

Putting his pipe into a large glass ash tray, Father Richard called toward the open door of his office. "Carlos." When a tall, gangly youth arrived, the Priest said, "Might we have some tea for myself and our guest, Carlos?"

"Of course, Father."

While they were waiting, Ennis noted several diplomas on the wall, one of which was from Oxford University. Before he could comment, tea arrived. Carlos served it in two elegant bone china cups, sitting on matching saucers. He placed powdered milk in the cup for Father Richard.

"I have learned to drink my tea without sugar. Since the bombings, it has become a precious commodity, to be used only on special occasions, assuming you can find it in the shops. We have to forego fresh milk, as well. Some of our military friends have managed to slip us some powdered milk for the children and, from time to time, to a grateful priest. An English officer, who doesn't like milk, gives me his powdered ration when he can. I imagine he has some other persons he also favors with the stuff."

Ennis indicated to Carlos that he would drink the tea as it was served.

"We may be bombed daily, but I still like to retain some of the elements of a civilized society in my life. Tea-time, and this tea service which was my mother's, connects me to my English heritage. If the Germans and Italians keep bombing us, I may be reduced to drinking hot water from a tin with no sugar, milk or even a lemon," Father Richard said almost apologetically, as he looked at his cup and took a careful sip of the piping hot tea. The drink was accompanied with scones. Putting the cup down, he apologized again for the lack of butter on the scones. "The War, you know."

Father Richard then continued with his exposition, spending the better part of an hour explaining how slaves were captured, redeemed and the horrors they lived through until redemption. During his discourse, Father Richard stirred his tea, steam rising, cooling the drink as it swirled upward. He took small bites of his scone. It was, as he had said, a regular and necessary ritual for him. Ennis waited until his tea cooled off on its own, meanwhile biting once again into his own scone, which was delicious.

The well-informed Priest continued, "For the Jews, captivity was especially nasty as they were constantly pressured to convert. Even, at times, through torture. Some gave in despite having other Jews to back them up spiritually. The burdens of brutal treatment and not knowing when release would come were overwhelming. I can only imagine it. Are you Jewish, by the way?"

"No, but I believe I may have had some Jewish ancestors who were slaves here during the year I gave you. They have the same name as my family had centuries ago."

"Ah, yes, let's find the exact year. That's why we are here. We can't be certain, you understand, Jim, because our writer did not give us a month, but we can come close. The Hebrew calendar is quirky," he smiled while explaining. "It has 13 months instead of our Christian 12. And there is a full month which acts as the Hebrew leap year, instead of only one day in February every four years, as we do. It takes 19 years in the Hebrew calendar to return to the same date, unlike our one year. It's really a very complicated system, best described as luni-solar. We use the earth's rotation around the sun as our reference for calculating time. The Jews basically follow the moon.

"I might also mention to you that the Jews had an organization which redeemed the enslaved captives. In English, it was called The Jewish Society for the Redemption of Captives. Well-to-do Jews and Jewish communities throughout Europe pooled their political resources and money. The money was used to create a fund to redeem poor Jews who were unable to raise the ransom for their release. The organization maintained a regular representative here in Malta to look after the welfare of Jewish captives as best he could. The Jews were solicitous of their brothers and sisters who were captives. It was not necessary that they knew who the persons were. If they were Jews, the Society worked diligently to release them.

"According to the list of Jewish religious obligations and duties, redemption of captives stands very high. It even takes solemn precedence over care for the poor and the elderly. For a Jew to be a captive is considered worse than starvation and death, and all Jews are absolutely obligated to redeem their captive brethren. Women and children first, of course.

"If Aaron's son, Jaime, was redeemed first, then Jaime had the obligation to redeem his father as soon as possible. If during his captivity Jaime reached his Bar Mitzvah age of 13, when a Jew is considered to become a man, it would have been a joyous event for all the Jews to celebrate: One of their own reaching manhood while a slave. The redemption of captives, in Hebrew, is *pidyon sheveim.*

"There were probably many dozens more Jews in that dungeon you went into, all awaiting negotiations for their release at the same time. And I'm sure that some of them must have poured out their hearts on that stone wall as your ancestor did. I think I'll go down there myself and do rubbings of whatever I can find. It has the makings of a good scholarly paper or a lecture on what went on with respect to the slaves of that period."

As he spoke, Father Richard pulled a thick book with a peeling, weather-worn black leather cover from a shelf, and peered into it. Beneath the dry, cracked leather was a reddish paper undercover.

The book smelled sharply of old paper, a vinegary aroma. Ennis could see it was printed in Hebrew. With an elegant gold fountain pen, the Priest made calculations on a pad on his desk.

"Here it is, Jim, the date, I mean. Give or take a year to account for the differences in the Hebrew calendar, and that we don't have a month, the year would be 1732, possibly 1733."

Ennis asked if there was any place where he could find out what happened to Aaron and James.

"Probably in London. The records of Salonica, Amsterdam and Livorno are under the control of the Italians and Germans." The priest looked at Ennis' uniform and smiled. "I would guess, Lieutenant, you would be *persona non grata* in any of those other cities."

Ennis nodded in agreement. He told Father Richard of the strange Spanish spelling he had seen on the inscription on the wall.

"It's Ladino," the priest said, "a language the Spanish and Portuguese Jews used. I don't know too much about its history, but it shouldn't be too difficult to manage for a Spanish speaker. It has some Mediterranean languages interspersed in it and it was spelled phonetically, which is why you have what you thought were misspellings. The grammar is old, pre-Cervantes, Don Quixote. That might be a little troublesome."

Ennis rose and reaching over the volumes of books and documents, shook the Priest's hand, thanking him for the orientation. "I'm on my way, Father, to do a rubbing. I'm sorry I can't send you some milk or sugar. I'm not stationed here, so I don't receive rations."

Father Richard waved a free hand at Ennis, saying, "I understand. Good luck in finding out what happened to Aaron and Jaime. I hope you find whatever it is you are looking for."

Jim left the church and returned to the dark dungeon after purchasing a torch to find his way in the darkness. As he placed the paper over the scratching on the wall, he realized he was standing where Aaron and Jaime had passed their lives as slaves. He felt a strange and warm closeness to these two captives, who had the misfortune to be caught by pirates on the high seas, forced to spend miserable years in this godless and desolate place. Then, he thought,

See how their religion sustained them, even to the celebration of an important ritual in the life of a boy becoming a man. Why is it that I have no such sustenance in my life?

After he completed the rubbing and was satisfied that it had captured all the scratches on the wall, Ennis took the time to look for other scratches. One, near to Aaron's, was in Arabic. He couldn't read it. *A prayer to Allah for release from this hell,* he surmised. There was one in better Castilian Spanish than Aaron's. It was a prayer to Jesus for help. Another, in German, said "Dear Sweet Jesus, please release me from this hell."

Enough! He was beginning to feel the anguish and turmoil of those poor souls. He folded the rubbing paper and placed it inside his jacket pocket, then turned the torch's beam toward the ancient, bowed stairway. He climbed his way into the sunlight just as the ritual of air raid warnings began screaming and he could hear the crunch and thud of bombs falling on the hapless citizens of modern Malta. He headed for the nearest air raid shelter.

9

THE CITY OF ZAMORA
MARCH 1493

Pedro Alvarez told Jaime that he had taken the young Henriques children to Zamora for their own safety. It was where Pedro's sister lived. As they made their way to that distant area of Spain, the two men were careful about what they said to one another, as the Queen's guards were within earshot. Zamora was close to the Portuguese border and Pedro's widowed sister had lived there for years. The town was notorious as a jumping off place for Jews seeking safety in liberal Portugal.

Pedro's sister, Maria, had received the children, Alicia and Manuel, from her brother without question. She had not been told but guessed correctly that they were fleeing the Inquisition. A woman in her 40s, Maria was dark haired, stout and a childless widow. Her curious neighbors were told that the children were her niece and nephew, come to Zamora to visit their aunt. She dispensed love and care as if the two fugitives were her own and tried, as best she could, to replace their lost parents.

As the travelers entered her home, she embraced Pedro. After being introduced to Jaime, she said, "Your family is back there, Don Jaime," pointing to the rear of her large home. "I have taken good care of them. In these past months, I have come to love them as my own. Go to them while Pedro and I put the guards up."

Jaime took Maria's hands, kissed them, and said, "I am forever grateful to you Doña Maria, for your kindness."

He headed down the hall toward the room where the children were lodged. He made sure the guards were not about. Maria was keeping them busy with her good cooking. Jaime knocked on the door, opened it and stepped inside. He was immediately assaulted by his siblings. They both cried out, "Jaime!" Manuel, who was 11, jumped on his elder brother, wrapping his legs around Jaime's middle. Alicia, who was 14, hugged Jaime while she was sobbing and crying, "Mama and Papa."

During the next half hour, Manuel and Alicia told their brother how the Inquisition's guards came to their home, took their parents away and then returned later to strip the house of all its assets. They related how Pedro Alvarez took them in tow after he learned the children were next to be arrested. Pedro learned their parents had been tortured and burnt alive after having confessed that they secretly practiced Judaism. The children were told that they would be brought to Maria's home to await Jaime's return from his voyage with the great Captain, Cristobal Colón. They trusted Pedro to do what was necessary.

Throughout their narrative, they both stopped from time to time, sobbing uncontrollably. Maria, they told Jaime, had treated them with the utmost kindness. Manuel, who was slender and looked younger than his 11 years, had straw-blonde hair and large brown eyes, which he rubbed vigorously. Between his tears, he said, "What's going to happen to us?"

Alicia was dark-haired with grey-green eyes and a body that was beginning to blossom. She looked at her brother and said, "Yes, Jaime, what's to happen next?".

"You are not to worry. The Queen is aware of the situation of the Henriques family. She has personally guaranteed her protection for all of us."

"What does that mean?" Alicia asked, her eyes red.

"It means we will return to Barcelona. The Queen has arranged for priests to interrogate us, to satisfy themselves that although Mama and Papa may have been guilty of secretly practicing Judaism, we are innocent of the charge."

Alicia stopped sobbing and looked at Jaime, her face filled with fear. "We can't do that, Jaime."

"What do you mean? Why not?"

"Mama was teaching me the secrets of the Jews. We are Jews. All of us are Jews. Our grandparents were, Aunt Sara and Uncle Carlos are, as are all of our cousins. We are Jews. Mama told me we never accepted the Church. If we return to Barcelona, they are sure to find out. Then what will become of us?"

Later, in Maria's large kitchen, sitting with only one feeble candle to illuminate the room, Jaime conversed with Pedro and his sister in a low whisper. After all, they were in this very deeply and could be arrested for helping Jews, even if they were good Christians. Jaime was still struggling with the idea that he was a Jew. They could speak, but only in soft whispers, as both guards were set up for the night in a barn close to the house.

"It was not such a secret. After I came to work for your grandparents, and they felt they could trust me, I always knew," Pedro told Jaime.

"Why didn't they tell me?"

"Because you would be spared if arrested. You could truthfully say you were innocent of such charges. It is always the women who keep such secrets, your father once told me, since they have less contact with the outside world and so were least likely to reveal the truth. Your father knew because he was retiring and was no longer active in the business world. But he told me that he always knew, even as a child and that it was something he was solemnly warned about; that he should never speak about it to anyone.

"Your family even has two cousins who became priests so they could gather information to alert the family if they came under suspicion. For years, I would buy, from a list your mother would give me, the special foods she needed. I am a good Christian, Don Jaime. It is my duty as a Christian to keep your family safe. If the Inquisitors have the slightest hint that you and the children are Jews, they'll apply torture to get a confession. I don't want to think of how young Manuel and Alicia will bear up under their torture."

The conversation had to be concluded. The barn door had opened with a rasping noise that cried out for an oiling of its hinges. One of the guards walked out of the barn, carrying a lantern to light his way to the outhouse.

"We will continue this tomorrow," Maria whispered, as the guard wandered about, looking for relief.

At ten in the evening of the next day, Pedro and Maria Alvarez and Jaime sat again on the heavy wooden chairs in Maria's kitchen. Pedro walked to the back door and peered toward the barn, as he had done the night before. Tonight, no candles were burning in the barn, and no one sought the outhouse. Satisfied the guards were asleep and could not hear the conversation past the kitchen's thick wooden door, Pedro returned to his seat.

"Now that you know all the facts, Don Jaime, I have to discuss the plans I have made without consulting you, because you were away at sea. Believe me when I say I was in anguish, having to make many decisions to keep all of us safe. When I brought the children here almost a year ago, I had a plan. But the Queen has now created a problem for us.

"What do you mean, Pedro?"

"Nearby, across the border in Portugal, is the town of Braganca. In that town lives your parent's old friend and cousin, José Pereira."

"Of course. His son and I used to play together."

"I want to bring all of us there, to safety. But to get there is the problem."

"I understand now," Jaime said. "The Queen has graciously provided us with two of her best soldiers for our safety. But it also ensures our return to Barcelona as soon as possible. And it certainly prevents us from making a trip across the border." As he said this, Jaime pointed with his chin to the barn where Maria had put up the two guards. "What do you suggest?"

"Last year, when Isabella and Ferdinand expelled all the Jews from Spain, the Pereiras, who never converted, went to Braganca and successfully established themselves there. Your father helped them by selling their property and sending the money to them, which is against the law. Today, José and his family live in Braganca openly as Jews. They live well with the money your father sent them.

"I plan to bring you and the children to the Pereiras in Portugal. Maria contacted them a few months ago and they were eager to help the children of their old friends and cousins. They owe a great debt to your father, as I explained. They are beholden to you and your brother and sister.

"There is a river nearby, the Douro. If we took it downstream, it would bring us to Portugal, into a region known as La Raya. It is filled with Jews. The Jews on the Spanish side stayed in Spain after the Expulsion, making believe they are good Christians. On the other side, the Portuguese side, live the openly practicing Jews who left Spain. Many on both sides are related to one another. They go back and forth across the river border.

"It is a 30-mile trip from here to the river. The other alternative would be to travel directly to Braganca, the main town in La Raya, which is 60 miles and more by land; a longer and much more dangerous journey. We could be arrested any place along the way. I am sure we could not stand any close investigation. What I am suggesting is the Douro route. With you away, I had to make some grave decisions on my own. I pray I was right."

"What about you and Maria? If we escape, you will most certainly suffer for helping us."

Pedro held his hand as if to say, 'wait.' He walked to the door, opened it and looked to the barn once again. Satisfied the guards were still asleep on their straw beds, he returned to his seat.

"When they arrested your parents, I was told by your cousins the priests that because of my long and dedicated relationship with your family, I was almost certainly next to be arrested. It was at that moment I decided to leave Spain, even though I am a faithful Christian. In these times, as you are quickly learning Don Jaime, there is much insanity and madness in all the Peninsula. Everyone is afraid of being denounced, even by their own family and friends. As I have learned, through torture innocent people are being falsely denounced as heretics. A person could relieve themselves of torture and pains by denouncing themselves and then others, whether the claims are true or not. Your parents, blessed be their souls, never implicated me to save themselves. But what if I was tortured and forced to falsely name my sister because I am not as strong as your parents? Maria is innocent of heresy. But they would torture her, too, and she might also confess to anything to stop the pain." Pedro smiled as he rubbed Maria's arm with a loving affection.

"It took a while to get Maria to understand the situation. She finally agreed that she also had to leave. I knew your mother was teaching Alicia your family secrets. The children also had to be saved from the horrors of torture and, of course, you too, upon your return. Everything has been taken care of to prevent that.

"Maria is a childless widow. She has sold her properties in Zamora and has to surrender them by the end of this month. She has assured the Pereiras she would take care of the children. José Pereira will need someone to help him in his growing business. I fit that position. He knows how well I served your family, and he is happy to have me. Besides, I no longer have employment since your parents..." Pedro stopped. He could not bring himself to talk of Jaime's parents as dead.

He continued with hesitation. "Our only worry is the guards. How could we proceed down the river without them knowing what we were doing? To make the river trip, Maria has contacted a Portuguese barge owner who regularly sails on the Duoro, bringing Spanish grapes to the wineries in Oporto, the last stop on the river before it empties into the sea. We could get off before that, as soon as we reach Portugal. From there, we can proceed by carriage to Braganca in safety. How does that sound to you?"

"I don't see too many alternatives. How do we deal with our two guards?"

"I have been thinking of that ever since the Queen assigned them to us for our safety. We tell the guards we want to delay our return to Barcelona for two or three days: we are tired from the long trip and the return journey will be worse since we will have two children to attend to. While we are regaining our strength, we arrange some diverting entertainment for our guardians. And while they are busy having a good time, we leave for Vega Terron. It's the last village in Spain before we get to the river.

"The last month before you returned to Barcelona, I sent a message to Maria to pack her clothes and all her assets and those of the children and deliver them in two locked chests to the barge captain. I have Maria's things and my assets, which I've saved over the years working in your family's service, in one chest. I took the liberty of taking all the jewelry, rings, gold and silver coins and chains belonging to you and your family, before the Inquisition took complete control of the house and all its contents. Everything of yours and the children's is locked in the other trunk."

"Can we trust the Captain?"

"Who know, Don Jaime? We can only hope we are dealing with a man of honor. We have no choice. If we lose all our goods but save our lives, then we are lucky. Should we be caught... I care not to think of it. The Captain comes highly recommended from several of Maria's commercial friends. He will be well paid. Half I have already given him in advance; the rest he receives when we get to Portugal. If he is treacherous, he will certainly lose some lucrative business among Maria's friends here in Zamora and others in the region: he will no longer have any grapes to carry to Oporto."

"You have done well, Pedro. I know why my father always trusted you."

ง๛ ๛

The guards happily agreed to a three-day delay, especially when Pedro said he would take them to the town's fanciest brothel, where he requested the well-paid proprietor to provide them with her best practitioners. That would keep the guards busy for at least two days.

Pedro bid them a happy time. They ignored him as they immediately began enjoying the pleasures of the brothel. Adding to their festivities, Pedro provided them with a gift of two bottles of the region's best and most potent brandy.

Two hours later, anyone on the streets of Zamora might have noticed Maria, her brother and their young niece and nephew, accompanied by a handsome young stranger, mounting a carriage. They had no luggage and were obviously heading for the countryside to enjoy the beautiful weather and a picnic. Everyone was smiling, and the children were chattering happily. Not until the carriage left the city did Pedro tap the driver on the shoulder and said, "We've changed our minds. Take us to Vega Terron."

The driver turned around, with a scowl spreading across his face. Before he could speak, Pedro handed him a leather pouch heavy with coins. It contained enough money to cover the 30 mile trip to Vega Terron and back again to Zamora. A generous tip was included. The driver inspected the pouch's contents, happily bouncing it on the palm of his hand and was satisfied with its heft. The scowl was replaced with a broad smile and a hasty, two-fingered salute. He turned around, snapped his whip across the backs of his two-mule team, and shouted, *"Hiyah, rapido, rapido."*

At Vega Terron, the Portuguese owner of the barge that would take them down the river to Portugal and safety awaited them. His flat-bottom barge, a *rabelo*, was loaded with grapes piled up into open bins. The fresh sweet-smelling fruit greeted the travelers even before they came aboard. There was barely enough room for passengers; they were unable to avoid stepping on grapes that had rolled to the deck from the overstuffed bins. Jaime noticed that the Captain's hands were stained red from long contact with the red grapes which would go into the making of Portuguese wines.

The children almost immediately began plucking grapes and filling themselves with the freshly picked fruit. Pedro saw with satisfaction that their two trunks were resting side by side on a pallet at the stern of the barge. The red sealing wax Maria had carefully placed over the locks had not been disturbed. Pedro signaled Jaime with a glance toward the trunks and a smiling nod to indicate that they were intact. Jaime returned the smile. He understood that so far, all was well.

As they sailed down the Douro, the peaceful valley was dotted with grassy-green terraced farms - *quintas* - rising high above the winding river. It was a peaceful contrast to Castile's turmoil. A gentle breeze fluttered across the bow and the sun shone on the grapes glistening with dew. Soon, flies swarmed around the fruit, competing with the children to enjoy its sweetness. The pleasant, quiet countryside was a sign that all would be well now that they were on their way to the safety of Braganca.

Maria opened her picnic basket, removing chicken and vegetables she had prepared the night before. There was also a bottle of red wine which was passed around and two large loaves of bread. She offered the Captain, who was at the tiller, to partake but he declined, preferring the sardines he had packed for his pleasure. As the barge rounded a curve, the terraced hills on each side framed an arc of shimmering lights of blue, green and yellow. A rainbow covered both shores of the river.

"Look, children," Maria cried out. "A rainbow, a good omen for the future.

When they reached shore, the Captain helped them unload the trunks. Pedro gave him a pouch with coins, the rest of the money promised. The Captain counted them. Satisfied that the amount was correct, he wished his passengers good luck, directing them to a place where they could find a carriage to take them to Braganca.

Pedro located a carriage for hire and gave the driver the address in Braganca where he wanted the driver to take them. They all loaded the trunks into the carriage and the passengers settled themselves inside. The driver called out to his team, and they were on their way to the house of the Pereiras in Portugal, safe from the Inquisition. Once settled in their new home, Pedro, Manuel and Alicia would be safely out of the reach of the Inquisition. They would incur Queen Isabella's anger; that could not be avoided under any plan. But now, in Portugal, they could proceed with religious instruction from a rabbi in Braganca. Pedro sat back, satisfied he had done whatever he could to save the Henriques children, as well as Maria and himself. But what about 21-year-old Jaime? How would he carry on? Back to sea most likely, but careful never to touch a Spanish port.

Jaime, the hard-headed seaman, was not too sure about the rainbow. During his months at sea, he had seen many rainbows, some of which were associated with terrible storms such as the one he had experienced on his return trip to Cádiz. At the time, neither he nor his fellow crewmembers thought of rainbows as good omens.

10

PORTUGAL
MARCH 19, 1497

They had been negotiating for a long while, Portugal's King Manoel and Ferdinand and Isabella of Aragon and Castile. Manoel had proposed marriage with their daughter, Juana of Aragon. It would be a perfect fit, Manoel pointed out. The two countries, which were of similar heritage, customs and language, occupied the Iberian Peninsula. They should merge, thereby establishing a strong dynasty and culture. It would be difficult for anyone to conquer them, protected as they were by the rugged and difficult-to-cross Pyrenees Mountains to the north, the natural boundary between Europe and Spain. And then there were the seas, the Atlantic and the Mediterranean on the remaining three sides. Invaders would have to think twice before trying to overcome a united Iberia, as the Arabs had done eight centuries earlier. The logic was evident, especially, as Manoel had pointed out, Portugal would be the trading and mercantile part of this new alliance and Spain would provide her warriors and navy for protection.

There was one strong obstacle, however. Isabella gave strict instructions to her emissary to the Portuguese Court: "Give King Manoel this letter. Be sure to tell him that our wishes are that as long as one Jew lives in Portugal, there will be no marriage between our families."

Manoel read the letter and understood the message. However, he also understood they were the wishes of a fanatic: he knew this point was not negotiable. While he was dedicated to the making of a union with Juana of Aragon, he was not, however, so quick to divest himself of his Jews, as had been the case with the Spanish royals. He was faced with a real dilemma. While Portugal was not a military power, it was one of Europe's great trading nations. Her merchant ships sailed to her colonies on the west coast of Africa, returning with gold, gems, slaves, wood and other treasures for Europe's consumption. Portuguese ships also called at the Mediterranean's important ports, trading with the Spanish, Italians, Greeks, North Africans, Arabs and the Ottoman Turks.

Recently, Portugal had even opened a maritime passage to India and China and was the only nation calling on Asian ports, by sailing around the southern tip of Africa's Cape of Good Hope into the Indian Ocean. Portuguese Jews had a strong hand in the booming commercial prosperity. It was not sound business for Manoel to throw his Jews out of the country, as the foolish Ferdinand and Isabella had done five years earlier. No. His was a better plan, one that would guarantee Portugal's prosperity and still satisfy those stubborn and fanatical Spaniards.

The King was aware that in 1492 when Jews were obliged to leave Spain, a large number of them, estimated to be over 60,000, had conveniently crossed the nearby borders into Portugal. They enlarged an already significant minority, adding to Portugal's prosperity. He couldn't let them go: he would keep them as converted Christians. That would resolve the problem raised by Isabella and Ferdinand. Now, he had to consider and work out a plan as to how he would go about doing that.

First, he decided that by end of December of this year, 1496, he would kidnap all the young Jewish children in his realm and forcibly convert them. Accordingly, soldiers and police swept throughout Portugal, seeking Jewish households. They took the children from their anguished parents and converted them. Then, they transported them to King Manoel's colonial island of Sao Tome, off the African coast. In the town of Braganca, two-year old Baruch Pereira was torn from his mother's arms. Fortuna Pereira cried for months, never recovering from the trauma. Manuel Henriques, now 15 years old, hid in the cellar with his sister, 18-year-old Alicia. Shaul Pereira, age 21 and engaged to marry Alicia, was off at work at his candle manufacturing shop, too old to be kidnapped anyway.

Then the duplicitous King assembled fleets of ships, and ordered the exile of the remainder of Portugal's Jews from his realm. As the mass of unfortunates jammed Portugal's ports, preparing to embark aboard those vessels, priests rushed to the docks, and forcibly converted every one of them.

By March 1497, Jews were no longer legally residents of Portugal, satisfying the demands of Isabella and Ferdinand. In Braganca, the Pereira and Henriques families were faced with the sad fact, as were all the Jews of Portugal, that with the quick scrawl of the royal quill, they had forcibly become Christ's newest children.

Manoel had his soft side. "No 'New Christians'," as they were now called, "will be denounced as heretics for practicing Jewish rituals for a period of 20 years," he generously decreed. After that, they would become liable to denunciation for "Judaizing."

Both Spain and Portugal were now vast prisons. By Royal Edict, the gates to freedom were shut on newly converted Jews. They were not permitted to leave Iberia. What Manoel had not considered however, was the history of his Jews. It was the stubborn attachment they had historically shown to their religion, even after their forced conversions. Eventually Portugal, faced with so many heretical Jews, in 1536 had to establish its own Inquisition based upon the Spanish model.

In Spain in 1492, Jews refusing to convert left by the thousands; possibly more than 200,00 of them. Most of those remaining were not strongly bound to their faith. They might have had a business or owned property they were not prepared to abandon. Or, they may have had close Christian family attachments they were reluctant to surrender. Some may have lacked any attachment to their religion. In 1497, however, Portuguese Jews were not afforded any of these options. The love of their faith still lay deep within them, despite the new religion they had been forced into. Then, unlike Spain's laws, they were granted a 20-year breathing period in Portugal. These historic differences between Spain and Portugal laid the groundwork for a vigorous religious underground in Portugal: a secret and hidden Jewish culture.

Portuguese New Christians would become famous; never able to throw off the 'stigma' of having once had Jewish antecedents. They traded throughout the Mediterranean, Western Europe and with the Portuguese and Spanish colonies of the New World. They were known as *La Nacion* amongst themselves. The Portuguese Nation, everybody else called them. Before 1492, Spain had already established an Inquisition to locate and erase all heresy among converted Jews. So far, the Portuguese had established no Inquisition. When it would be created, in 1536, it would be much fiercer than Spain's had ever been.

Because the Jews of Braganca and other towns had sold off all their assets in anticipation of their exile, they did not return to their old homes. Instead, they looked to Lisbon, Evora and Oporto, the country's major cities for business opportunities. Some went up into the mountains, establishing themselves in remote communities such as Belmonte, where they were not the focus of much attention and where they married only within a tight circle of certain families and friends. They would remain secretly Jewish for centuries.

Throughout the rest of Portugal, Jews were clandestinely teaching their children the tenets of the forbidden religion. Unlike Spain, where only a few stalwarts remained with the necessary energy and love for their faith, thousands of Portuguese Jews continued practicing their religion secretly. The country was a hotbed of crypto – secret – Jewry. As the generations passed, however, the basics of Judaism were slowly lost, eroded in time and by a lack of proper education in the tenets of Judaism.

Alicia Henriques, 18 years old, was preparing to marry Shaul Pereira, José's oldest son. She told Shaul that she intended to practice Judaism secretly, teaching it to their children. Shaul, whose family also secretly practiced Jewish rites, agreed. Her older brother, Jaime Henriques, was now sailing on Portuguese ships as a Christian officer, careful to keep clear of Spain and the long tendrils of the Inquisition. When the opportunity arose, he planned to settle down in a safe place.

One day, as he feared would eventually occur, a fellow seaman approached him, saying, "Don Jaime, do you remember me? I sailed on the *Santa Maria* with you and Admiral Colón. What are you doing here? We all thought you would continue sailing with the Admiral; he looked on you as one of his favorites."

Jaime made an unsatisfactory answer, and while there was no denunciation, he soon became well-known among his crew as the main who sailed as an officer with Don Cristobal Colón, the Admiral of the Ocean Sea. He felt that at any time he could be forcibly taken to Spain for the Inquisition's pleasure, a hefty reward winding up in the denouncer's pockets.

Around this time, during a stopover in Constantinople, he met a young Sephardic lady from a wealthy family. A year later he would leave the ship at that port, never to sail again. He became, with his father-in-law's help, the owner of a prosperous cloth-weaving factory.

Young Manuel Henriques had finished his apprenticeship as a shoemaker and was now on his own. He would eventually marry and name his first son Jaime, after his older brother. A generation later, Manuel's family was one of the leaders of crypto-Jewish families.

As time proceeded, some Jews managed to leave Portugal and establish Spanish and Portuguese communities throughout the world. Those who remained, stubbornly refused to completely surrender to Christianity. The result was that in 1536 the Portuguese King established his own Inquisition. He had approached the Pope earlier and was rebuked. It was finally granted under pressure and an acceptable bribe: Portugal was given the same powers Isabella and Ferdinand had received decades earlier. The Crown was to be the head of the Order and would decide when to begin its work. They would also select the head priests. Whatever funds were realized in fines and the confiscations of businesses and estates would be equally divided between Church and Crown. Portugal's Inquisition would become one of the most ferocious in the history of the Catholic Church.

11

NEW YORK UNIVERSITY
JANUARY 1942

It was cold. Very cold at 6th Avenue and West Fourth Street, reminding Jimmy Ennis of other New York winters when he'd left the subway and crossed the open area of Washington Square Park. He was in New York City again, to work with the marine architects on the final layouts for the submarines being built at the Electric Boat Company at Groton. America had been attacked by the Japanese at Pearl Harbor a month earlier, and the heads of Electric Boat were being pressured by the U.S. Navy to speed up their production of submarines for use in the War. That meant he and the other two U.S. Navy personnel assigned to Groton would be working double-time to get America's submarines launched and into the seas, ready for combat.

Before returning to Connecticut, Ennis was taking some time to visit his friend, Professor Miguel Garcia. The wind was merciless, relentlessly finding openings in his coat and sleeves, forcing icy chills into his body. He held his military cap firmly down on his head to keep it from blowing away. Speeding up his pace, Ennis carefully navigated his way around the shiny, uneven patches of frozen, diamond-hard ice, remnants of a snowstorm that had raged through New York City a week earlier. He battled the wind all the way across the open, unprotected Park to Washington Square East, fighting its strength to open the street door leading to the entrance of the University's Washington Square College of Arts and Sciences. He was grateful for the calming heat and the familiar smell of the school's cafeteria that engulfed him. He shook the chills away as he unbuttoned his coat and walked to the elevator.

Whenever Ennis came here, he was reminded that three decades earlier the top floors of the building next door, the Brown Building, was the scene of one of America's worst labor catastrophes: the Triangle Fire. Scores of innocent women died there in a tragic fire that should have been avoided. Reborn as a house of learning, the building was still sometimes referred to as "The Factory," by students who now walked its halls.

In addition to catching up with his old friend, Ennis' visit today was to make some sense of what he had discovered in Malta's basement dungeon a few months ago.

Professor Miguel Garcia was a first-generation American whose Cuban family had fled their island home in 1896, as political refugees from the Spaniards who were occupying the island. The Garcias were prominent activists among Cuba's wealthiest families who opposed Spanish colonial rule. They became an important source of intelligence for the U.S. government, helping American military during the Spanish-American War of 1898. Miguel's grandfather fought in the War, leading Americans to strategic armories and military posts. His uncles ran intelligence services for the invading forces. For their assistance, the family was awarded political asylum and American citizenship.

The family, which Ennis thought seemed always to have shadowy connections with the government, first landed in Tampa, a favorite place for Cuban refugees. Havana cigar makers had years earlier settled in nearby Ybor City, where they continued manufacturing their world-famous luxury cigars. Mysteriously, the family managed to recover the considerable fortune they had left behind, later settling in among the mansions and powerful politicians of Washington's suburban Georgetown. Garcias were still maintaining close relations with America's intelligence community.

As a young man fresh out of Princeton, Miguel Garcia gained a position as a non-military Spanish instructor at the United States Naval Academy. Just a few years older than his students, he was invited to accompany them to Army-Navy football games in New

York, Philadelphia, and Baltimore and to student parties on campus. Garcia developed a close relationship with one of his best students, James Ennis. After a while they were calling each other Mickey and Jimmy. Garcia had quietly disappeared during Ennis' last year at the Academy.

"Mr. Garcia got a government scholarship to study Spanish literature at Harvard," Ennis was told. Four years after Ennis graduated and began his stint as one of the Navy's consultants at Groton's Electric Boat Company, Mickey Garcia called him.

"I'm at the U.S. Naval War College in Newport, Rhode Island. I'm teaching Spanish to officers. They have these naval attaches who get posted to Spain or South America. Can't have them sitting on their asses in a Spanish-speaking country, unable to communicate with the folks they're supposed to be trying to pull information from," Garcia said. "We're practically neighbors, so we can get together some time."

Lucy and Jimmy Ennis would meet with Mickey and his wife Maria several weekends a year and on holidays like Thanksgiving and Christmas. Then Mickey left the War College for NYU, where he earned a PhD in Education while teaching Spanish at the University's Department of Romance Languages.

For all the years Jimmy Ennis knew Mickey Garcia, he always felt he did not fully understand his friend. There was a perplexing aura about Mickey that he never sought to explain. There were elements of his life and personality that eluded Ennis, and he always had the strong feeling that Mickey purposely wanted it that way. Ennis rode the elevator to the fourth floor and passed through the hallway door leading to Garcia's office. Garcia's secretary knew he was coming and ushered him in right away. The two men embraced, Latino style, Mickey's favorite way to greet a close friend.

"Mickey, you never get old."

"It's Maria's cooking," Mickey said, as he patted a non-existing paunch. He had the look of Spain about him, with his lean elongated face, Roman nose and dark hair and eyes and the olive-tinted skin of an Iberian.

"What are you doing in New York, Jimmy?"

"I'm spending the week here, working with Naval Architects Cox and Gibbs. I can't say any more than that. You understand?"

"I sure do."

"What have you been doing, besides teaching here?"

"I run three classes, three days a week. Then I go to Governor's Island twice a week and give courses to the military going on assignment to Spanish-speaking countries. You know; the language and the culture."

"How does it go?"

"Well, it's really a crash course, the basics, you know. I can only hope that once they get to their assignments they can pick up on the language and understand the differences between an Anglo and Latin society. They're mostly a bright bunch. I was going to suggest a walk to Little Italy or Chinatown for lunch, but it's dreadfully cold. So let's go to a place around the corner, on Waverly Place. It's a hangout for students. Some of the younger faculty go there too: better than eating in the cafeteria."

They walked the one block on Waverly Place to Rocky's, a restaurant/bar in the basement of an apartment house. The wind and cold attacked them all the way. When they opened the door to descend the stairs, a pleasant wall of heat greeted them, as did the friendly, yeasty smell of beer and roasted meat. The restaurant had a long bar along one wall, which sat eight people. A dozen round tables and two more long tables made up the dining area of the restaurant. A juke box took up part of a wall. It played popular music when fed the necessary coins. There were no menus: a blackboard leaning on a wall next to the bar advised customers what was available that day. One item never on the board was a well-known Rocky standard that all the regulars knew: Italian sausages on fresh crusty bread with a choice of sweet, mild, or hot sauce, served with a side of crispy French fries.

When he saw the two men enter, Rocky left his spot behind the bar and came over with two glasses of water, dining services wrapped in cloth napkins and his breezy greeting.

"Hello perfesser. How ya' been? Ain't seen ya in a while."

Rocky Palermo was a New Yorker of Italian descent and an ex-boxer who escaped the profession before it did bad things to his face and body. A small, balding man who fought welterweight class, he had saved his money to open a long-desired restaurant. Photographs on the wall behind the bar showed Rocky, 25-years younger, in different and menacing boxing poses.

"Have the sausage hero," Mickey advised. "There's a sweet sauce but I usually get the mild sauce. Hot is really hot."

Rocky nodded in agreement. "Two *salchichas*, mild sauce," he mumbled to himself as he scribbled the order on a green pad.

"Ya wanna New Orleans, perfesser?" Rocky asked in his New York accent, as he simultaneously ripped the written order from the pad and handed it to a passing waiter heading back toward the kitchen.

"Sure," Mickey said. And before Jimmy could ask what a New Orleans was, Mickey explained, "It's a mix of white wine and beer."

The two men settled in. Rocky's was busy. Jimmy noticed both men and women. *War time will soon thin out the men,"* Ennis mused, *"although Mickey won't get into the military because of his heart murmur."* The friends caught up on what life had been like since they had last met, several months earlier. After a short silence, Jimmy reached into his inside jacket pocket and pulled out the wall rubbing he had made in the Malta slave basement. He unfolded it and passed it across the table, explaining where he got it and for the first time, informing his friend that he had ancestors with the family name of Henriques.

"What do you make of this, Mickey? Are we dealing with an illiterate? Someone told me it's Ladino, some form of Spanish that Jews used a long time ago."

His friend looked at the writing and smiled. After a good long look, he set the rubbing aside. "That's right, Jimmy. It is Ladino and no, this man is not illiterate. In fact, he was probably able to speak six or seven languages. And probably was fluent in all of them, too."

"How can you tell that?" Jimmy asked, a little incredulous at Mickey's easy answer filled with such detail.

"Several ways. First, Ladino was spoken by Jews who had a Spanish or Portuguese family history. It's a mixture of Hebrew, Arabic, Turkish, Italian, Greek and French. The basic grammar and most of the words are Spanish. When this was etched into the wall,

Ladino was an important language, used throughout the Mediterranean basin, Latin America, and Western Europe. Even Christians and Moslems who had significant dealings with Jews, spoke it. Today, it's a dying language. If you had time to inspect all the scratches on that basement wall, I'm sure you would have found more writings like this one. Secondly, he comes from the Ottoman Empire; probably Istanbul, Izmir, or Salonica. And then, he is most certainly a descendant of Spanish or Portuguese religious refugees." Mickey looked at his friend with a broad grin.

"Mickey, what the hell are you, Sherlock Holmes? How do you know all this stuff?"

"Look," Mickey said, pointing to the rubbing. "See how he uses a 'k' to spell Cueva, instead of a 'c'? In the Turkish language used by the Ottomans, and their colonies throughout the Mediterranean, a 'c' is pronounced as a 'ch', like Charlie. So Jews substituted the 'k' to get the sound of a hard 'c'.

"And notice all the phonetic spelling, like the w for the u in Cueva. Obviously, Spanish is not his first language. But Ladino is. Next, he is a merchant who, with his son, was captured while at sea by Barbary pirates – the Knights of Malta. It was a tradition to travel with a son. It was the 18th Century version of getting a master's degree in Business Administration for the youngster. Persons of this type spoke many languages to be able to do business all over the Mediterranean. He probably spoke, or had a good knowledge of, Italian, Greek, Turkish, Arabic, Spanish and Portuguese ... and only God knows what else. He's obviously Jewish because he uses the Jewish calendar, as you explained to me. That's a fairly good profile of your prisoner, Aaron Henriques."

"I'm impressed. This man may have been my ancestor. I suppose I should find out if he was."

"It would certainly be an interesting thing to do. You could have been Spanish, way back. That's a thought. But tell me, why do you think he was an ancestor?"

"Because the Ennis family has traditionally said a man named Solomon Henriques came from London or Amsterdam to the English colonies before the Revolutionary War and he may have been the founder of the American Ennis branch. The name

Henriques was changed to Ennis; we don't know why or when, or by whom. I figure it was because he wanted to fit into an English culture. But that's only a guess."

"What you're telling me is curious. Jews from Spain and Portugal fled the Inquisition in the 16th and 17th Centuries and settled in Protestant countries like Holland and England. They are called Sephardim. Maybe you are a descendant of those folks."

After finishing their meal, Mickey asked, "Am I stepping into some area I'm not supposed to, if I ask what your next assignment might be?"

Jimmy thought a while. *There's that feeling again, that Mickey is more than he seems to be. His question was asked with a certain delicacy. Most people would not have asked if his next posting was a forbidden question. And at the Academy, on at least two occasions, I heard that the Garcia family was tight with military intelligence.*

"It's no secret. When I'm finished with Cox and Gibbs this week, I'll probably have a month's work or more in Groton tying up loose ends. With this War, the folks there are getting real pressure to build subs fast. With my years of working on them, I'm hoping to be posted to submarine duty, which I had already requested six months ago."

"Would you consider doing some intelligence work?"

"I don't know, Mickey. Never occurred to me. I don't know that I'm cut out for that kind of stuff. I don't think that's my line of work."

"It's not Mata Hari work. It's different. Let's go back to the office, where we can talk." Mickey nodded at the diners sitting near them, indicating what he had to say should be private.

Back at the Arts and Sciences building, Garcia rummaged through the many folders on his overcrowded desk. He finally located the one he was seeking. "Here it is!" he said with a tone of satisfaction.

"I get these kinds of requests often." He waved a two-page letter in front of Jimmy. "Naval Intelligence wants to know if I can recommend a highly-qualified Spanish speaker, preferably a naval officer in his late 20s or early 30s, who can translate and interpret

Spanish diplomatic messages. By the way, how's your French and German? Have you been keeping up on them on your own time?"

"Pretty good. I enjoy reading French and German magazines. It's sort of a hobby for me. If I spoke them daily, I'd be better at them."

"The two other languages are an extra lollypop for these people. I think you fit the bill. You have a gift for languages. Who knows where it could lead. Interested?"

"I don't know. What am I supposed to be doing? Am I qualified for that kind of work?"

"Sure you are. You were always one of my best students. I know you would be good at this. You would be reading stuff that comes into Intelligence agencies written in Spanish."

"Where would I be stationed?"

"That, I can't say. Washington at first, I would guess, so the big boys have a chance to look at you. Then South America, maybe Spain. If you go overseas, you'll probably have some diplomatic status."

"Could I take Lucy with me?"

"Probably. But I can't guarantee it. I only know that for the present they want a Spanish speaker."

"I'd have to discuss it with Lucy. I've been trained as an engineer. I was ready to go into submarine service. Combat. That's an important contribution I can make in this war. It might look as if I'm copping out of going into battle. How long do I have to make a decision?"

"This one has a Red Urgent on it. You probably have less than two weeks to decide. You're not the only one they'll be looking at. But if you want to do it, I'll make sure you're the only one out of this office, and I'll send a highly recommended letter on your behalf. Including your ability to speak other languages. Who knows, you might get to Spain and locate those ancestors of yours. Maybe we're distant relatives. And Jimmy, you should look at this as important work for the War. You may not be on the front lines, but keeping important people properly apprised of what's going on by translating or interpreting a foreign language into English, is just as important. Think about it."

12

LISBON
NOVEMBER 1, 1755

Gracia Henriques was excited. She awoke early this Saturday; an hour before the sun rose. The petite, handsome 41-year-old woman, who looked 10 years younger and was proud of her good looks, shook her husband Jaime awake and made her morning ablutions. Then, she carefully set out eleven place settings of dishes and silverware around her large dining room table in preparation for today's guests. The Pereiras would be coming, as would the Nuneses and the widower Manuel Calderon, the one all his friends called *Vilho Moises* (Old Moses.) Other guests were the Duartes and the Mendeses. All were members of Gracia's small circle of close friends. All shared the same forbidden secret: they practiced the religious rites of the Jews. The Henriques and Pereira families had ties that had been firmly established for over two centuries, going back to the days when their families lived in Castile.

Today was All Saints Day in Lisbon, a special Catholic religious holiday. Lisbon's churches would be crammed with worshippers lighting thousands of ritual candles. Most of Lisbon, except for Gracia, her husband and their friends would be in church. Many of those also not attending were Portugal's other crypto-Jews who also practiced their religion secretly. If caught, they faced torture and even death at the hands of the Inquisition.

First, Gracia's friends would meet in a small room the Henriques family had set aside for prayer. Gracia, as always, would lead the offering, saying prayers exalting the One God of the Universe. She used a handful of Hebrew words such as *Adonai*, one of the words for God. And *mitzvah*: a good deed. She could recite the *Shema* in Hebrew, the Jew's affirmation that there was only one God. Part of her rituals included the lighting of candles. Every Friday night, candles were secretly lit by women in the homes of Portugal's crypto-Jews.

Today, they would be meeting on a Saturday and during the day. This was unusual. Gracia and her friends knew this to be the Hebrew Shabbat, the special day of rest in the bible, when Jews all over the world prayed to God. This Saturday, few people would be around to denounce Gracia and her friends because most of Catholic Lisbon was praying in its many churches. It was a rare opportunity to pray on the Jewish Sabbath, just as other Jews would be doing, and Gracia was not going to allow it to pass by. As the sun rose, Gracia's friends began funneling into her spacious home. Her husband Jaime, tall, sandy-haired, and brown-eyed, greeted his guests as they passed through the door. "With most of our neighbors in Church, we are sure no one will notice us today," he said reassuringly.

"Later, Jaime will go to church so that he can be seen praying, to avoid any suspicion," Gracia advised her friends.

The Henriques family and those assembled were all New Christians, descendants of Jews forced to convert to Christianity in Portugal in 1497. Centuries later, their Portuguese neighbors were unable to forget that their fellow citizens were once Jews and considered them still tainted with the hateful religion of their ancestors. This recognition extended to placing barriers or outright denial of opportunities to join certain societies, hold positions in the military and government, or even travel outside of the country. New Christians could only leave Portugal if they left their family and assets behind, assuring their return. Nevertheless, for centuries a trickle of secret Jews had found ways to leave Portugal. They travelled abroad with their families, conceding the loss of all their assets, surrendering everything they owned in Portugal. Others were able to leave because over the years they had secretly squirreled funds abroad or had families and friends ready to care for them in their new homes.

They finished with their prayers, which over time had become distinctly different from those of their co-religionists throughout the world. That was because of the lack of instructors to teach them Hebrew and the necessary rituals. Cut off from world Jewry for centuries, their prayers would be mostly unrecognizable to those outside of the country, but they were sincere. Gracia's offerings still contained some basic Hebrew prayers such as the *Shema*. They also knew that on certain days they fed rivers with bread to expiate their sins. On other days, they fasted and on special days, always in the spring around Easter, they did not touch nor eat any bread. And they ate no pork or shellfish if they could avoid it. At times, they ate pork in public to show that they were good Catholics. When they all sat down to their meal, Gracia chanted two prayers. one for the blessing of wine, another for the blessing of bread.

Gracia had noted when she arose that morning, that the day was unusually still for this time of year. No wind was blowing, no birds chirping, and the neighborhood dogs, horses and mules were also strangely silent. At precisely 9:40 a.m., the dining room table shook, dishes rattled, silverware jumped as if dancing to the music of clatter. The sky darkened and turned a sickly yellow color. The diners were thrown from their chairs to the floor. A loud rumble, then a mighty chorus of thunderclaps accompanied by a storm of bricks and plaster showered down on them.

"My God!" cried old Moises Calderon. "The house is coming apart." He pointed to the wall leading to the street. It had separated where it had once met a side wall at right angles. One could see clearly to the roadway outside.

The silent animals were now howling. Horses and mules broke their tethers, neighing and braying as they ran free. Jaime could see a large opening in the ground, towards which a dog was running. Losing its balance, it fell into the chasm, yelping helplessly. The ground was undulating like a huge slithering beast.

Now there were screams from the few men, women and children who had not attended church this morning. It was the end of the world: walls tumbling down, people entombed under the brick, plaster, and wood of their own homes.

"Get out! Get out of the house and into the street," people were shouting.

One of the huge oak ceiling beams in the Henriques house split under the weight of a crumbling second floor. It came crashing down, pinning old Moises Calderon to the ground. Two men quickly pushed the beam aside and helped him, limping, into the street.

Outside, the scene was chaotic. Buildings had been flattened, reduced to heaps of rubble. The few people in the neighborhood who were not in church rushed into the streets, watching the ground moving beneath them. The sky returned to that pale and muddy yellow that Gracia could not remember ever seeing before. It frightened her. What was happening? Was the world coming to an end? Jaime had often told her that religious fanatics in the city were always predicting it, even to citing precise dates and hours and minutes. Was this the time?

God played no favorites this day. Churches collapsed too. Thousands of candles in churches throughout Lisbon fell to the floor or were flung through the air. Their flames devoured drapes, carpets, prayer books, wooden wall panels, doors, and pews. It consumed stained glass, the wood or ceramic statues of Saints and whatever else fires could hungrily convert to ashes. Soon, the whole city was burning. It was not merely confined to a single street, an avenue or even a section. All Lisbon was ablaze. And no one knew where to begin the fight to extinguish the conflagrations. Neither the needy nor the affluent, the young nor the old, the healthy nor the infirm, were spared. No one escaped the effects of this disaster.

The earthquake's main violence lasted only three and a half minutes. Its aftermath, however, remained for months and, in some cases, years. The quake was felt not only in Lisbon but in much of the Mediterranean. New World colonies in the Western Hemisphere experienced tsunami-like tides and flooding. At Lisbon's port, a wave reaching over 30 feet in height, beached ships on to dry land. It sank dozens more, clogging the harbor's passageways and docks. After-shocks, occurring when the shifting tectonic plates began settling, lasted for days, and destroyed most of the structures that had not already been wasted.

At night, people huddled together in open spaces for comfort and protection, as looters began roaming throughout the city. Frightening silhouettes of bandits darting back and forth seeking looting opportunities, were accented against a blazing, crimson night sky. After the fires were finally staunched, chaos set in. Municipal agencies were not operating. No police or soldiers were immediately available to maintain order. Water and food were not to be had at a fair price. People were shivering with nothing more than bedsheets, thin blankets or towels to keep them warm.

Gracia, Jaime and their friends all scurried to an open pasture, where there were no buildings to come crashing down on them. It was a safe meadow about a quarter mile from the Henriques home. They remained there for several hours while strong aftershocks continued to frighten them. When things were a little calmer, Jaime took his close friends Jorge and Delfina Pereira aside, and said, "The traditions of how my family helped the Pereiras, who then saved the Henriques children after their parents were murdered by the Inquisition, have kept us close. Now I have a plan to leave this damned place and save you with us."

José and Delfina moved closer. "What are you thinking, Jaime?" José asked.

"There is such confusion in this city now; we should take advantage of it. If we leave Lisbon now, no one will know and no one will care. There are no soldiers or policemen to check us or prevent us from leaving, something they are always required to do of New Christians. Everyone's busy now trying to keep alive. Let's go back to my house and get into the cellar. Praise God the looters have not found it."

"Found what, Jaime?" Delfina asked.

"Our savings, Gracia's and mine. They are behind a large fieldstone in the basement wall. If they are still there, it is enough to get us all out of here and sustain us for at least a year, maybe more. Will you come with us? I'll pay for everything."

"Where will we go?"

"Amsterdam, of course: so many of our people have already gone there. Then, perhaps, to London. We know that in both places we can live openly with other Jews and with real rabbis and synagogues."

"I don't know, Jaime. It's risky."

"Where's the risk, Jorge? Look around you, man. There's nothing left here. What difference if we start anew here or in Amsterdam? We will be able to leave with whatever assets we can carry with us. You know that in normal times it's illegal. In this confusion, we can walk out of this prison. Free! And no one is around to stop us. We may never have such an opportunity again."

Jorge Pereira looked at Jaime and Gracia. "Delfina and I have our children and many grandchildren here. We are too old to start over. You only have your sons Pedro and Carlos and a grandchild to care for. You and Gracia are younger than us, and stronger. We wish you good fortune. But we are staying here."

When they returned to their home, Gracia, Jaime and their son Pedro found that little was left of it, only a thick carpet of plaster and crumbled stone. Broken furniture, dishes, clothing and other debris remained where once their comfortable home stood. The rest of the neighborhood was unrecognizable. Only one house was standing. It leaned at a dangerous angle, ready to tumble down with the next aftershock

Their eldest son Carlos was at the site of the destruction, sifting through the wreckage while waiting for his family to return. The looters had already been there. The silverware and candlesticks had been stolen. They had hastily tossed the house's heavy beams, door jambs and the large dining room table into a large pile. A lifetime of hard work and dreams had been reduced to a triangle of rubble.

No one had tried going into the basement. Gracia, Jaime and their two sons walked through the ruins, trying to locate the stairway. Pedro found it. He stamped his feet with vigor and loose material gave way, tumbling down toward the basement. While Gracia remained above, the three men carefully descended into the basement. They were followed by a showering cascade of crumbled stone and dust. Illuminated by a shaft of daylight from above, Jaime found the iron lever he used to pry open the lids of heavy boxes. With it, he attacked a weathered fieldstone that made up part of the still-standing cellar wall. It came apart easily. Jaime shoved his arm into the space and pulled out two large leather knapsacks.

"They're here! The thieves didn't find them." He opened the pouches and saw his large hoard of silver and gold coins, precious gems, necklaces, rings and bracelets, together with the family's baptismal certificates. Drawing the leather strings on the pouches, Jaime and his sons left the cellar for the last time.

Upstairs, Gracia had found her sewing kit, some damaged clothing, and food. "Look at my dresses and your shirts and trousers. Torn. And they were only a few years old," she lamented.

"Don't worry, dear," Jaime said, his arm around his wife. "We'll put that to good fortune. First, we sew all the coins and the small gems into our clothing. There is enough here for two years of comfortable living, since the Pereiras are not coming with us."

Jaime revealed his plan. They would leave Lisbon immediately, cross the border into Spain and head for the port of Palos. From there, they would sail to France and then work their way north to Amsterdam. It was the classic escape route that many of Lisbon's New Christians were aware of and had always hoped they could avail themselves of at some time in the future. The fastest way out would have been to sail from Lisbon's port, but it was easy to see from reports they had received from people fleeing the port area, that it would take weeks, if not months, before the shattered harbor, blocked as it was by wrecked and beached vessels, could be cleared for normal and safe commerce. Jaime could not wait. All speed was necessary, while confusion ran not only throughout Lisbon, but in the wide area surrounding it.

"How long will it take to get to Amsterdam, Father?" Pedro asked.

"I don't know. Perhaps with all this chaos, two months or more. We will have to walk out of Portugal. I doubt we could find a horse or a coach available to buy until we get to Spain. Getting to the border may take more than a month." The two horses belonging to the Henriques' had bolted and were nowhere to be found. They may have been taken by looters. Jaime had given them up for lost.

"Then I have to stay," Carlos said. "With my wife with child in her third month, and the little one we have now, it will create difficulties and burdens that I can't even think of. We would be slowing you down. When you get to Amsterdam, let us know. Or I will contact the Portuguese community there to see if you have arrived. Once you are settled, I'll come out with my family."

"No! You must come. We cannot break up the family," Gracia cried.

"Mama, it's for the best. An infant and a pregnant woman will be a heavy liability and perhaps create some resentment among us. I don't want that."

"Gracia, don't argue. We must be practical. Carlos is right," Jaime said as he reached into one of his pouches. "This is approximately 10 percent of our fortune. Take it. The rest will be waiting for you when you get to Amsterdam. It should be an incentive for you to leave this prison that has no place for people of our faith. And here is your baptismal certificate. God knows you will need it. Look for the horses. They will be an asset if you can find them."

Carlos opened the cloth surrounding the jewelry. It contained pure gold coins, precious gems, diamond rings and bracelets, all part of the fortune Jaime had worked so hard to accumulate. Barely able to speak, he thanked his father.

"We will be reunited in Amsterdam," he promised. He kissed his parents and hugged 16-year-old Pedro. "Go with God, little brother. We will see each other again."

After Carlos left, Jaime told Gracia to sew the coins and small jewels into the clothes. "By wearing damaged clothing, we will look like all the other poor people wandering aimlessly with no particular destination in sight. Pedro, we have lots of work to do. Scuff up the knapsacks; make the leather look as if they are in such bad condition they should be thrown out. Then divide the rest of the jewelry into two parts and place them at the bottom of each of the sacks. On top of them, put clothing. Over the clothing, put items of food. You'll carry one pouch and I, the other. In the side pockets I will place our baptismal certificates and the small silver coins we will certainly need as we go along. That will save us from digging down into our pouches for money while others look at us and see what assets we are carrying."

Pedro began working on the pouches, scoring the finely tooled leather with sharp rocks, and rubbing dirt into it. When he was finished, the formerly fine pouches did indeed look as if they should be tossed into the rubble pile.

"Gracia, were you able to find any food in this mess?"

"Yes, Jaime. I found some coffee. And there is bread to eat, and a package of rice we can boil with potatoes and onions, garlic, and carrots. And some oranges! I also found two bottles of wine that were not broken and some cheese and a tin of sugar and another of salt. It's probably more than most of Lisbon has now. I'll look for more."

"Good. Then let's look as poor as we can and get started. The longer we stay here the more we become prey for thieves. And before we leave, we have to say goodbye to the Pereiras."

It was a tearful parting. Both families remembered the closeness born of assistance each had rendered to the other long ago. They kissed and hugged one another. Jaime told Jorge that Carlos was staying behind and that they should take care of each other as the two families had always done. They looked forward to meeting again in Amsterdam. But Jaime knew he would never see the Pereiras again. He handed Jorge a folded cloth with some jewelry inside.

"This is some of our savings. Take it. You will need them in all this mess." He gave Jorge and Delfina long kisses. "If you are ready to leave this hell, let us know. We will get you out; I promise you."

With that, Jaime, Gracia and Pedro took the first steps of their long and arduous trek out of Portugal. They walked amid the sounds of buildings crashing to the ground, the screams of the afflicted and heat of the crackling fires. Their difficult exodus from Portugal to freedom in Holland would later become a family legend, related by parents to their children and grandchildren for future generations.

As they proceeded south towards Spain, it became obvious that the earthquake was one of epic destruction. Many miles away from Lisbon, windows had been shattered and wooden buildings pulled from their foundations. Some structures were leaning precariously; some completely destroyed. There was now a resumption of frequent and strong aftershocks, each met with screams, flying debris and frightening noises.

Traveling only by day, the family lay on grass or in untilled open fields at night, trying to sleep. One of them was always on guard, to be alert to thieves among the many others of Lisbon's fleeing citizens. They kept to themselves, consuming only small amounts of the hidden food they brought with them, stretching it as much as they could because food was scarce even days away from Lisbon. They wondered when they would reach a place that had not been affected by this unbelievable upheaval.

Two days out of Lisbon, they began hearing tales from travelers of huge waves inundating the Spanish and North African coasts. News traveled much faster than the refugees. In two days they had covered only 10 miles, much less than Jaime had anticipated. He now realized the trip would be longer and even more arduous than he had expected. The roads were choked with thousands of refugees hauling carts behind them. Sick horses and mules moved slower than their owners could walk, slowing down normal travel. Roadsides were filled with the smell of dead animals, all of which had been worked to their limit and even more. Roadside inns were overcrowded and quickly running out of food and drink. Whatever the inns could offer was being sold at outrageous prices.

This difficult journey emphasized the strong attachment to their religious faith that propelled the Henriques family forward, away from the prison that was Portugal.

13

WASHINGTON D.C.
AND
BACK TO GIBRALTAR
OCTOBER 15, 1942

It wasn't until the fourth disturbing ring that Jim Ennis finally reached across his bed for the telephone. In the darkness of the room, he angled closer to his bed stand. Picking up the phone, he rasped a sleepy, "Hello?" into the speaker.

The caller on the other end spoke as if he were unaware that he had disturbed a sleeper in the dead of night. "Is this Lt. Commander James Ennis?" he asked. When the answer was "Yes," the caller requested his Navy serial number. It took a moment for Ennis to chase the sleep from his brain. When he finally whispered the correct number into the receiver, the caller continued, "There is an emergency, Sir. Please pack enough clothes for a few days." Within the hour, the impersonal voice advised, a staff car would be outside his suburban Washington apartment house in Bethesda, Maryland, to pick him up and take him to nearby Fort Meade.

Ennis switched on the bedside lamp, the light stabbing at his eyes. His alarm clock read 2:31 a.m. He felt a stirring on the other side of the bed: Lucy was awake, too. Her long blonde hair spread across her pillow, and the milky skin of her legs was exposed as she pushed her blanket away. Lucy looked at him through half-closed eyes, covered by a hand over her brow to reduce the lamp's harsh light. He thought how Lucy could always look attractive, even when she was half awake.

"Jimmy, what's that about?" she asked hoarsely, placing her other hand on a well-rounded stomach. She was seven months pregnant. Lucy Ennis was a Navy wife, aware that she always had to be ready to pack and move her home when her husband was reassigned to a new post. Since Jimmy was assigned to intelligence, she felt free from having to do that: he was home from work every day, except for the few times when he was required to spend a day or two away from home, usually in emergencies. It was better, she selfishly acknowledged, than having him roaming the Pacific seeking enemy ships to sink, putting himself in danger. And her going for weeks and months without word of where he was or what he was doing.

"It's some kind of emergency, honey. They told me to pack; I'm to be gone for a few days."

"Where are you going?"

"Fort Meade for now, but I'm sure I'll be going elsewhere from there. Go back to sleep. I don't have time for breakfast. I'll have some juice from the fridge. At this hour, I'm sure they'll be feeding me something."

Ennis took a quick shower and climbed into his uniform. *Mickey Garcia was right*, he thought, looking at himself in the mirror as he put on his jacket. The rank on his shoulder boards read Lt. Commander. *I made rank very fast in my new job as interpreter.* Packed, he gave Lucy a goodbye kiss and turned off the lamp. Standing by the bedroom door, he fingered the last button of his jacket, saying, "I'll try to get back to you soon. If you don't hear from me in two or three days, call Mickey Garcia. I have a feeling he'll know where I am. If not, I'm sure he knows where to find out. Don't worry about me. If it's really an emergency as they say, then I probably won't be able to get to you right away."

As he walked out the front door of his apartment house, Ennis saw a khaki-colored military sedan with a white star on the driver's door, its headlights piercing through the cold autumn darkness. Its motor was running in a soft purr.

Keeping warm inside the car were two Military Policemen. One, a Sergeant, stepped out of the car and opened the back door for Jimmy as he saluted.

"What's this all about, Sergeant?" Ennis asked, a frosty cloud rising from his mouth.

"I don't know, Commander. All I know is that we were ordered to pick you up and take you to Fort Meade, ASAP."

"OK then, Sergeant, let's go."

Settled in the back seat of the sedan, Ennis tried to sleep; but the nature of the 'emergency' intrigued him, creating different scenarios in his mind. In the darkness at three o'clock in the morning, the highway was empty. Since the War, the use of private cars had been restricted by the government. Doctors and other essential civilian services were given priority to purchase precious gasoline, which was needed to fight the war against America's enemies. A sticker with a black **A, B** or **C** on a windshield advised the gas station attendant where the driver belonged in the pecking order of gas distribution. At the bottom of the heap were those using cars for pleasure. This military car surely had some high priority: he noticed the driver wasn't paying attention to speed limits as he rushed to Fort Mead.

Arriving at the Fort's gate, the driver had a brief conversation with the guard, which Ennis could not hear. Then the driver rolled up the window and proceeded slowly along the street. Soon, they stopped at a dun-colored one-story wooden building. The Sergeant opened the door for him again. Waiting at the curb was another Sergeant, who greeted Ennis and asked for his military identification. Satisfied with what he saw, the Sergeant said, "This way, Commander," and escorted Ennis into the building and then down a long, dimly lit hallway, stopping at a door displaying only a number.

Inside the sparse office, lit as dimly as the hallway, sat three men: a one-star General; and two full Colonels. They did not identify themselves. There were, however, salutes. The three high ranking officers looked serious. Ennis noted an ash tray filled with half-smoked cigarettes. Two officers were nursing lit cigarettes, the General, a long cigar.

"Sit down, Commander. We're sorry to have to get you out of bed so early but we have an emergency on our hands," the General began. "We have been led to believe you're the one who can help us. You know Colonel Ellis Bosworth, of course?"

"Yes, Sir. He's the head of the French section where I am stationed. We often have coffee together. Sometimes, lunch."

"Well, Commander, he was scheduled to go to England in the next two hours. At eight o'clock last night, he fell in his shower and broke a leg. We've been looking for a substitute with appropriate military rank and language skills and according to Colonel Bosworth and some other well-placed sources, you seem to be the best one. How's your French, Commander?"

"Much better since I started working in the Spanish section, Sir. I wanted to get both languages on a par with one another, so I've been reading and listening to short wave broadcasts in French and using it the times I would meet with Colonel Bosworth. He encourages me with my French. A while ago, he asked me if I would be interested in transferring to the French section. Seems they need more qualified personnel to work with the French and Belgian Underground. I suppose I'm good enough for him to ask me."

"Our source and Colonel Bosworth think so, too," one of the Colonels said. "You better be good because we're handing you a big job. Your Spanish may also be needed. Your German is a big asset, too."

"What am I supposed to be doing?"

"You'll be briefed in London, where you'll be going in about an hour or so," the General said, taking over. "You'll be leaving right away."

Ennis was in a daze. He was told he could not call his wife, and then was swiftly ushered out of the room to a medical clinic in another wooden building on base. There, he received in just 15 minutes, shots for tetanus, cholera, smallpox, and he knew not what else. Then he was issued warm flying gear: a fur-lined leather flying jacket, woolen lined boots, and a thick, scratchy, woolen blanket. "Gets cold up there, Commander. You'll need them," a Sergeant advised as he passed out the material.

"We'll take care of your luggage, Sir. You'll have hot coffee on the plane, but you might want a sandwich and some fruit. Here's a package." The Sergeant handed Ennis a small cardboard box, which he did not open.

Ennis was swiftly ushered into a car and driven to the airport. He was starting to feel sick from the shots and tried to keep from vomiting. His left arm was aching, and he could feel heat rising from where so many needles had invaded his arm.

The car pulled into the cargo section of the airport. A C-47 cargo plane, painted in military olive drab and bearing U.S. Air Force markings, was waiting on the runway. Its two engines were already churning. The car ran right up to the steps at the passengers' entrance and Ennis, now feeling very dizzy, was helped up the ladder into the plane. There were eight other persons sitting inside the cabin, some of whom smiled and nodded at him as he entered, hunched under the plane's curved and low ceiling so his head would not bump up against it. The seats, which were uncomfortable for this long flight, were divided, ten on each side, lined up against both sides of the cabin, passengers facing one another. A Corporal, who looked and acted as if he should have been an officer, saluted him, led him to an unpadded metal seat, and told him to strap himself in. Ennis heard someone say the plane was usually used to drop paratroopers.

As they took off, the passengers could see the sun rising, lighting up the cabin with a soft orange light. Fifteen minutes into the flight, the Corporal passed hot coffee around. "We'll stop at Gander Field in Newfoundland, on the first leg of our flight. We gas up there, and then leave for London." He was shouting over the plane's two noisy engines.

The plane was not heated, and Ennis was grateful for the warm gear, pulling the blanket up and around his neck. He looked about. His fellow passengers were a mix of ranks and military services. There was a Marine Gunnery Sergeant, a Navy Lieutenant, two Army Colonels, two Chief Petty Officers and two Army Privates. Not much was being said, as the cabin was noisy.

After he drank the coffee, which helped settle his stomach, Ennis and most of the other passengers closed their eyes, trying to get some sleep. Ennis wondered if they were all on the same emergency or on different missions. No matter, he'd soon find what this was all about. An hour after they left Gander, he fell asleep. He felt a gentle shake, opened his eyes and through two slits he saw the Corporal. He could feel that his left arm was now hot and swollen from all the stuff they'd pumped into it. *Wherever I'm going, I'll bet there's no caviar and champagne.*

"We'll be landing in about 45 minutes, Commander. If you want some coffee, I can get you some."

"Thank you, Corporal, that's a good idea."

Ennis hadn't eaten the food package he had been given hours earlier. He now had hunger pangs. The dizziness was mostly gone. He groped for the box, opened it and inside was a sandwich wrapped in thin onion-skin paper and a shiny, ripe-red apple which gave off a fruity scent. He unfolded the paper covering the sandwich and took a bite. *Ham and cheese*, he thought, *better than K-rations*. His coffee arrived and the warmth of it washed his insides and settled some of his lingering stomach discomfort.

Turning sideways in his seat, he looked out of the window behind him. A blue-green sea reflected little shimmering fragments of light beneath the plane but up ahead, just past the whitecaps, there was land: Ireland, bright in the sunlight and lush green as he expected it would be. After all, wasn't it always called the Emerald Isle? They passed over land for some time and then there was more water. The Irish Sea, Wales, and then, England. He could see a port. The Corporal told him it was Bristol. He remembered his history. Bristol was Sir Francis Drake's home port.

Soon, the plane was descending, and the C-47 was making its landing approach. There was London, and below it, the River Thames looking like a silvery highway. As the plane bounced onto the tarmac, it rolled to a stop and cut its engines. Several cars were already waiting on the runway. His fellow passengers were quickly snapped up, heading in different directions. *So, they're on different missions.*

As Ennis descended the ladder, his arm still aflame with heat and pain, an Army Lieutenant called out his name. He saluted Ennis and then led him to a jeep. They rode silently to a building on the far side of the airport for another interview. This time, he was in a hastily created makeshift office that was obviously a file room. It had one scarred metal desk and one metal chair in front of the desk. Hanging from a chain was an overhead light bulb surrounded by a Kelly-green glass shade. Ennis observed that the Army was not as elegant as the Navy in its choice of meeting places. A full Colonel sat at the desk while Ennis stood. His instructions were terse and to the point.

"You are flying to Gibraltar, Commander, where you will meet with General Mark Clark. You are to be his translator and interpreter. General Clark is meeting with French General Henri Giraud, who claims to be the head of a resistance movement of Free French. We are going to invade North Africa soon. General Clark must convince Giraud that the French Vichy forces in North Africa should allow us to land our men without opposition. We're hoping that will save a lot of French and American lives. We've gone to a lot of trouble to bring Giraud out of his hiding place in southern France.

"Giraud, General Clark, three British commandos and yourself, will leave Gibraltar by submarine and land in Algeria at night. Giraud speaks no English, or so he says. You will be General Clarks' only translator. He also requested a Spanish speaker, because our operation – we call it 'Torch' - is close to Spanish Morocco. There's a possibility that Spanish dictator Francisco Franco might allow German troops to pass through Spain into Spanish Morocco to oppose our landing. General Clark wants to be able to immediately let the Spanish know that it is unacceptable to us and that they should remain neutral.

"We understand you speak both languages well, and German, too. That's why you were selected for this mission. Saves us the necessity of using other translators in case we need to speak with the Spaniards and Germans quickly, with the added asset that you are aware of everything that's happening and don't need another briefing. You come highly recommended, by the way."

"By whom, may I ask, Sir?"

"I don't know. I didn't handle that end of it. Just get ready with your personal effects. You are to leave immediately. England is only another step to your destination in Gibraltar. They want you there before nightfall."

"I'm as ready as I'll ever be, Sir." Ennis said as he scratched his swollen and fiery heated left shoulder. He felt the nausea returning. He didn't know if it was from the needles or his nervousness about the mission upon which he was now about to embark.

భ ళ

"Mickey, it's me, Lucy Ennis. Jimmy suggested I call you if I hadn't heard from him. It's been three days since he left here and there's no news. He said you'd know where he was. Can you let me know what's happening?"

"He's okay, Lucy. Don't go worrying about him."

"Mickey, I am worried. I'm his wife, for God's sake. How is it you know where Jimmy is?"

There was no answer.

Lucy was persistent, one of her many traits. She wanted more answers than she was getting. Her voice was rising. If Mickey Garcia could have seen Lucy Ennis, he would have known he was talking to a very anxious and upset wife.

"He's okay, Lucy. I assure you."

"Why did Jimmy ask me to call you?"

Garcia was not answering such delicate questions. "Everything's okay, Lucy. Not to worry. I have to go now, excuse me." There was a click and then the impersonal buzz of a dial tone.

"Dammit, Mickey you sonofabitch, you didn't answer my questions. How is it that you know where Jimmy is?"

But Lucy Ennis was talking into a dead phone.

14

GIBRALTAR
OCTOBER 1942

Since Jim's last visit to Gibraltar, the English had built another and more conveniently laid-out airport on the Rock. Because the area was so small, a roadway crossed the airport's runway. For this leg of his trip, he was flying on a comfortable and neutral Portuguese commercial airliner. His plane made a wide turn in its approach over the Mediterranean Sea, allowing long views of freighters and warships below. He also saw North Africa and, before they were descending, the faraway mountains of Granada in Spain, their snowy peaks reflecting a hazy sunlight to the west.

Once they landed, the ritual repeated: someone called his name, he pulled out his identification as requested and, after satisfaction and a hasty salute, he was hustled into a car and from there, into a room deep inside the tunnel that had been blasted into Gibraltar's rock to construct an office complex. It was clammy, bone-chilling, and uncomfortable.

No sooner had Ennis taken a seat in an office, than General Mark Clark appeared. Ennis rose and saluted. Clark returned the salute and then extended his hand. The General was tall, about six feet four inches, and lean, with a raw-boned hatchet face. He had the stereotypical look of a Texan, which he was not.

"They tell me you're Lt. Commander James Ennis. You speak French and Spanish, do you?"

"Yes, Sir."

"How do I address you? What do your friends call you? Jim? Jimmy?"

"I get called by both names, Sir."

"I like Jimmy. So now, Jimmy, here's what's going to happen." Clark looked around him, saw some clerks and his aides milling about, looking at Ennis with curiosity. He walked to the door and held it open. Then he said in a loud, firm voice, "I would like to be alone with the Commander. So please, everyone, leave. I'll call you when I need you."

Clark waited while the room emptied. When the last person left, he closed the door behind him and sat in a chair close to Ennis.

"Now, here's what's going to happen," he repeated. "Soon we will be invading Morocco, Tunisia and Algeria with thousands of our boys. Opposing us are about 125,000 or more French troops of the Vichy government. That includes artillery and air force. The Vichy are a quirky bunch. They are supposed to be independent of the Germans. But we all know that Vichy is really Germany's puppet. We know there are some French Generals who are German sympathizers and then, there are others who would like to throw in their hand with us. That's why we don't know if they are going to put up a fight or let us walk in unopposed. Obviously, we don't want a fight.

"In about an hour or so, a French General, Henri Giraud, will be arriving here. He claims to lead a Free French group who will follow him into our camp. We really don't know how influential he is, but he assures us that he has great political strength in North Africa.

"Giraud was captured by the Germans in 1940, escaped and was in hiding in southern France until we brought him here. He's supposed to be a big hero among the Free French. We'll soon see about that."

"Does he speak English, Sir?"

"Good question, Jimmy. He says no, but I doubt him. Now this is important. When you translate from one language to the other, I don't want you to say, 'the General says.' I want you to translate both of us as if the person you are translating, is speaking. Understand?"

"Yes, Sir, I do."

"Good. Now, we are leaving tonight, after Giraud gets here. We're going to Oran in Algeria, by submarine. We will be meeting with several high-ranking officers, commanders of the French forces opposing us. I am certain that at least one, if not all of them, speak English. I'll bet you a good steak dinner I'm right. But they're going to tell us they don't. I know that at least two of them attended artillery school in England for over a year. No matter. We'll go along with their fiction, if that's how they want to play it.

"Now, here's why I make these points. These French officers hate the British. They have no wish to become allied with them. A while ago, the Brits asked the French to turn over their navy to them, or at least remain neutral to keep the French fleet out of German hands. The French refused, so the Brits blew their navy to bits at *Mers-el Kabir* in Algeria, killing a lot of French soldiers, too. I guess the Brits had no other choice. If it was up to me, I would have done the same. Can't have all those good warships in German hands, to be used against us. That's why our invasion is strictly an American operation; the French will not cooperate with the English.

"I don't want you getting chummy with Giraud. Unless he speaks to you first, you are not to initiate any conversations with him. A submarine is a tight fit. We'll be aboard her for two days. I understand they are putting us in the officer's wardroom, which they tell me you need a shoehorn to get into. So, find a magazine to read or make believe you're asleep."

"I've been on submarines, Sir. I'll try to find a place for myself once I get aboard."

"You know submarines?"

"Yes, Sir. I was assigned to the Electric Boat Company as an engineer. They build subs. I sailed on many sea trials, and I've also served on a combat patrol here in Gibraltar a while back."

"I didn't know that. You're a good man to have around, Jimmy. I want you to stick to me like glue, like we were joined at the hip. Understand?"

"Yes, Sir."

"I have a note for you from a Commander McDonald. He'd like to see you at the Officers' Club. Get your ass back here in an hour."

ର୍ଚ୍ଚ ୨୯

Ian McDonald greeted Jim Ennis with a strong handshake. He was a full Commander now, and he must have just returned from a patrol because the grey submariner's pallor was showing on his face.

"I see they kicked you upstairs, old man," Ian said, pointing to Jim's shoulder boards.

"Yes. I guess they ran out of sailors to promote."

"I heard you were coming, so I asked when that would be, and they were very cagey. Finally, they let me send a note to your Yank office. Sit down, Jim. There's a tot of Scotch waiting for you."

The two men spoke, getting up to date in their personal lives. Then Ian said, "Chit-chat around here is that someone's going out in a sub tonight. It won't be on my *Undaunted*. We just got back and they're cleaning her up. I saw the *Seraph* getting a first-class cleaning; she's a bit bigger than my boat." McDonald waited for a comment. When there was none, he laughed. "Loose lips sink ships, I guess."

"I've got to go, Ian. They only gave me an hour with you."

ର୍ଚ୍ଚ ୨୯

When he returned to General Clark's office, General Giraud had just arrived on the hastily planned trip by submarine from his hiding place in Vichy France. Clark introduced the two men to one another. At least Giraud understood that much English.

General Henri Giraud was dressed in a rumpled civilian suit. His shirt looked as if he hadn't been out of it for a week. On his head was a grey, beat-up fedora, sweat-stained and crumpled at the crown. Yet he stood ramrod straight, emphasizing his rank, his face showing a sly smile of haughtiness for those around him. He was a tall, handsome man with a head of greying hair and a clipped, grey mustache. Despite his deplorable dress, he was imperious in manner and treated Jim Ennis as an inferior when he understood he was merely a translator and only a Lt. Commander.

After saluting the General and shaking his hand, trying to make their interview as warm as possible, Clark said, "You understand why you are here, General?"

"Yes. I am to coordinate the commanders of Vichy Forces in North Africa to allow an unopposed landing of American troops. You understand that for my cooperation, I am to be the Supreme Commander of all the Allied Forces in North Africa."

Clark was caught off balance. "That's impossible, General. The American Army cannot serve under a French commander. And I have no authority to speak for British forces on this subject."

"Then I cannot vouch for the leaders to follow me. My honor and the honor of France are involved here. I cannot agree to allow anyone but French forces to control or invade any French territory, especially to drop bombs on its sacred soil."

"Be sensible, General. Who would you say controls Paris, Cherbourg and Le Havre today?"

Giraud did not answer. He looked straight ahead, his face reddening; knowing Clark had made a valid, although sore, point. Clark was sorry for his harsh remark. He would have to apply some salve to save a heavily wounded pride.

"We would like you to help us get France back from the Germans so that Frenchmen can live free again. To do this, we must know who will follow you. You have some competition for leadership among your own people. General Charles De Gaulle in London says he leads the Free French forces. The two of you need to get together to work that out. For now, I am only concerned about who is with us and who is against us when we hit the beaches in North Africa in a few days. I want to save lives, both French and American. After that, you and De Gaulle can resolve France's military and political problems between yourselves. Right now, we are scheduled for a landing on November 8th."

Ennis noted that Giraud flinched when General Clark mentioned De Gaulle. But he quickly recovered and said, "We shall see where allegiances lie when we get to North Africa. But why did you wait to the last minute to let us know of the invasion?"

"Because, frankly, and it is no reflection on you, General, we don't know who we can trust in North Africa."

Giraud thought for a moment, then looked at Clark and nodded. "I agree, General," he said, "On that I cannot deny your concerns. They are genuine."

"Then, let's get ready. We were able to get a suitable uniform for you. You can change while we are in the submarine."

After the meeting with Giraud, General Clark took Ennis aside and said, "We will be traveling in an English sub commanded by an American captain and crew. Giraud hates the British and emphasized that he refuses to travel on an English ship. There was no other choice. We had to put up the Stars and Stripes on this English submarine to satisfy him. God, Jimmy, I hate all this political intrigue. You go to war to destroy the enemy. Someone wins, someone loses. I feel as if we're walking through a mine field."

The English sub, *Seraph*, had completed loading when Ennis, Generals Clark and Giraud and three British commandos were shown where to board. One of the commandos was a Lieutenant. The three of them were French Canadians, especially chosen because they had no English accent and spoke French. Clark carried with him a satchel loaded with gold coins. *Expense money or bribes? None of my business,* Ennis thought. *That's politics. It's not my place to know; I'm only here to concern myself with language.*

All the passengers were issued black jump suits without any insignia or rank. They fitted over their uniforms, so they would not be considered spies. They were also issued black woolen caps and gloves. The commandos were armed with Thompson submachine guns and two satchels loaded with replacement cartridges and hand grenades.

The sub was not a good fit for the tall passengers, as they moved throughout narrow passageways on the boat bending under low overheads and gingerly threading their way over watertight doors with sills a foot above the decks. The trip to Algeria was spent in silence, mostly in the wardroom. Giraud looked straight ahead, drinking coffee which he periodically renewed by silently holding an empty cup out towards a steward. He had taken a quick shower and looked impressive now that he had changed into his uniform. Clark and his commandos played poker.

After a while, Ennis felt the familiar movement of a submarine rising to the surface. Red lights came on in the interior cabins to help the passengers and crew accustom themselves to the nighttime darkness. The American submarine Captain, who Ennis knew from his days at Electric Boat, told him they should gather their gear and leave the sub through one of the outside deck hatches.

They surfaced off the coast of Algeria, near the city of Oran. On deck, warm and humid night air surrounded the boat. The *Seraph's* crew had already been busy setting out a black rubber life raft which they held tightly by its lines as it bounded on waves just below the sub's deck, only a few feet above the surf. Six men filed into the raft. The commandos rowed toward shore with a swiftness and expertise that led Ennis to believe this was not an unusual task for them.

Before they left the *Seraph*, the sub's Captain advised Clark that he would submerge and surface again the next day in the dark, to receive signals about when the party would return for a pickup.

No words were spoken as they paddled to shore. The only sound was the soft splashes of the surf running on to the beach ahead of them. The city of Oran was under a military curfew and only a few weak streetlights could be seen from the sea. As they came closer to shore, there were flashes of signal lights from the beach. One of the commandos, the Lieutenant, placed his oar across his lap and with a flashlight, responded to the signal. The commandos changed the raft's course to the right about 100 yards.

Before they reached the shore, two French soldiers awaited them, waist deep in water, instructing the men in English that was heavily accented, where they were to go. Despite the darkness, Ennis could make out a troop carrier off the beach, its lights switched off. The men got out of the raft, wading ashore the last few yards to the beach, the commandos dragging the raft behind them. A French soldier jumped off the troop carrier and showed them where the raft should be hidden, in back of the beach behind thick foliage. Two commandos would remain with the raft. A French army Captain introduced himself, explaining that he would accompany the party to a villa in the hills above the city. The four officers piled into the rear of the troop carrier.

As they drove along the darkened streets of Oran, the moon illuminated the facades of darkened window shops on what appeared to be a main street. One sign stunned Ennis:

A.Henriques et fils
Exporter et Importer

A. Henriques and Son
Export and Import

When he had time, Ennis thought excitedly, he would visit the Henriques office and see what he could gather about their family history. The sign was above the door of a substantial building.

The French troop carrier with its passengers proceeded up a hill. As they climbed higher, Ennis could see several Mosques and as he turned in his seat, he made out the beach below, white caps reflecting the moon as they washed toward shore. The *Seraph* was already disappearing beneath the waves.

They arrived at a large villa at the edge of a high parapet. In the moonlight, Ennis could see the building was painted white, topped on the roof with large curved ceramic orange tiles. The villa was cooled by a steady Mediterranean breeze. Inside, the house was large and tastefully furnished, obviously the home of a wealthy person. A group of a dozen high-ranking officers were gathered about. They all saluted Giraud, then shook his hand and seemed genuinely pleased to see him. He was a legend among the French since his escape from a German prison camp.

Giraud introduced Clark, but not the Commando or Ennis. Clark introduced Ennis as his interpreter and the Commando as his bodyguard. A large table was set up in the center of the room. It was filled with food and many wine bottles. The officers had not waited for their guests to begin drinking. Several empty bottles were already lying on their sides. An African soldier, dressed in a sparkling white tunic, black trousers, and mirror-bright shoes, acted as a waiter. He understood his task: maintain silence and keep up a steady flow of food and drink.

As soon as the newcomers were seated, he put glasses in their hands, offering a selection of white or red wine. There was even champagne, should they prefer it. Then he passed among the officers with a rolling cart piled high with food and large sliced loaves of crusty French bread. France's North African officers were not suffering the food shortages their fellow citizens were undergoing in Metropolitan France.

Giraud began the evening by explaining to the officers why he had come. Ennis softly repeated Giraud's presentation into Clark's ear. One officer addressed Clark.

"Are the British part of this invasion force?"

Clark knew the rank of the officer to whom he was responding. He was a Colonel. Clark had carefully studied the insignias of French military rank, and he could also tell an infantry officer from an engineer or an artillery officer by their badges.

"No, Colonel," Clark responded with emphasis. "There will only be the American Army. Of that, I can guarantee you."

The Colonel sat back in his seat, apparently satisfied with Clark's answer. But suddenly, all the officers began speaking amongst themselves. Giraud, who was the ranking officer, put up his hand, his order for them to be silent. Then he explained.

"The Americans will be invading North Africa in a few days. They want us to allow them to land unopposed. Then we are to join them in the fight against the Boche."

Giraud's statement set the officers buzzing amongst themselves again. They spoke, shouted, and yelled for a few moments. Clark needed no translations. These officers were not united.

When the banter quieted down, one officer asked, "How can we do that, General?"

A one-star General who had just finished chewing on a slice of ham, was standing in the corner. He swallowed, and shouted, "We are the army of the Vichy government. To do what you Americans propose is treason. It is a violation of law and of our honor as Frenchmen."

Another officer, a Colonel, looked at Clark and angrily asked him, "Who controls North Africa if we do this? North Africa is France. We cannot be the ones to agree to the loss of sovereignty over our sacred soil. Our individual honor will forever be blemished."

Clark looked at all the officers as he spoke through Ennis. "Neither the United States nor England wish to take North Africa away from France. But while there is a War, we must be responsible for the region, and it is our soldiers who will be fighting the Germans. And dying, I might add. Afterwards, we have no designs on North Africa."

"Impossible," shouted another officer. "We can never allow another country to control our territory and citizens. It is a violation of French honor."

"Be quiet, all of you," shouted a Colonel, who was now standing and raising his voice above the din. "The Americans are offering us a way to fight the Germans. There is where your honor is. We will have a hand at eliminating the German occupiers."

"I agree," said a tall Major, who rose as he spoke. "We have already lost whatever honor we had by capitulating to the Germans. Now we can restore it. We have to join the Americans and fight the Boche."

"Nonsense. We are soldiers, not politicians. All this talk of honor. Our loyalty is with our government, Vichy, and our leader, Marshall Petain; not with England or the Americans." Shouting this was a Colonel who looked to be the oldest man among this group of officers. Following these remarks, the officers began talking and then it deteriorated to renewed shouting among themselves, arms gesticulating, some faces red with rage.

Clark moved close to Ennis and asked, "What's happening, Jimmy?"

"There's still a lot of difference here, Sir. As of this moment, it seems as if we are not going to have all of them on our side."

Clark sat back in his seat and let out a sigh of frustration. "We need to know who is with us and who is going to put up opposition to our forces. I have to know if they are artillery or infantry, etcetera."

"Yes, Sir, I understand. I'll have the lists for you."

Giraud tried controlling the situation. In a loud voice, he demanded silence and a consensus as to how the officers would act on the day of the invasion. As expected, they were divided. Some officers sat silent, arms folded in defiance, an indication that they would not throw in with the Americans. Ennis noted where each officer stood. Giraud faced Clark and said, "General Clark, they will not act together to support the invasion. Some of these men will join you; others feel they are obligated to fight you."

It was obvious that Giraud would not pressure the officers to allow Americans to land at the beaches unopposed, unless Clark guaranteed he would become Supreme Allied Commander of North Africa. "My rank and honor require that position," he reiterated.

"Again, General, I don't speak for the British," Clark said, "and the United States would never put its troops under a French Commander. We have never done anything like that in our history and I have no authority to do that now. In fact, I might remind you that during our Revolutionary War your French Admiral, the Comte de Grasse, placed himself under the command of General Washington at the battle of Yorktown. When the English presented their swords in surrender to de Grasse, he refused to accept them, ordering the defeated English to give them to Washington."

General Giraud looked puzzled, as if he was unaware of that history. He replied, "Then I must at least command all French troops in North Africa. Anything less dishonors me and France." He was backing down, but not looking one bit defeated and still maintaining his haughty air.

"General, can you guarantee me that all these men here tonight will not fire on my troops when we come ashore?"

Giraud looked at the officers. Some nodded 'yes,' others 'no' and a few others did neither: they were still undecided. Ennis continued taking quick notes on a pad of the sides the officers were taking as some had changed positions since the first count.

"There is your answer, General Clark," Giraud said, making a gesture toward the officers.

"In that case, General, my government cannot back you, since you do not command the loyalty of all these officers, as you led us to believe."

"I would ask you to return me to France, General Clark."

"No, General. I'm afraid not. This was a one-way trip."

Giraud showed his first sign of emotion. It was anger. "Very well then, General Clark. I can only be an independent observer in this affair."

After the meeting, the Americans and the British Commando were driven to the home of Robert Murphy, the American government's representative in Algeria. By pre-arrangement, they would spend the night there until retrieved by the *Seraph*. Murphy had been responsible for arranging the meeting between the Americans and the French.

"We have made a grave error by alerting the French a few days in advance of our plans. But we were mistakenly assured that Giraud commanded everyone's loyalty," Clark noted, with obvious concern.

"Not to worry," Murphy explained. "Our sources have assured me that the Germans already knew about our plans. They have already admitted that they are in no position to give any real aid to French units in an invasion of North Africa. They don't have the men or the resources to oppose us and even if they had them, they are too far away to help. We can expect to encounter some units of the German air force and a few of their Battalions. That's about all.

"We had absolute confirmation of this, which we had already suspected for weeks. I didn't want to send you a message while you were at sea, for fear it would be picked up by the enemy. You'll stay here for now. One of my men is at the beach, making arrangements for you to be picked up tomorrow for your return to Gibraltar."

While the men were sitting in Murphy's living room, one of his aides came running into the house, panting as he spoke. "The French police are on their way here." Quickly, Murphy escorted his three guests downstairs into the wine cellar, turning out the lights as he ran back up the steps to return to the living room.

Both Clark and the British Commando drew pistols from their jackets and held them at the ready, pointing them toward the door. The Commando cocked his revolver, preparing it to be fired. When Clark saw that, he followed suit.

Upstairs, the Gendarmes knocked politely at the door. This was the home of an official of the American government and he had diplomatic immunity. Vichy was not at war with the United States, at least, not yet.

Murphy opened the front door and was greeted by a police officer in a blue uniform. He had a large smile and gave a formal salute. Murphy recognized the officer, who he knew had been assigned by the Vichy government to keep a close watch on the American envoy.

"Good evening, Sergeant Dubois. What can I do for you?" Murphy said.

"Pardon, Monsieur Murphy. We are looking for some smugglers. We had word that they were in this neighborhood. Perhaps you have seen or heard of some suspicious types here tonight?" The officer's tone was sarcastic. He knew some Americans had landed in Oran and had already met with French officers. He surmised that they were at Murphy's house. But there was little he could do about it. Murphy had diplomatic immunity. Dubois was not about to create a diplomatic crisis by breaking into Murphy's house. This visit was a necessity so he could tell his superiors he had checked the neighborhood, including the American envoy's house.

"I'm afraid not, Sergeant. I haven't been out all night."

"Sorry to bother you, then. If you should have word about these men, please let us know. And good night to you, sir." The officer made a polite salute, accompanied by another smile.

"I surely will, Sergeant Dubois. Good night to you."

Murphy watched the police car roll out of his driveway. Satisfied they were gone, he returned to the wine cellar and called for his relieved guests to come out.

After returning to Gibraltar, the officers in charge of the invasion of North Africa at least had a good idea of what to expect once they set their forces loose on the African continent.

15

SPAIN, JUST PAST
THE PORTUGUESE BORDER
1756

It had taken much longer to get to the Spanish border than Jaime Henriques had ever thought. The delicate Gracia required frequent stops to regain her strength after their long and tiring walks. Buying a horse in Portugal was impossible. None was to be had and even if one could be found, the price was exorbitant. They had not counted on the condition of the clogged roads that slowed up their progress. At night, rooms were never available; the family continued sleeping in the fields, even during rain, as did hundreds of others. In a way, it was a positive note: Jaime had figured on spending a portion of their funds for lodging and transportation. Since neither was available, he was conserving their treasure. So far, they looked as did the rest of the refugees: dressed in tattered clothes, dirty and almost penniless. No one was seriously disturbing them.

The roads were so jammed with refugees, the family decided to walk away from the crowds in an easterly direction. Then they turned south until they reached the northern banks of the Duoro River. At the river's edge, Jaime found a Spanish fisherman who had just off-loaded a cargo of fish. For a price, he agreed to bring them to the Spanish side. The boat reeked of fish and its decks were lined with gurry and fish heads, but they were finally on their way out of Portugal.

The world was different in Spain. Almost a month after they began their escape from Lisbon, they had finally rid themselves of Portugal, landing in an out-of-the-way place, where there were few refugees; no clogged roads. The fisherman showed Jaime where he could buy a beat-up wagon and a horse from a Spanish farmer at a reasonable price. They needn't walk any longer, a big help for Gracia. And at night, they could sleep in the wagon, which had a cover to keep them reasonably dry during a rainstorm.

They came upon a small pond, with no one about. They washed themselves completely for the first time in weeks and took out fresh clothes from their knapsacks. But they decided to get back into the old rags after washing and drying them. Who knew what the future held?

After a while on the road, they came upon a small country inn, where they ate their first hot meal in weeks and slept in beds. Jaime requested directions to Palos, where he planned to buy passage to France. The innkeeper explained how he could get to the main road that led to the port city.

Leaving the inn, Pedro asked, "Papa, if we are going to Amsterdam, why do we go to France?"

"Because, my son, the Dutch are at odds with the Spaniards and Amsterdam is also home to Protestants. No Protestants are permitted to live in Spain. They are heretics and can be arrested and turned over to the Inquisition. Probably no Spanish ship goes there directly from Spain anyway. Even if we could go directly, we might be suspected as heretics and arrested.

"We will walk or ride from France to Holland. You are not to tell anyone of our final destination. As far as anyone is concerned, we only go to family in France. Understand?"

"Yes, Papa."

After several miles, the Henriques family turned onto the main road leading to Palos. There, they were again thrown in with the crowds they had earlier avoided. Several soldiers had set up a roadblock across the congested roads, resulting in a long line of refugees that snaked its way as far as one could see. The soldiers were checking the refugees at different locations, to ensure that no heretics entered Spain.

A tall, unkempt soldier in a grimy uniform stopped them. He looked them over while leaning on his musket. He was in no hurry.

Observing their ragged clothes, he asked, "You are not Spanish?" It was more a statement than a question.

"No, we are Portuguese," Jaime responded. "We left Lisbon a while ago. There was a terrible earthquake there. We lost everything. Now we are going to France where we have family. We hope to start a new life there."

"We know about the earthquake. They felt it here and in Palos. The water rose over the piers and into the city. Hell of a thing. Never heard or seen anything like it. Some people say the Messiah is coming. Anyway, can I see your pass?"

"We have no pass."

"You have no pass! How in hell did you get past the border guards?"

"We passed no border guards. The roads were choked with refugees, so we went east. After several days, a fisherman took us across the river and so here we are, in Spain for the past three days."

"How do I know you are good Catholics? Only Catholics can enter Spain, you know. No Protestants, Jews or heretics can live here. No, they're not allowed in Spain. That's why we have these roadblocks."

"We know that. We have our baptismal certificates." Jaime reached into his knapsack and pulled out the documents. The soldier unfolded the certificates and scanned them, nodding. Jaime suspected the soldier could not read. The soldier handed back the papers and said, "You really should have a pass. I don't know. But you look all right; a good Catholic family are you all? Do you attend church faithfully?"

"Oh, yes," Gracia said in a sweet tone.

"How about you, young fella. You go to church too?"

"Yes, sir. Every Sunday," Pedro lied with conviction. In truth, church attendance was carried out at a minimum for the Henriques family. They attended the mandatory baptisms and communions, appearances for marriages and deaths of friends and on Holy Friday and Easter. There was also the occasional confession. To do otherwise could be dangerous, even fatal.

"I guess you're what you say you are. If you're going to Palos, don't travel alone. Find a group and go with them. It's not safe otherwise, especially at night. When you get to Palos, go to the Church of Santa Rosa de la Cruz. Ask for Father Vicente; he's young but he likes to be helpful."

Jaime reached into the pocket of his knapsack and came out with two small silver coins. He kept several there, for such situations. He handed them to the soldier, saying, "Thank you for your help and your kindness. I'm sorry we don't have larger ones for you."

The soldier looked at the coins and smiled. With a satisfied nod, he said, "I understand." He saluted the family and with a friendly wave he allowed them to proceed on their way. During these days of chaos, he expected to be receiving more of such *propinas*.

Following the soldier's advice, the Henriques family rode on to another inn. It was large and there were several groups milling around the courtyard, leaving for different cities. Jaime left his wagon to enquire about any that would be leaving for Palos. He saw many wagons and carriages which had gathered together. Among them were several Spaniards on horseback, who were obviously of the upper-class. They seemed to be familiar with the use of the swords and the pistols strapped to their waists. They accompanied the groups, offering protection in return for food and drink and a wagon to sleep in at night.

Jaime went into the inn. It was busy and noisy. The interior was set up with long wooden tables, which were filled with men drinking and singing or shouting. Jaime sat next to a man who seemed to be alone. "Are you traveling to Palos?" he asked.

"Yes, sir, I am. Most people here are. I'm with a group that's outside in the courtyard."

"Would they be interested in taking on another wagon?" Jaime ordered another ale for his new friend.

"Yes. Anything that would reduce the cost of our protection would be welcome."

After another drink for Jaime's new friend, the two men went outside, and Jaime was introduced to the leader of his friend's group. He was a short, burly but well-dressed man, obviously a man of quality. His name was Alfaro and he owned a team of fine horses with a sturdy, well-enclosed carriage in which his family was seated.

"I can't vouch for the other wagons and carriages," he advised Jaime, "but the señores who accompany us on horses are from the finest families in Palos and Cadiz. I know them. Don't concern yourself." The man went on, "I know these gentlemen. They are from my hometown. They are honorable men with good reputations. They would never travel with thieves or vagabonds. We will be safe."

The man also verified that Father Vicente of Santa Rosa de la Cruz was a good man and helpful to his congregants and strangers alike.

"Just before we leave, I'll let you know how much your share will be. We have to pay for food, lodgings and the protection of our *caballeros*." He pointed to the six men, who were tending to their horses. "They don't come cheap."

Days later, and without incident, they reached the port city of Palos. After some inquiry, Jaime, Gracia and Pedro found their way to the Church of Santa Rosa de la Cruz, where they sought out Father Vicente. Palos had several churches and Santa Rosa was one of the smaller, less important ones. But everyone knew the good Father Vicente and his eagerness to help the needy.

The family pulled into the courtyard of the church and asked for the Father. When he came out, he introduced himself with a smile that was genuine. He was a small, baldheaded man in his early thirties, perhaps a few extra inches over five feet tall. Jaime told him of the soldier who was kind to them on the road and advised them to look for him. Gracia related the results of the dreadful earthquake in Lisbon, describing the devastation and their personal loss.

"We heard of it, here. And we felt it, too," Father Vicente said, his voice filled with deep sympathy. "The sea came up above the piers and flooded this area. We were flooded for several days. Thank God, we were spared what you went through." Father Vicente crossed himself, his face directed to the sky. "You are not the first Portuguese to come here seeking help. Many who come here are penniless. It is sad to see people like that. How can I help you, my children?"

Jaime answered in an emotional ramble. "We have no pass, Father. We didn't know we needed one. We never thought about it. We want to buy passage to France to get to our family. We lost everything in Lisbon and hope to start a new life in France. But now we learn that without a pass we will not be permitted to buy passage on any ship. We can't go back to Lisbon; our house is nothing but rubble and dust. Everything we owned is gone." Jaime was just short of tears.

Father Vincente noted Jaime's distress. "Don't worry, children. I'll go with you when you purchase your passage. Do you have baptismal certificates?"

"Yes Father, we do." Jaime passed the certificates to the priest.

Father Vicente glanced at them and handed them back to Jaime. "You are a good Christian family hoping to start a new life. You must and will be helped. You can stay here at the church until the next boat to France leaves. Leave your wagon and horse in the courtyard. I will find places for you to sleep tonight, if not in the church, then with one of my parishioners. Tomorrow, we'll go to the pier after Mass and get the schedules for the sailings. Don't worry, you will get to see your family. I'll make sure of that."

The next day after Mass, which Jaime was careful to ensure that Gracia and Pedro attended with him, Father Vicente and Jaime walked to the docks of Palos. They passed across this part of Southern Spain where, 150 years earlier, Jaime's Spanish ancestor Felipe had bid his cousin and friend José Periera a tearful goodbye on his exile to Portugal. He tried to imagine what it was like on that day of exile: all those people waiting to be taken away from their homes. He recalled the legends of how Felipe helped José and then got caught up within the claws of the Inquisition himself. It was a story told to him many times by his father and grandfather and now he was in the same port on the very same soil. He was, in fact, on the very same beach, hoping to leave Iberia as so many others had sadly done, many decades before.

Father Vicente led Jaime to an office by the pier. Jaime felt confident that he was in good hands, since on their way several strollers stopped the young priest to greet him with smiles on their faces. Some people even requested blessings from him, which Father Vicente graciously performed. The short walk took longer than normal, because of all these pauses for blessings. *Surely, this is a priest people will listen to,* Jaime observed.

Finally, after many stops they arrived at an office close to the pier. The office manager came out from a place behind a counter and greeted the priest.

"Good morning, Father Vicente, good to see you. What can I do for you today?"

"Good morning, Don Francisco. This good Christian and his family are refugees from the misfortunes that occurred in Lisbon. They have lost everything and wish to start a new life with their family in France. He wants to buy passage to France for himself, his wife and young son."

"Does he have a pass?"

"No, my son. In all the confusion, he crossed into a part of Spain where there were no guards. They are simple people and know little of passes. He has baptismal certificates to show he is Portuguese and a good Christian." The priest looked at Jaime and said, "Show Don Francisco your certificates, my son."

Don Francisco looked at the papers, saying, "Without a pass, it's a little irregular. But if you vouch for them, I guess it's no problem. We don't suppose they're running from the Holy Inquisition, eh, do we Father?" Francisco said this with a wink and in a joking manner. Jaime smiled weakly, trying to show a reaction to Francisco's humor. Father Vicente remained impassive.

Francisco went back to his desk and called out to a clerk by name. "Salvador! Salvador! Let me know when the next ship leaves here for France."

Francisco then excused himself and told the two men to wait as he had to return to his work. A ship was leaving for one of Spain's colonies in the New World and Francisco had to quickly prepare the manifests.

Jaime and the priest sat on a wooden bench, their hands clasped and settled into their laps as they patiently waited. A half-hour later,

Salvador came out from behind a curtained alcove and asked, "How many persons will be leaving for France, Father?"

"Three. Is that not so, my son?"

"Yes, Father. Three," Jaime answered.

"Then they can leave for Brest tomorrow," Salvador smiled. "There's an unscheduled ship that leaves in the afternoon. Here is the price of passage." He passed a sheet of paper over to the priest.

Just then, Don Francisco came out from behind the curtain and was informed of the news. "Salvador, can the Captain be trusted?" Francisco asked. "These people are friends of Father Vicente. I want no harm to come to them."

"Yes, Don Francisco, the Captain is Jean Paul de la Croix."

"Ah, yes, Father. A fine Frenchman and a good Christian. He can be trusted. Your friends are safe with him. We hear so many tales of captains and crews stealing a passenger's property or selling them to pirates. No so with Captain de la Croix. They will be safe. Can you pay this?" he inquired of Jaime, showing him the bill.

Jaime held the paper before him and looked at the sum. "Yes, Don Francisco, I can. When do you need payment?"

"Bring the money with you tomorrow morning. You cannot board until passage is paid."

"You will have it before we sail in the afternoon."

Returning to the church, Father Vicente remarked that Jaime would have to sell his horse and wagon to purchase the necessary passage to France. The priest offered to find a man who would buy them at an honest price. Jaime told the priest that might not be necessary. Would the Father take Jaime to a jeweler where he could convert some bracelets into *pesos* to buy the passage?

That afternoon, the Henriques family ate a spare meal at the church. Father Vicente said blessings and prayers for the Henriques family on their coming trip. Then he took Jaime to a man who would buy jewelry in return for gold coins.

"Will you say confession before you leave?" Father Vicente asked.

"Yes Father, of course we will," Gracia assured the priest.

The family had expected the Father to ask them to make confession. They agreed they would each admit to having small amounts of food during their escape and failing to share it with their fellow refugees who were also needy. This was the truth. The family had come to like Father Vicente and his genuine desire to help whenever he could. Lying to him about some imagined sin would be deceitful, something they were not prepared to do. And confessing to their Judaism was absolutely out of the question.

After confession, Jaime took the priest aside and said, "Father Vicente, we thank you for what you have done for us, for making our stay with you a pleasant and a safe one. You are a good man. A man of God. Thank you for your blessings and good wishes for the rest of our journey. We want you to have our horse and wagon, for your convenience so that you may better help your fellow priests and your congregants."

"I cannot accept this, Jaime. How will you have enough money for yourself and your family when you start life anew? I was planning to bring you to a farmer who would buy your horse and wagon. You will have to sell them before you leave."

"We insist, Father. Throughout our travels, we have always made sure that we safely kept a fund for our passage to France. Put the horse and wagon to good use and please continue to remember us in your daily prayers."

The nest day, after attending mass with Father Vicente, Jaime, Gracia, and Pedro boarded a two-masted boat bound for France. They waved goodbye to the priest who was so kind and helpful to them. After the long trek from Lisbon, the Henriques family finally left Iberia behind them, with much of their fortune intact.

The good and kind Father Vicente was the beneficiary of the family's sincerest good wishes and a substantial donation. And Iberia was forever rid of three heretical Jews.

16

ORAN, ALGERIA
NOVEMBER 1942

On November 8, American soldiers stormed across the beaches of North Africa. General Clark and his staff, including Jim Ennis, came ashore with the third wave. Operation Torch concluded on November 16, when American troops mopped up the last of the few stubbornly resisting pockets of Vichy forces. As had been expected, not all French troops opposed the landings; yet there were still needless casualties on both sides, more among the defenders, because of those French officers who refused to surrender without a fight. French soldiers loyal to Vichy and their leader, Marshall Petain, held up the complete occupation by American forces both at the beaches and then for a short while, inland in the urban areas. Their air force put up a light defense with the help of the Luftwaffe.

When it was over, Morocco, Tunisia and Algeria were firmly in Allied hands. General Erwin Rommel's Afrika Korps was now sandwiched between the U.S. Army on the west and the English, Australians and New Zealanders on the East. And, as Ambassador Murphy had predicted, neither the Germans nor the Italians were in any real position to help their Vichy allies oppose the invasion of North Africa.

One morning when it was clear that General Clark would not need him, Ennis located a driver and a jeep to take him into Oran. They drove around several main streets until he spotted the sign he was looking for: *A. Henriques et fils.*

"Stop here, Corporal and wait for me," Ennis ordered as he walked out of the hot African sun into a large, cool, stone building lit with candles. A man with light brown hair and gray eyes was bending at some work behind a counter. As he stood up, Ennis could see he was of medium height, muscular and looked to be about 50 years old.

Ennis addressed him in French. "Are you Mr. Henriques?"

Jacques Henriques cast a puzzled look at Ennis. "Yes, I am. And you are an American, no? I can see that from your uniform."

"Yes. I am Lt. Commander James Ennis. And are you A. Henriques?"

"I'm Jacques Henriques. My father is Avraham Henriques. Your French is very good, Commander Ennis."

Ennis let the remark pass and their conversation continued in French, as Henriques added, "Excuse my office. Since you Americans liberated Oran, we have had no electricity. And a few nearby bombs have messed up my office quite a bit. As you can see, we've been cleaning up." Henriques pointed to the back of the building where a small army of men and women were sweeping up debris, mopping up standing water and stacking piles of loose papers and files on to dry counters, chairs, and tables.

"Perhaps I should return at a more convenient time. Although I don't know how long I'll be in Oran before they send me somewhere else."

"No, no. Stay, Commander. I want to thank an American for freeing us. Until you came, I thought I would be next to be shipped to France by our own Vichy government. From there, it would certainly have been to Germany or Poland to one of the camps. Many of us are already gone. I don't expect we'll ever get them back.

"But I thank you for saving our lives, those of us who are still here. I can prepare some coffee for us. I have a kerosene lamp in the back and can heat up some water. Please, don't say no. I just want to thank you, to let you know how much we appreciate your coming here to stop the deportations. Was there any particular reason you picked my shop to walk into?"

"Yes. My family name used to be Henriques. In my family, they say we were from Spain or Portugal."

"Are you Jewish then?"

"No, I'm not. But I was in Malta a while back and made a rubbing from an old slave headquarters. It was carved into the wall by someone named Aaron Henriques, during the year 1732 or 1733. He was kidnapped by pirates. I don't have the rubbing; it's at my home in the United States."

"Ah, our Henriques family from Salonica," Jacques explained. "He was captured by pirates with his son, Jaime. The son was released first and then got his father out. When did your family go to America?" Henriques passed a steaming cup of coffee to Ennis as he spoke. He opened a tin of canned milk, apologizing for the lack of fresh milk. He poured some into his own cup and offered the can to Ennis, who shook his head with a smile. The coffee was excellent.

"Before the Revolutionary War in America, I've been told," he said, resuming the conversation. "My father said we came from Amsterdam or London, then to Rhode Island."

"Then your family was probably once Jewish."

"That's what I'm beginning to think, but I have no proof. Where was your family from?"

"Portugal. They left Lisbon after the great earthquake of 1755. They went to Amsterdam and then, London. So, there are Henriques families in both those cities. We are all related. My, great-grandfather Samuel, was the grandson of Jaime and Gracia Henriques' son Pedro. Pedro later took the name, David. After the earthquake, they went to Amsterdam and from there to Paris during the Napoleonic Wars. They left another son, Carlos, behind. He never came out of Portugal, so I guess I have family there, too. I also have cousins in Paris, London, Amsterdam and Livorno, Italy. It seems I may now have one in America." He extended his hand again in friendship. "Now I have another reason to welcome you. What do I call you?"

"Jimmy is fine. Is one of your cousins in Amsterdam named Aarnald?"

"You know Aarnald?"

"No, but I saw his picture in an album in a Gibraltar gift shop. The lady said I look like him."

"Yes, I believe you do. Yes, you certainly do," Jacques said, tilting his head. After giving Jimmy a second and better look, he said, "You are a bit taller and have darker hair. Otherwise, she was correct."

"Is he safe?"

Jacques shrugged his shoulders, Gallic style, and raised his hands in frustration. "We don't know. We've tried to get news of him. We last heard he was in hiding in Rotterdam. The Germans round up Jews everywhere. We hear terrible stories of what happens to them when they are caught. We can only hope they are not true. Who can tell? We pray that Aarnald is safe."

"Is there anything I can do for you while I'm here?"

"Not that I can think of. Maybe you can restore my electricity?" Jacques laughed, knowing that it was impossible. "Will you come to my house for dinner? My father, Avraham, is here. He's the founder of this business. I came into it to be with him." Jacques swept a hand around the room. "He knows everything about the family and our history. He'll be pleased to see you. Maybe he can fit you into the family."

"I would like that; thank you." From the time Ennis walked into the shop he noticed Jacques had a yellow star sewn into his jacket, which was draped over a chair alongside the counter. It said JUIF. Jew, in French.

"Jacques," he asked, "Why are you wearing that yellow star?"

"The Vichy government makes all Jews wear it. The administrator for Oran says Algiers is France and French law says we must wear this badge, even if you Americans are here. It gets me angry.

"My son, Shimon, who is only 21, was at Bir Hakim with the French General Koenig and the Foreign Legion, fighting the Germans and the Italians. Shimon was one of 400 Jewish boys in a unit of the British army's Jewish Brigade. Koenig was assigned to the British left flank in an old French fort that was falling apart. About 100 Jewish soldiers were sent out with orders to lay mines in the area around General Koenig's fort to protect it, and then leave.

"The weapons they carried with them were only light arms. Then the Germans attacked. Now the boys became stranded with the French defenders and were caught up in a fierce battle, which became a three-week siege of Koenig's forces. With only their light weapons and grenades, they helped to hold off German tanks and dive bombers. During those three weeks, more than once the Jews refused German offers to surrender.

"When the Germans learned they were fighting Jews, they became ferocious. What saved those young men were the hundreds of mines they'd put down; the Germans couldn't get past them. Those boys suffered 75-percent casualties. Thank God, Shimon's wounds are now healed.

"After the battle was over, the Jewish soldiers, through their Major Boris, tried raising the flag of the Palestinian Jews, but a British officer made them take it down. General Koenig put it on his Jeep and ordered all his troops to salute that flag. Those Vichy lackeys you see here in Oran didn't fight for their country and they tell those who did and died for it, they must wear this badge of shame." Jacques pointed to the badge on his jacket.

What these people have gone through in their history: expulsion, kidnappings, this indignity of being ordered to lower a simple flag. Now this star business. And so much more. Why do they go on? It could all end for them so easily by just giving in. Ennis was now resolved to find out more about his family and the Jews. Yet he didn't know how to go about an investigation. For the present, he was an American Naval officer engaged in the fight to win the War. That took precedence over his curiosity about his family. He could, however, uproot an injustice now, here in Algeria, and that, he would do.

There was never a good time to see General Mark Clark. Every politician in Oran wanted him to do them a favor. Ennis was determined to get his boss to do something about the Star. He pulled aside his friend, the General's aide Major Barry Raines, and told him about the Jewish star, explaining that the Germans and the Vichy French governments made Jews wear them. Then he told Raines about Shimon Henriques and General Koenig at the Battle of Bir Hakim. Even though North Africa was now occupied by the British and Americans, the anti-Semitic laws of the Vichy government were still in effect.

"Hang in there, Jimmy. Wait, I'll get back to you."

Raines returned in twenty minutes. "Jimmy, can you get back here with your friend in two hours?"

"You bet, Barry!"

Two hours later, Ennis returned with Jacques Henriques in tow. One of General Clark's aides saw them and smiled. He looked to the far end of the room at a small, dark-haired man of about 40 years of age, bent over in his chair, looking at the floor, nervously twirling his hat with one hand and holding a cigarette in the other.

"Who's that, Jacques?" Jim asked.

"He's the aide to Yves Chatel, the Vichy representative in Oran. This rat's name is Alfonse le Blanc. They are both pro-German, real Nazis. And Jew haters. They couldn't wait until all the Jews of Oran were gone so they could divide up their property."

Five minutes later, Mark Clark and Major Raines walked in. After salutes, they both shook Ennis' hand vigorously.

"Hello, Jimmy," Clark said. "Introduce me to your friend."

"General Clark, this is Mr. Jacques Henriques, Sir. He lives here in Oran and has a business here, too. He might be a distant cousin. He speaks English."

"Is that so? Welcome to my headquarters, Mr. Henriques. I heard the story of your son at the siege of Bir Hakim. I would like to personally salute him. A fine soldier. Seventy-five-percent casualties. Imagine. Those brave men. Where is your son now? As I said, I'd like to salute him."

"He suffered some wounds, General, and was discharged from the British army. He's fine now. Recovered. He lives in Tel Aviv, in Palestine." Jacques Henriques was speaking in very good English, albeit with an accent.

"Too bad. I would have liked to have met him. From what I hear, he was a real hero. Tell me about that yellow star on your coat. Why do you wear it?"

"Our government makes us wear it, General."

"I wonder why? Have you done anything against your government to make them treat you differently like this?"

"No, General. All Jews wear the star simply because they are Jews and for no other reason."

Clark looked at le Blanc and asked Major Raines, "And who might this be, Barry?"

"The Vichy administrator's aide for Oran, Sir. Alfonse le Blanc."

"Does he speak English? "

"He sure does, Sir."

"Then get the sonofabitch over here."

Suddenly, the office became quiet. Typewriters stopped clacking; clerks stopped speaking to one another. The sound of desk drawers opening and closing ceased. Papers stopped shuffling. Personnel stopped working and all eyes were on General Clark.

When he was called, Le Blanc stood, then shuffled over to the General.

"Please, my General, may we go into your office for privacy? This is embarrassing, having to discuss these matters in front of everyone. After all, I am the assistant administrator of the city and..."

Clark cut him off. "No. We'll do this here and now. I want everyone in my command to know why brave men are fighting and dying for your country and why you people haven't lifted a finger to liberate it, and degrade your citizens for no good reason." Clark pointed to his clerks, who were moving closer to the wooden barrier dividing the workspace from the waiting room.

"Where is your boss, Yves Chatel? I asked him to come here, not you."

"He is busy with important administrative duties. I was sent here to appear for him."

Clark's face turned red with anger. "Well, I'm not happy that he ignores me. I am not used to people ignoring me. Nothing is more important than answering my call. But you can be sure that I'll deal with that later. And when you leave here, you tell your boss that I'm not pleased he decided something else was more important than my request to see him. I understand your boss has ordered cloth armbands with Jewish stars made for your Jewish citizens to wear. Is that correct?"

"Yes, my General."

"When you leave here, you are to immediately cancel that order. No one will be wearing those armbands or anything else denoting anyone's religion in the city. Am I clear on that?"

"Yes, my General." Le Blanc was now trembling and looking a bit confused.

"And you tell Mr. Chatel that he is not to use any government funds to pay for the armbands. I'm sure he'll have to pay a penalty for the cancellation. I will check to make sure my order is followed. Any penalty to be paid will come from Mr. Chatel's own pocket. Is that understood, Mr. Le Blanc?"

"Yes, my General."

"Now, Mr. Le Blanc," Clark continued with an edge of bitterness in his voice, "Will you please tell me why you are making French citizens, whose country is an ally of America and England, this man in particular, wear this star?"

"This is France, my General. The laws of France require all Jews to wear the star."

"Not anymore, it doesn't. Not since we took over this place." Clark's response was bitter. He looked to his aide, shaking his head incredulously. Le Blanc's face was showing fear. Standing many inches below the towering Clark, he held his hat close to his chest as if it could shield him from the General's anger.

"But my General, I don't make the laws. I only carry them out."

"Is this a just law, Mr. LeBlanc?

"They are Jews, General. Communists and anarchists. Bloodsuckers. Assassins of Christ. I don't understand why you defend them. They are enemies of France and of all good Christians."

"Nonsense! If you don't know why I defend them then I'll never be able to get you to understand. Frankly, I don't care to spend the time trying. Barry, please get me a scissor." Clark was shouting, visibly growing even angrier.

"Yes, Sir."

"Now, Mr. LeBlanc, do you see this scissor?"

"Yes, my General."

"I want you here and now, in the presence of my staff, to remove the star from this French citizen's coat, taking care not to damage it. If you do, I will personally make sure you replace it with a coat of equal value. And Mr. Le Blanc, you are to personally notify Mr. Chatel that every Jewish citizen in Oran can come to City Hall to have their stars removed by your employees. For those who cannot go to City Hall because they are sick or too young or too old, you are to send an employee to their homes to remove these stars.

"Your people are to treat these French citizens with respect. If I find anyone who does not, I will throw him in jail. That includes you and your boss, Chatel. And remember what I said about damages. Military law is in effect here, Mr. LeBlanc. I am more powerful than you or your Mr. Chatel. Make sure you carry out my orders exactly as I have set them out.

"And tell your boss there will be no more deportations of Jews or anyone else. Do you understand? And the next time I request his presence, he is not to send a subordinate. He is to come here directly, as I order."

Le Blanc made a silent, red-faced nod. A few office personnel clapped, stopping when they realized they were the only ones applauding. As Clark walked away, he heard the careful snipping of scissors. Le Blanc's face was still red, his hands trembling. He stopped working for a moment to light a cigarette to calm himself. He did not look at Jacques Henriques, his eyes focusing on carefully removing the badge. Finished, he kept his gaze down, donned his hat and in a small show of defiance, handed the star and scissors to Jacques almost as if it were a punch to his chest.

Barry Raines pulled Ennis aside and said, "I knew he was going to do something like that, Jimmy."

"How come?"

"Although the General is a Christian, his mother is a Jew."

17

AMSTERDAM
1756

The air in Amsterdam seemed freer than in any of the other places they had been to. Once Jaime, Gracia and Pedro reached Brest, they traveled easily and unmolested, by coach and foot through northern France until they reached the Burgundian port of Antwerp. There, they were told that the port of Rotterdam, in Holland, was just six miles away. They walked and rode to that city with great anticipation and impatience. Finally, they reached Amsterdam, where they were directed to its famed Jewish Quarter.

Jaime was amazed at what he saw. Men walked openly wearing religious skull caps. The Jews spoke Portuguese, Spanish and Ladino although some Jews spoke an unfamiliar guttural language. There were shops with Hebrew signs that were incomprehensible to him. But others bore legible signs with family names from Portugal: Mendes, Da Costa, Montes, Mendoza and de Leon. Some men wore silk shawls covering their shoulders, fringes swaying from the bottom, at the wearer's waist. Jaime had never seen one before, although he had heard of them and knew that they had a religious significance.

In this bustling city, Jaime was to learn that religious tracts were openly written and publicly circulated in Hebrew, Ladino, Spanish, Portuguese and Yiddish, a language he had never heard of. He was told that there was theatre in all these languages, as well as printed books.

Then Jaime saw a church just a few yards away from the Synagogue. It was a Catholic Church called Moses and Aaron.

"What a strange place," Jaime said to Gracia. "A church and a synagogue side-by-side and the church is named for two of our Patriarchs!"

The Dutch spoke a harsh language: guttural, not soft like the mellifluous Mediterranean Spanish and Portuguese. But they were a friendly people, and tolerant. They had given Jews citizenship, the first country in Europe to do so. That was more important than a barrier like language, which could easily be overcome. Unlike those in Lisbon, Dutch winters were icy cold and harsh. That also had to be gotten used to: small prices to pay for freedom.

The family had specifically been directed to the street called Visserplein, in the neighborhood known as Judenbruut, neither of which Jaime could properly pronounce. It was where the Spanish and Portuguese synagogue was located, in the heart of the Jewish Quarter. It was not called a synagogue, but an Esnoga. Later, he would learn that it was the Ladino word for synagogue. Ladino was the language Iberian Jews used among themselves in their exile around the world, or what scholars called "The Diaspora." The Esnoga also had a Hebrew name, Neve Shalom (Oasis of Peace), which neither Jaime nor Gracia could translate. And there were other things about this wonderful city he could not understand: the Yiddish speakers were Ashkenazi Jews; they had their own synagogue. But he hoped that in time he would understand it all in this marvelous place.

As he entered the main Synagogue, he noted the floors were covered with sand. Why? He didn't know, so he asked. There were several answers: a tradition carried from Spain and Portugal to quiet the footfalls, so Inquisitors would not hear Jews at prayer. Someone else said, "It is to remind us of our journey over the desert, when we left Egypt led by the Prophet Moses." Another person said, "God in the Bible said the Children of Israel shall be as numerous as the sands."

During religious services in this Esnoga, women sat in a balcony apart from men, taking no part in the service. During the secret ceremonies in Portugal, men and women always prayed together. In fact, it was often the women, not the men, who led the services. So many new things and so many strange words to learn!

The Quarter was not a place where Jews were confined or mistreated. There were no gates or walls surrounding the neighborhood. And there was prosperity here. Men and women dressed well and looked to be well-fed, like their Dutch neighbors. Shops were filled with plenty of meat, fowl and fish. Later, the Henriques family would be instructed as to the Jewish laws of *kashrut*, the ritual of food cleanliness, which they followed. There was even a Christian painter named Rembrandt Van Rijn who once, many years ago, lived near the synagogue and painted portraits and etched sympathetic likenesses of the neighborhood's Jews, even the rabbis: a practice unthinkable in Lisbon.

The Henriques family presented themselves at a building near the Esnoga which they had been directed to. It was run by the Hermandad, the Jewish brotherhood. Jaime felt uncomfortable when he heard that word, because that was also the short name often used for the Portuguese Inquisition. But he was soon put at ease. A friendly man named Moses Bueno de Mesquita, who spoke Spanish and Portuguese, was orienting the family. He was a slight man, about 60 years of age with greying, wiry hair and bright brown eyes. He immediately made the family comfortable. Jaime noted that he wore a skull cap and they weren't even in a synagogue at prayer. His office was filled with books, and the smell of paper and the leather that bound them into neat volumes permeated the room. There were familiar objects on shelves, a Menorah and a pair of candlesticks used to light the way for the coming of the Shabbat.

"Are you Spanish or Portuguese?" Moses Bueno de Mesquita asked.

"Portuguese. We come from Lisbon." Gracia replied.

"Portuguese is easier," Moses explained. "The Dutch are always at odds with Spain. So Spanish Jews say they are Portuguese. Makes it easier for them. Here are some rules you must follow. The Dutch are good to us. They grant us freedom to pray, and they have even granted us citizenship. But you must be careful not to say anything which attacks their religion. We are their guests, but we have had to deal with our religious problems to their satisfaction.

"A long time ago, one of our congregants, Baruch Spinoza, a brilliant boy from a fine Portuguese family, wrote of God and the

Bible in different ways than we teach. The Dutch were unhappy about this, since it also attacked their understanding of our Five Books of Moses, which is an important part of their religion. Spinoza was finally excommunicated from the Jewish community. To the Dutch, our Five Books of Moses are a sacred part of their beliefs. Spinoza's changing traditional concepts concerned the Dutch.

"The Dutch speak Nederlands, which is a form of German. You'll have to learn it to deal with them. In the Jewish quarter, you can get along with Ladino, Spanish or Portuguese. There are Jews from Eastern Europe here, too. They speak Yiddish. We call them Ashkenazim, from the German Duchies and the east, Poland and Russia. We are *Sephardim*, the Hebrew word for Spain.

"We need to get you settled. You plan to return to our faith, yes?"

"Yes, of course," Jaime said.

Bueno de Mesquita had already made a note in a large book. He had opened a new and blank page, titled: *Familia Henriques: Pai, Maie I filho.*

"If you return to our faith, you must attend classes for instruction in Judaism. I would expect that you have had none?"

Jaime looked to the floor. "Very little, except that we love our religion and have always refused to accept the Catholic faith."

"You're not different from many who come here. We will restore you to Judaism. When we first came here from Spain and Portugal many years ago, most of our people were like you. Only a few knew anything about our religion. We had to bring Rabbis from Eastern Europe, North Africa, Italy and the Ottoman Empire to help us. Now, we have our own Rabbis, who were born here. We learned and so will you." Moses Bueno de Mesquita coughed. He seemed to be looking for the right words.

"If you haven't already been, you will be required to become circumcised. This ritual is the pact that Abraham made with God. All healthy male Jews are required to undergo circumcision. You will have to do it before you appear in the synagogue. There you will, after proper orientation, publicly announce yourselves to the community as committed Jews."

Jaime looked at Pedro, who was puzzled as he did not understand this new word... "I'll explain later, Pedro," Jaime offered.

"What did you do in Lisbon?"

"I was a jeweler and I dealt in gold and silver."

"We have a mountain of jewelers here, most of whom have little or no inventory. Can you do anything else?"

"I brought fine jewelry and gold and silver coins with us."

"Enough to open a shop?"

"More than enough."

"Then we will look for a place for you to do business. Or perhaps, put you together with a partner. Which would you prefer?"

"I would prefer to work alone. My son Pedro, who is almost 16, was my apprentice in Lisbon. He can continue here. Could you suggest a good Hebrew name for him?"

"Yes. I think, after looking at him, that David would suit him well."

Jaime smiled down at his son. "Then from now on, you are David," he said proudly.

Moses continued. "Since you are Jaime, your Hebrew name should be Chaim. And Gracia is fine; your name needn't be changed. A great and outstanding woman of our religion, Doña Gracia de Mendes, bore that name before you. You can use it with pride."

Jaime rose from his seat, shook hands with Bueno de Mesquita and said, "Good. When do we start becoming Jews again?"

18

ORAN, 1943
AT THE HOME OF JACQUES HENRIQUES

Jacque Henriques' chauffer drove the shiny black pre-war Citroen sedan up a steep incline into the hills behind the city of Oran. The road was familiar to Ennis, who sat in the back seat of the car. He had traveled this road with General Mark Clark weeks earlier. While he couldn't locate the exact house where the meeting with the Vichy officers had been held, he did recognize many of the homes and Mosques along the road that he had passed that night, since the houses were large and obviously belonged to affluent families.

The car finally slowed down, turning into a curve that ran in front of a large, two-story villa, painted a light pastel blue with a bright, orange-tiled roof. As the car came to a stop, a tall man dressed entirely in white opened the car door and ushered Ennis into the house. Ennis stopped to look out over the city and to the ocean. The view was stunning.

The house was cool and smelled of freshly cut flowers. Jacques Henriques appeared from one of the several doors at the entrance level. He wore a white, long-sleeved shirt open at the collar, and dark pants that were crisply ironed and fit him perfectly. He held out a hand and greeted his guest with *"Bienvenue,* Jimmy," indicating that tonight they would be speaking French.

There was a clacking sound coming from the back of the house. Jacques noticed Ennis looking puzzled. "It's our generator," he explained. "We make our own electricity until the city gets powered up again. The Vichy government spitefully wouldn't allow us to put one up in our business. You need a permit to operate a generator in the city and Jewish names always seem to be at the bottom of the list when it comes to getting permission."

Jacques led his guest into a large, airy and sun-lit living room. A woman was standing by a cart, mixing drinks. She was introduced as Dora, Jacques' wife. She had jet-black hair pulled back tight in a bun, Spanish style. She was well-groomed, with a slender body and dark eyes. She immediately put Ennis at ease, by saying, "Welcome. Jacques said I should call you Jimmy, so I shall. We drink Pernod. Shall I pour some for you?"

"A pleasure to meet you, Dora. I've never had Pernod, but I'll be pleased to try it."

"We drink it with cold water, Jimmy, would you like it that way? Or I can give you some ice, too. The Americans are crazy for ice, I know."

"I'll drink it the way you do."

The Pernod poured from the bottle was colorless, but when Dora poured water into Jimmy's glass, it turned a cloudy, opaque white. She passed the glass to her guest, who sipped it cautiously, the anise flavor bursting in his mouth and rising to his nostrils. *It would take a while to get used to this drink,* he thought. Dora passed a glass to her husband and another to a distinguished-looking older man who sat in the corner of the room on a large plush sofa, surrounded by many large, puffy and gorgeously colored pillows of Arabic design.

"And this is my father, Avraham Henriques," Jacques announced, looking to the older man. "He is, as I told you, the family historian. Hopefully, he can answer some questions for you."

Ennis shook the old man's hand. It was smooth and soft, the hand of someone who had not known hard labor during his lifetime. He wore a short beard that was as grey as his thinning hair. His face was tanned from the African sun and lined with age. Ennis noted small holes in his white shirt, where a Star of David had once been sewn.

Avraham Henriques had green eyes that were fixed on Ennis, obviously observing this man who might possibly be a relative. He held out his Pernod in a salute and said, "We have to thank you for getting rid of those damned stars. It was a wonderful thing you did. The entire community will thank you when they learn what happened today."

"It didn't make sense. Wearing the stars, I mean."

"The coming to North Africa by the United States and the British has saved us. The French were systematically collecting us to turn us over to the Germans for only God knows what purpose. We were on that list put together by the Jew-hater Castel, the administrator of Oran. He was looking to take over our businesses and our houses. It was only a matter of time for us to be deported. The French told the Germans not to trouble themselves with rounding up Jews; they would do it gladly." The old man waved his hand as if to say, forget it.

"Jacques tells me that you have a rubbing of our family in Malta, which was scratched on a wall by Aaron, one of our ancestors. I would love to see it."

"When I get home, I'll make a copy and send it to you." *What resilience these people have. One of their ancestors is a prisoner in a stinking hellhole, and a descendant sits here in luxury. Who are these Jews? I never gave much thought to them before, but they are certainly an interesting bunch. I have to learn more about them when I have some time.*

"Thank you. I will look forward to that. They were finally redeemed, you know, Aaron and his son Jaime, for the going rate for Jewish prisoners. Young Jaime went first, sometime after his Bar Mitzvah, so he was considered an adult by our tradition. When he returned home to Salonica, he gathered up enough money to free his father. That is not only a son's solemn obligation, but it is also one for every Jew who is free: He must free those of us who are captives."

"So I've been told, and by a Catholic priest, no less." Jimmy Ennis smiled, hoping Avraham would catch the irony.

"Yes, the priests who study the Hebrew bible know such things. The story of the prisoners Aaron and Jaime are only one of the many stories of our family, including the one of the long trip from Lisbon to Amsterdam by another Jaime, his wife Gracia and their son Pedro who later became David, to reach freedom and return to our religion. Where did your family go when they went to America?"

"I've been told to Newport, in Rhode Island colony."

"Yes, yes, a few of our people went there after the Lisbon earthquake in 1755. They went to Newport because there was already a small but affluent colony of Portuguese and Spanish Jews there. Tell me, do you know how you came to have the name Ennis?"

"No, I haven't the slightest idea. I can only guess my ancestor wanted to fit in with all the English. Ennis sounds like a good English name."

"Makes sense," Avraham agreed. "We trace our family coming out of Portugal 200 years ago; before that, in Spain. We know that the Henriques family was originally Spanish and were the household attendants to the royal house of Castile. Henriques means 'Lord of the House.'

"An earlier ancestor, also named Jaime, was 21 when he sailed with Columbus as that wretched Queen Isabella's representative. He and his siblings fled to Portugal in 1493, when the Inquisition learned their parents practiced Judaism secretly and murdered them. Some others of our family fled to the Ottoman Empire, to Istanbul, Izmir and Salonica. That's where Aaron and Jaime came from: Salonica. Not the same Jaime in 1492, of course. Salonica today is known by its Greek name: Thessaloniki.

"In 1497, all the Jews of Portugal were forcibly converted to Christianity. They still maintained their love for our faith, however. Two-hundred years ago, during the Great Earthquake, our family escaped from Lisbon to forever be free of the hateful Inquisition.

"My grandfather several times removed, David Henriques, was almost 16 when he left Portugal with his parents in 1755. His name was Pedro then. They gave him the name of David when he arrived in Amsterdam, months later. When his father Jaime died in 1766, David took over the jewelry business that he had run with his father. A year later, he left for England with his mother, his wife Rebecca and their children, establishing himself as a jeweler to the English upper-class. There is still on Bond Street in London an exclusive jewelry establishment known as Henriques Brothers. They are of our family.

"When he was 17, David had married Rebecca Rodrigues of the Portuguese community. They had four sons, one of which we know immigrated to the English Colonies. His name was Solomon. Does that name sound familiar to you?"

"I am familiar with Solomon Ennis. He is one of my ancestors. Could he have been an Henriques?"

"Perhaps so. We might be related! If you notice the same names being repeated from generation to generation, it is because we Spanish and Portuguese Jews make it a point to perpetuate the names of our fathers and mothers over the generations. My son Jacques' real name is Jacob or Jacobo. Jaime gets Anglicized into James, like your name. Or Jacques in French, or Chaim in Hebrew. Our Solomon might very well be one of your ancestors. We shall see.

"Of the other three sons, we know one returned to Amsterdam, one remained in England and the last son went to France after the defeat of Napoleon. A generation later, one of his sons moved to Livorno, Italy and another to the Caribbean."

Avraham sighed. Ennis noted a glistening in the older man's eyes. Was it the beginning of tears?

"And there are members of our family in Amsterdam and Salonica now," Avraham continued. "We pray for them as the Nazis occupy those cities. We know what they are doing to Jews, even though the British and you Americans would rather shut your eyes to the mass murders." A tear rolled down his cheek. "As for all these people, we are related and we keep in touch, both as family and in business. Now we learn we may have family in the United States. I hope that is true. You would certainly be an asset to the Henriques family."

The old man reached into his jacket pocket and pulled out a pack of cigarettes. *Gitanes* was written across the sky-blue package that had a wispy cloud surrounding a picture of a Gypsy woman in a Flamenco pose. He drew out a cigarette and offered one to Ennis, who shook his head. Then he took a long cigarette holder from his pocket. It was exquisitely made of many inlaid stones which flashed like multi-colored beacons, reflecting the light. Inserting a cigarette, he lit it with a slim gold lighter and took a long drag.

"Dreadful," he said, now speaking in perfect English with an unaccountable accent. "These French *Gitanes* and *Gauloises* and the British Players don't compare to American or Turkish tobaccos. In wartime, however, we must settle."

"I'll make sure you get several cartons of American cigarettes," Ennis said. "Do you have a preference? Camels, Lucky Strike or Pall Mall?

"Thank you, Commander, any American cigarette will do. Aside from being a savior, you are also a provider. I do thank you." Avraham's thanks were accompanied with a broad and appreciative smile. "Now, we must find out what happened to the Henriques who went to Rhode Island and, more important, if you, Jimmy, are really an Henriques. Are there any Jews in your family?"

"I don't know. Certainly none that I know of."

"And you said there is a Solomon, no?"

"There is, back a few generations. I noted some other biblical names as well."

Dora called out in flawless Spanish, "Avraham, continue this business at dinner. Food is being laid out."

The two men stood. Avraham put his arm through Ennis's as they walked into the dining room, but he stood ramrod straight. "I'm 77 years old," he said. "I still keep my hand in the business, but if I can hang on to a young man as I walk, I relish the opportunity." He moved with a shuffle in Arab slippers of beautifully hand-tooled leather.

How easily they move from one culture to another, Ennis observed.

The dining room was a bit smaller than the living room. A large, three-foot high coffee urn made of gleaming brass and copper sat on a wooden sideboard by a wall. Dark oak beams ran across the 14-foot ceiling and housed two slow-moving fans that circulated air. A table made of the same dark wood, looked as if it could comfortably seat many more than a dozen guests; its edges were hand-carved in intricate designs. On shelves along the walls were polished copper trays, tea servers and cups, all of them in Arabic design. Two large paintings, perhaps six feet high and four feet across, dominated two walls. One was a scene of a bustling outdoor

Arab food market; the other portrayed an Arab *dhow*, sailing into a large cove filled with anchored sailing ships. Both paintings were of high professional quality and artfully executed. The dining room floor was made of tiles set out in an intricate design of cool blue and ocean green. The silverware and dishes were of a quality that Ennis had rarely seen.

The man who had opened the car door for Ennis now entered the dining room with a platter of lamb piled in slices, accompanied by a roasted leg. There were already dishes of vegetables on the table, and one that looked like porridge, which they called *cous cous*. Dora put a plate of warmed flat bread in front of her guest and said in Spanish, "Here, Jimmy, try this bread. It's called *pita*."

Jacques spoke to his wife in Spanish, "Dora, make sure our guest has enough lamb." Now Avraham took a bottle of wine and poured a cup for everyone. Then he took his glass and held it above his head, saying a short prayer in Hebrew. After he sipped the wine and set the cup on the table, he made another Hebrew prayer over the bread. Ennis noticed Jacques and Avraham were now wearing skull caps. Avraham offered an explanation in French.

"It is Friday night, Jimmy, the start of our Sabbath. We make these prayers to welcome Shabbat, as we call the Sabbath in Hebrew." The conversation continued in French, Spanish and English. Ennis noted that when they spoke to the man who brought in the food, they used Arabic. It was dazzling. Except for the Arabic, he could easily follow along.

Avraham wiped a drop of wine from the corner of his mouth. "Now, Jimmy, tell me about the oldest person you knew in your family. What was he like? What was his name? What did he tell you about the family?"

"That would be Grandpa Jim. I was named for him. He was, of course, an Ennis. He often told me that when our family came from either Spain or Portugal, our name was Henriques. And that one of the men in our family, Solomon Ennis, had fought and died in the Revolutionary War. I have to say, it was all very sketchy. No one could tell me much more about Solomon Ennis."

"Did your grandfather go to church?"

"Rarely. He used to say that his father told him religion caused problems and bad things for people and that's why he never went regularly. He would go to a wedding, or on Christmas, maybe Easter. That's about all."

Jimmy took a fork full of lamb, which was tender and delicious, filled with spices and flavors that were strange but pleasing to him. He could certainly enjoy this life.

19

THESSALONIKI, GREECE
JANUARY 1943

Colonel Stavros Matsarakis often performed this demeaning act. Each time he appeared before the German guards, he swallowed his large pride, lowering himself by playing the role of the humble, conquered Greek. It was a necessary ploy, needed to get past the guards and move freely around his occupied country. His Greek army had humiliated the Italians in Albania during the Greco-Italian War of 1940. The unwanted result was that Germany was forced to come to Italy's aid. Now the northern Macedonian city of Thessaloniki was in the grip of the despised SS and Gestapo, who were not as lenient as the former, easy-going Italian occupiers. It was because of the Nazis that the slender, mustachioed, and nervous Colonel Matsarakis had come to Thessaloniki. He was on a personal mission.

Fighting alongside him in that Italian campaign were those quirky Spanish-speaking Jews of Thessaloniki, members of the 50th Macedonian Brigade known as the Cohen Brigade because it was made up of Sephardic Jews, descendants of refugees from Spain and Portugal who had come to that city in 1492. Growing up in a small town, Matsarakis had little contact with Jews. But the ones he met in the army were his reliable and dependable comrades: privates, sergeants, and officers, all fighting like brave lions when the Greeks counterattacked against the Italians. More than once, they protected his flanks and saved him from capture. Even though the Greeks were greatly outnumbered at the battle of Klisura Pass inside

Albania, they routed the Italians. During the campaign, soldiers from Thessaloniki shared their blankets and food with fellow Greeks during the frigid winter. Now, after he had heard some troubling rumors about how the Nazis were treating the Jews, he promised himself he would do what he could for his comrades, the Spanish-speaking Jews of Thessaloniki's Cohen Brigade.

That time had come. He descended the Macedonian mountains, where he led a resistance group. The Colonel was bringing disturbing news about what the Germans were planning for Greek Jews. More than one German prisoner that he'd captured verified Jewish deportation to Poland and, after that, only God knows what was happening to them.

Today, he presented himself before the two German soldiers guarding the main entrance to Thessaloniki's Jewish Community office. Matsarakis was suitably dressed in shabby clothes, as were most of the rest of Greece's captive population. The soldiers stopped him, one of them speaking excellent Greek.

"What business do you have here with the Jews?" the guard asked.

"You speak Greek well," Colonel Matsarakis noted.

"I'm Bulgarian. Lived on the Greek border all my life. Volunteered for the German army. But what's your business here? Are you a Jew?"

"No, I'm not a Jew. I came here to see if I could buy some property from them. I understand they are selling properties."

"Let me see your identity papers," the guard demanded. Matsarakis reached into his pocket, pulling out papers kept together by a thick, red rubber band. There was a load of identification documents: ration cards, a driver's license, and his phony discharge as a sergeant from the Greek army. All the documents were excellent forgeries, showing his lean face with his dark, flowing mustache. He handed one to the guard.

"Everything seems to be in order, Mr. Poulos. You can go inside," the guard said after inspecting and returning the papers. "Good luck with the Jews," he added, laughing as Matsarakis headed up the stairs.

Once inside, he saw a building bursting with people dashing about. He asked to see "the Jewish priest." After a few moments, a young man, looking to be in his 20s, came into the waiting room.

"Rabbi Koretz is not here," he said. "I'm in charge in his absence. The Rabbi is away on some religious errands. I expect him back around 4 o'clock. What is your business with the Rabbi?"

Rabbi Zvi Koretz was an Ashkenazic Rabbi, retained by the Thessaloniki Jewish community to act as Chief Rabbi and represent them to the German occupiers. Tragically, the city's Jewish leaders mistakenly felt a German-speaking Rabbi would be more acceptable in negotiations with the occupiers than a Greek or Ladino speaker. In a show of contempt, the Germans sent the Rabbi to a concentration camp in 1941, then released him in 1942 so that he could be in Thessaloniki to help the Nazis oversee the final destruction of the 500-year-old Sephardic community of Salonica, as Thessaloniki was now known.

Rabbi Koretz was of little help. The Nazis had their plan for Greek Jews and Rabbi Koretz as well. It was the plan they had for all the Jews of Europe and a German-speaking rabbi wasn't changing their minds. If it wasn't helping in Germany, Poland, Russia or Austria, why should Greece be an exception?

"I don't think you can wait until tonight, young man. You are in great danger. The Germans have some plans for the Jews of this city. They are not pretty. You all need to act quickly."

"Who are you? How do I know what you say is true?"

"Are there any veterans from the Greco-Italian War in the building?"

"No, but the dentist Salvador Polo lives nearby. He was a Captain in the War."

"Good. Call him here. Quickly."

Waiting for Polo to arrive, Matsarakis noted some young boys in the office. He called them over and asked them their names and why they were not at school.

"I'm Dani Henriques. These are my two friends, Gabriel Crespi and Jacob Finzi. We can't go to school anymore. The Germans say Jews can't go to any schools. So we come here and help out in the office and whenever they can, the rabbis manage to spend some time teaching us."

"How old are you?"

"We're all 16."

"The Germans will be coming after you. Would you think about coming up to the mountains with me? To fight the Germans? I don't know what would happen to you if you were taken away, what they are planning to do. I don't see it as a good thing for you or any of the city's Jews, for that matter."

The boys began pondering the offer when Salvador Polo came in with the young man who was in charge, now identifying himself as David Moreno, a seminary student. Polo looked at the Colonel for a short moment and said, "Colonel Matsarakis, what are you doing here?" The question was accompanied with a strong handshake.

"Captain, good to see you. I could only wish that it was under better circumstances. I came to tell you what I've learned. The Germans have some plans for Jews. First they are going to put you all into the Baron de Hirsch hospital, like a jail. From there, they plan to deport you, by train, to Poland. After that, we hear stories – that I hope to God are not true. I want you to burn all the community's records as soon as possible. Without those records, the bastards will have a hard time rounding up Jews. Rabbi Barzelai in Athens has already refused to turn over the community records to the Germans and has promised to burn them if necessary."

"We can't do that without Rabbi Koretz's approval," David Moreno protested.

"Listen to me, young man. I came here at great risk to myself. Two of my men will be here later, also at risk to themselves, to burn your records. I can't wait around for approvals. If you want to save Jews, then listen to me and do as I say. If any of you want to return with me to the mountains, to fight Germans, you are welcome. We can use every healthy body available."

"Do women fight with you?" Dani Henriques asked.

"Yes, we have women fighting with us."

"Then I'll ask my sister Rachel. She's 18."

Polo thought a while and then said, "I'll try to get some of the men from the old 50th Macedonian Brigade. Anyway, at least I'll go with you, Colonel."

"Good, Captain Polo. I knew I could count on you and your men."

It was just after 10:30 in the morning when Colonel Matsarakis left, promising to return in the late afternoon. Dani, who had already decided he was going to leave with him that night, had a lot to do. First, he went home, looking for his sister. He told her what Colonel Matsarakis had said. She understood the peril facing the community and agreed to leave with her brother.

Then Dani went to see his father Chaim, a doctor who had his office and clinic a few streets from the Henriques home. After the German occupation, Jewish doctors were limited to treating only Jews, by order of the Gestapo. Dani's mother, Hannah, who acted as his father's nurse, was also at the office. Dani told them about Colonel Matsarakis. Rumors had previously come to Thessaloniki about camps where prisoners were savagely treated – even beaten to death. No one knew if they were really true. Unlike many in the Jewish community who chose not to believe them, Chaim and Hannah did not dismiss them. Even though Germany was the nation of Kant, Bach and Beethoven and the home of a great Western culture, Dani and his parents realized that if the daily treatment they were experiencing was any indication, the Germans were certainly able to do all the things they were hearing about. As far as they were concerned, it was not idle rumor.

"Dani," his parents said, "we cannot go to the mountains with you. Someone must care for your grandparents and your younger sisters. If you think it best, go with our blessings and take Rachel with you. Never forget who you are and where your family came from."

Dani had some more things to do before he returned to the community's office. He walked down to the harbor, along the road by the Gulf of Thessaloniki, its waters shimmering in the bright sun. It was the area the Jews called the Malecon, the sea wall where the White Tower, one of the city's iconic landmarks, was located. The outdoor café was no longer filled with Greeks sitting at tables enjoying the sights of the Gulf, sipping ouzo and raki, alcoholic drinks made with anise. They were no longer listening to Greek and Sephardic music played on guitars, lutes and Greek bouzoukis. There was no music at all. German soldiers took the place of the locals now, drinking the thick, syrupy Greek coffee served in small demi-tasse cups, speaking in a language foreign to Dani's ears. He spoke Ladino, French, Greek and Italian, the soft languages of the Mediterranean. They were now replaced by the harsh sounds of the Teutonic drawl.

He walked along the Malecon. Once, this place burst with energy. There were the Jewish fishermen, bringing in their catches to be sold at the famous Modiano Market. There, sweaty and muscular longshoremen and carters unloaded ships from around the world. Harbor pilots, too, would take time out from their work to have a cup of coffee as they awaited the next ship they would guide into port.

Today, the harbor was quiet. Docked were only two German Coast Guard cutters, swastikas flying from their masts. There was only one rusty commercial freighter in the Bay, its flag foreign to him. He continued on to his grandfather's office at the water's edge, at 11 Vassilios Heraklion. As the oldest son, he was by tradition named after his grandfather and when he walked inside, the two Danis kissed one another as they always did when they met.

"Nono," the grandson said in a whisper so that no one in the office could overhear. "I'm going up to the mountains." Then he explained Matsarakis' visit. The old man's eyes watered. He hugged his grandson close, so tight that the boy's breath was released. Dani had noticed recently that his Nono had aged much in the last months. Nono's hair had turned completely white, as had Dani's parents and his clothes, once always neat, clean and well-pressed, were now shabby, as were those of most of the Jews of Thessaloniki.

The office was quiet, just a few men sitting around smoking and chatting in Ladino. He remembered this place as being busy and bustling, filled with ship's officers, sailors and other mariners, with many languages filling the air. Nono was a ship's chandler, a supplier of the needs of those who sailed the seas. He also sold wood for the ovens and the stoves of the city. Now, by the Gestapo's law, he could only sell to Jews. He was, in effect, bankrupt.

After the boy finished speaking, the old man hugged him again. He put his hand on Dani's head and recited a Hebrew prayer, a benediction for his safety and hopes for a good fortune for the future. Then he reached into his desk drawer and pulled out a small blue box, handing it to his grandson.

"Dani, I've been meaning to give this to you at the proper time. I bought it in Livorno, Italy, some years ago. Take it now and wear it with pride when you are among the non-Jews."

Dani opened the box. In it was a small gold shield on a chain, with ten Roman numerals delicately cut into the shield. It was the Ten Commandments: *Los Diez Mandiamientos*. It had the pinkish color peculiar to Italian gold. The old man put it around his grandson's neck, fastened the clasp and patted it as it lay across the boy's chest. In Ladino, he said, *"Adio mi nieto, va con Dio."* Goodbye, my grandson, go with God.

There was one more place Dani would visit before trudging up the hill back to his home. It was near Nono's office, the Plaza Eleftheria. Freedom Square. Before the Greeks won the city from the Turkish army in the Balkan War of 1912, and changed its name, the Square was known as Placa Judeo, The Jew's Square. He was too young to remember that. In fact, he had yet to be born. But it was still a favorite place for the Spanish and Portuguese Sephardim. It was once filled with outdoor cafes and men sitting at tables under umbrellas to shade themselves from the hot Macedonian sun while they drank raki, Greek coffee and ouzo and sang the songs known as romanzas, which their ancestors had brought with them from Spain and Portugal. Here, one could hear bouzoukis and guitars and romanzas, with the familiar sound of a flamenco wail or even like the rabbis on Shabbat when they intoned a prayer to God. That was all gone. Even the name had been changed. Today, the Plaza was quiet, visited only by a few Greeks and Germans. Occasionally a café would have an entertainer or two. But it was no longer the center for the happy-go-lucky Sephardim of the city. Dani would miss all this.

"This was the greatest Jewish city in the Mediterranean," his father and Nono would always tell him. "It was here, in this city, that Jews were always the largest group amongst all others. In Salonica, under the Turks, Jews controlled the waterfront from ship to shore. Here, men studied to be rabbis and struggled to understand the mysteries of the Kabbalah. Christians and Muslims spoke our language, Ladino, and we were respected among all the citizens."

Despite his youth, Dani knew all this was gone, probably never to return. What would life be like here after the War? Hard to contemplate. The Henriques family had been here for almost 500 years. After the War, would they be able to continue on, in this special place?

◈ ◈

Dani and Rachel took only a few personal things, said a teary goodbye to their Nona, and headed to the community office. Rabbi Koretz had returned earlier than expected. He was not fond of the Colonel's plan but once the leaders of the community – called to the center by Moreno – learned what the Nazis had planned, they told the Colonel to go ahead. Koretz said "No." He knew what Rabbi Barzelai had planned to do in Athens.

"It will anger the Germans and cause reprisals. I cannot be responsible for that. There will be no burning of records."

Matsarakis looked at Koretz with an air of frustration. "I cannot order or force you to do this, Rabbi. But believe me, it is for the best."

Rabbi Koretz was adamant: there would be no burning of records. "I have spent time in a German concentration camp and do not care to return or have any members of this community become interned in one," Koretz insisted.

At 6.m., two Greek resistance fighters entered the building through an unguarded rear door, which had been left unlocked by Moreno. They were told there would be no burning of the records or the building. Matsarakis and his two soldiers gathered those who would accompany them to their mountain camp. Rabbi Koretz declined to go.

As the group slinked through the city, they all breathed easier when they reached its edge. Then they scurried up the hills leading from the city toward the Macedonian mountains. Dani Henriques, his sister Rachel, Captain Pinto, his fellow soldiers of the 50th Macedonian Brigade, the student David Moreno, and others who had decided to join the resistance fighters, looked back at their city. They said goodbye to this place that had been home to their ancestors for almost 500 years. They all knew in their hearts that for the Jews, this special city of Salonica would never be the same.

Three days later, word was received in the mountains that Rabbi Barzelai had burned the community records of Athens and the Germans were rounding up Jews with much difficulty and without any great success. Colonel Matsarakis' predictions, unfortunately, came true. The SS managed, after a great effort and with the help of Greek collaborators, to gather all of Salonica's Jewish leaders into the Esnoga known as the Shaul Synagogue. They made a sham of creating a protocol for the Jewish community. When it was over and the synagogue was empty, the Gestapo cynically blew it up, together with every other synagogue in the city but one, the newest of them all, the synagogue of the Monastir Jews who came to the city in the early '20s. The Red Cross used the building as a warehouse. Other buildings lovingly constructed years earlier, were also destroyed. Salonica's great libraries, containing Jewish religious and Kabbalistic thought and the Ladino literature of five centuries went up in smoke. Records of births, deaths, divorces, commercial transactions, religious tracts, essays, descriptions of public meetings, parties, political tracts and school records all disappeared as if they had never existed.

All the city's Jews were then ordered to move to the Baron de Hirsch hospital at the west side of the city, just as Matsarakis had predicted. It would become a ghetto, similar to the ones the Nazis had created all over Poland and Russia. The Nazis had been amazed when they entered Thessaloniki, to discover that the Jews of the city did not live in a ghetto. The Nazi's selection of the site for the city's ghetto was ironic. Baron de Hirsch was a well-known German-Jewish banker and philanthropist. Upon his death in 1908, his wife established this hospital in his memory, for the needs of the Jewish community. Now, it was jammed to overflowing with Thessaloniki's Jewish prisoners.

Soon the trains came. The terminal was near the hospital and the Jews were told they were going to Poland to work. They walked the short distance from the hospital to the railroad, believing they were headed for work camps.

Arriving at the camps, they underwent the same selection process other European Jews endured. The strong and sturdy longshoremen and fishermen were sent to work, some to the crematoriums. They learned how to use explosives in their work. They blew up a crematorium, an act which they paid for with their lives. Subsequently, Greek Jews who refused to work in the ovens were summarily executed. Within a short period, a few months in 1943, the Germans had wiped out a culture that stretched back to medieval Spain and Portugal and which could never be revived.

అ ఆ

Life in the mountains was hard for the Partisans. Food was scarce. If they were fortunate, they ate whatever few scraps friendly villagers could spare, which was always very little. The Nazis were forcing the Greeks to provide them with their harvests to feed their troops and their civilian population at home. German food production alone was unable to keep up with all its needs. Aside from German civilians, the Nazis fed a huge army, and there were hundreds of thousands of slave laborers who, even though provided with less calories than needed for healthy sustenance, had to be fed as well. As a result, all of Greece was starving, having to help make up Germany's shortfall.

On occasion when the Partisans attacked a German convoy containing a field kitchen, there was a feast. But it was obvious that even the German soldier was eating only just a little bit better than Greek civilians. They, however, were eating three meals a day, unlike the Partisans.

From time to time, English and American officers from the OSE and OSS would parachute into the mountains with radio equipment, arms, ammunition, and field rations. The dry food, eaten from boxes called K-rations, was mixed with hot water to create a hot sauce for a soup, or a pasta dish. It was food nevertheless, nutritious and it filled the belly. The cartons contained chocolate bars and cigarettes, which were always welcomed and became a means of trading between the Partisans and the villagers for small bits of meat or vegetables. At night, sitting before a fire, the English and American officers filled the Partisans with the latest news.

"The Germans are murdering Jews, Poles and Russians in astounding numbers, on a scale that we cannot believe. They maintain work camps where conditions are worse than merely bad. In these camps, political prisoners, homosexuals, Communists and religious dissenters are thrown together with Jews, Poles and Russians."

Dani and Rachel prayed for their family. Each time a new agent parachuted into the mountains with up-to-date news, any hope they held out for the family grew dimmer. One day a Greek Partisan who had sneaked into Thessaloniki to see his family, returned to camp with sad news: the city had been completely emptied of its Jews. They were sent north by train in cattle cars. The Jews of the smaller towns such as Larissa and Drama were in hiding. Those of Athens were being rounded up too, but many were in hiding with Christian friends. The Germans were frustrated, having much less success in rounding up Jews in Athens than they had in Thessaloniki because the Athens records of Jews had been destroyed by the community.

Dani and Rachel held each other, Rachel saying, "We will see them when the War is over." But she knew it was a false hope. The men they were fighting against showed little humanity or pity; why should their leaders be any better?

Once settled in the mountains, newcomers had to prove themselves. Rachel hauled water from springs or wells, helped with cooking and keeping the camp clean, which was difficult work because Partisan camps moved regularly to avoid discovery by the enemy. Captain Polo and his Jewish veterans were immediately integrated into fighting units and issued serviceable weapons. Dani and the other boys underwent the most minimal of military training. They learned by accompanying the fighters on raids. After some time, Dani and his friends were issued Italian rifles which had been captured, although some of them could not even be fired. They were told that after a raid, they were to pick up German weapons for their own use, and anything else that was useful.

The Greeks had one great advantage over the Germans: they had been raised in the mountains and knew them and the villagers intimately. After a while, the Germans used air patrols, radio-seeking equipment, radar and Greek traitors to locate the bands of Partisans roving throughout the hills. Lookouts were posted regularly, but on occasion German soldiers could surprise a group out on patrol or even in a large encampment. Once, enemy soldiers charged into a camp after killing the lookouts. Then they killed all 42 Partisans in a ferocious fire fight.

The leaders of Partisan groups were always thinking of ways to increase safety. The only proven method was to move the camps regularly. It was tiring but it kept the enemy guessing.

After a few months, Dani acquired a serviceable rifle, a German Mauser and a Luger pistol for himself. He was strong, but as with all his comrades, he was constantly hungry. He was becoming a good shot with both his pistol and rifle. As he watched many of his comrades being wounded or killed in raids, he wondered how long he could stay alive.

20

NEWPORT, RHODE ISLAND
MARCH 1774

The sun fought to shine through dark rain clouds on this cool and windy March day. The *King's Pleasure*, a three-masted sailing ship, had sailed past New York's Block Island after a New York stop, so seventeen-year-old Solomon Henriques knew he was close to his destination. He stood with other excited passengers along the ship's railing at the forepeak. They could now see something through the slate-blue haze that appeared to be land. It was dark green just beyond the shining reflection of water that dazzled him as it moved with each change of the ship's course.

The sun was coming through now and he could clearly see land. A rainbow arched above the water. *It pointed to Newport on Naragansett Bay*, he thought, his excitement rising. After a stormy Atlantic crossing, Solomon was finally here in Rhode Island, one of Great Britain's northernmost Colonies known collectively as New England.

From an early age, he had heard stories of the freedom colonists enjoyed in this place called America, and he told his father, David, about it and that he wanted to live there. David didn't want him to leave England. Solomon had just turned 17, but he was headstrong; he could see that there were very few opportunities in overcrowded London. It may have been the Empire's greatest city, but it was also where filthy streets were filled with beggars, the unemployed and the homeless. To a young man seeking to make a place in life, London could be depressing.

He had been working for years with his father as an apprentice, regularly handling money and accounts. He understood invoices and bills of accounts. He could easily find work in a city with a commercial reputation such as Newport, Rhode Island, which had a long history of welcoming men and women of all religions.

"My brothers have spoken about going elsewhere to live," he told his father. Adding to his argument, he said, "You were 17 when you married Mama, so I don't see 17 as being a child."

His father countered. "Your brothers would be close by in Europe, Solomon, just a few hundred miles away. The colonies are thousands of miles across an ocean and can only be reached by a long and expensive sea voyage."

Solomon ultimately prevailed. David reluctantly agreed, paying not only for his passage, but also a sum of money to get his son started in the New World. With his paternal blessings, David Henriques reminded his son, "Never forget you are a Jew. We have suffered too much over the centuries for you to surrender your heritage."

"I won't papa, I'll always be a Jew," Solomon said. His mother Rebecca remained at home, preferring not to see her son climb the gangplank and disappear from her life, perhaps forever. She had already said her goodbyes at the doorstep of their home.

At the pier, David and Solomon embraced and, without looking back, the lad walked up the gangplank to his ship. That had been more than five weeks ago. Today, he approached the New World where there were many opportunities and Jews weren't looked down on, as they were in Europe. As his ship sailed into Newport, he could see the masts of many vessels anchored in the Bay. This was a busy seaport. What was more important, it was a place of great opportunity.

When he disembarked from the *King's Pleasure*, he learned that the Jewish community had just finished building a fine new synagogue. He received directions to its location. David had told him that was where he would be helped, remembering how he and his parents were assisted those many years earlier by the Jewish community in Amsterdam after they had escaped from Lisbon's destruction.

The synagogue looked like none he had ever seen in London. His synagogue there, Bevis Marks, was made of heavy grey stones. It was large, with an ample interior made of dark wood. Newport's was a whitewashed building, modest in size, with clean architectural lines. The columns around the building were made of wood. There were 12 of them. *Could they represent the twelve Tribes of Israel he had learned about in religious school?* The synagogue was closed. Today was Wednesday. He would have to wait until Friday night, when there would be services celebrating the start of the Sabbath, before he could connect with the Jewish community. Until then, he had to find a place to live.

Walking through the city, he was impressed with what he saw. Newport was clean: there were few alleys piled up with filth and pigs and dogs rooting among the decay. Most buildings were made of sturdy wood, freshly painted and neatly laid out. The citizens of this town were well clad; only a few were dressed in rags as commonly seen in London. It seemed to him that everyone had a task to attend to. *Busy with business,* he observed. There was plenty to eat in Newport: its shops were filled with all kinds of food at what seemed to be much more reasonable prices than in London. The air was cleaner, too. London's air was most often smoggy and accompanied with a sooty, drizzly and hazy rain. Here, the air was scrubbed clean by fresh winds coming in from the Bay. After a while, Solomon saw a sign in a window offering a room for rent.

Mrs. Bailey, the landlady, was pleased to have this young man take the empty room on the second floor. After a quick inspection during which she asked many questions of the lad, she suggested, "If you're looking for a position, you'd best go to the waterfront. There's much work to be found for a serious young man such as yourself." She was certain Solomon was serious, since he had given her two weeks rent in advance.

Solomon was enjoying a cup of coffee at a nearby inn, where he learned from speaking with some citizens that among the most respected businessmen of Newport, several belonged to the Portuguese Nation, *La Nacion,* as he had been taught by his father. Among them were Jacob Rodriguez Rivera, his son-in-law Aaron Lopez, and Moses Levy and Moses Seixas. All these men, and others, had come to Newport – or their parents had – fleeing Spain and Portugal years earlier. They had, over time, established themselves in the city while returning to Judaism. It was just as Solomon's father had done in Amsterdam and London a generation earlier.

Rodriguez Rivera and Lopez had grown wealthy enjoying virtual monopolies with the production of whale oil, used to light New England's lamps. They owned the whaling ships that brought whale blubber to Newport, where it was then converted into whale oil. They also monopolized the soap trade, manufacturing the famous Castile Soap. On occasion, they dealt in slaves. They owned many ships, trading throughout the Caribbean for rum, sugar, and spices, and they traded in Europe as well, importing household and other goods for which Newport's citizens yearned.

Imagine: Jews as ship-owners! This was why Solomon had come to Newport. In London, he had heard merchants talk with great respect of fellow Sephardic Jews of the colonies in Newport, Savannah, Charleston, Philadelphia and New York who had become wealthy after fleeing Spain and Portugal.

Over time, Solomon also learned about a patriotic organization called "The Sons of Liberty." They vocally advocated political changes in England's colonial rule. There were branches in every colony: thirteen in all. The Sons, as they were popularly called, opposed the way the British ruled their colonies in America, especially what they considered to be unfair taxes on tea, paper and other products imported from England.

According to English law, colonists were forced to buy most household items directly from England. This forced the New Englanders to engage in a lively smuggling trade. Everyone knew that John Hancock of Boston, who was one of New England's richest men, earned much of his fortune through smuggling. Americans had no say in England's Parliament, which legislated these taxes and other laws affecting those in America. England countered with the argument that she had protected the colonists from the French and the Indians, fighting wars on their behalf, and that it was only fair that the colonies should share in the costs of those wars. "But," the Sons argued, "you tax us without anyone representing us in Parliament. We have no say in what you decide our taxes shall be."

The Sons of Liberty was not a secret organization. To the contrary, their members were everywhere; on street corners and in taverns, urging citizens to join them in protest. In the city of Boston, in Massachusetts, the larger colony to the north, their activities resulted in the Boston Massacre, as it was called, when English soldiers fired on street demonstrators, killing three of them. Hardly a massacre. The facts of the case were hazy as to who fired the first shot. The Sons of Liberty deftly exploited the situation. John Adams, a respected Boston lawyer and sympathizer with the Sons of Liberty, nevertheless defended the soldiers and won an acquittal on their behalf.

Solomon realized he had come to New England at a critical time in its history. He regularly attended meetings in which the abuses of English rule were denounced. Soon, he was accepting the Son's arguments against the Crown. He knew he would be forced to take sides and speak up, even as he quietly watched, fascinated, the birth of a colonial rebellion.

He found work at Aaron Lopez's Counting House. His knowledge of Spanish, French and Portuguese was an asset, as was his strong knowledge of business procedures and documents. The careful attention to business that his father had instilled in him was a talent greatly appreciated by Lopez's manager, Uriel de Leon. That beefy, middle-aged man, who was married to one of the Lopez daughters, took a liking to the new employee.

"You can start right away with verifying Bills of Lading," said de Leon, who was impressed with Solomon's knowledge of business and language skills. Solomon skipped some of the lower positions a new man had to learn on his way up in a Portuguese Counting House. "I'll look for you at Sabbath prayers," de Leon said, more as an order than a suggestion. Solomon was a member of *La Nacion*. That opened business and social doors for him. As such, he had to be regularly seen at the Esnoga, for who knows what young lady would take a liking to him?

The friends he was making at the coffee shops and inns were serious men. They met regularly at an inn where he relaxed following a day's work, after taking dinner at his boarding house. They were mostly older than Solomon, and many were members of the Sons of Liberty. It didn't take too long for the newcomer to become imbued with their fervor. First, he attended meetings where he learned all the complaints the colonists had against their King. Then, when they felt they could trust him, he was asked to become personally involved. He started with little things, such as helping collate pamphlets at the Sons' printing press, hidden deep in the cellar of a private house. Next, he gave speeches against the King's taxes and, finally, against the King himself and the soldiers patrolling the streets of Newport, causing its citizens to fear them.

The colonial Governor of Rhode Island prepared a list of trouble-making radicals in Newport, and they were closely watched. Solomon's name was on the list. One day, Walter Deaver, the leader of the Sons in Newport, approached Solomon and said, "Our friends in Governor Greene's office tell us he has prepared a list of those of us who are active in the Newport Sons. We understand that the Governors of every colony are also putting a similar list together at the behest of the government in London. You are on it. Some of us are planning to move to Boston or New York or Philadelphia. We have good friends in those cities. They'll find work for us. I'm going to New York with two of our brothers. I suggest you go to Boston… and change your name, because I'm sure this list will be circulated very soon. With a new name and a new home, they'll have a problem locating you."

The next day, Solomon spoke with Uriel de Leon. "I am on the Governor's list as an anti-government agitator. I could be arrested at any time. I don't want to see the Lopez family in trouble just because I work here. I've been told to leave Newport and go to Boston. I've also been told I need a new name."

"I appreciate your concern about the family," de Leon sympathized. "I know what you need to do. I'm sorry to see you leave; you had a good future here. I'll arrange to provide you with your wages up to date and something extra," he said with a wink. "It's a loan from the Lopez Company. You can pay it back when you have the money. And no interest on the loan, mind you. When will you be leaving?"

"I plan to leave right away. Tomorrow."

"Whatever you can't take with you, have it sent here. When you're settled, I'll forward it to you by one of our ships that call at Boston. You can leave on our ship *Prophet Elijah*; it sails at six tomorrow night.

"You say you need a new name. I suggest the name of one of our customers in Jamaica: Ennis. It's sort of close to Henriques. He's a plantation owner; grows sugar and ginger, in case anyone asks." De Leon wrote it down on a slip of paper and handed it to Solomon, continuing, "There are no synagogues in Boston. Moses Michael Hayes, our contact there, is a religious Jew. Hayes holds services in his large home for the few Jews who live in town. He's a good man and a faithful friend. He owns a successful trading house. Wait here; I'll give you his address and I'll write a note for you to give him. He might have a place in his firm."

De Leon held Solomon by his shoulders. "It's a great thing you're doing. Good luck and take care of yourself. Were it not for Sarah and the children…" De Leon stopped there. No sense in trying to make excuses. Anyway, Solomon would understand.

Solomon went to his rooms, packed the minimum amount of clothes and other articles he would immediately need. He put the rest into a large seaman's ditty bag, with instructions to his landlady to deliver them to Uriel de Leon and left her rent for an extra week.

The next day, he went to the inn that was the unofficial headquarters of the Sons of Liberty and sat in a back room until five o'clock. Then he walked the three bustling streets to the pier where the *Prophet Elijah* was making ready to sail for Boston. He looked around to make sure no one was following him. Satisfied he was not being watched, he made for the ship. As he boarded, the sailor who was at the gangway watch saluted him and said, "A passenger are you, sir?" Solomon said yes and offered up his new name.

The sailor checked this passenger's name off on a list and then said, "Solomon Ennis. Aye, sir. Welcome aboard, Master Ennis."

21

Mayfair, London
February 1944

Someone with lots of political power saw fit to pull Jim Ennis off the line after a successful year in the Pacific Ocean commanding the United States submarine, *Egret*. Today, he was winding his way through an old four-story mansion in London's Mayfair section, near Curzon Street. It was one of London's poshest neighborhoods. Neither the owner nor the builder of this Victorian pile would have recognized its once grand ballroom, or the three opulently spacious dining rooms. They, and some of the mansion's other large rooms, had been ruthlessly partitioned by bloodless civil servants. They were designed, using wall boards, into a warren of small, uncomfortable workspaces. Windows, twelve feet high, were crisscrossed with white strapping tape. It was certain evidence that the Germans, even this late in the conflict, had stubbornly refused to give up the idea that London needed to be bombed into submission to win this War.

He walked down a sunless corridor until he came to one of the few rooms that had not been altered. Instinctively, he knew who would be here. The doorplate read "Dr. M. Garcia." He didn't have to check the posting order in his hand to make sure he had the right door. He knocked, and went in after the familiar voice he was expecting told him to enter. This unaltered and comfortable room was obviously once a bedroom. It was roomy, lined with elaborate molding, sunny and cheerful despite the taped windows. Sitting behind a large Victorian desk was Mickey Garcia.

"Mickey, what in hell are you doing here?"

Garcia rose from his desk and embraced his friend, Latino style as he always did. "I'm working for the OSS. General Donovan himself recruited me," he answered, with a broad smile, indicating his job was some sort of political coup. "Couldn't get past the physical for service, because of my heart murmur. So here I am serving my country behind a desk, with pen and paper."

Ennis knew there was more to Mickey Garcia's job than working behind a desk for the "Good old USA." But he let it go. General William 'Wild Bill' Donovan was a famous WW I Medal of Honor winner, New York lawyer and Republican politician. He had persuaded President Roosevelt to make him head of a spy agency he would create and call the Office of Strategic Services (OSS). It would be based on the fabled British spy operations MI5, MI6 and SOE (Special Operations Executive.)

As the English had done, Donovan swept through America's colleges and universities to recruit his spies, reaping an army of unconventional and sometimes nerdy Underground agents. Among them were the intellectually talented, the brilliant odd-balls, crossword puzzle addicts, technical weirdos of all types and the multi-linguals. Most of the recruits came from the upper-classes, as did those of the English. Ennis was now thinking, *had Mickey recruited me that day at NYU as an interpreter for Donovan's OSS and again for my work with General Clark in North Africa?* If so, he now saw his old friend as a first-class manipulator.

"Sit down, Jimmy. You look flabbergasted."

"Frankly, Mickey, I am. Although I knew you would be here. My sixth sense." Ennis shrugged. "But why am I here?"

"I asked for you. I'm your handler here at the OSS."

"My handler? Does that mean you're making me a spy? A spy! Mickey, you know I belong in a submarine, helping out in the War in the Pacific."

"I have a more important job for you. I'm sending you to France to interview a German scientist and bring him here, if you're satisfied that he's genuine."

"That's impossible. What am I supposed to know about this Nazi's science expertise?"

"You speak German, you're an engineer, a submarine expert and you speak French, so you can get along with the French underground. Jimmy, this scientist is working on an air breathing system which allows a submarine to stay submerged for longer periods of time while also charging the batteries. Who better than you to understand what he is doing? I'm not downgrading your contribution as a submarine commander. But this guy wants to defect. This is more important than commanding a sub. I had sincerely hoped you would agree."

"What am I supposed to do?"

"We would drop you into France where you meet up with the French Underground. They take you to a designated place you don't know about, in case you get, er, caught. Then you can't reveal it even under torture. There, you meet this man, his name is Ernst Falkenberg. He works on this breathing system and wants to defect to our side. You must determine if he is genuine or if it's a trap. If you okay him, learn all about his system. We promised him asylum if he's genuine."

"Does 'drop me in' mean I'm parachuting into France? And maybe I'm going to be tortured?"

Mickey gave his friend a sheepish grin and said, "Look Jimmy, this has to be done. The Brits almost lost this War to Germany's U-Boats before we figured out ways to neutralize them. If the Germans can use this device, we could be back to 1942 before we got them under control. We can't have that. There are some things coming up very soon that I can't speak about. We can't delay them just because the U-Boats get strong again. We absolutely need a submarine-free Atlantic for the next stage of this War."

"I can't believe this, Mickey. You're making me a paratrooper and a spy. I could screw up here. I have no training for this." Ennis was shaking his head.

"We'll give you training. Show you how to jump safely with a parachute, handle a 45, a Thompson submachine gun and a British Sten gun. We'll also give you a cyanide capsule. You can be ready in three weeks."

"What in hell is cyanide for?" Jimmy practically roared as he half rose from his seat.

"In case the Gestapo catches you," Mickey said, in a decidedly lower tone than he had been using. He looked across the room at his friend, who looked as if he had just been struck by a baseball bat.

"Look, Jimmy, obviously no one can order you to do this. We looked at many candidates. You're the only one that has all the qualifications: expertise in submarines, technical background, speaking the necessary languages and young enough to undergo the rigors accompanying the mission. Think about it carefully, Jimmy. It's a very important job in a very crucial area of this rotten war. If you need time to think about it, I can only wait until tomorrow evening. No later than that. We need to act quickly on this matter."

Jim Ennis sat stunned, speechless. After a long pause, he asked, "Do you have any specifications on this miracle device?"

"As a matter of fact, I do," Mickey said. He slid open a drawer and pulled out a set of blueprints, handing them to Ennis. "They are not complete," he added. "That's why we need you to sort it out."

Ennis scanned the blueprints. "And what do they call this wonderful invention""

"It's called a schnorkel."

After another quick look through the blueprints, Ennis said, "MY first reaction is NO. I'm not cut out for all this spy crap. But I promise you I'll think about it. You'll hear from me before tomorrow night."

"Good. How is Lucy?"

"She's just fine. She told me that the next time I see you I should tell you she'll never forgive you for hanging up on her when I was sent to North Africa. And to call you a sonofabitch."

"I had to hang up, Jimmy. Suppose my phone line - or yours - wasn't secure. Your mission would have been compromised. You were being watched since the time you went to Gibraltar. Didn't you know that?"

"I never realized what a steel-hearted sonofabitch you were, Mickey."

22

Boston, Lexington and Concord
June 19, 1775

"On this day, April 19, 1775 we were ataked (sic) from behind barns, trees, hedges, buildings and hills. The rebels showed no respek (sic) for the rules of war, even ataking (sic) officers and non-commissioned officers, causing casualties among them. They refused to face us head on in battle. The rebels continued this ungentlemanly snyping (sic) which began at Concord and Lexington and lasted until we finally arrived at Boston sometime later. We suffered 273 casualties in the event."
    Sgt. Maj. E.J. Bogwood /s/

With this report from his Sergeant Major, General William Gage, Commander of the British Forces in Boston, was on notice that defeating the rebels was not the easy task he and the bureaucratic politicians at London's political headquarters at Whitehall had thought it would be. He was concerned, however, that a conglomerate of organized rebels from Massachusetts, Rhode Island, Maine, New Hampshire and Connecticut were now concentrated on the hills overlooking the village of Charlestown (Boston). They had to be eliminated. He could not have that rabble dangerously hovering above him, deciding on how he could move about.

Before descending on the villages of Lexington and Concord to collect weapons and ammunition stored in Royal arsenals, Gage also gave General William Howe the order to sweep the Heights clear of all its rebels. On the evening of June 16, Howe immediately began assembling his strike force. They would advance up the hill tomorrow morning at first light, and make the Rebels regret they had ever thought they could defy their King.

The New England volunteers were also at work, anticipating a British strike. The colonists were silently erecting their defensive breastworks at Breed's Hill under a blanket of darkness. Then they constructed another defensive position further back on the rise, at Bunker Hill. Finished before dawn, the men took time to relax before they knew the battle would surely begin.

His back leaning against the earthen breastworks, his musket clamped between his bent legs, his stock firmly planted into the soft earth and his musket's long barrel pointing to the sky, Solomon Ennis sat beside his friends, Billy Craig and Phineas Wooden. Both Billy and Phineas had come from Newport a few weeks after Solomon. Craig asked, "You as frightened as I am, Sol?"

"I sure am."

"Whatcha been thinkin' about?" asked Phineas.

"My wife, Miriam. We're expecting a baby in late October, maybe November."

"That's great," said Craig.

"Yes. They say a baby brings good luck, you know."

When Solomon Ennis left Newport, he had been courting Miriam Mendoza, the oldest daughter of one of Newport's leading merchants. She agreed to come to Boston chaperoned by her mother, to arrange for their marriage. Since Boston lacked a rabbi, the couple was required to marry before a Justice of the Peace. They vowed to be united in a religious ceremony at the first opportunity. Today, Miriam sat at home wondering how the oncoming battle, the news of which all New England was awaiting, would affect the Ennis family. When she knew she was with child, she asked Solomon what to name the baby. Now she wondered if her child would ever see his father.

"James," Solomon responded. "If it's a boy, we'll call him James after my grandpa, Jaime. If it's a girl, Grace after my grandma Gracia."

o 

As the first light of dawn illuminated the hills above him, General William Howe picked up his spyglass and drew it to its full length. Looking through it, he was shocked at what he saw: two sturdy and formidable earthwork defenses had been silently thrown up during the cover of night. He scanned the defensive walls with grudging admiration and thought, *we may think of these rebels as farmers and Yankee bumpkins, but I see in these impossible constructions a strong sense of purpose and dedication. I could not push my men to erect such defenses in one night and in complete silence, no less.*

Howe had been ordered to assault the hill and scrub it clean of the Yankee rabble. That he would do, using the world's finest and most disciplined army. *When these rebels see the steel of my boy's bayonets, they will flee like sheep scattering from the wolves. These earthworks will avail them very little.*

As Solomon and his friends were relaxing, they heard the distant sound of drums tattooing a marching beat. The three men rose. Standing by the wall they looked down the hill. Nothing was moving in front of them. The drums beat louder now and suddenly the top of a Battalion flag, fluttering upon a high pole, peeked above the hill. A golden eagle placed atop the pole flashed in the early morning sun, adding to the frightening event. Martial drummers were now beating louder, urging unseen soldiers on. Then they appeared: drummers and fifers first, at the head of the column, followed by the soldiers. Magnificent they were, too: a ruthless fighting, killing machine. They marched in lockstep; one solid unit firmly welded together through sheer blind discipline. Clad in bright red uniforms with white straps crossed along their chests, they all held their bayoneted muskets ominously across their bodies like a bold pattern on a bright cloth.

They were facing forward, ready to strike at their enemy. These fearful and legendary British bayonets were glinting in the morning sun, waiting to pierce a rebel's stomach and send him to hell. Every soldier knew his place in line as he marched together with his comrade. Their officers, magnificent astride their horses, urged them on. *This is truly a fearsome sight,* Solomon thought as he raised his musket and powder horn, placing them on the wall of the breastworks facing the oncoming soldiers.

Some men at the barricades now turned to run, but Solomon and Phineas put strong hands on their nearby comrade's shoulders. "Stand fast and wait for orders from Dr. Warren. All will be well," they shouted over the noise of the drums as they returned the men to their assigned places behind the earthworks. The British were now a wall, a solid line from one end of the hill across to the other. They seemed to be waiting for their Yankee adversaries to come out from behind their defenses to meet them: one wall facing another. That's not what happened. The Yankees remained behind their defenses, many of them taking a second look at their muskets, ensuring that they were loaded and ready to be fired. Their leader, Dr. Joseph Warren, stood about 60 feet away from Solomon, his sword drawn and held high above his head. He mounted the wall and shouted for all to hear, "Here come the lobsterbacks, lads! Hold your fire until I give the signal."

The Yankees called the British 'lobsterbacks' because of their crimson uniforms. Solomon looked around him. There was not a uniform among the defenders near him. A few of the older men, who had been placed far away on each end of the strategic flanks, were dressed in different uniforms. Once, years earlier, they wore them while they served their English king, in the wars against the French and their Indian allies.

"We are a ragged bunch, boys," Dr. Warren shouted. "We fight for our homes and for freedom. The Lobsterback fights for money."

Solomon, Billy and Phineas watched in awe as they saw England's finest soldiers advancing toward them. Warren waited until the British were closer, then dropped his sword and yelled, "Fire!" A volley of musket balls, aimed at the marching wall, struck the first line.

When the choking smoke of gunpowder rose like a curtain, a mass of men lay before the defenders. But a second disciplined column moved forward as if nothing had happened. Another deadly volley stopped the second wall, which now began wavering. Only a few soldiers continued forward now, seemingly unconcerned for their safety. These soldiers were picked off by individual sharp shooters. The rest of the attackers turned and scampered down the hill. The sharpshooters were now firing at officers on their horses and on foot.

"Load quickly, lads, it's not over yet. They'll be back," Dr. Warren shouted several times, making sure all could hear his command over the noise of rifle fire and the screams of the wounded and those about to die.

Soon, the drums beat again, followed by the fifes. A new line of fresh soldiers filled the gaps where their comrades had dropped. Coming forward, they stepped over the fallen dead, ignoring those on the ground who were wounded and moaning for help. A new volley of musket fire pierced the marching wall again and more men fell. The second wall soon came apart with the sharpshooting Yankees picking off soldiers and their officers. Again, the soldiers retreated down the hill. The bodies of the dead and wounded were piling up in the area in front of the defense works. Solomon turned. The defenders had suffered casualties as well. Around him were fallen men, some dead, others clutching an arm or a leg or trying to stop the bleeding from their wounds. His comrade Billy Craig, who had stood not more than three feet beside him, lay dead; a musket ball had entered his skull just above his right eye.

Someone in the ranks called out, "Dr. Warren, we're running out of powder and shot."

"After the next assault, fall back to Bunker Hill. There's powder and shot waiting for us there."

On the third assault, the British easily mounted the breastworks and began using their deadly bayonets. Dr. Warren was killed and the British quickly took Breed's Hill. Now, the New Englanders assembled for the next assault further back at Bunker Hill. There, they discovered there wasn't enough of the promised powder and shot to sustain a defense. The British stormed the second hill, bayonets finding their way into the helpless defender's bodies. The Americans had never seen a bayonet attack and were overwhelmed by its ferocity. They soon began hand to hand fighting. Many defenders escaped. When the fighting was over, General Howe declared a victory, although at the Battle of Breed's and Bunker Hills, he suffered almost eleven hundred casualties, including 100 officers killed. A tenth of his army, lost.

When Howe made his report to General Gage, he reluctantly emphasized, "When I look to the consequences of it, the loss of so many brave officers, I do it with horror: the success is too dearly bought."

The British were now committed to end this War as soon as possible to limit the losses they were experiencing.

ᆞ ᆞ

Solomon came home dragging his musket across the ground behind him. Miriam greeted him with tears. He had survived the battle but was covered with mud and dust from digging trenches. His face was black from the smoke of the gun powder of his musket's flash pan, placed so close to his face. Exhausted, he asked about her and the baby she was carrying and then he said sadly, "We lost Billy Craig."

Miriam put her hand to her mouth to stifle a cry. Young Billy, who always smiled and had good words for everyone he met, was one of Miriam's favorites of all of Solomon's friends. *How will his mother and sisters take the loss? It will be a difficult war,* she could see that now. Solomon stripped himself of his muddy clothes and fell into a deep exhausted sleep.

He will sleep a long time. He spent a night digging and then a day fighting. Miriam was a practical and realistic woman. Hard-headed, her brother Raphael had often told her. She had learned these attributes from her father, Gideon Mendoza, who himself was a hard-headed merchant. One must face life head on and not ignore its negatives. She had thought about this long and often whenever Solomon was away, training to fight. And now here it was, as everyone expected: War.

Miriam took her husband's clothes. They were the ones he always wore when he went for training. She was sure he would wear them into future battles, which was a certainty after today's clash. She washed them carefully and set them out to dry in the hot sun. Then she looked for her sewing kit. She rubbed her hands as she thought of what she was going to do.

The kit was on a high shelf, and she pulled it down. Opening it, she saw the eight-inch square of cloth which brought tears to her eyes. She had finished sewing it while Solomon was away fighting at the Heights. Now she reluctantly sewed it into the back part of the inside of his washed and dry shirt. It read:

I am a Jewish soldier. My Name is Solomon Ennis. I have died in the service of my country. Please bury me according to my religion and have someone recite the Kaddish over my grave. May God bless you in all your mercy for fulfilling my wishes.
Sewn by his wife Miriam Mendoza Ennis

23

Northern France
February 1944

"I read the specs on the schnorkel, Mickey," Jim Ennis advised Mickey Garcia, the day after their meeting in Mayfair. "This Falkenberg guy may have something. There are problems, though. I think you would have to slow the sub's speed to avoid damage to a long hose running deep into the water. Then, there's the obvious problem of the wake caused by the part that's on the surface. I have to see much more of what he has done before I can give you a final analysis."

"What did I tell you, Jimmy? You're the expert. That's why we need you."

"Yeah. Don't hand me that crap." The once happy relationship between Jimmy and Mickey was deteriorating fast. "There's something else here. He seems to know a lot about electronics. Where does this turncoat work?"

"At the Phillips Electronics factory in Eindhoven, Holland."

"That makes sense. What am I supposed to do besides figuring out the specs?"

"Well, a few things. First, determine if this new device has any real merit. Then convince yourself that he is not setting a trap to ensnare the Underground. After that, determine what else he is working on that may help us."

"Assuming that I would agree to go on this harebrained mission, how do I convince myself that it's not a trap to net a bunch of pesky Frenchmen and a dumb American?"

"Get him to do something that proves he's serious in wanting asylum and is ready to help us. He understands he gets no asylum unless he gives us something substantial. It's important that he understands that."

"This stuff about going in with a parachute; is it necessary?"

"Yes. We can't get you in any other way. When you're finished with your work, we get you out with a Lysander."

"What the hell is that?"

"A small plane the Brits use, that can land on a short grassy runway, and it flies under the radar to avoid detection. We try not to use them too often, so the Germans won't learn how to combat the plane. We'll train you in how to use a parachute safely. Even our women operators have to jump into Europe. What do you say?"

"I'm thinking about it."

"I'll get you out as soon as you finish your mission. You'll be under the protection of the Free French Underground all the time you're there. Give me an answer fast, Jimmy. If you say No, then I have to make arrangements for someone less qualified than you to go and I have to tell my boss I don't have confidence in this plan without you."

"I don't want to see the Germans getting any advantages over my submariners."

"Swell. From here on in, your code name is Teacher. That's what you will be called: Teacher."

Ꝯ ꝯ

At 5:30 a.m. on a cold drizzly morning smothered by a dismal fog, a young woman dressed in Navy blues pulled her black sedan up to the corner where Jim Ennis was standing. The car was dotted with shiny globules of condensation. She called out in a sing-song soprano voice overlain with a cockney accent, "Good Morning, Sir. Are you all ready and packed to go?"

"I am," Ennis answered.

Though she was barely five feet four, she took Ennis' large and heavy suitcase, handling it as if she were a burly Gunnery Sergeant and swung it, bouncing it into the car's boot. Then she slid into the driver's seat on the right-hand side, deftly slipped the car into gear and with her passenger safely in back, was on her way. The fog was so heavy Ennis could not see where she was heading. Obviously, she had no problem, turning here and there at corners and moving to the correct lanes at forks in the road. After half an hour, she pulled up to a large country mansion, swept out of her seat, opened the door to let her passenger out, hauled Ennis' luggage from the boot and laid it on the doorstep of this impressive building. "You'll be properly attended to, Sir," she said as she saluted him. Back in her car, she quickly drove off. The glow of watery dewdrops covered the car's taillights, shining like scores of red rubies as they dissolved into the fog.

Almost immediately, an English Sergeant Major appeared, saluting Ennis. "Welcome Sir," he said. Another man, looking like a civilian waiter, took up the luggage. "Follow me, Sir, please," the Sergeant said. Entering a large hall, Ennis saw a long, winding staircase, about 40 feet above the entryway, flowing down from an upper floor. The Sergeant directed him to a desk in front of the stairway. A Corporal requested identification. He checked to verify that what he held in his hand matched the information he was looking at in a large loose-leaf book. Satisfied with the results of his search, the identification was returned.

"That way, Sir," the Corporal said, pointing to a door. It was all very precise and military. The Sergeant Major opened a heavy and intricately carved door, which led to a large room lined with glass windows and a riot of colorful plants lining the walls. He was in an atrium. Steel folding chairs were set out in three lines, six chairs to a row. Some chairs were already filled, a few with women. Ennis never thought much about women operatives dropping into France the way he was told he had to. Or firing a Tommy Gun or a British Sten gun. Or learning hand-to-hand combat, or how to kill a man with one crisp blow, silently and efficiently. He took an aisle seat in the back row, sat down on the cold steel of the chair, and waited, for what he didn't know. In the next ten minutes, three more men and a woman sat down. Ennis counted 12 people all together.

Finally, a very tall, athletic-looking British Lt. Colonel strode in. He was wearing khaki colored battle fatigues and high combat boots. His greying hair was closely cropped. He stood next to a dais and introduced himself as Colonel Gridley-Smyth. He looked to be about 45 and wore the military patch of the legendary British commandos. Next to him stood Mickey Garcia, who was in civilian clothes. Mickey was not introduced.

The Colonel began his orientation by saying, "I represent the SOE, the Special Operations Executive. You have all been selected for our concentrated three-week course, training to operate behind enemy lines. Those of you holding military rank will find life here similar to what boot camp was like when you entered the service. Those without military experience may feel you have lost your dignity. No matter. Whatever goes on here is for your safety and will allow you to perform your mission in the best way possible. Sergeants and Corporals will be most of your teachers. They will exhort you, perhaps even curse at you. You who are officers are never, ever, to pull rank. In this place, you will be treated as if you were in basic training and your teachers are only doing their jobs to train you to come back from your mission alive. We have learned that using impolite language makes an important point easier for you to accept and remember. Know always that the Sergeants and Corporals are your friends. They are dedicated to keeping you alive and safe. Follow their instructions and you'll be okay."

Gridley-Smythe paused, looking over the group before resuming his talk. "You each have a code name. It is the only name you will use among yourselves while you are here and on your mission. You are not to discuss the facts of your personal lives with your fellow trainees. This is for your protection and that of your comrades, should you be caught by the enemy. While you are here, you will be monitored carefully and often. If we feel you cannot carry out your mission properly, you will be asked to leave the course.

"You have all signed the Official Secrets Act and are not to reveal what went on here during your stay, however short it may be. If we ask you to leave, it is because we feel you may be easily discovered in your mission. We do not want you to suffer the anguish you may be subjected to should you be so unfortunate as to be caught. You are training for a joint British and American enterprise. You will see others while you are here, undergoing longer and more rigorous training. They are the Jedburghs, named after the Scottish city whose fierce warriors fought the English with great courage and tenacity. You are all being trained for one specific mission only; the Jedburghs are training for complicated long-term missions. Now, I turn you over to the administrator of your program, Dr. Miguel Garcia, who represents the American OSS, the Office of Strategic Services."

Mickey moved over to the dais and said, "I will repeat the Colonel's warning. You are a very interesting group. Normally, you would be pleased to learn more about the people you will be spending time with during the next three weeks. You are not to discuss your real names with anyone, nor your positions in your lives before you came here. The more you know about your comrades, the more vulnerable they will become should you be interrogated by the enemy. You all have code names. Leave it at that.

"During the next three weeks, you will see me everywhere. I'll be watching you, making sure you are absorbing what we are teaching you. Should you have any questions or suggestions, feel free to speak with me. Tonight, I have arranged a fine dinner, complete with some excellent wine. Starting tomorrow, everyone is on military rations."

The next three weeks were crammed with long 14-to-16-hour days. The group made jumps from a high tower in simulated parachute drops. They learned how to hit the ground properly when they landed, to soften contact and minimize injuries. After several jumps from a tower, the candidates were herded on to a bus and driven to a landing field near Manchester. This was the parachute training center at Ringway, where they made actual drops from a balloon and an aircraft, at the same height as the one they were expected to make jumping into Europe.

Continuing with their studies at the mansion, the candidates received instruction in firearms, hand-to-hand combat, how to kill a man silently with a sharp, hard blow to certain spots on his neck and head, and Morse code, which Ennis excelled at, having learned it at the Naval Academy. They were taught how to send coded messages, operate a shortwave set, set up its aerial and how, when eating in a restaurant and cutting into food with a knife, you were not to move your fork to your right hand, a sure giveaway that you were an American and not the Frenchman you were trying to be.

It was a dizzying three weeks, and Ennis hoped he could remember everything he had learned. Every time he saw Mickey at the sessions, he silently cursed him. If Mickey looked his way, Jimmy turned away.

Finally, the course was completed. On the night before they were to make their drops, each person was visited in their room by an auditor for a last-minute check of equipment.

"Please leave all personal letters, photographs, club memberships, behind." Ennis' auditor was Mickey Garcia, who brought a large box into the room with him.

"You will be wearing these, Jimmy. Leave your regular clothes behind in this box."

Mickey opened the box. A complete set of clothes, underwear to shoes, was removed. "These were all made in France. We don't want anyone noticing an American cut to your clothes, do we? Here are your identification and rationing cards. They are first class and the best forgeries we can make."

Mickey paused. "Jimmy, I know you're angry with me, first because of how I dealt with Lucy and then I pushed you into this. It's war, Jimmy. I accepted a role that requires me to be ruthless and put personal attachments aside. I must be cold-blooded. Suppose someone was listening to my conversation with Lucy? And I told her where you were? You might be dead today. And I picked you for this job because you are the best qualified to do it. I didn't relish putting you in harm's way; it's not something I can decide based on our friendship. A job must be done. It's up to me to put the best person in position to do it."

For the first time, Mickey told Ennis where he would be dropped. "You'll be parachuting into northern France, on the border with Belgium. It's the closest we can get you to Holland with an Underground group we can rely on. Distances in Europe are not far, unlike in the States. The Dutch Underground has some security problems I can't discuss with you. If I sent you to Holland, you might not come out. Falkenberg must also know that, because he turned himself in to the French, not the Dutch.

"Our defector works in Holland. It's not far from your drop. He'll be doing all the traveling that's necessary. You'll not be required to go to Holland. We waited until the last moment to tell you where you are going for your own protection."

Garcia handed Ennis a small glass container containing three pills. "The big one is a knockout drop you might want to use on an enemy. The second one is Benzedrine. It'll keep you awake if you haven't slept in a few days. The last one is cyanide. If you are captured, you are to use it at your discretion. It's very powerful. Works fast and they say it is painless."

Mickey headed for the door, held out his hand and said, "Goodnight, Jimmy. Go with God. I hope to see you back here safely in a few weeks."

Jimmy took Mickey's hand and then hugged his friend hard.

The next evening, a British Hudson bomber, painted a dull, non-reflecting black and lacking all markings, was waiting for Ennis and three other operatives. Jimmy could see two other bombers alongside, and his classmates piling into them. The groups were dropping into different zones in France, Belgium and Holland. A Sergeant was waiting for Ennis and his group on the runway. He made a final check of his passengers' parachute straps, ensuring they were properly surrounding the jumper's body; the helmet's chin straps were in place, and the Thompson machine guns were slung across their bodies on straps circling their necks. Satisfied that all was well, he helped everyone into the plane, which was obviously once a bomber. The pilot and co-pilot entered the plane through a forward entry and the sergeant followed the jumpers. The pilot called the tower and requested permission to take off. In a few minutes, they were on their way. Passing over France, they were pelted with anti-aircraft fire. At one point, it sounded as if someone was throwing gravel or rocks at the plane.

"Flak from the anti-aircraft guns," said the Sergeant who would be supervising their jump, smiling as if it were an everyday banal event.

When a red light in the cabin turned yellow, the Sergeant rose from his seat, fell to his knees, and opened a trap door on the floor of the plane. Ennis knew it was called the Joe Hole. A loud noise and sudden gush of freezing wind filled the plane. A canister with supplies was dropped first. "Can't 'ave the canister following you and landing on your 'ead, Sir. Can we?" The Sergeant pushed the heavy supplies through the Joe Hole.

Ennis was the first to go. He sat astride the opening; his feet caught in the swirl of the moving plane. He felt a tap on his shoulder, saw the yellow light turn green, and had that now-familiar metallic taste of fear in his mouth. The Sergeant tapped him on the shoulder again and shouted, "Go! Good luck, Sir."

Ennis dropped into an inky-black sky. When the chute opened, he felt a strong tug at his body, as he was lifted several feet. His drop was uneventful; he had learned his lessons well. After gathering the chute, he saw another one which was dropped further east to ensure it wouldn't land on him. He wondered how it was that the Germans didn't see the parachutes or hear the engines of the drop planes. The parachutes opened at 600 feet, the lowest at which one could open safely. It exposed you to the minimum of time in the air. If the chute failed to open, there was no time for a safety to be employed.

He looked for and found the signal light he was told to expect. He headed toward the beam and was met by three men carrying Sten guns.

"*Bienvenue a' France,* Teacher," one man whispered. The other man explained in halting English that the second parachute was attached to the canister, which was swiftly recovered. It contained small arms and ammunition, medical supplies and medicine and cold food rations for the Underground fighters. The parachutes were gathered and Martin, the man who greeted Ennis and the group's leader, explained in halting English that they had many uses for the parachute.

Martin learned that Teacher spoke excellent French when he was asked in that language, "Where is Falkenberg? I want to see him right away."

"Immediately," Martin responded with a happy smile. At last London was sending people who could properly speak the language of his country. He led Ennis to a hay wagon and piled the canister, Ennis and the chutes into the back of the wagon, where space had been created to hide people and strategic materials.

"Teacher, if we stop, do not get out under any circumstances unless I open up the back. It is important that you follow those instructions. Understood?"

"Yes."

The space was cramped, damp and smelled of moldy hay. Ennis consoled himself that according to Mickey Garcia, Martin could be trusted. He knew what he was doing and there were good reasons for hiding out in such disorder.

They were stopped twice. Ennis could hear German soldiers speaking. "Where are you headed?" and "What's in the wagon?" Once, a soldier poked at the hay with a rifle and told his comrade, "What a stench, Heinz. These French must be hard up to try to sell this shit."

He finished his remarks with a laugh and said, "Go on with this shit; get going to wherever it is you are headed."

Yes, Ennis thought, *Martin knows his business.* They finally arrived at a farmhouse. The wagon drove into a large barn. Martin told Teacher to get out. Two men emptied the secret space of its contents. Then they directed Teacher to a door that had been concealed by a dozen oversized bales of hay. Inside, there was a large room where several men and two women were sitting. There was the smell of coffee, which Ennis welcomed. Martin laid his Sten gun aside and sat down at the table, slapping its top, a signal for coffee, which he indicated should also be served to the new man who accompanied them.

"Everyone," Martin said, "this is Teacher, he speaks excellent French. He is a brother sent from London to take care of our Nazi guest, Herr Falkenberg."

Teacher was greeted with 'welcome' and 'good to see you.' The welcome was genuine, especially since Teacher came accompanied with supplies, was going to take a defector off their hands and spoke good French, the latter a definite plus. The Brits were always sending operatives who couldn't even say "*bonjour*" properly. How could anyone expect such a fool to go into town and try to pass himself off as a Frenchman? It put everyone in danger.

Ennis took the coffee offered by one of the women and smiled his thanks. She seemed to be in her late teens and was dressed in khaki army fatigues. The coffee was hot, which was the best he could say for it. She went to the back of the room where she opened a door to a small, unlit and windowless room with just enough space to hold an army cot and a chair.

"Here is your Herr Falkenberg, Teacher," the young girl said.

Teacher stepped inside. One of the men gave him an oil lamp which lit up the room. Teacher closed the door, theatrically unbuttoning the holster to his 45, laying back the flap. Falkenberg was shielding his eyes, trying to accommodate himself to the light, but he didn't fail to notice that the handle of the 45 was exposed. He looked like a trapped ferret, with a long nose which came to a point. His face was long and thin, and his deep-black eyes darted about. His ears stood out from his head. There was at least a three-days growth of beard on his face. He was about 45 years old and filled with fear. Hardly an advertisement for the fair Aryan race the Nazis were advertising to the world.

In good German, Teacher said, "I have been told you want to defect."

Falkenberg was surprised. He was certain he was going to have to deal with his interrogator in limited English or in French. Now, he felt a bit more relaxed. The tenseness in his face and shoulders disappeared.

"Yes," he answered, "and I don't know why I have been treated like this."

"The French Underground is not exactly running the Ritz Carlton Hotel, Herr Falkenberg. They don't know what to make of you. Certainly not until we determine how to deal with you. May I see the rest of your schnorkel plans? I was only given some of them."

"Certainly... er, what is your name?"

"Teacher."

"The leader, the one who calls himself Martin. He has my papers, Teacher."

Ennis called out for Falkenberg's briefcase. When it was produced the German, with trembling hands, opened the case and from it took the blueprints, handing them to his interrogator.

Ennis looked at them, and said, "Have you been able to work out the problems I see here?"

"They are working on them in Holland. One of the problems is establishing the correct air mixture so the diesels will operate efficiently. Now they overwhelm the engines, using up too much oxygen in the U-boat."

"I can see that. How long will it take to fix it?"

"I don't know. If I am not there, I can't say, except to tell you that there are some talented scientists in my section. Probably in three or at most, six months, if they concentrate on the problem."

"What else are you working on?"

"An electronic guidance system. I don't know what the purpose is. I heard rumors that they are working on it to use in some kind of jet propulsion system. This will guide them to where they want them to go."

"When do you have to be back to work?"

"1 have to be back in Eindhoven in three days. I took a week's leave when I was told you would be coming. But I don't want to go back.'

Ennis first ignored the answer. After a long pause, he asked, "Why don't you want to go back?"

"Eventually they'll know that another copy of the plans was made. They do a review every three months. In 15 days, they'll know that I made copies because I had to sign out for them. They'll want to know the purpose of it. That's why I don't want to go back."

"One of the reasons I'm here is to determine if you are leading us into a trap or if you are a genuine defector. I'm supposed to find out if you are really a serious defector."

"I am, you can believe that as sure as the sun rises every day."

Teacher opened the door and said, "May I have some coffee for our guest?" He left the door open until the coffee was delivered. He thanked the server, closed the door, and handed the cup to Falkenberg, who greedily took a sip.

"Now, Herr Ernst Falkenberg, I must know why you want to defect. Every reason, mind you."

"It's simple. I have a girlfriend, you see. We have been together for several years. Before the War, even. I never thought of marrying her. I always knew she was hiding something from me. I thought it might be that she had another lover before me and maybe she had a child hidden away somewhere.

"It turns out her grandparents were Jewish. The Gestapo is going to find this out, since they are investigating some of her cousins. When it's discovered, I am in trouble for harboring a Jew. Damn her! Had I known years ago, I would have dumped her."

"You have no political or moral reasons for defecting, other than your girlfriend?" Ennis asked, disgust for this creature in his voice.

"No. I am not a Nazi, you understand. But I am a German. I do this because I will certainly be under suspicion and would be sent to jail or maybe worse."

"Will you work for the British and the Americans as a scientist and reveal all you know about what you are working on for Germany?"

"Yes," Falkenberg said as he sipped his coffee, now certain he would receive the asylum he so urgently needed to save himself.

"Then I have to put you to a test."

"Anything, Teacher."

"You will have to return to Eindhoven."

"No, I can't do that. I told you, I'm in danger there."

"You have no choice. If you don't, I can't help you as a defector. If you go back, you can do everything I ask of you in less than 15 days."

"What is you want me to go back for?"

"How are your contacts with the Gestapo?"

"I am not close with them. No one is close with those savages. However, there is one man, Bruno, he's one of those who monitors the factory. He seems to be a decent chap. We have lunch together sometimes in the factory's cafeteria and even take coffee together during work breaks."

"I want to find out where a certain man is. If the Gestapo has him, I want to know where. And everything about his current situation. And then I want you to bring me all the material you have on this electronic guidance system and anything else that may be new that you are working on."

"I can do that. I'll have to do it before they start their check."

"Good. Get cleaned up. You are going back right away. Once we have the information, you'll contact the man who brought you here and I'll guarantee your safety."

"Of whom am I supposed to be inquiring?"

"Aarnald Henriques. He was last known to be under Gestapo custody in Amsterdam."

24

Dorchester Heights
June 1775 - March 1776

General George Washington took command of the Continental Army on July 3, 1775. He arrived at the camp site at Dorchester Heights, which overlooked Boston and its important harbor. The British army lay spread out below him. The English navy was anchored offshore. The two armies were at a stalemate: the Continentals dared not attack the British and the British refused to battle the rebels in another uphill attack. Even though General Howe knew he would win, he was fearful of the appalling losses he could incur, based on his past experience.

Almost at once, despite his bearing and reputation which afforded him a positive greeting, Washington had great misgivings at having accepted this important post. The six-foot-three Virginian towered over his men, most of whom barely reached five-feet eight, the average American's height. It was not difficult for the men to be in awe of their new commander and feel positive about him. On Washington's part, he had to be charitable to consider that what he had been given to command was an army.

There was no standard uniform among his men. Washington arrived in a fine uniform, resplendent with gold epaulets and buttons. He was a contrast to his soldiers, who wore dun colored hunting shirts into battle. His officers were made up mostly of a rag-tag group of politicians with little or no military experience. As was the tradition of the time, these politicians stitched together groups of citizens from their communities into what they called battalions, regiments or other combat units. The politicians were then elected by the men they gathered, to act as officers even though they lacked any significant military experience.

Then, there were those with the financial ability to raise, pay for and equip groups of local men to entice them to volunteer for military service. Aside from their being elected as officers – for which they also lacked all qualifications – such wealthy persons would often have the units named after them. This followed the centuries-old British tradition of gathering an Army together.

Washington did have a few men with military experience, but they were scarce. Like Washington, some had seen combat during the French and Indian Wars more than a decade earlier. A few had seen action as soldiers in foreign wars in Europe or had actually served in the English army.

Washington also inherited a political problem: The state militias. Those colonies which did send their militia to serve, insisted that it control their use. Some states even refused to send any militia at all, arguing that their men were needed to defend their citizens in case of an English invasion. In any event, Washington would soon learn militias were generally useless: they ran away at the first sight of British and Hessian mercenaries attacking with their fearsome bayonets. Washington's army had little training at handling themselves in any kind of European-style combat.

Another problem was that his troops had no sense of sanitation. Washington's new home lacked proper latrines and serious illness soon began spreading among the ranks. One of his first orders was to clean up the camp, create sanitary conditions and vaccinate the men against smallpox, the great decimator of 18th Century armies in the field.

Fortunately, Washington did have one great asset: 25-year-old Henry Knox. The young, overweight, former Boston bookdealer had no military training or experience, until the Battle of Breed's and Bunker Hills. There, for the first time, he effectively directed artillery at the attacking British. Because of his political leanings, Knox had to flee Boston, leaving his bookshop behind to be destroyed by his enemies. He was a self-taught genius in the science of engineering and in the art of the use of cannon and artillery. He learned them all from the books on the shelves of his shop.

In 1775, Fort Ticonderoga, originally built by the French on New York's Lake Champlain, fell to the Continental Army after Ethan Allen and his Green Mountain Boys ousted the British. Cannons and ordinance now lay at the Fort, silent but still under the control of the Continental Army. Knox advised Washington that he was sure he could transport the Fort's many cannons to Dorchester Heights. They could be used to end the stalemate between the colonists and the English. Washington liked the idea and approved Knox's request to move the cannons to the Heights. Knox assembled the men, mules and horses needed to transport the ordinance.

Solomon Ennis and his comrade Phineas Wooden were among the soldiers selected by Knox to retrieve the cannons. It was a grand undertaking. Fort Ticonderoga lay 300 miles to the west. There were no major roads running directly from the Fort to Boston. The trip to the Fort was uneventful, but on the return trek to Dorchester Heights on December 5, winter had begun to set in. The men faced daily temperatures that ranged from freezing to below zero. Fifty-nine cannons were retrieved, part of the 60 tons of ordinance, spare parts, and other equipment they would have to haul over frozen, hard-as-rock meadows.

Lacking roads, depending only on ice and snow to bear that huge weight, the soldiers pressed forward, exacting all the energy their beasts had, to carry the cargo forward. Solomon and Phineas, like most of the soldiers, had no winter clothes and their shoes were not fit to keep their feet warm. Yet the men worked with the mules and horses, slowly dragging the heavy load toward their destination. Knox and his men arrived at the Heights on January 23, 1776, having performed one of the most amazing accomplishments of human endeavor during the Revolutionary War.

Solomon suffered minor frostbite to his feet during the trek and was given leave by his commanding officer until a physician could pronounce him fit for active duty. During his father's absence, six pounds, six ounces James Ennis was born. Miriam was sad that Solomon was not present at the birth of their son, but she understood his commitment to his new country, which was also being born. When he finally did arrive home, Solomon was pleased to have the time away from camp to be with his family while recuperating. He wrote to his parents, informing them of the birth of their grandson, detailing the color of his eyes, hair and skin.

He also informed David, the new grandfather, that, "While there was no rabbi at camp, nor a *mohel* (ritual circumciser) available, I found a physician who had previously performed circumcisions on adults for health reasons. As the doctor did his work, I read the appropriate prayers from the same prayer book you pressed into my hand, Father, as I left London. You would have been proud to see me recite the blessings over my new-born son."

Solomon expressed hope that the grandparents were pleased to have a Jewish grandson and that the time would come when they would get to see and hold him. In the meantime, there were some excellent artists among the troops; as soon as he could, he would have one do a drawing for the new grandparents to see what little James looked like. Solomon emphasized that they named the boy James after his grandfather, Jaime. "I am now a soldier in the Continental Army," he wrote further, "and I serve under General George Washington," who, he added, "is a very great gentleman."

"A soldier in Washington's army is not like being one in the King's army," he wrote. "We all fight for freedom," he emphasized. "This is a new society. We must accommodate ourselves to it. Soon, when enough of our brothers and sisters come here from across the sea to start a new life, we will have our own rabbis and a regular Jewish life, so that our children shall never forget their heritage." With that thought, Solomon closed his letter, stating his great love for his parents. He sealed the envelope and addressed it.

There was a process during the hostilities in the Colonies in which letters from America were sent to England. First, a ship transported them to the neutral Dutch island of St. Eustatius in the West Indies. From there, a ship of a neutral nation brought the letters to England. It was a long and tedious route, but the only one available during the War. Solomon's letter took eight months to reach London. It was the third and last one the Henriques family would ever receive from their American son.

ᘐ ᘒ

Henry Knox now set about expertly placing his formidable 59 cannons to overlook the Boston harbor and the city itself, which now lay perilously beneath their menacing presence. Knox's artillery had the reach to also strike at the British navy's vessels offshore, should they try getting in close enough to support the British army. General Gage understood he was in great danger, living beneath the power of Washington's artillery, which was ready to inflict immense damage to his forces. He decided to evacuate Boston, sending some of his troops to Canada. With the rest of his fighting force, he then proceeded south to New York City.

By March 15, Gage's evacuation of Boston was complete. Washington now began making plans to also move south, to defend New York. Solomon Ennis, who had spent the winter with his family while the injuries to his feet healed, would soon be returning to service.

On the last day of March, a Sergeant from Solomon's battalion knocked on his door and ordered him to appear before a doctor to determine his fitness for military duty. Washington needed all the men he could muster for his move on New York.

✑ ✒

"You seem to be okay, young fella. Do your feet hurt?" the doctor asked Solomon.

"No, sir."

"Can you feel the pin I'm sticking you with?"

"Yes, Sir, I surely can."

"Then I'm gonna mark you fit for military duty, lad. Take this paper to your company commander and good luck to you, young man." The doctor scribbled some words on a paper and handed it to Solomon.

When he returned home, Solomon told Miriam he had to return to duty. He had signed up for a year and that wouldn't be over until the last day of September. In terms of the War, things had been quiet for a while. Soldiers had little to do since the British left Boston. They cleaned up the encampment and took inventory of the army's equipment, cleaning and repairing them. Soldiers were counted in their units, so Washington would know how many men he could rely on for his defense of New York. The final count was an unpleasant surprise. It was many thousands less than Washington had expected; an unwelcome and ominous beginning to his decision to defend New York City.

Solomon came home on the second of April and said, "Miriam, we will be leaving for New York in a few days. I don't know when I'll be back." He kissed and hugged her and young James. He put whatever he needed into a knapsack, together with the bread and cakes Miriam had baked for him, and slung the knapsack across his shoulder.

"Wait," Miriam said. "I have your shirt and trousers that you always wear when on duty." She went to a basket and pulled them out. She looked inside the shirt to assure herself that the statement she had carefully stitched into it was still there. It was.

Wiping a tear from her face, because she didn't want Solomon to leave with a last memory of her crying, she carefully folded the shirt so that her needle work was covered over. With her back to Solomon, she wiped one more tear away and then stuffed the clothing into his knapsack. She hugged her husband and then handed young James to his father for his farewell kiss.

"Goodbye, my dear husband. Go with God. I will be here with our son, awaiting your return." With that, Solomon Ennis, just over 19 years of age, husband, father and foot soldier in George Washington's Continental Army, was on his way.

On the Fourth of April 1776, Miriam Ennis and several dozen wives stood at Dorchester Heights and looked below. They saw less than 10,000 soldiers of Washington's slap-dash army march off to New York City to battle the world's most formidable army. The day was clear and from the Heights, one could look out for miles across the land and east to the ocean. The Continental Army marched out of Boston to the tune of martial music as the British had done weeks earlier. Yet Miriam noted that when the British left, they did so in good order, wearing clean, starched uniforms that were bright red, marching in unison to the music of drums, fifes and the strange sound of Scottish bagpipes.

The American forces were a jumbled mass of grey, brown, white, black, and green trousers and shirts. They would arrive in New York City readying themselves for the first consequential battle of the Revolutionary War. As she stood at the edge of the Hill, Miriam heard one of the wives beside her say in a thick, Irish brogue, "I head this morning that 4,000 men refused to extend their enlistments."

Miriam felt a shiver throughout her body and although it was a balmy spring day, she wrapped her shawl around herself and little James, who she held tightly in her arms.

25

German-Occupied France
1944

Ernst Falkenberg was true to his word. He returned in four days, managing to bring with him three boxes of blueprints, drawings, written comments on tests performed for the schnorkel, the electronic guidance system and some other material concerning experiments on rockets. Aarnald Henriques, he told the Teacher, had been under arrest in the Gestapo's Amsterdam headquarters for almost a month.

"Aarnald, I found out, was the second in command of an Underground cell operating out of Rotterdam. The number one man was killed in a fire fight. Pressure was put on Aarnald to get information. They say he has revealed nothing, so the day after tomorrow they are moving him and some others to Paris where the Gestapo is known to be more efficient in its interrogations. After they finish with him, it's the cemetery." Falkenberg drew a forefinger across his neck, emphasizing the fate of the resistance fighter.

"Do you know the route they are taking?" Martin, the Underground leader asked.

"If you give me a map, I can show you." After a map was spread out before him, Falkenberg, with a shaky finger, traced the route from Holland through Belgium and into France.

"It's only 10 miles from here," Martin remarked.

"By the way," Falkenberg said, "you didn't tell me this Aarnald fellow was a Jew. My Gestapo friend was very curious about me wanting to know about a Jew. In the future, I do nothing where Jews are involved. They are a nasty bunch and get you into trouble. You almost got me into the hands of the Gestapo.'

Martin slapped Falkenberg hard across the face, shouting, "Bastard!"

Falkenberg stepped back, holding his hand to his face. "You can't change the fact that all of my contacts with Jews have been unfortunate for me," he yelled at the top of his voice.

"Do you know how they are moving the men?" Ennis asked, ignoring the German scientist's outburst.

"Yes," he replied while rubbing his face, now a cherry red where Martin had struck him. "In a truck, with soldiers and four motorcycles as an escort."

"This had better not be a trap. If it is, you are the first to get a bullet. And I know where to put it so it takes a while to finish you off." After he said this, Ennis was surprised he could say such a thing. He realized what Mickey Garcia had put him into was not a game but something deadly serious.

Looking at Martin, Ennis asked, "Can we attack that convoy?"

"I don't know, Teacher. They are Dutch. They have nothing to do with us."

"They are in the fight against the Boche, as you are. And the Gestapo is using France to transport him to Paris, where he will be tortured and then killed."

"You have a point. But I can't order my people. The best I can do is ask for volunteers. I'll be the first. You go outside with that scum, Falkenberg. There may be some talk you wouldn't like to hear."

After 10-minutes, Martin walked into the courtyard where Ennis and Falkenberg were sitting in the shell of an old Ford sedan. "Including you and myself, I can put together 12 men. The women will come too; they are sure whoever the Boche are moving, those people will need medical treatment."

Two days later, with the partisans hiding behind trees and thick bushes lining the road, the Gestapo's caravan appeared just as Falkenberg has predicted. First, two motorcycles, each with a man armed with a submachine gun riding in the attached side car, roared down the road. Then came a rickety open-roofed army truck, its sides also open and protected only by flimsy wooden slats that swayed with each turn in the road. Ennis could see at least two soldiers standing inside, rifles hanging on their shoulders by straps. He observed that they seemed to be confident that there would be no trouble. Behind the truck, were two more motorcycles without side cars. So far, Falkenberg was living up to his word.

Martin spread his partisans about a hundred yards along the road. They were to start firing when he blew a whistle, as had previously been arranged. Ennis and two other men were detailed to quickly dispatch the soldiers in the truck. From experience, Martin knew that during such an attack the soldiers would try to massacre their prisoners. He had warned the men assigned to the truck that the soldiers had to be dispatched quickly and decisively.

Martin blew his whistle. The first two leading motorcycles were swiftly taken out. One motorcycle ran up a small grade by the side of the road, striking a tree. Its two passengers were thrown to the ground and quickly gunned down. The other cycle rolled to a stop and its occupants also neatly machine-gunned by one of Martin's men. The following two cyclists were dispatched similarly. Fortunately, their motor bikes traveled just a few feet once the men were thrown off. The bikes soon stopped, intact.

Ennis engaged his Thompson. He had never killed anyone face-to-face before. Yes, he had sunk ships as a submarine Captain. He had set up the ships, fired the torpedoes that killed hundreds of men. But that was impersonal. It was not looking at a victim face-to-face as he watched him die only a few feet away. They taught him at commando school to put those thoughts aside, to be vicious. If not, he would be the one to die and maybe not so pleasantly. He would lose the prisoners in the truck if he wasn't dispassionate. That feeling returned: the tightness around his chest and the metallic taste of fear. The killing had to be done.

He and the two partisans crept up to the truck which had foolishly slowed down. It must have been driven by an inexperienced driver, Ennis thought. Instead of speeding up when the first two motorcycles had been hit, he slowed to look at them. The four soldiers inside the truck, taken by surprise, barely had time to aim their weapons. They were quickly put away.

Martin, after running alongside the slowing truck, came up to the cab's open window. Using his pistol, he swiftly put bullets into the heads of the truck's driver and a passenger. It was a surgical strike. Ennis was impressed. The Germans were so surprised they had fired no shots. *Martin knows his business,* Ennis mused.

He and Martin climbed into the truck, followed by the women carrying medical kits and water-filled canteens. "*Mon Dieu! Les batards,*" Martin shouted.

What they saw was pitiful. Ten prisoners lay on the truck's floor, their hands tied behind their backs, their feet secured with leather straps. Two of them, one a young girl in her teens, had died after being loaded aboard in Amsterdam. All the prisoners were covered with dried blood, urine, and feces. Two men and a woman wore the Yellow Star that said, JUDE. When the young French women boarded the truck, they cried at the sight. They freed hands and feet at once and began ministering to the prisoners.

Martin told Ennis, "As often as I see things like this, I can never get used to them."

"Aarnald Henriques," Ennis whispered as he walked among the prisoners. A man in a corner weakly raised his head. Ennis could not recognize him. His swollen face was a purple-green, the result of bruises from many beatings. Two of his front teeth were broken, his lips badly split. His arms and legs were pocked with cigarette burns. He looked as if he had not eaten for days. One of the women gave him a cup of water, which he swallowed in great gulps, much of it spilling down his chest.

Martin began shouting, "Quick, quick! We must get out of here."

What happened next impressed Ennis even more. The motorcycle with the sidecar that struck the tree was wrecked beyond repair. Its gas tank was emptied of fuel, which was placed into two empty wine bottles. The truck's fuel tank was emptied into several jerry cans. A few drops of gasoline were left in both tanks, however. The dead soldiers were stripped of all weapons, ammunition, boots and anything else Martin's people could use, including uniforms. After the rescued prisoners were placed in wagons that had been brought along, all the dead soldiers were thrown into the truck with the unserviceable motorcycle, lifted by four of the strongest partisans. As Martin's volunteers rode away, three men riding the three captured and serviceable motorcycles followed. Before they rode off, lit matches were thrown into the gas tanks of the motorcycle and truck. Two men threw Molotov cocktails on to the truck. They were the wine bottles filled with gasoline, lit with rags as wicks. The truck and its contents blew up in a huge corona of flames.

If left to burn untended, it would be difficult to identify anything. No one was staying behind to watch. The whole operation took just over 15 minutes. None of Martin's people was injured and they left, saving eight lives, salvaging a large haul of useful equipment and some needed future transportation. They took the bodies of the two dead prisoners for a later burial.

అ అ

The next night, a gull-winged Lysander airplane was scheduled to pick up Ennis and Falkenberg. Resistance fighters were preparing landing lights, a set of twelve fires created by pyres of dry twigs and brush. The fires were set 40 feet apart, six on each side of a makeshift runway along a flat, grassy area in a dry meadow. They were landing lights to define the runway. It was a clear night with a full, bright and yellow moon, perfect for the plane's pickup. Lysander pilots carried no navigational equipment. A full moon and signal lights were all that were necessary to locate a landing field. The plane, designed to land and take off on short runways, could only carry two passengers. As it settled, the motor continued running for a quick departure. The pilot opened the door. Ennis shouted over the noisy engine.

"Take these two back," he said, pointing to Henriques and Falkenberg. "On your next pickup, I'll be coming with three boxes."

"I'll try to send someone tomorrow," the pilot responded. "The moon is still full. Listen on your radio for a confirmation."

His two passengers crawled into the back of the plane for an uncomfortable flight to England. The pilot slammed his door shut, gunned his engine and guided his plane forward as blades of grass thrown up by the plane's propellers rained on those standing nearby. The plane rose quickly, its black silhouette looking like a large marsh bird soaring across a bright harvest moon, and disappeared into the dark night.

Martin's men killed the fires, mounted their cars and took off. In a few hours, a German patrol would discover the area with its burnt landing fires and rutted tracks left by the Lysander's wheels. The Resistance never used the same landing site twice in a row, stymying German efforts to capture a Lysander, its pilot, and occupants.

Now Ennis would get on the short-wave radio to arrange for a pickup the next night.

26

Long Island, New York
August 1776

From the first, Solomon Ennis noticed that New York City was unlike Boston and its Heights. New York was flat. At least the lower part by the Bay was. Then he observed the city's two great rivers, one running along the east side: the East River. The other, flowing along the west side had two names: the Hudson, or the North River. It was not really a river, but an estuary running as far north as Albany. The two waterways met at the city's southern end, a place called the Battery, which was triangular in shape and laced with artillery to discourage an attack on the city from the sea. After the waters met, they coursed into New York Harbor, running south and dissolving into the Atlantic Ocean.

It took no great understanding of military tactics to realize that the English Navy, the world's largest and most powerful, could send many ships into this harbor and then move them up both rivers, bombarding defenders who would be caught in the middle between two fiery rains of sure destruction. After all, the distance between these two rivers at the Battery, someone told Solomon, was less than a mile.

To the west, were the shores of the fellow colony, New Jersey. To the east, lay Long Island, with its farms. The slender island of Manhattan, located between both rivers, was a juicy target for Britain's expert naval gunners. Washington had to admit that he had made a mistake and could not realistically put up a defense for New York City.

Washington decided to move his forces across the East River to Long Island, away from this impossible position. There were no large cities on that side of the river, only small agricultural settlements. It was a rural section of the colony filled with farms and dairies. Many of the owners were descendants of the original Dutch settlers of New Amsterdam who came there in the early 1600s. In fact, the name of Brooklyn, one of the sections, was Dutch for "Broken Hills."

Solomon's unit was assigned to encamp at Brooklyn Heights, located along the eastern bank of the East River. The Heights rose above the river with a grand view of New York, its harbor and beyond to Staten Island at the southwest. One morning as he awoke, Solomon began putting his kit together for the day. Then he saw it, to the south: a sight which at once filled him with wonder and dread.

Hundreds of English ships of war, of all sizes and purposes, emerged from the early morning mist. Many were sailing toward the East River, others toward the southern end of Long Island, to a place called Coney Island.

Solomon nudged Phineas Wooden awake, urging him to look at the ships. Soon, all the men in the company were standing in silence at the edge of the Heights, looking at this unbelievable sight. None of them knew it, but this armada was the greatest ever assembled by the Royal Navy. The sight of such an assembly drew fear into their hearts, exactly what it was intended to do.

That day, August 27th, the Battle of Long Island began. The British landed thousands of soldiers, who marched north across Long Island toward the Continental strongholds. With excellent intelligence gathered from Loyalist farmers, the British trapped their enemy and almost completely wiped them out. Were it not for a contingent of Maryland units, under the command of Major William Smallwood, who fought a heroic delaying action, allowing their comrades to make a retreat, the War might have ended that day. As it was, the British captured several high-ranking officers and large contingents of colonials. Solomon and his comrades were soon outmaneuvered and overwhelmed by the troops, which included Hessians from the German Duchy of Hesse, hired by King

George to fight alongside English soldiers. They pushed the Continentals back toward the banks of the East River.

Overwhelmed by the sheer numbers of enemy troops, after two days of fighting Washington and his generals agreed that the only way out for the battered Americans was to retreat back across the East River to New York City. The maneuver was successfully carried out by New England's doughty Gloucester fishermen, commanded by Colonel John Glover. His professional sailors, using the cover of night and aided by a heavy rain, thick fog and silenced oars abundantly wrapped in rags, calmly rowed thousands of Continental soldiers across the East River to the New York side. It was a miraculous escape.

Solomon, Phineas, and their comrades, with their commander George Washington, were among the last to be rowed to safety. They were part of the holding guard to protect the evacuation. Before they boarded the last boats, the rear guard stoked large campfires to dupe the British into believing an army of men was still encamped and prepared to meet them in battle.

A lone British guard stumbled upon the last boat as it was leaving Brooklyn's shores. He fired a useless shot. Washington, who was one of the last to leave, had already saved all he could of his retreating army. Once ashore in Manhattan, the soldiers pushed north, pursued by the British and Hessians.

Instead of keeping up pressure on the defeated and retreating enemy, the British army dallied at Murry Hill, where General Howe took a tea break with Mrs. Murray, proprietress of the farm at that location. This allowed the broken band of Continentals to scamper to the northern tip of Manhattan. After Howe's rest, the British continued their pursuit.

Pushing their way north, the Americans followed old Indian and farm trails. Retreating soldiers were able to keep their pursuers at bay, always a mile or two ahead of them. Halfway up the island of Manhattan, at Harlem Heights, a group of American soldiers stopped. They gathered behind a large and sturdy stone wall and were ordered to hold the advancing British, giving their comrades enough time to move further away from their pursuers. They picked a good location, setting up a defensive position behind a well-constructed and stout stone wall located at the peak of a hill. The Hudson River was to their right, a natural barrier to prevent an end attack from that position.

As the British marched up the hill, they were met with a rain of musket balls from the defenders. A stiff battle ensued, which delayed the pursuers. The smell of smoke from gun barrels of both defenders and attackers filled the air. During the skirmish, Solomon spied three Hessians soldiers in the bushes moving along the American left flank, trying to infiltrate from that side. As he stood, he knew instantly he had made a mistake. He had exposed himself to enemy fire. Then he felt it: a blow to his left leg below the knee as if someone had punched him hard. He fell, clutching his leg. The day he was wounded, Solomon's enlistment was over. He could have left the battle at midnight and returned home to his wife and son.

"Phineas," he shouted, "I'm hit."

"Stay where you are, Sol, I'll get to ye in a moment."

Crawling behind the protection of the wall, Phineas sidled up to his mate. He looked at Solomon's wound. It didn't look good. But he made no comment. He removed a scarf from around his neck and tied it tight above the site of Solomon's wound, staunching the flow of blood.

"Does it hurt, Sol?" he asked.

"Not too bad."

"Can ye move?"

"I think so."

"Then get up the hill to that ledge where yer out of range of them Lobsterback's rifles. From there, as soon as I'm finished here, I'll get ye up to the main camp. There's sure to be a doctor there."

A half hour later, the two men reached the clearing that had been converted into a makeshift medical camp. Confusion reigned. Three doctors and a few volunteer soldiers, who were assisting them, were overwhelmed with treating the large number of wounded soldiers laying on the ground. Phineas left Solomon with an aide and returned to the fighting. After an hour, a doctor with a European accent that Solomon could not place tended to his wound.

"There's not much I can do for you now, soldier," the doctor said, a touch of apology in his voice. "All our medical supplies were abandoned when we retreated from Long Island. I'll remove the tourniquet and put a fresh dressing on it. I don't even have any laudanum to relieve your pain. That musket ball must come out. I heard we will soon be crossing the river into New Jersey. There are sure to be doctors there who can help you. We'll be sending all the wounded who are able to walk, down to the river soon, for a speedy evacuation to New Jersey."

After cleaning the wound and dressing it, the doctor put Solomon in a group of other wounded men who had been helped and were waiting to go on to New Jersey. Solomon fell asleep as he waited, for how long, he didn't know. He was awakened by Phineas, who told him they would now be heading towards the riverbank for evacuation. Phineas would also be leaving with the soldiers heading to New Jersey. Another group was staying behind at the crest of a high hill in a place they were calling Fort Washington. They felt it was impregnable.

Solomon looked at his leg. The doctor had done his job well. Aside from the blood on his pants from the initial wound, he was no longer bleeding. Good luck. But now he was in pain and needed help to walk down that steep hill to the shore where the boats were waiting. Phineas found a stout broken branch from a nearby tree and gave it to Solomon to use as a cane. Then he lifted his friend from the ground, put Solomon's right arm around his neck and they began the arduous descent to the river's edge.

It was not easy going and took them over 15 minutes to travel downhill along an old rocky Indian trail, each step a shock to Solomon's leg. By the time they reached the boat ferrying the wounded across the river, Solomon's leg was wet: the wound had opened during the difficult trek and was bleeding again.

"They're only lettin' wounded on this here boat, Sol. I'm right behind you in the next one and I'll ketch up with ye on the other side," Phineas said. As they looked behind them, the friends could see a battle ensuing at Fort Washington. The Fort was not as defensible as had been thought. Many men were dying; many more taken prisoner.

"Better to die than be taken a British prisoner," Phineas said. The English were not known for treating captured soldiers who were not officers with any kind of basic care.

It took a while to fill the boat with the wounded. Now Solomon could feel the warm blood dripping down his leg. He didn't know how much he had lost. Then he looked to the floor beside his feet. Blood was pooling there. He applied another tourniquet. By the time the evacuees reached New Jersey, Solomon had to fight to stay awake. Then he was put into a wagon. Phineas caught up with him and put a new tourniquet on his leg. He didn't like what he saw, but smiled, "You'll be fine, Sol. I'll get ye to the first doc I can find."

At the village of Newark, the retreating caravan stopped for food and water. Phineas jumped out of the wagon and ran into a nearby tavern where a group of men surrounded a bar.

"Is there a doctor around here?" he shouted from the doorway.

"On the other side of the street, soldier boy," one of the patrons said, pointing a beer mug in the doctor's direction. "His name is Witherspoon."

Phineas dashed back to the wagon and pulled Solomon out. "Come on, Sol, we're getting ye to a doc."

Solomon barely had enough strength to walk. Phineas slung him over his shoulder, blood dripping onto his clothing. Arriving at the doctor's house, he shouted for help. A young man in his late 20s, came out, looked at the two men and directed Phineas to bring Solomon to a table in a back room. It was filled with books and various skeletal portions of the human body. Dr. Alexander Weatherspoon, graduate of William and Mary College and the College of Pennsylvania, where he had learned the arts of medicine and healing, immediately removed Solomon's pants and asked Phineas to leave the room and wait outside while he examined the patient.

"Can you hear me, young man?" the doctor asked, as he inspected the wound, carefully removing the tourniquet and bandages. Blood was dripping profusely on to the wooden table.

"Yes sir, I can," Solomon answered in a weak voice. But he was drifting back and forth into unconsciousness. His eyes were closing;

the lids were heavy weights he could not control. The ceiling above him was spinning.

"When were you wounded?"

Solomon wasn't answering. The doctor repeated the question several times, raising his voice until Solomon answered.

"A few days ago, maybe two or three." He could barely speak. The doctor took his hands and rubbed them vigorously. Solomon responded to the rubs.

"How long have you been bleeding like this?"

"Several hours. Maybe more. I can't really tell. I fell asleep. Am I going to die?"

Dr. Witherspoon didn't answer. He looked at the wound again, this time with greater care. He didn't like what he saw.

"Has a doctor seen you?"

"Yes, in New York. But he said he couldn't do anything for me since all his equipment was lost in the battle. He said the musket ball had to come out."

"Yes, I can see that."

"Doctor, I know I'm going to die." Solomon paused, drifting off again He shook his head to force his return to consciousness. "Please give all my clothes, my stockings and my shoes to my friend Phineas. Winter is coming and he'll need them. I'm a Jew, doctor, and I request a Jewish burial."

There was not much Dr. Witherspoon could do. If he tried to remove the bullet, it would surely cause more bleeding and certain death. He tried unsuccessfully to stop the bleeding and guessed that at first the ball had barely nicked a large artery, but it had opened wider under stress when Solomon walked down to the river to his evacuation.

Twenty minutes after entering Dr. Witherspoon's office, Solomon Ennis was pronounced dead. During the time he was alive, the doctor wrote down much detailed information about his patient and his short life, filling three long sheets of paper. He called to Phineas, who was waiting on a chair on a porch outside the building. He told him the news.

"He wanted you to have his clothing. He knew you would need them with winter coming on. Let's remove them. I'll wrap him in a sheet."

As the doctor removed Solomon's shirt, he noticed Miriam's stitching. Silently and without Phineas noting, he carefully cut the tightly sewn threads with a scalpel and folded Miriam's work, putting it aside. Then, he noticed the dead man's circumcision.

"Private, did you know your friend was a Jew?"

"Yes Sir, I did. Makes no difference to me. He was a good and dependable mate. He never let me down, never. I'll have to write to his wife and let her know about this here tragedy. What will we do with the body?"

"Don't worry about that. I'll bury him in the woods back of my house and put up a marker so that if you want to move him later, you can locate him."

"I'll come back soon as I can, Doctor, to move him to Boston."

Phineas thanked the doctor and offered to pay for his services, which obviously would have been an extreme hardship. Doctor Witherspoon refused. Phineas took the clothing, gently folding them, and placed them in his shoulder bag. They would have to be washed to remove his companion's blood and sewn to cover the hole where the musket ball had cut into Solomon's leg.

He trotted out of the office, having a long distance to go to catch up with his retreating unit. There was such confusion among the ranks that Phineas did not report Solomon's death. It was his intention to do so once the troops settled. He would, however, write to Miriam to let her know of the sad news, as soon as the army took a break on its long road to a permanent encampment on the Pennsylvania side of the Delaware River.

Doctor Witherspoon fattened up his notes while his conversation with Solomon was still fresh in his mind. He had asked his patient many questions, most of which were answered. The doctor knew of no Jews nearby who could help him with a proper burial. He would have to go to New York City to find one, so that this young man could have the Jewish burial he wanted. There were Jews in New York, he knew that, and he heard they even had a synagogue; the place where they met to worship.

It would have to wait, however. The British were in control of the city and Witherspoon was a well-known and outspoken rebel sympathizer. One of his relatives was a signer of the Declaration of Independence. Bringing an enemy soldier to be buried in a British-controlled city was risky. Anyway, Jews would be leaving the city with the rest of the anti-monarchists.

Removing Solomon Henriques would have to wait until the English left New York City, which he hoped and prayed would happen soon. Then he would go to the city and make proper arrangements to bury the body after he removed it from the field. He gave Miriam's stitching one more gentle fold, stuffed the papers he had written about Solomon between them and placed it all in a large envelope. He set it on the top shelf of one of his three tall office cabinets, the one behind his desk. The one everyone knew not to go into.

Before the War was over, Dr. Alexander Witherspoon would bury ten Continental soldiers, four British officers, three British privates and a Corporal and six Hessian privates. All of them were placed next to Solomon in the grassy fields in the back of his house. His military cemetery became famous among the citizens of Newark and its environs. Solomon Ennis' grave was the only one without a cross to mark it.

ℒ ℒ

At the first opportunity Phineas had, and before Washington's fleeing army finally settled on the western banks of the Delaware, he wrote a letter to Miriam. He had yet to report the death to his commanding officer.

Dear Miriam,
I hate to tell you the sad news that yer deer husband and my best
friend Sol was wounded on the 1ˢᵗ of Sept. at the battle of Harlem
Hgts. He died 3 days later from his wounds in Newark New Jersy.
He is buried here in New Jersy. I will bring him back home. He
always spoke of luv for yew and yer son James. When I return to

Boston ye can always count on me to help. Sol wuz like my brother.
I will miss him.
Yours, Phineas Wooden

Phineas asked his commanding officer if he knew when the next wagons were returning to Boston. He wanted to send the letter to Miriam. They would be leaving after lunch, he was told. One wagon was making a final loading at the back of the mess tent.

"You tell Mrs. Ennis that Sol was a damn good soldier and had the respect of all his comrades." Phineas told Willy Seton, the wagon driver, as he struck his pipe across a tree to clean it of its burnt ashes.

"A damn shame, this company losing one of its best men," Willy exclaimed.

"Willy, you see that Mrs. Ennis gets this letter. Tell her that her husband Sol was killed in the battle of Harlem Heights."

"I sure will, pal."

The wagon left for Boston. Willy Seton headed north, remaining on the New Jersey side of the Hudson River, away from the British, until he could get to upstate New York where, clear of the enemy, he would find a ferry to safely cross the river. From there, he would meet up with the road to Boston. His horses galloping parallel to the river, Seton enjoyed the air, which was cool and dry, with the sight of the leaves that were just beginning to turn color. In another week or so, the Hudson River Valley would be gorgeously ablaze with autumn colors.

As he drove along, two British frigates on the river spotted the wagon. Satisfied it belong to the enemy, they fired several accurate salvos at it, making direct hits. Six wounded men, the driver, two horses and every bit of paper in the wagon were burnt to cinders.

27

Normandy, France
June 5, 1944

They gathered in a cave: half a dozen French Underground fighters in front of a wireless radio operating on batteries, their faces glowing from the dial's lights. They bent over, straining to hear the BBC announcer from London, speaking in French. He was delivering several un-meaningful short lines selected from poetry or classic French texts. Each one was a special call to action for a specific resistance group. The listeners became animated as lines from a familiar poem called out to them. It was London's order to destroy all the telephone and electric poles along a main highway leading to the beaches of Normandy and its nearby German military camp.

The fighters knew what they had to do. Each person had a pre-assigned task. One woman in her twenties went to the back of the cave and returned toting a box filled with dynamite sticks, which she began tying into clusters. Others would place them at the base of the phone and electric poles. One man opened a box full of fuses, separating then into useful bunches. Another inspected flashlights and lanterns, to insure there would be proper lighting for everyone to perform their special tasks. A man sitting on a bench in the far corner gathered several sub-machine guns, rifles and pistols, making sure they were properly cleaned and loaded. He handed them out to every member in the cell. They slung them around their shoulders or pocketed them into holsters around their waists.

The man at the bench was Marcel Henriques and he had joined the group only a month earlier, coming to them from the *Maquis*:

resistance fighters operating out of the mountains of central France. *Maquisards,* as they were called, were a mix of Communists, Jews, labor leaders, Christian dissenters, other groups the Germans detested and men and women who refused to be conscripted into the German work force. The Germans were always on the lookout for the *Maquisards,* as they were openly resistance fighters, unlike Urban Underground groups in France's largest cities, who were not so visible. Urban groups usually engaged in a specific act of sabotage, then melted back into the city's life.

As a Jew, Henriques posed a great risk for the rest of his new group. Should they be caught, they could expect severe retribution from the Gestapo for harboring a Jew. Marcel had received word that his mother, who was in hiding in nearby Cherbourg with a family friend, was very sick. The note he received said, "Your sainted mother is gravely ill. I cannot see her lasting more than a few weeks at best." It was signed Emily Dupres, a close Christian friend of the Henriques family.

At great danger to himself, Marcel came down from the mountain, heading for Cherbourg. Traveling a long distance, he was constantly in danger of being discovered at any of a dozen check points. He arrived at Normandy in time to be with his mother at the end. In a secret ceremony, he recited the *Kaddish,* the Jewish prayer for the dead, over her grave, even though he lacked the necessary ten men to intone it. Where would he find ten Jews today in Cherbourg? Then he headed for his new group. Returning to the mountains was too dangerous. Not wanting to push his luck by making the long trip back, he used an introduction from his leader to Francois Charre, the head of the Normandy group. Since he had much more direct combat experience than Charre's group, they reluctantly accepted him.

Tonight, Francois Charre felt less apprehensive about his new *Maquisard.* This last order he received over the wireless, he was sure, presaged the long-awaited invasion of Europe. *Once the British and Americans were ashore,* he thought, *this Henriques fellow will be less of a liability. And he did have more experience fighting the Boche out in the open than any of us did. We could probably learn much from him. For now, we have a task and it was an important one. We are to destroy all the telephone and electric poles in the area and cut off communications and power to the Boche camp and everyone else in Normandy. Henriques was already checking out our weapons, making sure they were cleaned and loaded so that everyone had a dependable weapon. Jew or not, he was still a Frenchman and, as all of us, fighting to rid France of the despised Boche.*

As they walked toward the highway on foot, more people who had heard the call over the air joined them. Soon, Charre's group grew to 45 resistance fighters. Their retreat would be a fast and orderly escape, facilitated by cars arriving at the scene later. Falling to their knees and covered by the dark of the night, they used blankets and jackets to cover the flashlights and lanterns, lights they needed to do the job of connecting wires to fuses and explosives. Men and women began tying dynamite sticks to the base of every telephone and electric pole running to the beaches of Normandy. From time to time, German patrol cars passed by. Work would stop, not continuing until a lookout called, "All Clear."

Explosive experts from another resistance cell linked the poles together with sets of the long fuses provided them. Then *plastique*, highly explosive putty, was slapped on to the base of the poles. After that was done, silent hand signals ordered everyone away from the poles to a safe cover away from the ditches, far from the highway. Using plungers, the experts blew up the poles, which dropped as if they were soldiers mowed down by a machine gun. Wires snapped, whipping through the air as they sparked. Condensers exploded. It didn't take long for German soldiers to respond. As resistance fighters began leaving the scene, sirens were blaring and bright search lights swept the area where the poles once stood.

Marcel pulled aside three men and a woman to stand with him. He pushed everyone back into a ditch which now contained fallen electric poles that were still sparking; they would be used as defensive barriers. As disoriented groups of German soldiers ran by them, the little group put out a wall of heavy automatic fire, allowing their comrades to make an orderly retreat. The Germans now became more integrated. Henriques signaled a retreat. Running to catch up with the rest of their group, they were now receiving heavy fire. Marcel ordered them to stop and return fire.

239

Their weapons functioned perfectly; Marcel had seen to that. No jammed Sten guns, no useless weapons among the group. And he had been careful to ensure that everyone had enough ammunition in their knapsacks. Soon, two more men came up beside them, helping to hold back "the dirty Boche," they shouted. Henriques could hear automobile ignitions starting up at the top of the hill and then the roar of engines on the getaway cars.

"To the cars," he shouted. Everyone jumped up from the ground and headed to the crest of the hill where a car awaited them. All but one had taken off. As they scrambled up the rise, Henriques was the last, his back to the car, facing the pursuing Germans. "Go, go," he urged the retreaters, waving them on. As the men and women piled into the car, they awaited Henriques, who was struck with a bullet as he reached the crest of the hill. He fell to the ground. "Let's go," shouted the driver. One man sitting in the back seat put the barrel of a Sten gun to the driver's head. "Bastard. You wait until we pick up that man. Where is your honor? He saved us."

They pulled Marcel into the car. He was bleeding from a shoulder wound, and in shock. He managed to whisper, very low, "Thank you, my friends."

28

A Military Hospital in London
1944

Jim Ennis stood motionless over a sleeping Aarnald Henriques for several minutes before Henriques opened his eyes and forced a weak smile.

It had been a full month before Ennis had returned to England from France. He missed the next day's Lysander pickup, which was purposely cancelled. German Army patrols were out in full force looking for clandestine drops. The Gestapo was also out on their own accord, searching for their important defector, the treasonous Jew-lover, Ernst Falkenberg. He had been allowed to slip through their hands through their own laxity. And, of course, there was that troublesome resistance Jew, Henriques.

Ennis had to wait until the next full moon to return to England. Moving all the while, one step ahead of the Gestapo, he slept in 14 different beds during his one-month wait.

Aarnald's condition had improved in that time, but one could see that he still needed care. His face was gaunt and continued to show discoloration from his beatings. But it had filled out somewhat with the hospital's good nutrition. He would never again look like the man whose picture Ennis had seen in that Gibraltar gift shop years earlier: the Gestapo had seen to that. Ennis introduced himself.

"You're the man who rescued me," Henriques said. "I don't remember much after they put me in the truck. They struck me on the head in Amsterdam. Your name is Teacher, right? They told me a naval officer rescued me. That's how I figured it was you. The uniform." Aarnald pointed to Ennis' clothes.

"Yes, that's me. I'm Teacher. And now that we're in London, I can tell you my real name. I'm Lt. Commander James Ennis. Call me Jimmy."

Henriques extended a hand. It was shaky and cold; he placed another cold and bony hand over James Ennis' hand, holding it as firmly as he could. Ennis could see that there was still a lot of frailty in this man. His thin, bony wrist was peeking out from beyond a wide, dark blue pajama sleeve. The cigarette burns were still there, but they were fading.

"I thank you for rescuing me," Henriques said. "I was certain I was headed for the end. You have made a friend of me. I'll never forget you. I don't know how much longer I could have held out. I gave my cyanide capsule to a fellow prisoner who used it two days later."

"Well, I was just as pleased to save you. I sent word of your rescue to your family in Oran, Avraham and Jacques. They were worried about you. They didn't know what happened to you. I understand your whole family was sent to the camps."

"Yes, I knew that. I don't hold out any hope for them. How is it you know my family in North Africa?"

"I met them when I was stationed there a while ago. I think we may be related. There are Henriques in my family a least a hundred fifty years ago. They came from Spain or Portugal and then lived in Amsterdam and London, according to family lore. No one in my family has ever told me we were Jewish. Your cousin Avraham says my family history definitely fits such a background.

"You know how I found out about you? I saw a photograph of you in a shop in Gibraltar. You were at a convention of Jewish leaders in 1938, sitting around with a bunch of men, enjoying some coffee. The lady who showed me the photograph said we look alike."

"Yes, we all met in Gibraltar that year. We came from all over Europe, some 40 of us, and we all had stories to tell about how things were deteriorating. The Italians were living in a fascist state; Mussolini signed laws preventing Jews from studying at the universities. Our German cousins weren't there because they couldn't leave their country. What was happening there was unbelievable. Spain was still at war; that kept them from attending. The Poles and Hungarians and we Dutch were watching the rise of anti-Jewish politicians. Right here in England, the fascist Sir Oswald Mosely marched with his gangsters in Whitechapel, London's Jewish section. It ended up in a street brawl.

"The only bright spots were Switzerland and Turkey, which were neutral countries. The world wouldn't pay attention to any of those nasty things that were happening. Now we are paying a big price.

"The concentration camps have two purposes: slave labor, to work a person until he is useless and then, to murder him. Again, no one pays attention. They can't believe a civilized society could be capable of such things. But they are. And they continue, with no one to stop them. In the Underground we receive regular reports of these atrocities. We send them on to England and America. You know what they say? 'It's an exaggeration.'"

Ennis stood quietly beside Aarnald. There was not much he could say. He hadn't known much about the Jews and their history, but he was learning. He could see Aarnald was agitated, not a good thing for a man recuperating from injuries that could have killed him. He changed the subject, hoping he would not be thought of as another insensitive American.

He told Aarnald of his Henriques background and the search he was making. "I want to see you get better, Aarnald. What are you going to do when you leave the hospital?"

"My government in exile, here in London, has work for me. They've been here to see me. When I get out of the hospital, I'll do some Dutch-language radio broadcasts over the BBC, some writing and some espionage work. I'll be fine.

"You know, Commander, we have a family bible that begins with our origins in Spain and Portugal in the 1400s and goes up to the present. I packed it away when I went underground. Are you serious about finding your ancestors?"

"Yes, I am. The more I learn about them, the more I want to know."

"The book is safe in a bank vault in the Hague, in the custody of a friend of mine. When we kick the Nazis out of Holland, you might want to look at it. Maybe we can add your family's story to the pages. I will be forever grateful to you for rescuing me and if you really are an Henriques, you belong in the book. Anyway, for me at least, you'll always be an honorary Henriques."

"I'll take you up on seeing that book, Aarnald. Don't wait too long to get your good looks back."

୬ ৶

Although Ennis had been in London for three days, being debriefed on his mission, he had yet to meet with Mickey Garcia. He was told Mickey had also been on a mission outside of England and as he left the hospital, Ennis looked at his watch. Mickey should have returned by now and would be waiting for him.

Jimmy walked across Green Park towards Mayfair. In the park, crews were cleaning up the damage from last night's air raid. The rear of a German bomber rose above the ground, its swastika prominently showing on its tail. Ennis wondered if anyone survived that crash. The rest of the plane, from engine to middle, was almost completely pulverized. He marveled at how the Germans were so persistent in their belief that they could demoralize Londoners with air raids. It hadn't worked over the years; why would it work now?

As he entered Mickey Garcia's office, he encountered a red-faced and angry man. Today, there were no bear hugs. Instead, there was a loud slam by Mickey's fist hitting the desk.

"Jimmy, just who in hell authorized you to put that Dutch tulip on the plane and leave yourself behind for a month?"

"I did it on my own initiative, Mickey."

"Your own initiative! What would have happened if the Gestapo caught you? You're in their hands and the plans you had would be gone, too!"

"The Underground kept the plans safe until I left. And if they caught me, what do I know? Nothing. I wanted to get Henriques out because he is one of the top men in the Dutch Underground and you don't want him in the Gestapo's hands. Eventually he would have had to break. He admitted as much to me. He gave his last cyanide capsule to a friend who soon used it. Besides, according to you, I was to make all the decisions based on what I saw on the ground. I made them. I'm sorry if you weren't happy with them. Anyway, I have to leave you. I have to sit with the submarine people again to figure out this schnorkel thing you got me into. I'm on my way."

Mickey quieted down, the reddish color receding from his face. "I suppose you have a point," he said quietly. "Where are you going after you finish up here in London?"

"I'm surprised you don't know. Unless you have something cooked up for me, I'd like to get back to my submarine patrols, where I belong. Thanks to you, everyone thinks I make a good translator and spy. I think they're going to put me in some office looking at documents and telling the brass what they mean."

"That's not so terrible. It's important work. I keep telling you that. Didn't you think when I got you assigned to General Clark in North Africa, that you were doing important work?"

"So it was you who assigned me there. Somehow, I thought so at the time. Who else looks out for my welfare by dropping me out of planes and teaching me to be a killer?"

"For me, Jimmy, it was always finding the best man for the job."

"Well, this best man made what he deemed to be the best decision based on what he knew. And besides," Ennis said as he turned his back on Mickey and walked toward the door, "the Dutch tulip, as you call him, might be a relative."

29

A Courthouse
Springfield, Massachusetts
1784

Miriam Ennis had been carefully coached by her attorney, Caleb Bull, as to how to answer the judge's questions. She had retained counselor Bull to represent her at this hearing before the Court. Bull's fees were paid by Angus Duff, Miriam's friend, who hoped to marry her after a positive Court decision.

Miriam had fallen on hard times after her husband, Solomon, disappeared during the fall of 1776. Two years later, the family assistance she was receiving stopped when Miriam's mother and father were killed in the bombardment of Newport by British naval and land forces. With a young child to care for, Miriam took to sewing to earn her way. Soon, she became so successful she was hiring several young women to assist her in expertly patching old clothes and fashioning new ones for the wealthy.

On a trip to Boston, Angus Duff, a big, sturdy Scotsman with blue eyes and sandy blonde hair, met Miriam Ennis. He was a maker of uniforms for the Continental Army. He was impressed with her sewing skills and her little business and persuaded her to move to his hometown of Springfield, Massachusetts, where he could guarantee her enough work to insure her a comfortable life. The two would eventually fall in love, but a cloud hung over their heads: Solomon Ennis. Was he still alive? Had he become a prisoner of the British? Did he die in captivity? Had he been killed in battle? No one knew. Every inquiry Miriam made was of no use.

It had been eight years since Miriam had last heard from Solomon and one year since the War ended. If he had survived as a prisoner, which was unlikely from the tales she had heard about how the English treated their captives on the prison ships in Wallabout Bay in Brooklyn, by now he should certainly have returned home. But he hadn't. After so many years of hoping, Miriam had finally given up.

She was petitioning the court to apply the benefits of a law which allowed her to declare Solomon Ennis legally dead, as there had been no word of him or his whereabouts for over seven years. About to appear before a judge of the State Court of Massachusetts, Miriam sat nervously on a rude wooden bench in the courtroom. Angus Duff was gently holding her hand, trying to import some confidence to her. The judge sat behind his bench high above everyone in the courtroom, which was crowded with petitioners, some suing one another, others waiting for a trial. And like Miriam, there would be those petitioning the court for all sorts of individual relief. Miriam was not pleased to have to let this mob know all about her personal affairs. She understood that she had no choice if she were to clean up this part of her personal life. Angus Duff wanted to marry her, and she wanted to be his wife. She had been alone too long. Her husband and her parents were gone, and she had long ago put aside the hope of comfort from her faith. Other than her son, she was alone in the world. And now Angus was offering her a new life.

Miriam heard the Bailiff call her name. "The petition of Mrs. Miriam Ennis, nee Mendoza, to declare her husband Solomon legally deceased. Petitioner step forward please."

Attorney Bull put his hand under Miriam's elbow and gently led her to the head of the courtroom, directly in front of the judge, who looked down from his bench. He peered over the glasses perched on the end of his nose at the papers containing the petition filed in this matter. Then he addressed Caleb Bull, standing beside Miriam.

"I've read your petition, Counselor. It seems complete and meets the requirements under law. I would, however, like to ask your client some questions."

"Of course, your Honor. My client would be pleased to answer any of your questions."

"You are Mrs. Miriam Ennis?"

"I am, Judge."

"Where and when were you married?"

"We were married in Boston, 1775."

"When was the last time you saw your husband?"

"In April 1776, sir. Before he left for New York with General Washington and the Continental Army."

"Have you had any word from him since that time?"

"None, your Honor."

"What efforts did you make to locate your husband?"

"After the Battle of Long Island, some of my husband's fellow soldiers who were wounded, returned to Boston. I asked them what they knew about Solomon. The only thing I was able to learn was that his close friend, Phineas Wooden, took him to a doctor because Solomon had suffered wounds. Exactly where the doctor was, nobody could remember. There was much confusion, they told me. They were retreating.

"My husband's friend, Mr. Wooden, died with other soldiers; something about bad food before they ever got to Pennsylvania at Valley Forge. I never got to meet or speak with him. So I have no idea what happened, or even if they ever went to a doctor."

"Your petition says you were born in Newport, Rhode Island and had family there. Why didn't you go to live with your family?"

"If Solomon were to return, Sir, the first place he would come to would be home to Boston. I wanted to be there when – if – he returned. Then my parents died when Newport was invaded by the British."

The judge sat back in his chair, scribbled something on Bull's petition. "I'm granting the petition, Counselor Bull. I just marked it 'So Ordered.' Take it to the clerk and have him enter it appropriately." The judge looked at Miriam and as he struck his gavel said, "Mrs. Ennis, you are now a free woman. Good luck to you."

Three weeks later, at a sedate ceremony presided over by a local Justice of the Peace, Miriam Ennis nee Mendoza, married Angus Duff at a civil wedding held in one of Springfield's better taverns. Young James Ennis, eight years old and a bit bewildered at what was happening, was there. For the past few years, Angus Duff had treated the boy as if he was his son. James had never known his father and it was natural that Angus, who loved the boy, would be the logical substitute.

Angus was not a man to go to church, but when he did on Christmas or Easter, James accompanied him. Miriam always remained at home and never complained that her Jewish son went to church. She thought the fact that Angus treated him as a son and James accepted him as a father, was more important to keep a harmonious relationship in the family. Although Angus wanted to adopt the boy and give him the name of Duff, Miriam insisted that he remain Ennis. It would be his only connection to his Judaism and his biological father. But James Ennis knew little, if anything, of the Jewish religion or of his father, Solomon Henriques Ennis.

30

New Jersey
1812

The death notice in a New Jersey village's newspaper was only of local interest. It briefly detailed the life and death of a prominent Newark physician.

DECEASED: Dr. Alexander Witherspoon, *63, a leading resident of Newark, N.J., a graduate of William and Mary College and the College of the Pennsylvania School of Medicine. For many years Dr. Witherspoon was Newark's only physician. In 1776 and all during the Revolutionary War, Dr. Witherspoon treated soldiers of the Continental Army as they retreated from the Battle of Long Island to safety in Pennsylvania.*

Later in 1778, after the Battle of Monmouth, Dr. Witherspoon tended to both retreating British and Hessian troops and the pursuing Americans. It was well known that the doctor maintained a famous military cemetery on his property, containing American, Hessian and English soldiers.

Dr. Witherspoon was a member of the Presbyterian Church, acting as a board member for over 25 years. He was active in local affairs and charitable organizations.

He was related to New Jersey's signer of the Declaration of Independence, the Rev. James Witherspoon.

The citizens of Newark were aware that Dr. Witherspoon often treated the poor and needy without compensation.

The doctor is survived by his wife of 33 years, Heather Daley Witherspoon; a son, the Reverend Horace Witherspoon; a daughter Penelope Witherspoon White and five grandchildren.

Services will be held at the Presbyterian Church. Burial at the Military Cemetery on the Witherspoon property, according to the doctor's wishes.

It fell to The Reverend Horace Witherspoon to straighten out his father's affairs. He was the older child and Minister of the Presbyterian Church in nearby Elizabethtown. There was much work to do. The easiest task was to sell his father's medical equipment to the two other doctors who had lately struck roots in the growing town. Then he turned over personal medical records to his father's patients, most of whom he knew as a boy growing up in Newark. Finally, he had to tackle the most difficult problem: going through his father's personal papers and financial situation.

Aside from the careful maintenance of his medical practice, Alexander Witherspoon was not a man to keep his personal records in any kind of logical order. This meant rummaging through the three large oak cabinets in the doctor's office. One of them had always been off-limits to the family. That was the one behind his desk. It was never locked, yet everyone knew they were not to go into it. *Perhaps mother knew what it contained. If she did, she never let on*, Horace thought.

The cabinet was eight feet high and had three doors, starting from the top to the last one which was two feet off the ground. Standing on a wooden office chair, Horace opened the door to the top one first. There was a jumble of papers inside; they were in no special order and covered with deep accumulated layers of grey dust. It had obviously not been gone through for many years.

After removing the dust, some of which came out like hunks of plucked flannel, Horace began removing the contents. Much of what he found were letters received over many years from patients thanking him for the free or much-reduced fees he charged them for treatment. *Father didn't want us to know who they were.* Horace smiled at the thought. There were snippets of yellowed newspaper articles, none of which seemed important. He found a small book, which he dusted off. It contained names of several families the doctor had been regularly helping with loans, which appeared never to have been repaid. The names were familiar to Horace. After so many years, many of the patients named in the book had died. Of those remaining, there would be no pressing for payment.

Then he saw it: an age-browned envelope in a corner, buried beneath all the many papers. *It must have been one of the first things father squirreled away here,* Horace thought. He lifted it. It was soft, obviously a fabric inside. He dusted and then opened the envelope, removing its contents. It was a piece of fabric, with a legend stitched into it. He slid it out and as he unfolded it, some papers fell out. He stepped down from the chair, retrieved the papers and set them aside. He read what had been stitched into the fabric.

As a religious man, he was deeply moved by the sincerity of the stitched message. Then he opened the three pages that had fallen from its folds. Horace recognized his father's handwriting. The notes he was reading detailed the treatment of a 19-year-old soldier, Solomon Ennis. There was a complete narrative of the young soldier's life and that his last wish, after giving his clothes to his friend, was to be buried as a Jew, just as the stitching had requested. At the end of the narrative, Dr. Witherspoon wrote that he would comply with Ennis' wishes, but since there were no Jews in Newark, he would have to go to New York. As that city was now occupied by the British, he wrote, he would have to wait until the situation changed.

Horace knew Ennis had never been re-interred. As a child and an adolescent, before he left Newark to study at the seminary in Philadelphia, he often walked through his father's famous cemetery and he remembered that the name Ennis was on one of the grave markers, a weather-faded wooden tablet. He always wondered why of all the graves; this was the only one not bearing a cross. Now he understood.

He rose from the chair and walked to the back of the house. There it was, still there: the grave of Solomon Ennis. He was right; it had never been removed. The Reverend Horace Witherspoon made a decision on the spot. *I'll have to take care of this. It's a moral and religious duty to get his remains properly interred.*

The next night, after leaving Newark and before returning to his home in nearby Elizabethtown, Rev. Witherspoon knocked on the door of Samuel Cox, a friend and one of his parishioners. Cora Cox answered the door and called out to her husband, "Sam, Horace is here. Can I get you some tea, Horace?"

"Yes, thank you Cora."

Sam Cox entered his living room, buttoning the bottom two levels of his waist coat. Finished, he extended his hand. "Is there something wrong, Horace?" He was looking at the hall clock and noted that it was past seven p.m. on a gloomy Spring evening. "Please, sit down Horace."

"Sam, I just came to get some information. I know you deal in business with some Jews in New York City. What can you tell me about them?"

"What do you want to know?"

"Anything you can tell me."

"Well, they're a small, closely-knit group. They have a building where they worship, a synagogue they call it. It's on Mill Street. They're mostly good people, careful to carry on with their religion. There are some rascals among them, I must say. Same as any other group. Some of the families are descended from people who suffered greatly under the Spanish and Portuguese Inquisitions."

Horace then showed Sam Cox the stitching and his father's notes. After Sam read them, the Minister said, "Ennis is still buried in my father's cemetery. Do you know if the Jews in New York have a cemetery?"

"I don't know. I've often heard them say that when one of them dies, they must be buried quickly, within a day or two and only in their own cemeteries."

"Do you think you can make contact for me with one of your Jewish friends, so we can arrange for a proper Jewish burial for that soldier?"

"Yes, I believe I can try, and I'll go with you when you're ready. You're right, Horace, it's a religious duty we owe to this soldier, who fought and died for his country."

"Do you think they'll take Private Ennis' body? I want to carry out the wishes of this young man... .and my father."

৯০ ৵৵

Mr. Henry Fisher had been born in Frankfort, Germany. He had been known in his native country as Heinrich Fischler and there was no denying his Teutonic accent. After he became an American citizen, he wished to be known as Henry Fisher. He was a middle-aged man with light brown hair that was thinning. He greeted his two visitors with a friendly smile but was puzzled to meet Sam's friend, who was introduced as the Reverend Horace Witherspoon. Why had Sam Cox come to his shop with a Christian minister?

"Good to see you, Sam," Fisher said. "You came before I expected you. I have some wonderful silk shawls from Spain and some good shoes from Italy, too. I know they'll interest you."

"I'm not here on business, Henry, though I'll have a look at your merchandise later. My friend and Pastor, Reverend Witherspoon, has a story to tell you and I thought you might be able to help him."

Fisher's business was carried out in a large building, a combination warehouse and office. The three men were sitting in the office. Fisher swung around in his wooden swivel chair and thrust his legs beneath his desk. He folded his arms across his chest and asked his visitors if they wanted some coffee. Sam and Horace nodded their heads: it was an opportunity to make this visit less formal than it might have been. After an employee passed coffee all around, Horace related the story of Solomon Ennis. He showed Fisher the stitching and Dr. Witherspoon's three-page narrative.

"This young patriot is now buried in the field in back of my father's house. As you can see from reading my father's notes, he intended to comply with Solomon's wishes. He never got around to it. It's time to fulfill that request."

"Yes, yes, I see, and I agree. You have to understand, Reverend, that in our religion, a non-Jew cannot be buried in a Jewish cemetery."

"What does that mean, Mr. Fisher?"

Fisher paused for a while, reached inside an open desk drawer, and pulled out three cigars, offering two to his guests. Only Sam Cox took up the offer. It was obvious that Fisher was looking for the right words. He remained silent as he lit his cigar and, tilting his head upward, he watched the first puffs of blue smoke rise above his head. Satisfied that he finally had the right words, he explained.

"Well, I'm not a rabbi, you understand, Reverend, and it's a little complicated, but I'm sure the person in charge of any Jewish cemetery must be satisfied that a person to be buried there is really

Jewish. Under our religious law, that means that the religion of a child comes from its mother; that the child has a Jewish mother. You see, that's where the Jewishness comes from, the mother.

"You have a good start with this," he continued, picking up the stitching and holding it out. "And the circumcision helps, too. I think whoever is in charge with the burials is still going to want to be satisfied that this young man had a Jewish mother."

"So, where do we start, Mr. Fisher?" Horace asked.

"With our *Hazzan*. That's the Hebrew word for Cantor. Which is where I'll take you now." Fisher rose from his chair, reached for his hat that was hanging on a wall peg and drained the last of his coffee in a few quick movements. After shouting to someone at the back of the warehouse that he would be gone for a short while, he gestured to his guests with a hand towards the door, that they all would be leaving.

"This problem is one that we can work on together, to satisfy a religious duty," Fisher advised his two visitors as they stepped into a busy Manhattan Street.

ᔕ ᔐ

New York City's Jewish community was small, but vigorous. It was composed mainly of shop keepers, a few national and international traders, landowners, and some physicians, but it had yet to muster the wherewithal to hire the services of an ordained Rabbi. New York's Spanish and Portuguese Jews were proud to be known as descendants of the first Jewish community in North America, tracing its beginnings to 1654, when 23 of them found their way to Dutch New Amsterdam after being ousted from the Dutch colony of Recife by the Portuguese. On their way to Holland, they were captured by Spanish pirates, then rescued by a Frenchman, whose ship made for New Amsterdam, where the Jews were landed.

Jews from Germany, Poland and England followed them over time, making up the majority of the congregation. Today, Witherspoon and Cox would be taken to meet with Benjamin Pinto, who acted as the community's religious leader. He was the *Hazzan* and assumed many of the roles of a rabbi, which he was not. To meet with Pinto, the three men walked the few blocks to Mill Street, where the Jews had their synagogue. The building was surrounded by a gleaming white picket fence. Fisher opened the gate, and they entered the yard leading to the synagogue's entrance. Since Pinto was not a rabbi, the congregation and others in New York's Gentile community addressed him with the respectful title of Reverend.

On Friday, the men found Pinto preparing for the evening Sabbath services, which would begin at sundown. Fisher asked the *hazzan* to excuse the interruption: he introduced the men to Pinto, explaining that they were on a mission to fulfill a *mitzvah*, a Jewish religious duty or good deed, even though they were not Jews.

"I'm sorry I can't offer you gentlemen coffee or tea, but I am alone today and not very handy in the kitchen," Pinto said.

Horace looked around the building to take in the surroundings. He had never been in a synagogue before. It was small and neat. The interior was lined with wood. Wooden benches were stretched out along the walls, facing the center of the room where a reader's platform, also constructed of wood, was located. It had a reading stand and seats behind the stand for half a dozen persons. Facing the Cantor, about 30 feet away, was a wall with an ark and two doors built into it. Above the ark were Hebrew letters and an oil lamp was burning.

Pinto, noticing Horace's curiosity, said, "You have not been to a synagogue before, Reverend Witherspoon?"

"No, I'm afraid not. This is my first time."

"We also call it an Esnoga, a Ladino term. It is the language we brought with us from Spain. It's peculiar to us Sephardic Jews. The ark faces east, toward Jerusalem," Pinto had long experience working with the Christian community and felt comfortable with non-Jews. He could see Horace was sympathetic to Jews. Else why would he come here on a mission to fulfill a Jewish wish?

"Might I bring my congregation here to see this?" Horace asked.

"Of course. Now, what can I do to help you?"

Horace showed Pinto the stitching and the narrative his father had prepared. He explained that he wanted to carry out his father's wishes. He said it was right that this young man who died for his country, should be buried according to his wishes.

Pinto agreed. He read the narrative again, this time very carefully and then he asked, "Reverend Witherspoon, do we know who his mother was?"

"I'm afraid not."

"I have to resolve that issue before I can authorize a burial. Sometimes we have children of a marriage of a Jewish father to a Christian mother. The young ones are raised as Jews, attend services, observe all the Jewish laws, including circumcision for the boys but, unfortunately for them, according to our law they cannot be considered Jews. Only if their mothers are of our faith, or they undergo conversion. These are people who love our religion and are faithful to our precepts but, unfortunately, unless they convert, they cannot be buried in a Jewish cemetery. In fact, we maintain a separate burial ground for them."

"I don't understand. But that's not the issue. What can be done here?"

"The situation is not hopeless. Your father writes the man's original family name was Henriques and that he was born in London. I can write to the Spanish and Portuguese Synagogue there and try to determine his background. I have no doubt this man is legally Jewish according to our *halacha*, that's our Jewish law. My feelings, however, mean little in face of facts. I'll get on it right away."

Ȿ Ȿ

The Reverend Benjamin Pinto wrote a long letter to the rabbi of the Spanish and Portuguese Synagogue at Bevis Marks, London. He had correctly assumed that the Henriques family were members of this congregation, which also had as its founding members Jews of Spanish and Portuguese origin.

In his letter, he attached a copy of Dr. Witherspoon's narrative and the wishes that appeared on the fabric stitched into Private Ennis' shirt by his wife Miriam. He requested such information as would allow him to bury Private Ennis, who was unknown to the Jews of New York.

Pinto arranged for his letter to leave on the next ship bound for London. That would be on June 16th. On June 18th, the naval war known as the War of 1812 between the United States and Great Britain, was officially declared. The ship carrying the letter was seized by the British Navy since it was bound for England flying the American flag. Letters and non-military cargo the ship was carrying, were released after a while. However, after much bureaucratic fussing and handling, it would take almost a year to reach its addressee in London.

31

New York City
1815

The *Mazatlan*, a three-masted vessel of Spanish registry and a neutral ship, dropped anchor in New York Harbor. She was carrying among her cargo a letter from London addressed to the Reverend Benjamin Pinto. It was a response to his inquiry about Solomon Ennis, a/k/a Henriques. Pinto's letter to London and its answer took almost three years due to the hostilities between the United States and Great Britain. Pinto eagerly opened the letter.

"Yes," wrote the rabbi, Jeshurun Carasso Millan, of London's Bevis Marks synagogue, verifying that the Henriques family was still members and were sad to receive the news of Solomon's death.

> *"A brother, Aaron, his wife and children and Aaron's 85-year-old mother Rebecca, who has recently deceased, have been active members of our congregation. The brother was sad to hear of Solomon's death as the many letters and inquiries they had sent to Boston over the years were never answered. The family has arranged for a memorial plaque to be placed on one of the synagogue's walls, after learning of his death.*
>
> *"Our synagogue records verified that Solomon was the son of David Henriques, who died in 1809, and his mother verified, just before she died, that her son was a Bar Mitzvah at the synagogue. Congregational records verified the rite. And indeed, his mother, of blessed memory, was not only Jewish, but because of her age, one of our most venerable members at Bevis Marks. Records*

further revealed that Solomon left the congregation for Rhode Island colony in 1774 and that he was no longer required to engage in synagogue activities such as holding office, carrying the Torah on certain Jewish holidays and other solemn religious duties.

"I pray that this answers your enquiry and wish you and your congregation well."

Reverend Pinto sighed with a satisfied smile. At last, after all these years, his guess about Solomon Ennis had proven correct. Now he would go to his synagogue's Board of Directors to request the burial of a non-member who was nevertheless a patriot who died in the service of his country and lacked any family to tend to his body. Pinto did not expect any controversy.

He opened his desk drawer, pulled out a sheet of cream-colored writing paper, dipped a pen into an inkpot and wrote a note to the Reverend Horace Witherspoon at Elizabethtown, New Jersey.

During the long delay, Witherspoon had regularly inquired about any response from London, even to making personal visits to Mill Street. He even brought some of his congregants with him to see the synagogue. Over the years, the two Reverends had become good friends.

Now, Witherspoon received the good news. He read Benjamin Pinto's letter again, giving it to Samuel Cox, who was also elated.

"Dear Horace,

After a long delay due to the War between our country and England, we have finally received an answer in the matter of our Solomon Ennis. His mother was Jewish and his proper burial may proceed. All that lacks at present is the Board's approval for a non-member's burial.

I shall be in further touch with you. Please make the necessary arrangements for the remains to be brought to New York City.

I look forward to seeing you again.

Yrs, etc., Benj. Pinto, Hazzan,

Cong. Kahal Kadosh, Shearith Israel.

Horace Witherspoon quickly arranged to disinter Solomon Ennis' remains. Since he was not buried in a coffin, but in sailcloth, new lengths of three stiffened sail cloths were used to wrap the remains of the dead hero for transfer. Witherspoon personally arranged and paid for the casket, which the Reverend Pinto advised him should be "a plain pine box."

Reverend Witherspoon was learning more about the Jews. A plain pine box, indeed. Sam Cox arranged and paid for a carter to bring the body to New York, where Benjamin Pinto received it, gathering the ten members of his congregation necessary to properly recite the prayer for the dead, pursuant to Jewish law. The group of ten men was called a *minyan* in Hebrew. The men were eager to participate when they learned Ennis had died defending his retreating comrades at the battle of Harlem Heights, just a few miles north of where the burial grounds lay.

As Pinto knew they would, the synagogue's directors unanimously agreed to arrange for a plot and burial in their cemetery. Pinto advised Witherspoon and Cox of the date and invited them to be present.

The funeral party left for the cemetery at Chatham Square. Although it was once a rural outskirt of New York City, Witherspoon could see it was no longer so. It was becoming a part of the commercial and residential section of a city rapidly expanding to the north.

Prayers were said over the body on a dreary day, while a misty drizzle fell. Tiny individual and dewy crystals settled along the shoulders and hats of the men. The last request of Solomon Ennis and his wife, Miriam, were finally carried out after almost 40 years.

The two men from New Jersey stood by respectfully as they watched the burial ceremony, taking pleasure in knowing they helped make the young man's wishes come true. They had participated in the making of what the Jews called a *mitzvah.*

Cantor Pinto recited the prayers in Hebrew. The ten men from the synagogue joined in the prayers. When they concluded, two grave diggers gently placed Solomon Ennis' coffin, smelling of freshly sawn wood, into a grave they had prepared earlier that day. Then they shoveled the dark, moist earth back to where they had recently removed it. When they finished, a curved mound of fresh earth remained where an open grave once stood.

The Board of Directors had also agreed to pay for and place a tombstone at the site. That would come in a year, in a ceremony known as an unveiling. It would bear the name Solomon Henriques Ennis, Hero of the American Revolution, with the dates of his birth and death and that he was born in London, England and died at the battle of Harlem Heights.

Witherspoon and Cox shook Reverend Pinto's hand, thanking him for making a Jewish burial for Solomon Ennis. Then they shook hands with each of the ten congregants, thanking them for their participation in the burial service. Witherspoon noted that one of the congregants placed a small American flag into the soft earth of the burial site.

As they left the cemetery, the Reverend Pinto said, "Don't forget, Horace. I expect you and more of your congregants at Shearith Israel so they may see our synagogue."

❧ ☙

On a bright and cold December day in 1823, Angus Duff suffered a heart attack on the floor of his cutting room. He fell with a thud, frightening the workers nearest him. Two of his workers lifted him and carried him, unconscious, to his office. They placed him on the chaise lounge he often had used to take afternoon naps during his long working day.

He never awoke. He died within the hour, minutes before a doctor could tend to him. Both he and James, by working hard, had seen their business grow during the past 25 years. Angus Duff and Co. was now regularly making uniforms for all of America's services: Army, Navy, Marines and Coast Guard. The company would also fashion, if you could afford it, a fine made-to-order set of clothes for men. Bespoke, they called it: trousers, shirts, jackets, and elegant women's clothes too, including elaborate one-of-a-kind evening gowns.

Miriam Mendoza Duff would die three years later, leaving instructions with the local Jewish community she was to be buried as a Jewess. Many years before her death, she had been quietly visiting the community as regularly as she could, careful not to allow her religion to create an imbalance in her family.

When she first began visiting Springfield's small and informal community, Miriam was greeted with great respect. She was well known as one of the affluent members of the city. Surprised and delighted, members of the Jewish community were pleased to admit her into their small, struggling family, which had neither synagogue nor rabbi. Miriam was quiet. Without special notice, she began helping the community with its dozen or so families. She had a leaky roof fixed, ordered prayer books and materials for the children's religious school, supplied food and drink for communal events, even bringing rabbis to Springfield on holy days. She was an essential part of the congregation's activities and had more than satisfied the congregation that she was a Jewess, as they had neither rabbi nor cantor to say otherwise

"I am leaving instructions for my burial," she advised the congregation's leader, Isaac Levy, whom she and Angus had known well from their business dealings. "Make sure it is done according to our customs," she emphasized.

"Of course, Miriam," he assured her. "Is there anything else?"

"Yes, Isaac. I am leaving a sum of money to the congregation. Mr. Ashworth, our attorney, will notify you as to the amount after my death. The only proviso I make is that it be used to strengthen this congregation's dedication to our religion. I would like to see you purchase a permanent home."

"Of course. I will advise the Board of your wishes. They will try to carry them out."

Miriam told Angus what she had done about her funeral arrangements. She drew a promise from him that he would not interfere. He knew she had been attending prayer services, that could never be a secret, but it was never discussed. It was of no matter, however, to the irreligious Scotsman who, in any case, died before Miriam.

While lingering on her sickbed during the days before she died, she finally spoke to her son James concerning the story of his biological father, Solomon Henriques Ennis.

"Your father and I are both Jews. My family came to Newport from Amsterdam. Your father came to America from London. His family, as mine, originally came from Spain and Portugal. Your father joined the Sons of Liberty in Newport, which preached separation from England.

"Your father changed his name from Henriques to Ennis because the English were looking to arrest him. He went off to war in 1776, just after you were born. I never heard from him after he left. I believe he was killed in the Battle of Long Island, but I don't really know. You were named James according to your father's wishes, after his grandfather, your great-grandfather Jaime Henriques. Your father held you in his arms, kissed you and loved you for only a short time before he went off to war. He had great pleasure knowing that he had a son.

"When I met Angus Duff, he was, anxious to be good to us. He has always treated you as if you were his own son and you have accepted that love. He truly loved me. I could not ask for a better man to care for us.

"You have received no Jewish education, as I felt it would interfere with our new family situation. You are now married, with a young son and a daughter. What you do with them is up to you. I would hope you might raise them as Jews. But since I gave you no Jewish education, I doubt you could easily do that. But you might try."

Upon Miriam's death, Isaac Levy explained to James that "according to Jewish custom, James, she must be buried as soon as possible, and in a simple pine box."

"I know, Isaac. You do what has to be done. She was a good woman and I want her wishes to be carried out."

Many of the city's citizens failed to attend Miriam's funeral service. It was not for lack of respect; it was because her interment outside of the city occurred so swiftly after her death, they were unaware of the funeral. Christian Springfield was used to viewing a deceased in his or her open casket, surrounded by flowers and weeping mourners, with a burial perhaps as long as a week after demise.

Isaac Levy performed the service, attended by close friends who knew Miriam was dying and were in daily contact with the Duff family. Every woman in the congregation stood beside her casket, weeping for a lost sister and friend. Many men of the congregation were also in attendance. Later, James received sincere regrets on Miriam's death from Springfield's Christian citizens who expressed sorrow they did not attend the ceremony.

Since there was no Jewish cemetery in Springfield, Miriam's body was sent to Newport, the city of her birth.

The lawyer, Mortimer Ashworth, told Isaac Levy of the financial arrangements that Miriam had made for the congregation. The sum was much larger than Levy had ever anticipated. The congregation decided to do two things to remember Miriam. They ordered a large tombstone inscribed in English, Hebrew and Portuguese. The other act to perpetuate her memory was to establish a religious school in her name, with the intention to further the Jewish education of children and adults.

Over the years, the endowment grew with other gifts but as the congregation enlarged, few people were old enough to remember her. Miriam's tombstone in Newport stood tall in a corner of the graveyard, with the odd, un-Jewish name of Miriam Mendoza Duff, written in three languages, one of which was Portuguese, which no one could read or translate.

James didn't know how to even begin raising his children as Jews. Upon Miriam's death, he became sole owner of Angus Duff and Co., inheriting the entire business interests of his mother and the earlier deceased Angus. For some time, he had been living an affluent life with his wife and children. Now he had become elevated to one of Springfield's leading manufacturers and the sole employer of many of its citizens.

He would tell his children about the family history. As far as religion was concerned, he gave little thought to it. Angus Duff had raised him without religion. Better to leave it that way. Besides, how would the people of Springfield take to one of their leading citizens suddenly announcing that he was a Jew? That part he would leave out when he related to his children the tale of the Henriques family's migration to America and its hero ancestor.

He did recall, however, that Miriam Duff was buried in a Jewish cemetery and went once to Newport to see it. Once only.

As generations passed, even the tale of ancestor Solomon Ennis, the Revolutionary War hero, became hazy. It also separated from the story of the Henriques immigrant.

32

San Francisco, California
1851

Carlos Henriques, the son who stayed behind after the Great Lisbon Earthquake of 1755, never made it to Amsterdam. Instead, he remained in Lisbon, prospering as the city was rebuilding. When his father Jaime left Portugal, he had given Carlos 36 pieces of expensive jewelry. It was a small fortune in earthquake-ravaged Lisbon and with those assets, Carlos opened a trading enterprise, calling it The Thirty-Six Company.

Traditionally, England and Portugal had developed strong trade treaties since the 14th Century, so Carlos could easily import English goods for the Portuguese, who were now hungrily replacing what they had lost in the earthquake. The Thirty-Six Company was a great success, and the now affluent family was regularly making business trips to London.

Yet in Lisbon, the connotation of 'New Christian' never left them. The family secretly practiced Judaism as had their ancestors, but they slowly lost the memory of the Jewish ancestry to the cloudy past. In the early 1800s, because of their strong connection with England, every member of the Henriques family was fluent in English, was a non-attending member of the Catholic Church, and had only wispy and hazy reminders that their family had at one time been Jewish. Their continuing attachment to the still crypto-Jewish Pereira family was forever that reminder. The Henriques family, aware of the Inquisition's past examinations into the lives of New Christians, was careful to give them no cause for any charges of heresy.

Almost 100 years after the Lisbon earthquake, another Carlos Henriques, the great-great-grandson of Jaime, learned that gold had been discovered in America; in a place called Northern California. On his business trips to London, he saw that suppliers of mining materials were busy filling orders for the Californians' equipment. And he heard merchants complain that they were running out of stock. He decided he would go to America with a load of cargo, to see what opportunities were available. The worst that might happen was that he would sell his stock and make a handsome profit. If he wasn't happy in America, he could always return to Lisbon, his pockets filled with American gold.

The year was 1851 and after a tiresome nine-month voyage by land and sea, Carlos came ashore in San Francisco. He was now calling himself Charles and already had decided he had no intention of soiling himself by mining for gold. At 26, Charles was darkly handsome, with hazel eyes and a smile that told you he was trustworthy. He was elegant, always careful to ensure his hair was properly styled; he dressed in a long pearl-grey frock coat and wore a tall, dark opera hat. He spoke excellent and cultured English, which caused people on their first meeting to believe he was an Englishman.

Carlos stood out among the scruffy miners and most merchants. He was recognized as a person to always be addressed as Sir. Immediately, the astute young man could see that San Francisco was not like Lisbon. This was a big, booming city, free of Lisbon's stolid and stuffy social order. A man could come here from anywhere, penniless and lacking education, and yet with hard work, rise to the heights of social and financial importance. Your ancestor's blood line counted for little in San Francisco. What propelled you to the top was your success in accumulating large sums of money. No one in San Francisco ever asked anyone for a *Certificado de Limpieza de Sangre*.

Charles Henriques quickly assessed the financial situation in this growing city and knew he had made the right decision when he was 6,000 miles away in Lisbon. There was little to be earned in the actual mining for gold. Only a few fortunate men hit it big. The larger lodes had been depleted long before his arrival or were under the tight control of the up-and-coming millionaires. The rest of the miners worked punishing hours at hard labor, hoping to pull out small amounts of gold from the ground. This allowed them to break even or, considering the money they had put into purchasing equipment and the long hours spent digging and panning along the mountain mill races, do only somewhat better.

Money in San Francisco was to be made by supplying the miners with what they needed in the camps. Charles had brought with him a large cargo of work clothes, picks, axes, shovels, boots, tents, and mining lamps. He immediately rented commercial space beneath a tent in an outdoor market in the section of the city known as the Barbary Coast. Within three days, needy miners, like crows in a corn field, had plucked him clean, buying everything he had put out for sale, including the three wooden crates the cargo was shipped in.

The buyer of the first crate told Charles, "I'm gonna convert this here crate into my home. Cheap and decent rooms are hard to find along the Barbary Coast, Mr. Henriques."

Charles took the cue. He would no longer sell the empty crates. Instead, he fixed them up, found an empty lot, and rented them out. Soon, he was partnering with a real estate broker, building houses, the apartments of which were rented out to San Franciscans hungry for a private and comfortable place to retire to at the end of a busy day.

Charles used his profits to purchase more goods, build more homes and establish an office in a hastily erected wooden building. He began making small and carefully placed loans to men trying to establish themselves in the city, which was growing fast. He was determined to grow with San Francisco.

As loans were paid off, the interest was plowed back into the business. Charles was now bringing in a line of fine clothing for himself and others of affluence. In this raw young city with muddy streets, where tents served as shops, hotels, and churches, he stood out among the city's citizens and was regularly called upon to provide mining equipment, housing, and business loans.

Other men also understood what Charles had foreseen about San Francisco: that it would soon become a great city. They established banks, shops, office buildings, an opera house and built grand homes. Charles naturally fit in with this visionary group. They were mostly Americans from the East Coast and the Midwest, although here were also Frenchmen, Chinese and Englishmen. Australians who watched their gold strike peter out, moved on to California with great hopes of attaining success there. Germans and Central Europeans came too, some of whom were Jewish.

Charles had heard about Jews but had never met any, other than if you counted the New Christians of Lisbon to which the Henriques family belonged – as did their cousins the Pereiras. He regularly found himself dealing with the Jews of San Francisco. They were an odd bunch. Someone told him that they were fussy about what they ate and some among them refused to work on Saturdays. What that meant, he was not too sure. If they didn't work on Saturday, yet were successful, then perhaps they were a group to be carefully watched and maybe even emulated.

The younger generation of Jews was more open, and it was with them that Charles began to cultivate friendships in business and socially. One man, Wilhelm Steglitz, who took to calling himself William, or Bill to his friends, was the youngest son of a family that came from Austria and was involved in shipping. Charles had often used them to transport his goods to San Francisco.

One day, Bill invited Charles to his home, where a string quartet was performing a concert of classical music. Many of the invitees were people Charles dealt with in his businesses. It was a cultural event. Evenings such as these were occurring more often in San Francisco, and the Jews were always among the leading sponsors and participants in these events.

Bill greeted Charles and introduced him to his family. It was here that Charles met Bill's sister, the lovely Marthe Steiglitz. He was at once struck by her beauty and grace. With her coal-black eyes and auburn hair that flowed down below her shoulders and across her milky white skin, he deemed her to be perfect. During the recital, he could not take his eyes off her. He vowed to meet her again and spend time with her. Indeed, that night he determined to make her his wife.

As the guests left, Charles pulled his friend aside. "Bill," he said, "I would like to see your sister again. What can you arrange for me?"

Bill paused and said, "I don't know, Charles."

"What do you mean? What's the problem?"

"You're not Jewish, that's the problem. You're a Christian, Charles. My parents would discourage any friendship between you and Marthe."

"That's silly. I'm not a Christian. I don't go to or belong to any church."

"Were you ever baptized?"

"Yes, of course I was. Everyone in Lisbon gets baptized. I hardly ever set foot in a church, and when I did it was to attend something a friend was celebrating."

"Well, I'll try. But don't expect me to be successful."

That night, Charles could not sleep. He was thinking of Marthe, her face firmly etched in his mind. He was unable to accept that a matter of religion could keep them apart. He never thought much about religion. It was never an important part of his life, or that of his family. Then he sat up, remembering: He was what they called in Lisbon a New Christian. He had heard that term often. His father told him that at one time, a hundred years earlier, the Henriques family had secretly been Jews although they no longer practiced that religion.

Charles created a scenario in his mind. He would tell Bill that he was Jewish; that his family had not practiced the religion for a long time. That would resolve the problem. Everyone would be happy. He was pleased he had worked out a solution and couldn't wait until the next time he saw his friend to tell him this. And as he finally settled into a satisfied slumber, he also created a fantasy where he met with Marthe and she said, "Charles, I'm so happy there are no barriers between us. I know father will be pleased to have you as a son-in-law."

But that was only a fantasy he had created, a dream of how he wanted it to be, not as it really was.

"Bill, my family were Jews decades ago. That should satisfy your family."

"Are you making this up, Charles?"

"No. My father told me we used to be Jews."

"Give me time to work this out. Can you prove it?"

"What kind of proof do you need? But it's true. Portugal is filled with families like mine. It's an historical fact."

The Jewish community of San Francisco had a rabbi, Dr. Emile Gotfeldt, a learned Hungarian who had studied to become a rabbi at the Jewish Seminary in Berlin. Bill Steiglitz made an appointment to see him.

"Rabbi, I have a friend who says his family was once Jewish. He wants to become friendly with my sister. I don't know what to do."

"Where is he from, Wilhelm?" the rabbi asked, in his strong German accent.

"Lisbon, Portugal."

"Ah, yes. It could be. Many Portuguese Jews were forced to convert, centuries ago. Many continued praying in secret. Some of them, when caught, paid with their lives. Does he practice our religion?"

"No, Rabbi. He told me what you said of the Jews of Lisbon. I didn't believe it. I thought he was making it up so that he could see Marthe."

"Perhaps you should have our friend see me. Do your parents know about this?"

"No."

"Then tell them of the problem. I can't do anything without their permission."

The Steiglitz family was not pleased with Charles Henriques' attentions toward their daughter. They did, however, assent to Rabbi Gotfeldt's probing the situation.

In a dark study filled with Jewish ritual objects he had never seen before, Charles sat before the rabbi. He felt like a butterfly pinned to a table, awaiting dissection.

"You are not Jewish, Mr. Henriques?"

"No, I am not. My father told me that generations ago we were Jewish, but we were forced to change our religion."

"I see. Unfortunately, that does not make you a Jew, unless you can prove your mother was Jewish."

"She may have been, I can't be sure. What's so important about being a Jew?"

"The Steiglitz family takes the position that their daughter cannot marry outside of their religion. So for them, it is important. To be a Jew you must have descended from a Jewish mother. That is our law."

"How does Marthe feel about this?"

"She has to follow her parent's wishes. She will only marry within the faith."

"Suppose I become a Jew?"

"That would help. But I cannot convert you just because you want to marry Marthe. I can only convert you because you are sincere about wanting to follow the tenets of our religion."

"But I know nothing of the religion."

"Then you must learn about it to decide if you are sincere in your wish to convert."

"How long will this take?"

"A year, perhaps more. And then, only if you are sincere about converting can the process begin."

"I don't think I can wait that long, sir."

Several months later, Charles Henriques and Marthe Steiglitz eloped. Her family refused to accept the marriage and disowned her. "She cannot come into this house ever again," Marthe's father shouted. Then, in an irretrievable and dramatic act, which sealed him off from his daughter and her children, he tore a portion of his clothes, the traditional act of mourning for the Jewish dead.

William, the brother who had introduced them, was the only member of the family to maintain contact with Marthe. Eventually, she and Charles had two children, Charles Jr. and William. The boys, who were born of a Jewish mother, were Jews. Marthe insured their religious upbringing, careful to join a different synagogue than the one her parents attended. Charles Jr. would go into the ever-growing business with his father and William studied to become a physician. After graduating in 1898, William volunteered his services during the Spanish American War. He was assigned to combat duty, attending the wounded at the battle for control of San Juan Hill, in Cuba. He caught the attention of Colonel Theodore Roosevelt.

One evening after the battle had ended, his officers, known as the Rough Riders, were sitting around enjoying a quiet time; playing cards, having a smoke, and drinking. Roosevelt asked William what he planned to do when he returned to civilian life.

"I'm returning to San Francisco, Colonel, to practice medicine."

"I've had my eye on you since San Juan Hill. You were very cool under fire. I liked that about you. You might think about coming East and practicing medicine in New York. I can help you get started. Think about it; there are great opportunities in New York for a young man like you. And I know many people who can help you."

William returned to San Francisco and discussed Theodore Roosevelt's offer with his parents. "The Roosevelts stand high in New York society. The Colonel says he can help me. I know it will be good for my career, so I've decided to go to New York."

William became an attendee at some of the Roosevelt events. At one of the home gatherings in Oyster Bay, he met Patricia Reynolds, a distant Roosevelt cousin. After a year-long courtship, they married. Teddy Roosevelt, now president of the United States, arranged for William to become a lecturer at Columbia University's medical school.

William's only daughter Martha was ignorant of her father's religious origins. He had become a close associate of the President, advising him on medical matters. He went on to become a leading and internationally recognized specialist in traumatic injuries and taught the subject at Columbia.

During their lifetimes, neither Charles Henriques Jr. of San Francisco nor Dr. William Henriques of New York had ever met or knew anything about any member of the Ennis family. William's granddaughter, Dorothy, would learn of her Jewish background while going through family letters she had found in an old trunk. She returned to Judaism after moving to Omaha, Nebraska, where she taught psychology at the University of Nebraska.

33

Charleston, South Carolina
December 8, 1861

Gerard Simon Henriques pushed his desk drawer shut and let out a sigh of frustration, as he sat back in his chair. Henriques, at 52 but looking much younger, was the elected chairman of Charleston's Third Regiment, the Light Dragoons, an elite volunteer military group led by the upper-class and flamboyant lawyer, Henry le Duc. The officers of the Dragoons consisted of the affluent members of Charleston's society. It was even open to prominent Israelites, such as Gerard. They mostly engaged in showy Sunday and holiday military exercises.

Henriques, who was also a Lt. Colonel in the Light Dragoons, had been charged with procuring proper uniforms for the part-time amateur warriors. Engaging in battle atop prancing steeds requires the kind of gorgeous uniform distinguishing officers from the prosaic foot soldier below. Angus Duff and Co., of Springfield, Massachusetts, had been recommended as the manufacturers of finely tailored uniforms. Duff had an excellent reputation, having supplied the U.S. government with uniforms since the Revolutionary War.

Willard Ennis, the company's president, was vacationing in the south. Before he left his home in Springfield, Willard decided to drop in on Henriques himself, instead of sending one of his sales representatives, known as a drummer. What called his attention to the letter of inquiry about uniform pricing, was that it was signed by an Henriques, a name Willards's late father, James, had told him was historically connected with the Ennis family.

"Gordon," Gerard Henriques called out to an office employee, "I'm expecting a gentleman in about half an hour. Run down to Maria's Restaurant and have the chef prepare two fish dishes for lunch. And not to forget the good French wine I like."

"Yes, sir," Gordon said as he left on his errand.

Arriving a few minutes earlier than expected, Ennis was led into the Henriques office by a secretary. The two men introduced themselves, exchanged business cards and shook hands. It was all very proper and even though it was a cool December day, the office was a bit stuffy, which Henriques noticed. He opened his shuttered window and welcomed a cool breeze into the room. Ennis took the time to notice the excellent furnishings and fine paintings on the wall; this office belonged to a person who was affluent. Willard could always tell much by what people put on their walls for others to see.

After discussing the uniforms and their prices, Henriques said, with sadness in his voice, "Since I first made inquiries of your company, the situation in this state has turned grave. We may soon be involved in a war, Mr. Ennis. The citizens of South Carolina are close to seceding from the Union, together with our sister states of Louisiana and Mississippi. That may require us to negate any contract we agree to with your company."

"Are you South Carolinians that serious about your position, that you would leave the Union?"

"I'm afraid so, sir. At this very moment there are over a thousand men in this town who are ready to take Fort Sumter by force. It's at the entrance to Charleston's harbor. You can see the Fort from the Battery, at the end of town. Very strategic it is, Mr. Ennis."

"Well then," Ennis said, "I suppose it would be useless to make uniforms for your Dragoons. I'm making uniforms for the United States government, and you are looking to secede from it. I certainly pray we are not in a war. That's unimaginable to me; Americans killing each other."

"I agree. But please be my guest for lunch, Mr. Ennis. I've arranged for some excellent local fish and a good French wine."

"Sounds fine. You might be wondering why I, the owner of the company, came to see you instead of sending one of my salesmen."

"As a matter of fact, I did, sir."

"Well, according to family tradition, our family name was originally Henriques. How it came to be Ennis no one knows for sure. I thought I might get some insight from you. We might even be related; Henriques is not a common family name in the United States."

Over lunch, Gerard Henriques explained that his family came to Charleston from the island of Barbados in the early 1800s. "My grandfather Jacob, everyone called him Jack, ran a sugar plantation for one of my grandmother's brothers, who lived in England. Grandmother was a Rivera. The family changed their name to Rivers; more Anglo, you know. The plantation was put up for security for a debt her brother owed and couldn't pay, so he lost the plantation and with it went grandfather's position."

Gerard took a small sip of wine. Noticing that Willard's glass was empty, he filled it up, continuing with his story.

"My grandparents originally went to Barbados from London, where they were both born. Before that, the family were Dutch and, of course, Portuguese. When the plantation was lost, they came to Charleston, where they had some relatives. Many Spanish and Portuguese Jews had already settled in Savannah, Charleston, and New Orleans. We have all the information documented in letters, birth and death certificates."

"So, your family came from Portugal before Holland?" Willard emphasized.

"The Henriques family originated in Spain and then went on to Portugal. Like our family, some of us settled in the South: Charleston, Savannah, and New Orleans. Today we are all over."

"I had no idea. My father told me we came from London and before that, Amsterdam."

"That sounds right. Usually, when they left Portugal and Spain they went first to Holland, and then some went to England. How did you come by the name, Ennis?"

"No one in the family really knows. But an Ennis fought in the Revolutionary War and was a hero. But I haven't been able to verify anything else."

"Good for him! We could use someone like him in Charleston. You are Jewish, of course. Most Henriques are."

"No, we are not."

"Sounds as if your ancestors might have wanted to bury their past."

"I've thought of that, too, but Solomon Ennis became a soldier in the Revolutionary War and was killed in combat. Doesn't sound like the kind of man who would want to hide his past."

"No, you're right. "I'm going to give this information to my father; maybe he can help you."

"I must leave to return to Springfield tonight. Should you have any information for me, write to my office in Springfield. I would appreciate any information you might dig up."

That evening, while visiting his parents, Gerard Henriques related his luncheon conversation to his father, Armand.

"Gerard, there is a family bible that I have been told about," Armand explained. "The family that remained in Amsterdam owns it. It traces our family all the way back to Spain, through Portugal and Amsterdam. Your friend might want to see it. He might find out something about himself."

ൟ ൶

Mr. Williard Ennis

Dear Willard,

My father is convinced we are related. So, I may be addressing you as a distant cousin. He says the Henriques family of Amsterdam has a family bible with entries going back to Spain and Portugal, covering the move to Amsterdam, London and beyond. You might want to avail yourself of the information in that bible.

By now you are aware that my state has seceded from the Union. War is certainly in the offing. I pray to God our families do not face each other in battle. I hope we may soon see each other again as friends and not as enemies.

> *Yours faithfully,*
> *Gerard Simon Henriques*

War did start. The Ennis' in the north and the Henriques family in the south each provided their men to fight in their respective armies. They would face each other in battle, as did others who were brothers, sons, cousins, fathers, and friends.

૭ ൴

Willard Ennis became even richer by manufacturing uniforms for the Union forces during the Civil War. His son, Todd, took over the management of Angus Duff and Co. in 1870, when Willard passed away. Although the company had survived some economic panics, Todd lost the business in 1878 because of the decline in government contracts, and watched as his home and many of his household items went under the auctioneer's hammer.

Because the Ennis family had been good employers and good citizens in the community, Todd was able to find work in Springfield's city government. He became Town Recorder and so continued to be close to the city's citizens, as his father and grandfather had been. He worked hard to help win the government's slate at election time. He was rewarded by being installed as head of an influential political club, where he doled out charity, political favors and controlled the decisions as to who in his ward would run for various elected offices. One of his sons, John, demonstrated a shrewd political talent, eventually becoming a political power in Springfield.

First, John gained a seat on the City Council, then he was sent to the State legislature, where he distinguished himself with his ability to successfully act as a conciliator between political parties. Finally, he was elected to the United States Congress, representing his district for 26 years, until his death.

John had three sons and a daughter. His youngest was born in 1913. The two older boys were named John Jr, and Solomon. Both of these sons, and his daughter Donna, died in the influenza epidemic of 1917. The youngest child, James Ennis, survived that pestilence. When he was 16, he told his politically powerful father that he wanted to enter the United States Naval Academy at Annapolis, Maryland. He could earn an engineer's degree and serve his country in the military. That was not a problem: his father easily arranged an appointment.

In 1931, James received his appointment as a Cadet. In that same year, Congressman John Ennis died. It left James the last surviving member of the Ennis family. As planned, he would make the United States Navy his career.

The story of Solomon Ennis was now cloudy, at best. Except for his name and that he fought and died in the Revolutionary War, not much more was known about the founder of the Ennis family. Where was he buried? Where did he die? No one knew; no one had answers.

Ensign James Ennis graduated in 1935 with a degree in Marine Engineering. Along the way, he earned Honors in Spanish. After two years at sea, he was assigned to teach engineering at the Academy.

In December 1938, now a Lieutenant, Jg., James was re-assigned as an engineering consultant to the Electric Boat Company of Groton, Connecticut, manufacturers of submarines for the U.S. Navy. He would remain there until America entered the war with Japan in 1941.

34

Cold Harbor, Virginia
June 12, 1864

Local tradition has it that the name Cold Harbor, a town close to Mechanicsville, Virginia, evolved because the village's only tavern served no hot meal for weary travelers.

Confederate General Robert E. Lee and Union General Ulysses S. Grant locked horns at Cold Harbor on May 31, 1864. Their armies faced each other in one of the worst bloodbaths of the Civil War. In less than two weeks of desperate combat, almost 13,000 causalities were suffered, 7,300 in the first hour. One Southern officer, after observing this butchery, remarked to his commanding officer, "It was not war, Sir, but pure murder."

Although the South was considered the victor at Cold Harbor, it was a pyrrhic victory. The Confederacy had lost so many irreplaceable soldiers and equipment, it would enjoy no more significant victories. From the last day of this battle, the South began slowly sliding to its final defeat.

Each side took prisoners during these days of violence. Claude Henriques, Captain, Third Regiment Charleston Light Dragoons (Volunteers) sat on the grass at the base of a hill, surrounded by three dozen of his fellow Confederates who had also been captured by Yankees. They'd been trapped after they retreated into a *cul de sac* during the last day of battle. Ten armed Union soldiers stood nearby to ensure there would be no escapes.

Claude knew nothing about the protocol for prisoners. He would ask, as soon as things settled down, if he could send word to his parents, Gerard and Abigail Henriques in Charleston, to let them know he was all right. Gerard, now a full Colonel, was serving with Charleston's Home Guard. Learning that Claude was a prisoner would be another blow to the Henriques family, which had already lost most of its assets during the war.

Claude hoped the Yankees would at least be gallant enough to allow him to contact his family. Southerners in the same circumstances would certainly allow an officer to send home a note letting his family know he had survived the battle, suffering only a slight wound. He had taken some wooden splinters in his left arm, which were removed immediately and were now of little or no consequence. He wanted to let his family know he was in much better condition than many of those he now saw scattered about him. He was sure his family would be worrying, once they saw the casualty statistics.

Looking around, he realized how fortunate he was to have survived this dreadful battle relatively unscathed. As far as he could see, the living on both sides of this hellish fight, were nursing their wounds. Some were sitting on the ground, heads resting on knees; others were laying on their sides, evidence of blood from wounds turning dark brown and spotting their shredded clothing. *Is that sobbing I hear? It's all right, these men have a right to cry. They're crying not only for themselves, but for their dead comrades. And the dead were piled up in high, cold, impersonal heaps, blue uniforms atop grey, grey atop blue. It's true: in death there are no political differences.*

A Yankee officer walked by, ordering the prisoners to their feet. He was young and handsome. *He could be one of us instead of being a Yankee,* Henriques thought. The officer used his saber, pointing at his prisoners to direct them into a line. It was not a menacing gesture, but merely a useful method to consolidate men into some sort of a tight and manageable group.

"We'll be moving soon," the Yankee officer informed his prisoners. Beckoning to his guards, he said, "Move this group over there. We'll be putting them together with some others down the road and we'll march them all off to a prison camp soon." *He seems very efficient,* Claude thought, *perhaps even sympathetic toward his prisoner's situation. Maybe he was thinking that he might have been a prisoner and hoped some Southern officer would treat him kindly.*

Claude Henriques stood up, reached into his shirt pocket and pulled out a long, dark cigar. It was his last. He lit it and savored its calming effect and familiar taste. *If I don't smoke it now, some Yankee soldier will take it from me. Yankee loot, spoils of war, what they call 'liberating,'* he thought, smiling to himself. He was only 25 years old, but he'd seen enough dying and wounded to cover more than several lifetimes. The hair at his temples was beginning to show some grey. It had been months since he enjoyed a decent haircut, having been on the run all that time. The smooth, boyish face that had accompanied him when he joined the Confederate Army in 1862 was beginning to show deep worry lines.

As they began moving in the direction ordered by the Yankee officer, he noted a soldier having difficulty standing. He stopped, clamped the cigar tightly between his teeth and put out his hands to help the man to his feet, noticing blood stains around the soldier's left calf.

"Thank ye kindly, Cap'n," the soldier said.

"How old are you, soldier?"

"Seventeen, Sir. This here's my first battle."

"Well, there you go, soldier. Why don't you have a tourniquet around your leg?"

"Cap'n, Sir, I didn't have time to put one on."

"Well then, let's stop the bleeding and let's get you something to help you walk with."

Henriques wrapped his scarf tightly around the soldier's calf. He looked around and saw an oak tree that had suffered a cannon blast. He ripped off a sturdy branch from the fallen tree and gave it to the disabled soldier to use as a walking stick as, under guard, they proceeded together. He noted that many prisoners had difficulty walking. That was why they were caught: they couldn't run away. Instead of retreating as he could have, Henriques had stayed behind to help his badly wounded Major and was captured with the dying man as they hid beneath a grove of trees.

A few hundred yards away, more prisoners were being herded into carefully corralled groups. The same Union Lieutenant, now on horseback, had been designated the task of joining all the prisoners together and overseeing them until they were put on trains heading for the internment camps. Prisoners were funneling in from several locations across the now silent battlefield. Henriques was surprised to see so many Confederate prisoners. He was not sure who had won this battle. Whichever side it was had paid a steep price for the victory.

The Lieutenant moved his horse closer to the marchers, as he found it easier to manage them that way, handling them as if he were a cowhand tending a herd of cattle. A Yankee Major came to inspect the Lieutenant's work. A look of distaste formed across his face.

"Are you having trouble here, Lieutenant? If so, why? Shouldn't we be further along with these prisoners? The Confederates are mopping up nearby. We must retreat from this position as soon as possible."

"Sir, we need to get these prisoners some water, and medical treatment," the Lieutenant answered, his voice dripping with frustration.

"We don't have time for that, Lieutenant. I want these Rebels out of here now. I want them away from this battlefield before other Rebels free them and then you'll find them facing you again on the front lines."

"Sir, we may be having to deal with a lot of dead soldiers on the way to the prison camp if we don't give them some basic care here and now. I don't want to be responsible for a lot of dead men when we could be avoiding that."

"You will do just as I ordered, Lieutenant. I don't need any unnecessary observations from you. Our mission for the moment is to quickly get these men out of here and on the road and into prison camps."

The Major pulled on his horse's reins, turned and rode away. He came across a Captain standing nearby, stopped his horse and called down to him. "Captain, that Lieutenant back there on horseback, with the prisoners... what's his name?"

"Ennis, Sir. That's First Lieutenant Richard Ennis. One of our best. He's with the First Springfield Massachusetts Volunteers."

35

Bergen-Belsen Concentration Camp
April 15, 1945

The British Army had no idea of what its soldiers would find at Bergen-Belsen when they negotiated with high-ranking German army officers for the surrender of what the Germans called a "prison camp." Both sides sat for several frustrating days working out the terms of the camp's surrender. During these meetings, many sadistic SS officers took advantage of the dithering delay by abandoning their posts and disappearing into the surrounding countryside. They would escape the punishment doled out to those guards who remained behind.

On the 15th of April 1945, elements of the British 11th Armored Division, accompanied by two Canadian Armored units, arrived at the camp's gates, which the soldiers found closed. Major David Henriques, sitting high up in the cab of his armored car, the first in the line of vehicles, addressed the guards at the gates in fluent German.

"Why are the gates closed? We made arrangements with your superiors to enter this camp unopposed."

"We have locked them to keep the prisoners from escaping, Sir," an overstuffed Sergeant answered, while making a proper Teutonic salute and clicking his heels. The other guards nodded in agreement, saluting, and smiling.

"Stand aside. We're going in." Switching to English, Henriques issued an order to his driver. "Corporal, smash the gate down. Run through it."

The large vehicle easily smashed through the wood and wire gate. Slowly, troops dropped from the rear of the carrier and with automatic weapons at the ready, began carefully edging their way inside the camp. Major Henriques' vehicle followed them at a slow pace. He was, in turn, followed by five half-tracks carrying more troops. Among them were Canadians, who were now also jumping from their trucks.

As they began to sweep through the camp, the soldiers stopped, in shock. Behind the buildings dead bodies, looking like skeletons, were stacked in piles several feet high. Half-naked and obviously starving inmates were sitting on the ground, powerless to muster enough energy to stand to greet their liberators.

Sergeant Howard Crawford ran back alongside the troop carrier in which his commanding officer was riding. He looked up and shouted over the engine's clatter, "Major 'Enriques, Sir, you ain't gonna believe what I just seen, Sir. It's like some sorta 'ell, I tell ya."

"What are you saying, Sergeant?"

"Over there, sir. Thousands o' dead. Like a bunch o' dead fish. Piled on top o' each other at the beach. I almost threw up, I did, Sir."

Major David Henriques climbed down from his armored carrier. He motioned for the rest of the vehicles to stop where they were. Once all engines were off and he was away from the fumes of the diesel engines, he was overwhelmed with the smell of dead bodies and human waste. He stood before the heaps of the remains of what were once human beings. Faces, no more than skulls with skin stretched over them, gazed into space, mouths open and teeth showing as if in a macabre grin or a silent shriek of pain.

"Sergeant," Henriques shouted, "get the medics in here, and quickly."

"Yes, Sir. I will. Right away, Sir." Sgt. Crawford was anxious to get away from this charnel house. He ran out of the camp looking for the medics who would have been on the last line of trucks waiting to enter the camp.

Henriques stepped into a nearby wooden barracks. The stench was overpowering. No strong light was able to pass through the filth-encrusted glass windows. In the gloom, he saw men sitting on the edges of wooden bunks. They stared at him quietly, not knowing what to make of this man in a different uniform than that of the hated SS. He was not shouting or barking commands. In any event, they no longer had the physical power to respond to any commands. Henriques stared back. As his eyes adjusted, he could see that many of them wore yellow stars on their shirts. He knew what that meant. He turned and left the barracks, stopping at the doorway outside. He leaned against the side of the building, buried his head in the crook of his arm, and began to cry.

The rat-a-tat sound of automatic fire alerted him. Instinctively, he brought his Sten gun to his chest, preparing to engage in combat. Then he saw Sergeant Crawford running up to him with a doctor and some corpsmen.

"What's happening, Sergeant. Are we getting some opposition?"

"No, Sir. It's our boys. They're shooting the guards. The prisoners are pointin' out men and our boys are finishing 'em off. Some of the stronger prisoners are also 'avin' a go at the guards, too, Sir."

"Where are they? That has to stop. They're prisoners of war; we don't kill prisoners."

"Back o' that concrete building, Sir. That's where our boys are at. Beggin' your pardon, Sir, I think you'll 'ave an 'ard time tryin' to stop 'em."

Henriques dashed several yards to the concrete building. It was a crematorium and still smoldering, radiating heat combined with the stench of burning flesh. Several dead German soldiers lay in a heap in front of the building. Others, looking frightened, their heads held high over their heads, were shouting, "*Bitte, bittle kamarade.*"

"Stop all firing," Henriques shouted.

A young lieutenant, his pistol still smoking, said, "Major, go inside and look at what's in there. Then tell us to stop firing. Sir."

Henriques walked into a dimly lit hallway. This was the site of the odor of burnt flesh. There was a row of eight ovens, their doors opened, smoke from the inside billowing at him. He covered his face with his handkerchief to fight the smell of burning flesh and walked past each of the ovens. He saw the same horrors in all of them: Human bones and half-burnt bodies that were not yet completely incinerated. They had obviously been dumped into the ovens in haste, just before the British arrived. The Major swallowed hard, as tears came to his eyes again. This was too much for any human to experience in one day. He couldn't imagine how those who had to live through this for months and years had felt. He went outside and took a deep breath. Then he found the Lieutenant again.

"Lieutenant, stop the shootings. Then make these bastards dig ditches deep enough to bury all these corpses. They are not to use any equipment or machines to dig the graves. Just shovels. If they can't find shovels, then they'll use their helmets or their hands.

"Before these corpses are buried, see if there is any way we can get documentation on these people. Both the Germans and the prisoners. Get all the information you can on these butchers. I'm sure the courts will want them to explain what all this is about."

As he was speaking, an SS Colonel approached Henriques. He saluted, clicked his heels and offered a wide smile. He said, speaking in German, "Good morning, Major. One of my guards tells me that you speak excellent German. I am pleased about that. We are to be considered prisoners of war and expect you to treat us as such." He spoke as if he were a professor lecturing one of his young students.

Henriques mustered all his energy to act as a proper English officer charged with the duty of protecting prisoners of war. He addressed the SS officer, "Colonel, we are told that you had the gates closed to prevent these people from escaping. Could you explain to me how it is that you expect them to escape? They can hardly stand."

"They are mostly Jews, Major. You know how the Jews are. They can always find ways to do what they want. That's why the gate was closed. We did not want them roaming around the countryside making trouble among the population – stealing from them, terrorizing them. And you must order your troops to stop shooting my men. They are offering no resistance. And the prisoners, too. They are attacking my men. At least six were killed by them. That is an intolerable situation."

"You are the only prisoners here, Colonel. These people you call prisoners have been kidnapped by you. I doubt any one of them individually has the strength to leave the camp or create any trouble in the countryside, as you claim they might do. And I will make a full report to my superiors about what I found here."

"I am sure, Major, that you will include the fact that we have prevented all Jews from pillaging the area, which is why we have them under our control," the German insisted, although now with a less superior smile.

"I will not, Colonel, for if I did, I would have to include myself as one of those pillagers."

"You are a Jew?" the German swallowed hard. "I heard the English and Americans had Jews in their armies, but officers..." The Colonel stepped back just as a jeep pulled up. It was the English Commanding Officer, a full Colonel, who asked "What's going on here, Henriques?"

"With all due respect Sir, I suggest the Colonel look around the camp. I'm too sick to describe it to you."

The Colonel waved the jeep's driver on and said, "You wait here, Henriques, with that German officer, 'til I get back."

Ten minutes later, the Colonel returned, red-faced and in a rage. He addressed Henriques. "You tell this monster what I'm saying because I don't speak his damned language. This is the most outrageous thing I have ever seen. My men are telling me that I haven't seen it all. I'm going to make a full report here." He looked at the German, and said with contempt, "And you and your men have some real explaining to do."

Turning to Henriques, he further ordered, "Henriques, get the medics here. And get graves dug. We need food and clothing for these poor devils."

"I've already done that, Sir. Assistance is on its way. And Sir, I've ordered all the graves to be dug with shovels. They are not to use machines."

"Good idea, Major. Make sure this Colonel has a hand in digging, too."

At that point, the German officer, who obviously understood English, said, "Colonel, I am a German officer. As a prisoner of war, I am not to do that type of work. And my men are not to be used as grave diggers."

"Since you had a hand in the deaths of these people, Colonel, you should help bury them. If you wish to lodge a complaint, you are entitled to do so after you finish the burial detail. As the highest-ranking German officer here, you will personally command the detail and also be involved in the digging. I expect it will be done with the greatest efficiency, for which you Germans are well noted.

"I apologize to you, Henriques, for my outrage. I have never seen such a thing as this in all my life. Such uncivilized behavior is inexcusable. Inexcusable!"

☙ ☘

Two years later in Nuremburg, Germany, at the trial of Bergen-Belsen's guards, the camp's former prisoners testified as to the treatment they received at the hands of the defendants. David Henriques, now a civilian; his commanding officer, now a General; and Sergeant Crawford were summoned by the Court to testify as to what they found when they entered the confines of Bergen-Belsen. The German defense was that as guards and soldiers they were merely following the orders of their superiors.

It was an eight-day trial. After seeing the displays of photographs and hearing graphic testimony, many spectators left in haste, their hands drawn to their mouths. Many were seen wiping tears from their eyes. At the conclusion of the trial, two guards were acquitted. Five were sentenced to 20 years imprisonment for their activities at the camp, and the German Colonel to life.

After serving three years, all five guards were released. Their Colonel followed them five years later. David Henriques and his General were outraged when they heard the news. Somehow, Sergeant Crawford was not surprised, especially since the Court stated that the English commanding officer violated the Geneva Convention by obliging the Gestapo Colonel to perform manual labor. Afterwards, Henriques and his commanding officer issued a joint statement to the press: "There was no Geneva Convention to protect the poor skeletons who failed to survive the brutal and inhuman treatment from their vicious captors."

At the War's end, Henriques left the army, returning to his studies at Oxford. He had been a reader in Mathematics. In 1947, after completing his mathematics studies, he began reading in History, trying to understand what he had seen at Bergen-Belsen. He was determined to explain it to the world. Ten years later, after he had been teaching History at Oxford for five years, he was also writing extensively about the Holocaust, as it had come to be known.

By 1960, he was one of the leading academicians on the subject, teaching the political and social bases of the aberrations leading to the Holocaust. He would receive many honors from his and other governments for his work.

David Henriques was the son of Byron Henriques, a partner with his brother Morris of Henriques Brothers, one of the oldest jewelers engaged in business on London's famous Bond Street. They often told their clients that their family originally came to London from Amsterdam, and Portugal before that.

The Henriques brothers were purveyors of fine jewelry by appointment to her Majesty, Queen Elizabeth II. In 1983, David Henriques was dubbed Knight of the Realm by Queen Elizabeth. On the sign leading to the entrance to his father's celebrated shop was inscribed:

Henriques Brothers Purveyors to the Crown
London and Amsterdam since 1781

36

Thessaloniki, Greece
June 1945

The Partisans came down from the mountains, victorious over the despised Nazis. They were a fierce and ragged-looking bunch, weapons slung over their shoulders, dressed in torn clothes, rags tied around their feet, substituting for boots. They smelled of the sheep and goats they'd lived with during the last months of their final fight against the Nazis.

Despite their victory, war in Greece was not yet over. Yes, the Germans were gone, defeated, but a new and nasty Civil War was brooding. The Communist DSE, which had also resisted the Germans, were now threatening to focus their energies on overthrowing the democratic Greek government. They were backed by the Yugoslavian dictator Marshal Tito and the Communist governments of Bulgaria and Albania. However, the United States and England stood firmly behind the current Greek government.

Dani Henriques had enough of war. His beloved sister, Rachel, had been killed when a surprise attack on her camp resulted in a desperate firefight. Of the 200 partisans caught unawares in the camp, less than two dozen managed an escape.

"Rachel fought like a tiger, until she ran out of ammunition," survivor Sabetai Levy told Dani. "She was not taken alive. I saw her fall. When I went to her side, she was already dead. Benny Mordoh was beside her. Dead too, he was. He was holding her hand."

It was a fear all women had: that the Germans would take them prisoner, their fate too ugly to consider. At least Rachel didn't suffer that indignity. No. Dani had enough of war; it made him at the age of 19 more like a man of 30. Both his mind and body were hard. He had seen death and had dealt it out, too. He wanted no more of it. For the present, he would dedicate himself to locating his family.

As the tired men came into the city, they went to the homes they had known, grown up in, and lived in before the War. That's when returning Jewish soldiers received their first shock: their homes no longer belonged to their families. Greeks were now living in them. They contemptuously waved deeds in front of the faces of the Jewish warriors. These represented the purchases of homes from the German occupiers. No matter they had stolen them from the Jews. Often, Greeks slammed doors on the faces of those who had fought the Nazis, while they sat quietly and meekly at home in the city. Dani's home and his father's clinic were now occupied by strangers who claimed legal ownership.

The next blow was seeing the almost complete destruction of Jewish Thessaloniki. The Nazis had blown up 38 of the city's 39 synagogues. Only one, the Monastir Synagogue, the newest of them, located at the western end of the city toward the Vardar River, survived intact. The Red Cross had appropriated it for use as a warehouse.

The men finally faced the reality that in a city in which Jews once represented an important and significant element of the population, they no longer existed. The story of the 500 years in which Jews enjoyed their lives in this place, suddenly disappeared: records of births, deaths and divorces disappeared. Jewish tracts, literary activity, plays, discourses, Kabbalistic treatises and religious texts were reduced to ashes. Records of the decisions of the community's religious courts were gone, as were deeds to homes, commercial transactions, and the long lists of recorded trading associations. It was as if the Jews of Thessaloniki had never existed, and that the Mediterranean's largest and most prestigious Jewish city was merely a myth.

The Greek government made facilities available for the returning Partisan fighters. Those who were not fighting for the DSE were given a small stipend and a barracks to live in until they could make their own way.

Menahem Abulafia, a concentration camp survivor, told Dani that he had seen his grandfather Daniel and grandmother Boulisa, sent off to the side, to the area meant for those destined for the gas chambers. In his heart, Dani always knew they had not survived, but the verification saddened him. He only hoped his parents, Chaim and Hannah and his little sisters Leah and Rebecca, had survived. He would stay in Thessaloniki until the last of the survivors returned, or he learned of their deaths.

Gradually, the pitifully few survivors returned from the camps, some in small groups, others, alone. Eventually, only 1,200 of the 56,000 Jews who had been deported from Thessaloniki returned. Jewish organizations soon descended on the city. They came with rabbis, doctors, and social workers. Dani found work with HIAS, the Hebrew Immigration Aid Society. It took him out of the barracks. Now he could eat kosher meals for the first time in years and every two weeks he had a few drachmas that he had earned. Through his job, he could question the returnees to learn if they knew anything about his family.

One day, his father returned with other men, stumbling off the back of a truck into the facility. He was very thin, only a grey wisp of hair covered his almost bare head. Dani ran over to him, overjoyed to see his father. There was deep sadness in Chaim's eyes.

"Papa, it's me, Dani!"

"Dani. I hardly recognized you. You've grown. And you're so thin."

"I grew four inches in the last years. What of Mama and Leah and Rebecca?"

"Leah and Rebecca are gone. All the young children were murdered right away. Your mother and I were separated, but she went with those women who were sent to work. I have had no word of her since then. I've asked survivors, but no one can help. And Rachel, where is she?"

"Dead, Papa. Killed in a battle in the mountains."

Chaim was quiet. The lovely young Rachel, always smiling and happy. Dead at war when she should have been at school. She'd wanted to be a doctor, like her father and work beside him at his clinic. All those dreams, done and over with now.

Dani noticed Chaim was wearing a shirt, a ragged striped pajama top like those issued to prisoners. Chaim's came only two-thirds down his forearm. He kept pulling on the wide sleeve, trying unsuccessfully to cover the numbers tattooed on his lower left arm. Dani had learned earlier that many survivors considered the numbers a matter of shame. The boy took his father and gently guided him into the communal dining room.

"Papa, let's have lunch together. Go. Wait for me in the dining room. I'll meet you in a few minutes. I have something to do first."

Dani went to the Jewish community's storeroom, where he saw Sonia Kahn, who was in charge of clothing. "Sonia," he said in Ladino, "I need two long-sleeved shirts immediately."

"For you, my son?" Sonia asked. She was a 28-year-old, chain-smoking American, who came to Greece working for HIAS. She spoke Ladino as she was the American-born daughter of the Calderons, immigrants from Turkey who had come to America just before World War 1. Sonia was thin and a war widow. Her husband Bob died in the first wave on the beaches of Normandy on D-day. To forget her loss, she worked hard to bring comfort to the depressed and rootless returnees. She became depressed herself when she was unable to help.

"What size are you, Dani? You look like a large."

"It's not for me, Sonia. With God's blessings, my father showed up this morning at our camp. He had no decent shirt. I figure he's a size or two smaller than me. He needs to cover the numbers on his arm. His shirt doesn't do it."

"I understand. I see that all the time," Sonia said sadly as she turned into the door leading to the storeroom. After rummaging around, she came out with two shirts. They were not new, but they were clean, starched and ironed.

"Here, *Pasha*," she used the Ladino term of endearment for a male. "For your father, in honor of his return. I thank God for you that he survived." Sonia, as Americans say, 'always wore her heart on her sleeve.'

Returning to the dining room, Dani found his father was already devouring and relishing a once-familiar dish so long denied him: *bamya*, okra smothered in a thick, spicy tomato sauce. Dani put the shirts on the bench next to his father. "For you, papa."

He would not let his father sleep in the barracks with the other returnees. He brought him to the small room allotted him by HIAS and put him in the room's only bed, while he slept on the floor. It was no hardship. He had for years slept in much less comfortable places in the mountains.

છ જી

After long consultations, the rabbis had agreed to strongly encourage single male and female survivors to marry one another. They did not want the women to be alone. Only God knows what they had gone through; no one ever discussed it. It was a strictly unmentionable subject. Marriage was the best and maybe the only solution for a bad situation. Dani was deemed too young, since most of the women were much older than him. Chaim refused, claiming that he still held out hope that Hannah had survived.

One day, Dani came to his father and said, "Papa, I am sure there will be no more survivors showing up. I have arranged for Greek passports for us. HIAS will pay our way to Bari, Italy, where there are ships going to Palestine. We can start a new life there. There is nothing left for us, here in Thessaloniki. It's over. Everything is gone; there are only memories. We need to admit it. We need to go on. In Palestine, we can live with other Jews who are looking to create a new and strong Jewish state."

Chaim thought for a while. "Dani, you are right. You should go. But I stay here until I find out what happened to your mother. I will continue as a doctor, working for HIAS. I make enough to take care of myself until I know what happened to Mama. Write to me when you get to Palestine, so I'll know where you are. Eventually, one way or another, I'll get to Palestine and be with you. I promise that."

Dani had a British soldier's backpack which Sonia had given him. She filled it with a pair of pants, shoes, two shirts, three pairs of underwear and a woolen sweater. "I would give you more but would have a lot of explaining to do for giving out so much to one person... who was not even a refugee."

After filling the backpack, she kissed her *pasha*, and led him to her room where they spent the evening together. Sonia cried softly when Dani held her. She had not known a man since before her husband was killed in Normandy. She rose at dawn, immediately lit a cigarette, then woke Dani and kissed him. After breakfast, she smoothed out his hair and said, "Good luck to you, *Pasha*.

And so, once again, Dani Henriques left his father behind. After a bus ride to the south, he arrived in the Greek port of Piraeus, where he had been told to go to an appointed place. There, he met a man from one of the Jewish agencies who gave him a paper allowing him to board a ship in Bari, Italy. The ship was *La Linda*.

In Piraeus, he boarded a Greek freighter that carried many passengers west across the Adriatic Sea. Arriving in Bari, he and several other selected passengers were put on trucks and driven dockside, to the waiting *La Linda*.

୨୭ ଓ୧

One had to overlook the rickety condition of *La Linda*. Her mission was what was important. She was bringing concentration camp survivors to a place where Jews had been longing to be for over 2,000 years; a place where they could rule themselves. Where the police, firemen, janitors and even the street corner prostitutes were Jewish. The people who were traveling with Dani thought they were going to a Jewish paradise.

The 45-year-old *La Linda* had enjoyed life as a medium-sized and luxurious Spanish cruise ship. During the Spanish Civil War, she had been appropriated by the dictator General Francisco Franco for use as a troop ship. *La Linda* ferried Moroccan soldiers of the Spanish Foreign Legion across the Strait of Gibraltar to Spain, to fight a decisive and bloody battle on the grounds and in the classrooms and science laboratories of the University of Madrid. That was in 1938.

Now, she was docked at a Bari pier. Hundreds of passengers were lined up waiting impatiently to board her and get on their way to Palestine. Rust ran down her sides. No one had bothered to give *La Linda* a beauty makeover. Her portholes were surrounded by bulging rust-encrusted flakes that crumbled to the touch. One of her cargo booms was obviously inoperative: it was broken at the heel, swinging dangerously loose. Two seamen were working hard to capture and secure it.

La Linda was no longer Spanish: she had been purchased by a shadowy Liberian corporation formed by a group of anonymous, wealthy American Jews. The United States had passed laws making it illegal to sell arms or assist, in any way, any of the contentious groups at war with one another in Palestine.

The British were unsuccessful in their attempts to ensure that Jews did not exceed the limits of entry imposed by their government for immigration to Palestine. *La Linda* was proof of England's inability to stop the illegal flow. She now flew the Liberian flag, her home port was Monrovia, and while the fading letters on her bow and stern read *La Linda*, that would change once the voyage got underway. The crew would place her new name, *Mt. Horeb*, fore and aft, in English and Hebrew.

La Linda belonged to the squadron of aging, broken down, unwanted, cast-off vessels resuscitated to a minimum degree of seaworthiness and then selected to run the British blockade that was preventing homeless Jews from entering Palestine.

Someone, presumably the ship's Captain, was standing at the foot of the gangway speaking to a uniformed Italian official through an interpreter. Both the Italians and the French had been turning blind eyes at these blockade runners. They sympathized with the survivors, who the British would not allow into Palestine. That didn't mean they sanctioned unseaworthy ships leaving their ports. They had to be satisfied that any ship leaving their country was seaworthy and would reach its destination safely.

Bari was a popular port for the refugees because it was close to Palestine and easy for refugees to reach from Germany and Poland. Jewish agencies and illegal Underground groups spirited Jews from displaced person camps and brought them there. There were so many refugees in Bari that some had to be taken to Marseilles in France, which became an alternate route to Palestine.

The uniformed officer seemed satisfied with whatever it was that he required of this ship. He signed some papers, saluted the Captain, and said, "*Buona Fortuna.*" He was supposed to be aware of the ship's destination, which was listed as Beirut, Lebanon. But he knew where she was really going. The Captain returned the salute, signed documents which he handed to the Italian and shook his hand in an extra gesture of friendship. Then he waved to the upper deck.

A dozen or more crew members, women among them, descended the gangway and in a babble of languages, mostly Yiddish, Polish, German, and French, began leading the passengers onto the ship. Most of them carried all they owned in pitiful bundles tied with cord. Some had peeling cardboard valises; others came aboard with nothing but what they wore.

37

Bethesda, Maryland and Norfolk, Virginia
1945-1951

Lucy Ennis was happy. Jimmy had written to her: a short letter said he was coming home at last.

Since he had gone to North Africa in 1942, Lucy had seen him only briefly on three occasions. Last spring, she gave birth to a second child, a girl. They named her Rachel. While Jimmy was at war, the rest of the Ennis family was safe in Bethesda, two miles from Lucy's parents, Grandma and Grandpa Peters. Michael, the older child, was a precocious two and a half years old.

The War was coming to an end in Europe. That left the remaining conflict against the Japanese in the Pacific. Jimmy hinted in his letter he would not be participating in it.

Aside from the assaults on Pearl Harbor and Japanese occupation of some remote islands in Alaska, the contiguous forty-eight states of America had been free of the horrible trials of war that Europeans and Asians had experienced over the past years. Americans had not known the terrors of night-time air raids, nor had they experienced arrests and roundups by police and the military or hard labor in prison camps. True, the country had imprisoned its Japanese citizens. For most Americans, that was far removed on the Pacific Coast and maybe, some mistakenly thought, necessary.

Most of Europe was almost starving because of poor harvests and the great need of the German regime to feed an army, it's civilian population and the huge number of slave laborers, who, had they been free, would be on farms tilling the fields and reaping fat harvests. In contrast, Americans were eating regularly. True, food was rationed in the States, but butter and other oils were still available, as were sugar, meat, fish and fowl. All were available in reduced amounts, and they were expensive.

Americans were exhorted to voluntarily eschew meat one day a week; 'Meatless Tuesday' they called it. Compared to Europeans living under German occupation, Americans lived in luxury. Their cities were not crumbling under the crunch of bombs and their children were not sleeping in bomb shelters.

Jimmy Ennis was coming home from Europe and, as he wrote his wife, he was being sent to an unknown post to work as an engineer. As a military wife, Lucy knew she would soon have to be packing to re-locate to another city. It was a small inconvenience. The important thing was that Jimmy would be home, safe with his family. They would be together, eating together, traveling together and spending time together as a family unit for the first time. Lucy shook her head every time she realized that Jimmy had never seen his daughter Rachel except in photographs.

Ennis was assigned to the Navy base at Norfolk, Virginia. It was American's largest naval shipyard, where the government would be decommissioning surplus military vessels that were no longer needed to haul supplies across oceans to help defeat an enemy. The future was bright for the Ennis family: Jimmy was advancing in the Navy. He was now a full Commander, hoping realistically to attain a Captaincy, although in peacetime that might be slow in coming. His work at Norfolk looked to be of a lengthy tenure. The family could welcome some stability in their new home.

One evening during their Norfolk assignment, Jimmy and Lucy sat down and talked about their children's future. They agreed they should both have the best education available. Lucy was teaching English at a local high school and with the extra income, they could afford to set aside a monthly amount as an education fund for them. Lucy's parents made a handsome gift to get the fund started and Jimmy wrote a book about his mission with the OSS, Lucy making a substantial contribution as editor. The book was a mild success and earned the family extra income.

America would soon be enjoying peace. People could buy cars, enabling them to move from urban apartment houses to one-family homes in the suburbs. Workers in America's factories came home on Fridays, their pay envelopes thick with money to be spent on toaster ovens, TV sets and vacations. America's merchants responded by erecting suburban shopping centers, where customers could be conveniently and easily relieved of their cash.

The Korean War, which erupted in June of 1950 and lasted until 1953 did not interrupt the happy time Americans were enjoying. There was no rationing or tightening of belts as the country had experienced during World War II. Years later, the Korean War would be called the Forgotten War.

Jim wasn't sent abroad during the Korean War. He had been reassigned to the construction of America's powerful and more modern aircraft carriers and submarines. The Ennis family had much to look forward to in the coming years; in a peaceful and prosperous America, with two children prepared to reap the rewards as citizens of a serene and undisturbed America.

ఞ ఞ

From the first time he had read about the far-off possibility of outfitting an American submarine with an atomic power plant, Jim Ennis knew he would somehow be involved in its construction. He had dreamt on several occasions that he was standing in front of a draftsman's table, looking at blueprints for the new and innovative submarine. If they were going to construct this great dream, it would probably be in Groton and, of course, built by the Electric Boat Company. If it was to happen, then it was certain that he would be associated with it. Lucy would be pleased; she would be returning to Groton where they still had old friends from Jim's tour. Yes, he was sure that this was another of those events in his life: presaging things which turned out to be true; what his psychologist friend had called "precognition."

Soon afterwards, he read another account about the maverick Navy officer who was proposing the plan. Although Ennis had never met him, he knew Captain Hyman Rickover's reputation: a tough Academy graduate; an outspoken, difficult-to-work-with curmudgeon, who always managed to get his own way. Yet through the years he had successfully completed every task the Navy had given him.

Twice, he had been denied promotion to Admiral. Being passed over that way was a polite signal that it was time for the candidate to retire from the service. The Navy's Review Board, which handled promotions, was packed with men Rickover had personal issues with during his career. Perhaps Ennis thought, it didn't help that the man was born a Polish Jew, even though Rickover became a Christian in early adulthood. Ennis had been learning all about the difficulties Jews faced and could understand what Rickover might have been experiencing. He may have converted, but he was still 'the Jew.'

President Harry Truman wasn't saddled with the Review Board's hang-ups. He personally intervened to break the ice blocking Rickover's promotion. First, Truman issued a presidential order to proceed immediately with the design and the building of an atomic submarine. Then, with a snub at the Review Board, ignoring them completely, he put Captain Hyman Rickover in charge of the entire project. A major project of this sort was always headed by an Admiral. But Harry Truman was not a man to let tradition or personal animosities stand in his way. Especially in the construction of an important military objective, such as an atomic powered submarine. With Rickover in charge of this operation, Truman put everyone on notice that Rickover was not retiring. Then, Truman sent his Secretary of the Navy to pressure the Review Board, "and those snooty Admirals," to promote Rickover to Admiral. When it was all over, Rickover, while working on the new submarine, became an Admiral and went on to be the longest serving officer in America's naval history.

For now, Ennis had his duty station: he was one of several engineers helping to build an aircraft carrier at the Navy's mammoth shipyard in Norfolk, Virginia. He was grateful for this duty. It kept him in a community where Lucy and his young children, Michael and Rachel, could live comparatively stable lives. His work allowed him to leave for home at a reasonably civil hour. He enjoyed spending his evenings with Lucy, watching his children grow, answering their questions, spending weekends with them and Lucy at the beach, and being present to discuss the children's progress with their teachers during open school week.

He had done his duty for the Navy and his country: working at Groton, the submarine patrols in the Mediterranean and then the Pacific, jumping into France 600 feet above ground to minimize his descent so the Germans couldn't find him, doing a spate of translating for General Clark in Africa and then for other officers as Americans fought their way across Europe toward Germany. This was time he had earned, to enjoy being with his family. Any engineer working on a complicated project like an atomic submarine might have to dedicate seven days a week and probably 16 hours a day married to his drafting board instead of his wife and family. Yet he also knew what being at Groton meant to Lucy.

The secret, sealed order finally came, as he knew it would, ordering him to The Electric Boat Company at Groton, Connecticut, for an interview. The order read, "With the possibility of leading to work on the construction of an atomic powered submarine."

He wasn't surprised. At least he wasn't being sent overseas again, away from his family. A full Commander now, he wondered what his role would be. He soon found out. On the day after he arrived at Groton, he was sitting across from Captain Hyman Rickover himself, being interviewed about every aspect of his life.

Sitting in Rickover's Spartan office, Ennis saw a slender man with closely cropped grey hair sitting behind an uncluttered desk. He had slightly bulging eyes that showed little trace of humor. It was easy to see he was a man dedicated to successfully accomplishing whatever tasks he undertook.

"I am personally interviewing every person involved with the construction and operation of this submarine," Rickover informed Ennis, "from the boat's cook to her Commander. And, of course, all the people involved in its design and construction. I'm calling the boat the *Nautilus*, after Captain Nemo's submarine in Jules Verne's novel 'Twenty-Thousand Leagues Beneath the Sea.' There have been other ships with that name in the history of our Navy," he observed, while flipping open Ennis' 201, his personnel file.

"I liked what I've been reading about you. That's why I called you here. You have good submarine experience, practical and

307

theoretical. You've had some other interesting experiences, which show me you're versatile. I like that. But I must say, frankly, there's something here I don't like," Rickover said as he ruffled through Jimmy's file. "You don't follow orders."

Rickover looked Jimmy in the eye and saw no reaction. *Good, he's leaving it up to me to tell him what I mean. I like that; he doesn't step in where he doesn't belong.* Rickover continued.

"You understand, Commander, that whenever I give an order, it has to be obeyed and without question." Rickover paused to receive an answer.

"Of course I do, Captain."

"When you were on your mission to France for the OSS during the War, you were supposed to return after you completed your task. Instead, you chose to send someone else to England in your place and then had to wait a month to return. You did not follow orders. Do you have anything to tell me about that?"

"Yes, Sir. The plane returning to England could only accommodate two passengers. I had to send the defector back. That was why I was sent to France. The other passenger was a Dutch Underground leader who had a lot of information in his head. If the Germans caught him, they would either get it out of him or kill him. Then there were also some large boxes of blueprints and notes. They took up the space of a second passenger.

"I was sent to France to evaluate the defector; to see if he was genuine or leading us into a trap. I also had to bring back those boxes. I had to make an on-the-spot decision. It was my call. I sent the defector and the Dutchman back. I should have made it back the next night, but the Germans were scouring all the possible landing spots. They were real sore about this scientist defecting and were out in force looking for him. Then, they were red-faced about having a top resistance fighter stolen from them.

"Leaving the next night would have been risky. So the boxes and I had to wait till the next full moon. I hadn't anticipated that reaction from the Germans. The Underground should have told me to expect it, but they didn't." Ennis paused for Rickover to say something.

"Have you told me all of your reasons, Commander?"

Mickey, that bastard! He probably put in his report that Aarnold Henriques was possibly my relative. I might as well get it out. The worse that will happen is that I go back to Norfolk and that's not so bad. Ennis took a deep breath and said, "No, Sir. It's possible the Dutchman was a relative."

"Commander. You jeopardized a mission for a relative?"

"No, Sir. His possibly being a relative had no basis for my decision. First, his being a relative was only a remote possibility. He was an important person to get back to London and safety. Much more important than I was. I was the man on the spot. Henriques had all the information about the Dutch Underground. The number one man had been killed. This man had taken over and knew everything about their activities.

"I believe I made the right decision. Anyway, I didn't consider myself under military orders. I was the man sent to France to assess the situation and based on what I learned, to then make the proper decisions. Acting on those assessments, and according to the authority I was given and what I knew at the time, I made one.

"If I left the Dutchman behind and he was caught and then forced to reveal what he knew, I most certainly would have been criticized for not protecting him. I also had to take into consideration that he had no cyanide capsule to escape torture. He told me he gave his last one to a comrade he knew couldn't stand up to the Gestapo's torture. Not that most of us could, anyway." Ennis looked to Rickover for a reaction to his last remark. There wasn't any.

"Once I saw the inhuman way those prisoners were treated by the Gestapo, I knew he would eventually crack and give out what he knew. I had no choice. There was another factor I had to consider. He was badly beaten and needed immediate medical attention. There was no way he could get that in France. If he remained there in hiding, he most certainly would have died. He was so bad that when I got to England a month later, he was still in the hospital. He spent three more weeks after that in confinement."

Rickover was silent for a long time, rubbing his chin several times. Then he said, "So. You've convinced me you can make difficult decisions on the spot. That's a good quality. Have you had other situations like that during your career, Commander?"

"Yes, Sir. When I was a submarine Commander in the Pacific, after I followed and attacked enemy vessels, on several occasions I would have only one or two torpedoes left. I had to pick one Japanese ship out of three or four, trying to determine the most damage I could inflict with what I had left."

"What resulted from your decision?"

"One time we sunk a tanker. She went up like a dry Christmas tree on New Year's Day."

"Interesting. I can probably order you to work on this project. I would hope it interests you enough that you would want to be on the team that constructs the world's first atomic powered vessel without such an order."

"I would like to work on it. How long would this project take?"

"I estimate four to five years."

"I would be in Groton all the while?" Jimmy was thinking of how happy Lucy would be back in Groton.

"Yes. Or certainly from time to time, working across the river, nearby in New London."

"I'd like to come aboard, Sir."

"Good, Commander. Get yourself to Groton in two weeks. I'll cut the orders. Glad to have you aboard." Rickover extended his hand.

Was that a smile Ennis saw on Rickover's face?

38

Sailing Across the Adriatic Sea as an Illegal
1946

As Dani Henriques boarded *La Linda,* he knew instinctively this would be a troubled voyage. Leaving the pier, he heard her engines straining to produce power. After they left port, the engines broke down twice, just as they had passed twelve miles outside of Barri, well into international waters. The ship was bobbing, dead in the water. Yet the Captain refused any tug assistance on both occasions; it would have meant returning to Bari and unknown consequences with the authorities that he was unwilling to accept. Passengers could hear the sound of men pounding away in the engine room; metallic pings skimming across the calm and silent sea. Dani also became aware that this ship was dangerously overcrowded: men, women and children were jammed on the outside main deck. It was the best place to escape the heat and foul orders which were difficult to bear: seasickness and overflowing toilets had become endemic below.

Walking along on what was once an elegant promenade deck, he could hardly make out its teak planks. He carefully picked his way through a sleeping and reclining mass of people, to get from one end of the ship to the other. Climbing to an upper deck, he finally found a place where he could have some reasonable comfort. He sat down and fell asleep, waking an hour later, when he felt the heavy vibrations of the ship's engines passing through his body. *La Linda* was starting up, moving on her way; reborn.

But now, the ship was behind schedule. The sun was rising, the dawn a pink glow and she was barely out of sight of Bari. She should have stolen out of the harbor under the protective cover of a moonless night and been well out to sea by now. Instead, *La Linda* was barely twelve miles outside the harbor, according to what a crew member told Dani. There were no English ships nearby. That was a good sign. At least for now, the British did not know where they were. But *La Linda* was supposed to reach a Palestinian beach in the dead of night. That was impossible now. Landing during the day was risky. All the passengers might be gathered up by a British patrol that would easily see the ship coming in daylight, even when it was still miles off the coast.

La Linda's crew was an international mix, mostly volunteers. All eight American members had either served in the U.S. Navy or the Merchant Marines during the War, some as officers. The skipper, Emmanuel Bruen, was an English Jew who had legitimately earned his Captain's license, graduating from a French Maritime Academy. One of the crew's French volunteers said the skipper had commanded a Canadian Corvette during the War, hunting German U-Boats in the North Atlantic.

Because she was so overloaded, *La Linda* was having difficulty maintaining stability. The Captain wanted to land as soon as possible. But that would be difficult. Her timetable had been altered because of engine failure. He had to stop the ship and send a radio message to Palestine to coordinate a new night-time approach.

La Linda was now the *Mt. Horeb*. The crew took advantage of the ship's idling to throw large, whitewashed canvasses fore and aft, secured by sturdy two-inch heaving lines. The ship's new name covered the old one. Dani knew from his years fighting Germans what a friend the cover of darkness could be. Sitting out here in the open, in the middle of the sea on a bright and cloudless day, he felt vulnerable. As the ship drifted in the water, the sun beat down on passengers and crew.

Dani was not the only one aboard the *Mt. Horeb* who was concerned. In the wheelhouse, Captain Bruen had already noticed a thin, tail-like formation of black smoke rising far aft of his ship. Spotting his binoculars on the site, he was certain that what he was seeing was an English Corvette. Not taking chances, Bruen ordered his engines full ahead. It was now a race to Palestine, and there was no doubt that the Corvette was swifter than the aged *Mt. Horeb*.

Once within sight of Palestine, there might be two reception committees awaiting the ship and its passengers: one most certainly the now rescheduled Haganah, the Jewish Underground, hiding at an arranged location on a beach somewhere between Haifa and the old Roman city of Caesarea. They were ready to take the ship's ragged passengers and swiftly distribute them through Palestine, away from the snooping British.

The other group that could be waiting for the *Mt. Horeb* were the unwanted 'greeters,' the English military who, to date, had no real information about where the ship would be landing. The English were, however, receiving radio reports from the pursuing Corvette of the ship's current position at sea. A truck full of English soldiers was now moving along the coastal road, hoping to catch *Mt. Horeb* as she landed in Palestine. Another truck, a mobile British radio-tracking vehicle, was picking up the Corvette's signals and relaying them on to the unit patrolling the seaside highway.

Strike groups of the Haganah, also picking up the signals being sent to the radio truck, were ordered to put the tracker out of commission. Once successful at that task, the patrolling British would be unaware as to where the ship could be expected to land. They would be reduced to visual observations at night.

Two jeeps, filled with Haganah fighters, pulled up alongside the radio truck, its circular antennae rotating above the roof. Firing at the antennae, they severed it at its base, rendering it useless. Using a loudspeaker, the Jews warned the British to remain in the truck. If they tried to leave, they would be shot. The doors did not open. Two men descended from the Jeeps and with their Sten guns, shredded all four of the truck's tires. A spare tire bolted to the truck's rear was removed and likewise shot to pieces.

ം ൈ

All this violence, secrecy, and illegal attempts to bring Jews to Palestine resulted from England's ambiguous position toward Jewish immigration to Palestine. Awarded the Mandate to govern the territory by the League of Nations after World War I, successive English governments took the position that Jewish immigration should be severely limited. It was a political stance taken to satisfy the region's Arabs, who were supplying the British Empire with much needed oil to run its industries, light the lamps in the homes of its citizens and fuel its military adventures.

The Jewish world had its position, too. Leaders pointed to the Balfour Declaration, issued almost 40 years earlier by Lord Arthur Balfour who was then England's Foreign Secretary. He prepared a letter in which the English government took the position that it was in favor of the establishment of a Jewish homeland in Palestine. England's present stance was ambiguous but weighted in favor of limiting Jewish immigration to the region. Jews caught illegally entering Palestine were shipped to the nearby English colony of Cyprus. There, they were interned in camps reminiscent of Nazi concentration camps: barbed wire, searchlight and armed guards were visible everywhere. The British were intent on maintaining this policy to the extreme, even to using force, sometimes resulting in the death of hapless illegals.

This is what Dani knew he was facing. He had years of experience fighting those who opposed Jews and he would not allow himself to be transported to a camp like a criminal. Through one of the crew members, he was taken to see the Second Mate.

"I was with the Greek Resistance during the War," he explained. "I am ready to fight here if you need me."

"I hope we won't need you. But I'll keep you in mind. Can you handle a Sten gun?" the Mate asked.

"Of course. And Mausers, Lugers and American Thompsons."

"Okay. If we get stopped, come up to the bridge right away. We'll see if we can use you. In the meantime, stay alert."

Now, as the *Mt. Horeb* slowed her weigh, passengers could see the night lights of Palestine rising out of the sea along the highway beside the shore. Later, they would see the lights of homes nestled high among the towering hills of Haifa to their left. People rose from the deck, jamming the railings, shouting, and singing.

It was impossible for the crew to get them quiet. The *Mt. Horeb* pulled as close as she could to the shore, which was now about two miles away. Through his binoculars, Captain Bruen could see the running lights of the British Corvette aft of him and gaining. He had

314

ordered all the ship's lights, including the running lights, extinguished. This was in violation of international law concerned with safety at sea. Earlier blockade runners had done this. It had successfully kept the British from locating them in the dark.

But there would never be enough time for all of Bruen's passengers to debark onto smaller boats to get ashore before the British would catch up to them. There was only one decision to make; the one he had been seriously thinking about since his engines had failed outside Bari. The one he kept to himself.

His passengers were more important than this old, worn-out ship. She had had her years. Now, it was over. He would ground her, something no Captain cares to do to his ship. It's like killing a member of the family. It had to be done, however. With great reluctance, he ordered on the ship's telegraph, "Engines full ahead."

The engine room complied. The *Mt. Horeb* moved quickly until her stem plowed forward through the shallows and her bow settled firmly onto the Palestinian beach. Then with a deep sadness on his face, he rang the telegraph with signaled orders from the bridge to the engine room: "All engines stop."

Immediately, the crew dropped ship's ladders set out on the gangway and opened the lower doors to the port side, to let the passengers out. The ship's stern, now in shallow water, allowed the more adventurous to safely jump into the surf, avoiding the clutter gathering forward. From the shore, Jewish volunteers waded into the water to hurry passengers on to waiting buses, trucks, cars and even taxis.

Dani climbed the ladder to the bridge. The Mate introduced him to the Captain. "We can count on him to fight," the Mate explained.

"We may have one. Look down the road. There's a truck load of what looks like soldiers coming at us from the right." Captain Bruen gave his binoculars to the Mate, seeking confirmation. The Mate, after looking in that direction, agreed with the Captain. Bruen opened a closet door and handed a rifle to the Mate. Then he gave Dani an English Webley pistol.

"I hope you know how to use this, son," he said. It was an old revolver, in use at the beginning of the 20th Century during South Africa's Boer War. Then he gave Dani a handful of bullets.

"I've used newer versions of this revolver. If it works, I'll manage, Captain."

"Oh, it works all right. I've used it on several occasions. There's to be no firing unless the Brits fire first, understand?"

"Yes, sir."

"Then stay with us here. The crew leaves last. Let's hope we have enough time to get out of here before the soldiers show up."

The Captain had some last-minute business to attend to. He removed his Masters' license from behind a glass frame on a wall, breaking the glass to do so. Then he wrapped his license, the ship's passenger and crew lists, the ship's rough and smooth logs, the secret codes, and frequencies used for sending messages to the waiting volunteers ashore, and the ownership and insurance papers into an oil cloth, stuffing them into a denim gym bag which he tied with a rope, leaving a loop that he could hang around his shoulder. Then he cried out, "I'm ready. Let's go!"

As passengers left, the *Mt. Horeb* lightened, her stern bobbing in the surf. The passengers were screaming and crying with joy. Some were singing '*Hatikvah*,' the Jew's anthem of hope, sung whenever they'd dreamed of living in a country of their own. The crew descended to the lower deck, moving late stragglers into the arms of volunteers standing hip deep in the water. The stern was rising and now the crew could clearly see the headlights of a truck racing down the ocean road.

With no more passengers on the ship, the crew waded across the water into a waiting bus. By the time the British arrived, their rifles at the ready, preparing to enter into mayhem with the passengers, there was no one to greet them. They had arrived so late; they couldn't even see the lights of the buses and cars that were carrying Palestine's newest illegal citizens away.

The soldiers scampered aboard the ship and found nothing but empty cans, boxes, bottles, newspapers, old sheets and towels and a ragged cloth doll left behind by a child who had been exhorted by a parent to leave in haste. The bridge was empty of any identification of its crew, its officers, passengers, or anything else. Except for the loss of a ship, which probably had only one more decent crossing left in her, the landing operation was a success.

৯০ ৶

In this new country, everyone tried to be helpful about where a new resident should be placed in Jewish society. The most popular and obvious were the collectives – the *Kibbutzim* or *Moshavim*. They were generally for farmers and dairy men who tilled the soil or cared for cows and sheep. There were also collectives for writers, artists, and makers of items in small manufacturing. Dani was not cut out for that. He wanted to continue his studies, but he didn't have any idea how to go about getting into school. Besides, he had no money for tuition. The volunteers arranged for short-term living, but he would soon have to find a regular place for himself in his new and strange country.

He was issued false identity papers, so he could travel. Then someone told him about the Haganah, the illegal Underground military arm of the Jewish community. It was the defense force protecting Jews from the Arabs who attacked them on their farms and in the cities. They were the volunteers who helped the passengers off the *Mt. Horeb*. He might get started there until he could find himself a university.

He spoke the halting Hebrew he had learned years ago at school in Thessaloniki. It was good enough to be able to do basic things; he would get better at it, he knew. He also spoke Spanish, French and Greek. With all that, he should be able to get around, although he noted on the ship that he would have been much better off had he spoken German or Yiddish.

Someone introduced him to a local leader of the Haganah.

"Can you handle any kind of arms?" the man asked him, looking at Dani carefully. This young man might be an English informer looking to get into a forbidden Haganah group to turn them in.

"I fought with the Greek resistance for three years," Dani answered.

The local leader was impressed. But even if this young man was genuine, he had to convince himself that this was not just bravado. He took Dani to the back of a shop and into a storeroom. He handed him a Sten gun.

"Can you take this apart and put it together?"

"Sure." Dani promptly did that in the dim storeroom, with a speed that impressed the leader.

"Come back in an hour," the man said.

Returning as requested, Dani saw the leader and another man waiting for him.

"I'm Pepo Mitrani. What's your name?" the man asked in Ladino with a hint of skepticism in his voice.

"Dani Henriques."

"Who is your father?"

"Dr. Chaim Henriques. He ran one of the clinics in Salonica. My grandfather was Daniel Henriques. He had an office on the waterfront at 11 Vassilios Heraklion."

A big grin spread across Mitrani's face as he jumped up and hugged Dani. "*Hermano*," he shouted. "How did you survive?"

"In the mountains with the Partisans."

"I knew your father and grandfather. Your father treated my mother." Pepo's smile turned grave. "What happened to your family?"

"My three sisters are dead, as are my grandparents. Father survived the camps. He is still in Salonica, hoping to get news about my mother."

"He must come here. Salonica is no more for us," Pepo said solemnly. As most Jews he, too, persisted in using the city's old name rather than the newer Greek Thessaloniki.

"He won't do that until he gets word of what happened to my mother."

Pepo Mitrani became Dani's mentor. He introduced him to Haifa's maritime community: it was made up of Sephardic Jews from Salonica who immigrated with their families to Palestine before WW II, to help the British build and operate the new and modern seaport of Haifa. As they had once been essential to maritime life in Salonica, these men were now important in Haifa's port. They stayed in Palestine, continuing to contribute to Haifa's maritime success.

"Dani, what do you want to study?" Pepo asked.

"At home I wanted to be an engineer."

"How were your marks at school?"

"I was a good student."

"Good. After some tutoring, we'll get you into the Technion Institute. You'll also be a member of the Haganah. When we need you, we'll call on you for help. You must be ready to defend your brothers and sisters."

"I'll do that."

"I believe you have a cousin in Tel Aviv. His name is Shimon Henriques. He is important in the Haganah."

And so, Dani became a member of the circle of expatriate Sephardim living in Haifa and a member of the Haganah with a cousin in Tel Aviv he would look up when he had the time. Many longshoremen knew Dani's grandfather and related stories about the old man during the happy days, which Dani was pleased to hear. Somehow his tuition was paid. He didn't ask how, but he guessed it was longshoremen, the Haganah, or both. He now had money to buy books, supplies and clothing. Suitably dressed, he attended Haifa's Technion Institute, the Middle East's finest scientific school which was associated with Albert Einstein and other noted world-renowned scientists. His fortunes were on an upswing, and he wrote to his father, imploring him to come to Palestine.

"Surely, Papa," he noted, "there will always be a place here for a fine doctor such as yourself."

But Chaim would not come yet. He wrote back, "Every month, one or two people are still returning to the city. I cannot leave until I have world of what happened to your mother or there are no more people returning."

One day, when Dani returned to his room, he found a note under his door. It was written by Pepo. "Dani- get down to the Longshoreman's office right away. We need you."

Arabs were on the rampage and Haganah was calling in its chips. Dani would once again be toting a weapon.

ॐ ॐ

It was nighttime. Thirty Haganah men descended from three bread and milk delivery trucks. The leader was a young French officer, Major Shimon Henriques. He was short, about five-feet-eight, and very thin. He wore the khaki shorts of a desert military fighter, topped with high khaki knee socks. Shimon Henriques may have looked like an adolescent, but he had the leader's rare quality of getting men to follow him into danger.

Dani's introduction to his cousin would come later. For now, the task at hand was to relieve a Kibbutz bordering on the Sea of Galilee. One of its Arab employees had a wage dispute with the Collective and decided to settle it by attacking the farm.

The rattling of automatic fire, explosions and flames lit up the sky. It looked to Dani as if the settlers were taking a beating. Scurrying through heavy underbrush, the rescue team could see about forty Arabs, who were directing heavy fire into the Kibbutz' main building. This was where most of the defenders were located. Quietly, Shimon Henriques ordered ten men to take up positions behind the invaders. Then he set up mortar squads on each side of the Arabs, ordering his men to fire only on his signal. Dani was with the remaining group that was to fire into the invaders as the mortars rained down on them.

It was a good plan. As soon as mortars dropped, the invaders broke ranks and ran, firing blindly into the night. They killed one Israeli and wounded two others. The men Henriques had assigned to the rear caught them as they ran off. Of the 40 or so invaders, only 11 escaped, leaving their equipment behind. It would contribute to Haganah's sparse arsenal.

The Israelis entered the Kibbutz to treat the wounded and carry their dead comrade for burial. Over a cup of steaming tea, Dani introduced himself to Shimon.

"From Salonica," Shimon said in Ladino. "We heard things were not too good there."

"No. Almost the entire community was wiped out."

"Where are you living?"

"Nearby, in Haifa. I'm studying engineering at the Technion."

"When you finish your studies, let me know. As soon as the English leave and we establish a legitimate army, I could use an engineer in my reserve group. Interested?"

"Yes, Major."

"*Hermanicao*, I am always Shimon to you."

39

Michael Ennis
1958

Michael Ennis exhibited a high level of curiosity and intelligence at an early age. He and his sister Rachel were known as 'Navy Brats,' the children of military parents who moved around a lot. During his young life, Michael lived in Washington, DC; Bethesda, Maryland; Norfolk, Virginia, Groton, Connecticut and Boston, Massachusetts. As a boy and teenager, it was difficult for him to make lasting friendships. He spent much of his time reading. Wherever he lived, the local library became one of his regular hangouts.

Listening to the stories his father told him of the origins of the Ennis family, led Michael to read heavily about the Revolutionary War. There was nothing he could find about the Henriques family in the American Colonies. He consulted genealogical charts for Ennis. With all this research, Michael progressed no further than his father's scant understanding of the beginnings of the Ennis and Henriques families.

One day, Michael came across a genealogical book explaining that prior to 1820, there were no central repositories for passenger lists landing in an American port. It meant, the book explained, that if any passenger lists still existed for the pre-Revolutionary War period, they might possibly be found in either local museums, libraries, the basement of a courthouse or in a City Hall. They might also be found overseas. For Michael, that would mean London or Amsterdam, both out of his reach economically. There was also the possibility that a passenger list might be stored in someone's home in a dusty attic, among a forgotten pile of other papers.

One summer when he was 16, Michael took the bus to Newport, Rhode Island from his home in Norfolk. There, he went straight to City Hall and looked up the old colonial tax records for the city of Newport. Solomon Henriques was listed as a taxpayer. There was no listing for Solomon Ennis. Checking the current local phone book, he found no Henriques, but there was a family named Ennis. After calling and explaining the purpose of his inquiry, the family told him that there was no one in their Newport family who went back to the Revolutionary War. Nor could he establish that they were in any way related to him.

Next, he visited the well-known Redwood Library and Athenaeum, one of America's oldest libraries. As he stepped inside, he noticed the old building's several fireplaces and the old shelves stacked with rows upon rows of books. He imagined Solomon coming here, sitting close to one of the fireplaces on a cold day, reading a book and trying to keep warm.

"Might you have ships' manifests and passenger lists for the period around the Revolutionary War?" he asked the librarian.

"No," was her reply, as she pointed out the window, "but you might try our Court House down the way. Take Touro Street just a few blocks until you get to 45 Washington Square. They may have records of the sort you're looking for in their archives."

After a short walk during which the hot hazy sun reflected off the Narraganset River to his left, Michael approached a desk in the Court House lobby and asked the guard there if he could look at the archives.

"What's the purpose, young man?"

"It's research I'm doing for a school project."

The guard sent him to the top floor, telling him he should ask for a Miss Maria Malfetano, which Michael did. He had to wait, as there was no one regularly in charge of the archives, which were locked. In 15 minutes, Miss Malfetano came into the waiting room jingling at least 20 keys on a large steel ring. She was a young lady dressed in a pleated tartan plaid skirt and was the Court's newest clerk. Tending to the archives was one of the extra duties for a freshman clerk.

It was obvious that she did not often enter this room, as she had to try almost half a dozen keys before she found the one that opened the door. She smiled at Michael.

"What is it you're looking for? Hardly anyone ever comes up here. I do have a list at my desk of whatever's in our archives. I memorized it. Tell me what you're looking for and I can probably direct you to it and save you some time."

"Passenger lists around 1775, for ships going from Newport to Boston."

"That's a tall order. We don't have records for ships that far back. But I do know what you might try. The two biggest ship owners at the time were Jacob Rodriguez Rivera and Aaron Lopez. There were others, but those two were the main shippers. I've seen their records in here. You'll find them along that wall," she said as she pointed to the back of the gloomy room.

"They might have duplicate passenger lists. I suggest you start with them first. We keep them in chronological order, so you can go directly to the period you're interested in right away. If there's nothing there, I can suggest some other shippers who might help.

"You'll find me in Room 436, that's my office. You are not to mark any documents, mind you. We'll have to have your name and address, because you'll need to fill out a formal request to read any files. Here are the forms. You can't get started 'til you've filled them out and give them to me. You may make photocopies if you wish. Twenty cents a page. When you're finished let me know, so I can lock up after you and help you with any copies you might care to make." Malfetano turned a switch on, and the room suddenly bloomed when a series of fluorescents flicked into a bright light.

There it was, just as she had suggested. He found them in Aaron Lopez' records, which he had gone to after an unsuccessful search of the Rodriguez-Rivera papers. It was a folder with passenger lists. Solomon was one of 12 passengers bound for Boston the night he left Newport. He read:

Passenger, Master Solomon Ennis, unaccompanied, bound for Boston on the sloop Prophet Elijah.

So, he's not yet 21, Michael surmised. *He's listed as Master, meaning he had not yet reached 21. Everything points to this Solomon, being both Henriques and Ennis.*

A further search of the Lopez records revealed an earned salary payment a day earlier, of two pounds to Solomon Henriques, *in liquidation of all claims for his earned wages,* as well as a generous loan of five pounds. No interest to be charged. The entry was signed by Uriel de Leon, Chief Clerk. Further along in the documents, several weeks later, Uriel de Leon made another entry concerning Solomon: *the landlady of Solomon Henriques delivered a seaman's ditty bag to our office, to be held by us for the young man as he requested.*

Michael's research now unearthed clear proof that Solomon Henriques' name was changed on the same day he set sail for Boston. This was something new. It was also known that on the same day Solomon Henriques was receiving his wages, he got a loan from his obviously sympathetic employer.

As he read more documents, Michael learned that Lopez and Rodriguez-Rivera, as patriots to the Revolution, made their sailing vessels available to the Continental Congress during the War.

None of this proved Solomon Henriques or Ennis was a Jew. Michael read further and found a letter from a Boston client, one Moses Hayes. It was directed to Uriel de Leon, informing him that he *had hired Solomon Ennis, the young man you referred to me. I am pleased with his abilities.* Hayes thanked de Leon for sending the young man to him. And there it was! Like a lightning bolt accompanied with a thunderclap: Hayes goes on to tell de Leon that Solomon attends Friday night Sabbath services at his home with "great frequency."

So, our ancestor was a Jew! But the trail ended there, cold, tantalizing, and frustrating. What had happened to Solomon after he reached Boston and began working for Hayes?

When Michael showed his father copies of what he had found, James Ennis lauded his son's research efforts. "But we're no further on in finding out how and where he died and most important: where is he buried?"

Michael had to agree. He had to accept the fact that he had no idea about how to continue his research from the point he had already uncovered.

ℜ ℜ

When he was 18, Michael entered Columbia University. It was his first solid and lasting relationship with people his own age. Some of his classmates were Jews. After a while one of them, Sylvia Beckman, invited him to her home on Manhattan's Upper West Side, for a Friday night dinner. This was his introduction to the Jewish Sabbath and the mystery of the *Shekinah*, God's feminine guardian. Traditionally, she is assigned to care for and protect the Jews in their long wandering exile from the Holy Land. He was impressed with the ritual lighting of candles and its accompanied blessings; the gathering of an entire family to enjoy a meal together in a religious setting. He liked that time was taken to bless bread and wine before partaking of them. For someone who was not raised with any religious beliefs or a regular weekly assembly of family for meals – because the head of the house was away on his country's business – it was a revelation. After that first dinner, Michael mentioned to Sylvia's father the history of the Ennis-Enriques families.

"Ah," Beckman said, "Sephardim. Spanish Jews. You might go to the Jewish Encyclopedia to learn about the Henriques family. I don't know much about the Sephardim. Check it out and let me know what you find."

Beckman was being polite; he never expected to see Michael again. But from that time, feeling such comfort at the Friday night ritual, Michael wheedled invitations as often as he could to Sabbath dinners at Sylvia's home. He and Sylvia were now seeing each other exclusively. After a few dinners, Michael told Sylvia's father, "You know, Mr. Beckman, I followed your advice and checked out the Henriques family in the Encyclopedia Judaica at the University's library. "

"And what did you find?

"That some of them are a distinguished English family with branches in the West Indies. Several members served in the English military as officers during World War II. One of them was a Major in the Armored Corps, who was among those who liberated the Bergen-Belsen concentration camp. He now teaches about the Holocaust at Oxford.

"There are even Henriques in Italy. I imagine they are all related. My father told me that he met some in North Africa when he was stationed there during the War. And he knows an Henriques in Amsterdam"

"Well, Michael," Mr. Beckman said with a smile, "looks as if you may have some notable ancestors in your family tree."

Sylvia's father, Albert Beckman, was not quite six years old in 1903, when he accompanied his parents to the United States from their home in London. Beckman's father Morris had been invited by an uncle to help run a printing business in New York City. The uncle's only son had no interest in taking over the enterprise. Morris was a fast learner and soon ran the business while his elderly uncle enjoyed a much-deserved retirement. Eventually, he bought the shop from his uncle and steered it into a business with over a hundred employees. It became one of New York's most successful printers. Albert stepped into his father's shoes when Morris retired.

As Michael became a regular visitor to the Beckman's apartment, Sylvia's father could see the young man and his daughter were more than friendly classmates. He liked Michael, who was obviously now serious about his relationship with Sylvia. Albert was pleased that Michael asked intelligent questions about the Jewish religion, but Michael wasn't a Jew and that posed a problem for a man who had taken for granted that his daughter would marry within the religion. He had expected to have the pleasure of taking his grandchildren to his synagogue; watching with pride as they grew and following them as they passed through the Jewish rites marking childhood, adolescence, adulthood, and marriage. Beckman was hoping Michael would either get tired of his research and disappear or, perhaps, convert.

Michael was now in law school and Beckman realized he had a dilemma. Michael and Sylvia had been dating for four years and

Albert Beckman had done little to discourage them. Sylvia was happy and in a way that was important. At least Michael was someone Beckman could respect, and his father was a high-ranking member of the Navy.

So Beckman said to Michael, "I can't answer all your questions Michael. Maybe I should introduce you to my rabbi, who has better answers than I do." Beckman was hoping the meeting with the rabbi would lead to conversion.

The synagogue was a large space surrounded by 12 stained-glass windows, each one representing one of the Twelve Tribes of Israel. But attention was focused on the wall containing an Ark. It protected the scrolls containing the Laws of Moses, behind a pair of doors. After pointing out the Eternal Light glowing atop the Ark, the rabbi explained that portions of the scrolls were read to the congregation each Saturday morning, as well as on Tuesdays and Thursdays.

Michael attended his first service and while everything was foreign to him, he appreciated the order in the Synagogue and the prayers that he was able to read through the prayer book's English translations. He was even happier when Rabbi Stein, an older man, suggested he get together with one of his younger assistant rabbis, who could help him with his questions.

That's how Michael met Leonard Mosher, only three years older than he, lately out of the Jewish Theological Seminary and a man obviously on the road to an important career in the rabbinate. They became more than teacher and student: they became fast friends, attending movies and concerts together, Michael with Sylvia and Leonard with his new wife Paula.

One day Michael told Leonard about his efforts to solve the mystery of Solomon Ennis. The rabbi studied Michael carefully, then asked, "So what are you planning to do about it?"

"Len, for a long time I've been thinking I want to become an Henriques and a Jew."

"That's quite a plan. Do you realize what being a Jew means?"

"I believe so. I've read a lot of history about the Jews. You and I have talked a lot about Jewish history and rituals. I think I know what it means."

"If you're asking me to convert you, then by tradition, you know, I am obliged to turn you down. Three times, no less." The rabbi smiled as he made a record of Michael's request into a small notebook he kept in his jacket pocket.

"I know that, and I would like you to start me on a conversion course right away. Consider yourself asked three times. When do we start?"

"You may not realize it Michael, but for the past few months you have already begun the process."

40

Grandma Miriam's Grave
1962

For a long while, Jim Ennis had had an itch to visit Grandma Miriam's grave. Not that he ever knew her. She was the family legend who had died a hundred years earlier. He didn't even know where she was buried. When he was eleven years old, his father told him that he had visited her grave. But Jim couldn't remember where his father had said it was. Maybe her tombstone would reveal some more clues as to the Henriques connection with the Ennis family. Visiting her grave would concretize the history of his family. She was a real person with a Spanish name and somewhere under a tombstone, she may be wondering why none of her descendants are paying attention to her.

The logical place to start would be Springfield, Massachusetts, Jimmy's birthplace. He had not been there since he was 18, preparing to leave home to attend the Naval Academy at Annapolis. That was in the 1930s: so long ago it seemed to be another lifetime. He was a runny-nosed kid then, with little meat on his bones. In those days, digging up the history of his family was certainly not one of his priorities.

During the summer of 1962, Jim had earned a long leave. He and Lucy packed luggage for a ten-day motor trip. They loaded it in the trunk of their Pontiac sedan and began the drive to Springfield. Aside from seeking the grave, it would also be a nostalgic trip for Jim, and an opportunity to show Lucy where he had grown up.

Before the Civil War, the Ennis family, among the wealthiest in the city, had built a two-story, 20 room mansion in Springfield's

Maple Heights-Ridgewood district. That neighborhood was the finest in town and the old Ennis house was now one of the many carefully preserved 19th Century homes.

The name Ennis, which had been carved in granite above the main entrance, was still there. Jimmy had never lived in that house. By the time he was born, the family fortune had been lost, as was their ownership of this home. He remembered, he told Lucy, as a boy walking by and seeing the name on the building and wondering what it was like for his ancestors to have lived there and to have been counted among Springfield's wealthiest citizens.

The eight-room house where he grew up was closer to the Connecticut River. A few houses down from the new Ennis home lived a 60-year-old retired sailor. Shelby Pines lived with his daughter and son-in-law. He kept a one-masted sailboat moored on the river, and he had often invited Jimmy to sail with him. While they were on the river, the old sailor filled the young boy with exciting tales of the sea. Pines taught Jimmy how to sail. Jimmy fell in love with the river and boats. He was anxious to see the oceans the old man had described to him, and the large freighters that sailed across them. That would come later, when he finished high school and entered the Naval Academy. Jimmy would never lose his love for the sea.

"Let's see where you grew up," Lucy requested. They drove up to the old Ennis house, two stories high, wooden construction with a tiled roof and five stone steps up from the street. Jim rang the doorbell. A young boy, perhaps 15, answered the call.

"I'm Jim Ennis. I used to live here. I was wondering if I could show my wife the house where I grew up?"

The boy looked at the couple with doubt. But seeing Jim in his Navy uniform he asked, "Was your father Congressman Ennis, sir?"

"Yes, he was."

"My grandpa bought this house from your father's estate. They said the Congressman had a son at the Naval Academy. Was that you?"

"Yes, it was."

"Come in. I'm all alone. My folks are at work, and Charlie, that's my sister Charlene, she's still at school. I suppose it's all right to let you in."

Lucy and Jim stepped into the house. On the street floor, a cheerful dining room replaced Congressman's Ellis' old home office which once housed his scarred Cherrywood desk, a bank of wooden file cabinets and bookshelves which were filled with copies of the U.S. Constitution and the laws of the federal government. There used to be pictures of Abraham Lincoln and Teddy Roosevelt on the wall.

The living room had changed too. Now, there were many paintings and prints on the walls and there was a piano where once stood a large oak sideboard. Stowed below the sideboard, Jimmy's mother had kept her holiday dishes and the good silver service that had survived the auction of the belongings of the Ennis family's better days. The kitchen had been modernized by the new owners, but the new appliances were in the same spaces the old ones had once occupied.

They walked up a carpeted stairway to the second floor. Jimmy noticed that a creak in the third step had disappeared. They stopped at the first room at the top of the steps. The door was closed. Jimmy didn't try to open it. It was a teenager's sanctuary he would not invade.

"This was my bedroom," he announced.

"It's mine now," the boy said, making no move to invite his guests inside. The room was his private place, obviously off-limits to all adults, including his parents. There was even a sign on the door, declaring this place as "Off Limits."

In the bathroom, Jimmy showed Lucy a small hole in the medicine cabinet. "One morning I misfired with my air rifle. I was punished for it," he recalled, with a smile that brought him back decades.

He explained to his wife and their young host the way things had been when the Ennis family held sway here. In his first year at Annapolis, Jim's father died. The estate sold the house. Since Jimmy was the only heir, his mother having preceded his father by several years, the proceeds were held in trust for him until he reached the age of 21. Jimmy had become the last in the Ennis family line.

๛ ๛

Jim had a plan to locate Grandma Miriam's grave. He would contact the oldest congregation in Springfield and get them to open their cemetery so he could finally see where she was resting. But it wasn't that easy, as the congregation's rabbi, Lionel Rabinowitz, explained.

"The first formal congregation in Springfield wasn't established until 1887, long after your ancestor died. Even then, they only had a small building. A cemetery didn't come for five more years. Your great grandmother's body would have been sent to Newport, or perhaps, Boston. That's if she wanted a Jewish burial. So that's where you'll have to go if you are looking for her grave.

"I can tell you, Commander Ennis, that we are presently preparing a history of the Jews of Springfield. Only a few Jewish families lived here in the 1820s. They had no formal congregation. They met mostly on holidays or when there was a significant religious event. We do know that they maintained a Sunday School for the youngsters.

"Most of the Jews were itinerant merchants. There were two Jewish doctors living here at the time, and we had a Jewish lawyer, too. All the professionals were married to non-Jews. Some of the folks who were children at that time, wrote memoirs of early Jewish life in Springfield when they were in their later years. We're putting it all together in an album. I've read most of the papers of the records of the Jews in this city: your great-grandmother Miriam is most prominently mentioned in the memoirs of those who remembered her. She seems to have been known generally as Miss Miriam. And from what I've been reading, she was a fine, remarkable woman who helped in every way she could, with money, clothing, shoes, food, even bringing rabbis to Springfield from time to time. When we have finished compiling all the notes and congregational minutes, I can send copies to you."

"I would really appreciate It," Emmis said, writing his address on a small notepad and handing the page to the rabbi. "I believe we should be starting at Newport to look for Miriam. And I'll look forward to hearing from you, rabbi."

At Newport, they consulted with the rabbi of the city's famous Touro Synagogue. After a check of the community's graves, he said, "Yes, Miriam Mendoza Duff is buried in our cemetery. Our records show that she was born here in Newport and was a member of the well-known Mendoza family."

James and Lucy entered the graveyard with the Rabbi, who showed them where Grandma Miriam's grave was located. The etchings in the upright tombstone were fading but could still be read.

> *Miriam Mendoza Duff*
> *Born 1758 – Died 1842*
> *Loving Wife of Angus Duff*
> *Beloved Mother of James*
> *A Daughter of Israel*
> *And a great dispenser of charity*
> *May She rest in peace.*

There was also a line in Portuguese and Hebrew, which Jimmy could not read.

"Her parents are also buried here," the rabbi added. "They both died during the Revolutionary War when the British naval forces bombarded Newport. Here they are: Gideon and Penina Mendoza."

James ran his hands softly over the two neatly carved headstones which lay side by side. *They were his Jewish ancestors, come across the sea just as Solomon Henriques had done. They also wanted to start a new and better life in the Colonies.* The rabbi interrupted his thoughts.

"Their son, Rafael, is there," the rabbi said, pointing to a gravestone a little further away. "He was killed in the War of 1812. He's your great uncle, a few times removed."

"What about any of the Henriques or Ennis? Are they buried here?"

The rabbi shrugged. "Those names are not familiar to me at all. We have no one buried here with those names."

୨୦ ୶

Two weeks after returning from their New England trip, Ennis received a phone call from Rabbi Rabinowitz in Springfield. "Is this Commander Ennis? This is the long-distance operator calling for him. Rabbi Rabinowitz is calling for you sir, from Springfield, Massachusetts."

"This is Commander Ennis."

"Commander? Rabbi Rabinowitz here. I'm calling to let you know that we found more notes about your ancestor, and we will be sending you copies of what we found. You might like to hear some of the comments beforehand."

"Sure Rabbi. But before you begin, your hunch was right. I found Grandma Miriam's grave in Newport, as well as her mother, father and brother."

"I'm pleased that's resolved for you. To get back to the notes: the first one is from an excerpt by Gregory Belasco who was 14 when she died. Fifty years later, he remembered her quite well. He said,

"I remember Miss Miriam in those days when we had no rabbi or synagogue in Springfield. There were only a few Jewish families and our parents tried hard to educate us and teach us about our Jewish heritage. Miss Miriam, that's what we all called her, would come to someone's house on Sunday mornings and sit with us children to teach us about our history. She was a great lady who everyone respected. She bought prayer books for us and on Sundays she made sure we all had cookies and milk. And more than once she brought a rabbi to Springfield for a High Holiday service. When a new boy was born, Miss Miriam always made sure that a circumciser came to perform the circumcision ritual. When I needed a new pair of shoes because mine had holes in the bottom, she quietly bought me a pair."

"That's great," Jimmy shouted into the telephone.

"Here's another person who recalled your ancestor, commander. Her name is Elizabeth Mallow. She wrote her memorandum in 1898."

"Miss Miriam would make clothing for the poor among us when we had an important event, regardless of their religion, and always did so quietly. It was Miss Miriam that paid the rent for the rooms we would meet in on the Holy Days. I know this because my uncle was her lawyer and I heard him tell my parents that this was so. That was after she died. Later, my uncle told me she liked to be quiet about the good things she did for us. She made him promise that so long as she was alive, he was to tell no one of what she did for the community. I remember he told me she once gave a Catholic Church money, to help rebuild after a fire.

Miss Miriam always seemed sad. I remember that she only smiled when she was with us children. It was as if she was holding some secret inside her that hurt her. We all knew that she had a son. We never could understand why she never brought him to be with us."

"There it is Commander. These notes in greater detail and other comments will be going out to you by mail. Oh, yes, by the way, I checked to see if there were any mentions of an Ennis or Henriques family. There is none."

"Rabbi, thank you for your efforts. I really appreciate it."

"Glad to have helped, Commander. I felt like a real detective digging up all this information about your family and helping you find them. I felt good about it."

Jimmy wrote to the Rabbi, thanking him again for his efforts, enclosing a check for the synagogue. It was to be a contribution in the names of Miriam Mendoza Duff and Gideon, Penina and Raphael Mendoza.

Unfortunately, the mystery of Solomon Henriques/Ennis was still unresolved. Where was he buried? How did he die? And when did he die?

41

Dorothy Bedford nee Henriques
1967

Dorothy Bedford was handed the telegram as she left class, on her way to her office. She had recently been appointed Adjunct Professor of Psychology at the University of Nebraska and was settling into an academic routine of teaching and research. The telegram was from her sister, Marie.

Mother passed away last night. Funeral in 2 days. Await your presence. Marie.

Dorothy was a single parent. She and Emery Bedford had been divorced; was it three or four years ago? She could never recall, exactly. As a psychologist, Dorothy knew there were reasons for that lapse, which she didn't care to investigate. For now, she would have to arrange for her 12-year-old daughter Victoria to stay with a friend while she was in San Francisco attending her mother's funeral. She managed to wheedle one week's emergency leave from the head of her department.

Dorothy and Marie were the last of the Henriques family of San Francisco. Their father, Charles Henriques III, had died five years earlier. Marie, a lawyer, was five years older than her sister, and a childless widow. The sisters had little contact with their family in New York City. Dorothy wondered if those Henriques had received notice of their Aunt Blanche Henrique's death. She would find out once she got to San Francisco.

Marie met Dorothy at the airport. The sisters hugged one another tearfully, partly because they'd lost their mother, partly because they'd not seen each other for more than a year.

As Marie pulled out of the airport parking lot, she asked Dorothy how long she could stay in San Francisco.

"I managed to get a week's leave from my department. I left Victoria with a friend. I can't stay longer than that," Dorothy answered.

Marie made a wry face. "There's a lot of Mom's stuff to go through. I don't want to be making the decisions about what to keep and what to throw out. We should start making an inventory right away."

Charles Henriques III, had been in bad health for several years before he died. Unable to run the family business, he sold it. The bulk of the proceeds went to Blanche Henriques, his wife. He also established two well-endowed trusts for his daughters. Now, according to the terms of Blanche's will, her estate was divided equally between her two daughters. As her beneficiaries, the girls had become millionaires. But Blanche's personal items still had to be inventoried, either to be kept or sold.

First, there was the funeral to attend to. Their mother, in her usual competent manner, had made all the arrangements through her lawyer years earlier. Flowers from her friends filled the room at the funeral parlor and if they themselves were too fragile to attend, their representatives were there.

The work for the sisters began when they started the inventory. First, they went through the pockets of each of their mother's jackets, coats, sweaters, slacks, and housecoats. They came up with a treasure trove of loose cash, expensive pens, uncashed checks, and some interesting jewelry.

Inside a bedroom closet, Dorothy found a small cardboard box. Opening it, she saw it was filled with letters. She lifted the box on to her mother's bed and nestled beside it. Her glasses were settled on her chest, held by hangers. She set them over her eyes and plunged her hand into the opening of the box. She pulled out a letter at random and looked at the date: 1911. She set it aside and retrieved another one, dated 1876. A third letter was dated 1899.

Dorothy turned the box upside down, emptying it of its contents and excitedly called out, "Marie, come here. I've found something!"

Her sister, who had been inventorying the furniture in her mother's sitting room, rushed in. "What is it?"

She sat on the bed next to her sister, who was separating letters from receipts for purchases, missives from workers suggesting work in the house and other miscellaneous papers.

"Dorothy, what are they?"

"Marie, they're letters. Old letters. Many old letters. Here, help me count them."

The women counted 121 letters. It took a while, but they put them in chronological order. The oldest dated April 12, 1851. It was from their great-great grandfather Charles Henriques, written to his sweetheart, Marthe Steiglitz.

The sisters took turns reading the letters aloud.

April 12th 1851
My Dearest Marthe,

I know how distressing this issue of our religious difference is. I wrote to my parents in Lisbon to clarify the issue of our religion. They say that the Henriques family has always been Jewish... that we have secretly practiced Judaism since 1497 and that some of our family left Portugal in 1755 after The Great Earthquake. To be caught practicing Judaism in Portugal meant punishment - sometimes death on certain occasions. Which is why the secrecy. So, you see, I am Jewish. This should satisfy your parents.

I love you and am unable to think of a life without you.

Your loving Charles

The next letter was written by William, Marthe's brother, two weeks following Charles' letter.

April 26th 1851
Marthe,

I told Mama and Papa what Charles told you about his family's religion. Unfortunately, they are not convinced that he is a Jew. They will not change their minds and told me to tell you that you are not to see Charles again.

I saw the letter Charles received from his parents and I am convinced that what they wrote is true. But Mama and Papa won't accept it. Charles will not stop trying to see you. You have to decide.

Charles is a good man. He is certain to contact you. You have to decide what to do.

Your loving brother, William

May 2d 1851
My Darling,

Your parents are insistent on keeping us apart. I will not accept it. If you love me, then meet me at Antonio's restaurant tomorrow night at six. I hope with all my heart that you will be there. Your presence will assure me that you love me as much as I love you.

Your loving, Charles

May 3d 1851
My dearest Marthe,

I cannot express to you the joy I felt when I saw you enter Antonio's last night. Seeing you once again, I was sure my love for you is real and not an infatuation.

When can we meet again? I await your reply.
Your loving, Charles

There were later letters from her brother William, in which he related news of the family who had rejected Marthe following her elopement. Then there were letters from her children. Young William, named for Marthe's brother, wrote from Chicago where he attended college and later, medical school. Letters described how, after graduation, he would volunteer for the Army, to go to Cuba during the Spanish-American War.

There were letters from her other son, Charles, Jr., who remained in San Francisco to go into business with his father. Charles' letters were written while he was in college in Austin, Texas. He wrote other letters from vacation venues.

William wrote his parents to tell them that he had caught the attention of Colonel Theodore Roosevelt, commander of the famous Rough Riders, who urged him to come to New York where he would help William in his medical career.

William would briefly return to San Francisco and then go on to New York. Three years later, he wrote to his parents to tell them that he was marrying a distant Roosevelt relative. When Theodore Roosevelt became president, William was on his medical staff.

There were no more letters after this one. Americans had stopped writing letters and keeping diaries. But it was likely that their mother had kept a diary. Blanche Henriques was one of the older generations. But searching for that would come later.

At dinner that night, Dorothy asked Marie, "Did you ever follow up on investigating if we are related to the Henriques family of New York?" she asked.

"I don't know. I think we should do something about it. How is it that we lost touch with our uncle and cousins in New York?"

"Dorothy, New York is a long way from San Francisco. Especially in the days before the airplane. You had to travel more than three days by train to get to New York during grandpa's time. I remember grandfather telling me that they did go to New York once and saw William Henriques, who introduced the family to President Theodore Roosevelt. We just lost touch afterwards. That's all I can say about that."

ϟ ϟ

When Dorothy went back to Omaha, she took the letters and her mother's diary, which she found after a long search. Over the next two years she read them again and again, making careful notes of what the writers were saying. She also made many psychological and insightful comments and, of course, she followed the history of Henriques family through genealogical charts, making the connection between Michael and her family. Her book was shaping up. She included a final detailed chapter with tips on how her readers could trace their ancestors, encouraging them by telling of her success in locating family members.

Dorothy was surprised to learn that the Jews of Spain, Portugal, Southern France, and Southern Italy represented over 90 percent of Europe's Jewish population at the time of the Spanish expulsion in 1492. They were the ancestors of Jews who found their way into Eastern Europe. Families currently living in Poland and Russia were probably unaware of their Latin ancestors.

Dorothy also learned that in Eastern Europe, the early minutes of old synagogues were written in Spanish and Portuguese. Centuries later, only Yiddish was spoken and used in the synagogue and the community. Had any Henriques found their way East? That was for another time. Another book perhaps.

When she thought the book ready to be published, she walked to the University of Nebraska's publishing offices and deposited the manuscript with one of its editors. Six months later, an editor called to tell her that her book had been accepted and would be going to press after some editing.

"Do you have a final title for your book?" the editor asked.

Dorothy was prepared; it wasn't the first time this had come to her attention. "How about "The Henriques Family: A Study in Tears and Joys?"

"I'll give it to the managing editor," the editor responded.

Within six months, Dorothy's book became a best seller. Americans were thirsty to learn about the past generations of their families. Dorothy Bedford was helping to show them how to start; that you didn't have to be a professional genealogist to track your family. She became a celebrity, appearing on television and radio. Newspapers and magazines carried interviews with her.

Along the way, she met her Henriques family and began gathering material for a second book.

42

La Buena, New Mexico
1968

Manuel Henriques Maldonado arrived at the Friday night religious service a few minutes late. He spotted a seat on the long wooden bench in the back row by the wall. *If I slip in quietly back there*, he thought, *no one would pay too much attention to me*. Sliding into the space, he was a little jittery, unsure of what his visit would accomplish. He had been thinking of coming here for a long time, finally gathering enough courage to attend this Jewish service which was regularly advertised in the Religious Services section of the local newspaper.

He didn't know what would be expected of him: how to behave in this strange place. In churches, the few times he did attend, he knelt before the altar and crossed himself as he had been taught to do from childhood. From what he had been reading about Jews, he knew they never knelt as part of their service, and certainly never made the sign of the cross. What he did notice was that there were no statues or images in this sanctuary. It was bare of any symbols, except for a Star of David carved on the dais where prayers were being read.

Manuel tried to follow the service; it was mostly in English. But when the leader spoke in Hebrew, Manuel was lost. The service lasted an hour and a half, ending with blessings over bread and wine. That was followed by socializing in a large hall. The congregants were obviously a closely-knit group. Many were middle-aged, others looked like college students. There were a few youngsters in their teens and some even younger scattered about. An array of cakes, fruits, soft drinks, coffee and tea was set out and there was friendly chatting. Henriques Maldonado learned that this was called an Oneg Shabbat in Hebrew.

Myron Greenberg, the congregant who assumed the post of the synagogue's official greeter, approached the stranger as he sipped a cup of coffee while standing alone in a corner of the social hall. Congregation *Bet Ha Shomer* was home to 65 families (too small to afford a rabbi) in this New Mexican town of *La Buena*. Some congregants owned shops *on La Buena's* Main Street, famous for its untouched architecture harkening back to the time when Spain was colonial master of New Mexico. *La Buena* was also home to Merritt College, a school specializing in mining and agriculture. Some of the synagogue's members taught at the college or were students there. Manuel noticed two or three elderly couples who he assumed were retirees or, perhaps, tourists.

"Good evening. Welcome to our Temple. Is this your first visit to our synagogue? I don't recall having seen you before," Myron said, his hand extended in a friendly greeting toward Manuel. "I'm Myron Greenberg. Everyone calls me Mike."

Mike was hoping this gentleman was a newcomer to town and perhaps a potential member with a wife and child or two to be enrolled in the religious school. "Please, have some cake with your coffee," Mike continued. "Are you Jewish?"

"No, I'm not. But I've been wanting to learn about your religion for a while. My mother, before she died, said we were Jewish a long time ago. When she was alive, she lit candles every Friday night. My mother also told us not to eat pork and I never saw her in church. Later, I read somewhere that lighting candles on Friday nights was a Jewish ritual."

"Yes, it is one of our rituals. Where was your family from?"

"Spain, of course. We came here as settlers in the 1600s, with the *Conquistadores,* exactly the date, I don't know. We settled here in New Mexico, near Albuquerque. Then we moved further north. I came to *La Buena* after I graduated from college in Colorado, to find work in the computer department of Merritt College. The rest of my family still lives in a town called Aurora; it's not far from Taos."

"We get a few people here from time to time, telling us a similar story," Mike said. "You may have had a Jewish ancestor way back in your family history. Did you have Jewish objects around the house?"

"I wouldn't know what's Jewish or not. My mother had what she called a candelabra; she would light a lot of candles on it for many days during the winter, around Christmas time. She said it had something to do with a miracle for the Jews. Then she also had the old silver candle sticks she used to light the Friday night candles. I remember at some time of the year, in the fall, she would fast for a whole day. And she recited strange words, some of which I recognized sitting here tonight! She also wore what I later learned was a Jewish star, which she was always careful to keep under her blouse so no one could see it. My sister has one, too."

Henriques Maldonado paused, and then said, "My mother would tell us a story of how Jews were hounded by the Inquisition, so they left Lisbon to escape them because they'd found out a branch of our family was practicing Jewish customs. They joined a group that was settling here in New Mexico during the 1600s. My mother said the Henriques and Pereira families were very close in Spain and Portugal. But that's not so here, as far as I can remember. There are some Pereiras in Albuquerque, but they don't seem to be close to the Henriques family nowadays. It's a family tradition, though. How true it is, I don't know. I can't say. And the basis of the association has never been explained to me." He took a deep breath, looked Mike Greenberg in the eye, and after hesitating said, "Is it all right if I come to your services?"

"Of course. You are always welcome."

Henriques Maldonado then held Greenberg by his arm while looking into eyes with a strange seriousness. In a low voice and with an assurance that no one else could hear him, he said, "I took a DNA test. According to what they found; I have Jewish ancestry."

Mike stared at his visitor. "That's real interesting. How accurate are these tests? They're new, so I don't know too much about them, other than some professors at Emory University in Atlanta began working with it."

"The company that made the tests says I can depend on the results."

"No kidding?"

"Does that mean if I want to join the congregation, I can?"

"Well, I don't know. There are some of our religious laws that must be followed for a person to be considered a Jew. We call it *halacha*. That's Hebrew for the law. I'm not the one that's really up on that. Some of our members know more about this than I do."

"There are hundreds, maybe thousands like me, living in Albuquerque, Santa Fe, Taos, all over these mountains. I learned, after my mother died, that many pray in secret. As Jews, I mean. It's a secret their families have kept for hundreds of years. Some of the people I know have told me they want to return to the Jewish religion. But they don't know how to go about it."

Mike looked at Manuel. "I think you might want to talk to Marty Grant. He teaches history at the college." Greenberg guided him to a very tall blond-haired man in his late 40s with a sharp nose and lavender-colored eyes.

"Marty," Greenberg said, interrupting a conversation, "there's a man here you might be interested in speaking with." He introduced him to Manuel and the two men shook hands. Grant said he'd recognized Manuel from the administration office at the college. After hearing Manuel's story, Grant said, "That's a hell of a tale. How often do you go back to see your family?"

"I'm planning to go back next month. My brother's getting married. In a town that's about 60 miles from here."

"I'd like to go back with you. I'd be interested in seeing what goes on in your community."

"Yes, I can arrange for you to come to my brother's wedding and meet our family and friends."

❧ ❧

The mountains of New Mexico are noted for their breathtaking beauty. Manuel Henriques Maldonado and Marty Grant arrived at Aurora during the night. The wedding would be held the next day in the early afternoon. Grant stepped outside his motel room, standing in the cool fresh air, and looked at the sky. The motel was high in the mountains. The usual loom of a city's night lights, its lampposts and neon signs always obscuring the heavens for city dwellers, was absent. The sky was like black paint, glossy and shiny-bright: alive. Marty felt the universe was setting itself to music. Stars shone above him as he remembered during his childhood, when his family vacationed in the Pennsylvania countryside during summers. He felt as if the stars were so close, he could reach up and pull them down.

This was a magical place the crypto-Jews had picked to settle when they came from Spain. Yet why had these secret Jews who accompanied the Conquistadors as outwardly observant Christians, chosen to settle in this out-of-the-way place, over fifteen hundred miles from Mexico City, which was the center of civil and religious power, wealth, and personal opportunity?

The wedding was a low-key affair. The groom, who seemed nervous, was five years younger than Manuel and a close look-alike. The bride, a pert young lady, was from the same town as the Henriques Maldonado family. The guests, mostly family and close friends, emphasized that their families had been close for centuries, beginning when New Mexico was *Nuevo España*, under Spanish colonial rule. The residents of Aurora usually married among themselves, or their friends and families located in nearby towns.

When Manuel introduced Marty to the guests, they welcomed him with handshakes and smiles. Many of these people had never met a Jew before and were wary to speak to him about their personal lives.

A Protestant minister, who was a Justice of the Peace, in his 60s with a wrinkled brow, a sun-tanned face and snowy white hair, married the couple. After the ceremony, the guests sat down to a meal. Upon learning that Marty Grant was Jewish, the minister, Pastor Samuel Rios, remarked that his family had been Jewish generations earlier.

"Many of the people in these small mountain towns have similar family histories as mine, including the families of our bride and groom. They have long familial associations with each other over centuries. When the Americans took New Mexico away from the Mexicans, Protestant ministers came to these mountains with Spanish bibles and lured some of us away from the Catholic Church. Under Spanish rule, the church didn't permit us to read the bible; the priests read it to us and interpreted its meaning, from which we were not permitted to deviate. Now we are free to do that.

"Since we became American citizens, our young men have fought in two World Wars and Korea, and we have had close and direct contact with Jews. These so-called 'Christ killers', as they were depicted by the Catholic priests, created confusion, since the Jews they met in the army and in business were not the devils they had warned us about.

"Some of our Catholic women prayed to St. Esther; *Santa Esterita* they called her. It infuriated the priests. "There is no St. Esther," they would shout in frustration. But the women persisted. It was their way of injecting a Jew among the Catholic saints, making it permissible to pray to her."

"Why is this area filled with so many families like these?" Grant asked.

"Converted Jews in Spain and Portugal who continued to practice their religion secretly had to find a way to escape the Spanish and Portuguese Inquisitions. By law, converted Jews – New Christians as they were known – were not permitted to leave Spain or Portugal or even settle in the new lands in America. Inquisitors had been locating the heretical secret Jews and torturing and even killing them. The converted Jews found ways to get around the law, migrating to Spain's colony which eventually became Mexico. It was three thousand miles away, across an unfriendly ocean to the New World. Jews hoped to rid themselves of that hated Inquisition by leaving it behind."

The Reverend paused, snapped a crisp roll in two, and took a small bite before he continued. "In effect, they were divorcing themselves from the horrors of the Inquisition and the unfair civil laws aimed at them. At one time, it was necessary to have a certificate to show you were four generations from your family's conversion, in order to serve in the army or hold a government job or even travel outside of Spain or Portugal. It was called *limpieza de sangre*. The purity of blood."

Pastor Rios let out a frustrating sigh. "When they arrived here, to their surprise these secret Jews learned that the Inquisition had preceded them. It had already been installed in Mexico City, the center of Spain's financial, religious, and political power. The Inquisition was continuing its nasty work here, even to jailing the Governor of New Spain and killing all the members of his large family, for the heretical act of practicing Judaism.

"The Jewish settlers resolved the problem by moving to these out-of-the-way places in the mountainous area around Santa Fe and farther north. In those days, it would have taken several long and arduous months for civil and religious authorities to travel the 1500 miles from Mexico City up these mountains by mule or on foot. There were few roads leading to this area. Then too, there was the real danger of thieves and Indians attacking any caravans heading up the mountains.

"You can imagine, once here, these families were basically on their own. The secret Jews among the settlers kept to themselves, trying not to marry their Christian neighbors. When a priest or civil officials did get here, any heresy or necessary legal work to report took months, even years to notify the authorities in Mexico City. Then, they had to wait many more months for a response. By the time an answer could be received, a heretic could disappear. Or even die."

Pastor Rios smiled. "Every time I relate this tale to visitors, I marvel at how fascinated they are by the story. So, they were relatively safe from the civil and religious snoopers who were trying to see what these colonists were up to. Over time, without any rabbis to guide them, they forgot most of the essence of Judaism, but they still remembered they had been Jews and continued to think of themselves that way. They kept it a secret from anyone who was not within their close and special circle of family and friends. Often, even from the male children until they reached maturity. The secret was kept by the women, who passed it among themselves.

Woman stayed at home and were not engaged in commerce, so they had less contact with strangers and less opportunity to mistakenly reveal who they really were.

"Come to my office tomorrow morning. Anyone can tell you where I am. I'll take you to a Catholic cemetery where you'll see tombstones with a cross, a Star of David, and the deceased's name in English, Spanish, and Hebrew. Without fear of punishment or chastisement from the community, some of our people have recently decided to come out in the open. Despite that, many are still wary; they fear the old stigma of Judaism may fall upon them and their families. If you have a camera, bring it with you tomorrow; you can photograph these tombstones."

Everyone at the wedding learned that Marty Grant was Jewish. Some of the guests refused to talk religion with him. Others, less wary, invited him to their homes to show him candlesticks, menorahs, even silver Torah pointers called *yads* in Hebrew, *punteros* in Spanish. One family, the Valencias, showed him a lengthy family tree going back to Spain before Columbus. There was a big story here in these mountains, the slow unveiling of secrets tightly held for hundreds of years.

When he returned to *La Buena*, Marty related to his fellow congregants what Pastor Rios had told him, the homes he had visited and the Catholic graveyards he had seen with Jewish tombstones. There were many questions thrown at him. Some congregants wanted the synagogue to help these people come back to Judaism. But Marty felt that might be unwise. "We might help only if these people come to us, sincerely wanting to change their religion."

Two weeks after the wedding, Henriques Maldonado came to a Friday night service with three friends. After services, the curious congregants sat with their visitors. Regina Carvajal, a bright and attractive young lady in her late teens, and a student at Merritt College, spoke for her two friends who were shy and didn't seem to want to engage in too much conversation. Roberto Cardona and Sarah Pisaro remained silent while the spunky Regina answered the questions tossed her way. Marty Grant had previously advised the congregants that silence and secrecy was part of the way they practiced their religion. The congregants were not to be concerned by their guest's silence.

They were called conversos or forzados: forced Jews. In Hebrew they were anusim. That word was new to them. One of the congregants heard Sarah Pisaro whisper to Regina Carvajal that they would bring that new Hebrew word back with them.

"We want to be Jews," Regina said. "We've talked about it for a long time. That's what we want to do."

"It's not that simple," explained Irwin Bender, head of the congregation's Ritual Committee. Irwin had studied at an Orthodox religious day school while growing up in Chicago. Absent a rabbi, he was acknowledged by everyone as the community's religious authority. When a holiday was nearing and the local newspaper, radio and television station wanted to explain how La Buena's Jewish citizens would celebrate it, it was Irwin Bender, Professor of English Literature at Merritt College they always interviewed. He could be counted on to set forth an authentic explanation of the meaning of the holiday and how and why Jews would be celebrating it.

"Can you prove all the women in your family – going back to the 1500s – were Jewish?" Irwin asked.

"That's impossible," Regina countered.

"Well then, you and your friends would have to undergo a conversion. We can help you with it if that's what you truly wish."

"For hundreds of years, our family knew we were Jews. Now you make us convert? That's an insult!"

"I'm sorry," Irwin said. "That's the law. As I said, I didn't make it. I just follow it as best I can. You are always welcome to come here and pray with us. But we can't accept you as Jews without a conversion."

☙ ❧

The revelation outside of New Mexico of these communities, with their long-kept religious secrets, was a minor sensation within academic circles. Most rabbis did not take kindly to the news, although there were some who wanted to help the group return to their heritage. Then it was revealed that similar communities existed in Colorado, Arizona, Texas and Nevada, all states that were once part of New Spain. It was soon discovered that the Spanish still spoken among the mountain's anusim contained Ladino, a dialect used by Spain's Jews centuries ago. Ladino was still being spoken by Jewish citizens of Spanish heritage along the Mediterranean Basin, Israel, South America and even in the United States.

Marty Grant's curiosity impelled him to continue investigating the crypto-Jewish communities of the Southwest. He studied the newly unearthed groups in nearby states. He wrote books and several papers, until he became a leading academic scholar on the subject.

New Mexican crypto-Jews, as they were now being called, were puzzled as to what to do with their secrets now revealed. Some, in their curiosity, only wished to learn more about their family histories and leave it at that. They drew family trees that ran all the way back to medieval Spain.

Others refused to accept their ancestry and would continue to remain true Christians, disregarding what any examination of their backgrounds might reveal.

Many were not upset that the secret of their Jewish heritage was now out in the open. Manuel Henriques Maldonado and several of his family and friends were determined to learn more about Judaism with the possibility of converting. Both Regina Carvajal and Henriques Maldonado became regular attendants at the Temple and were welcomed by the congregants. They bought a Hebrew language program on tape, which they shared, and became better at the language than most of the congregants. They volunteered at synagogue fund-raising events and sponsored Friday night Onegs. They brought other anusim to services, encouraging them to learn more about Judaism.

Regina became so proficient at Hebrew that she taught basic classes at the congregation's small Religious School. From time to time, she even tutored adults privately. For those who did not know their backgrounds, Regina and Manuel appeared to be regular congregants at Temple *Beth Ha Shomer*.

The more the two studied, the more they became fascinated with Judaism. One day, three years after they began their quest to understand their roots, they drove to Sante Fe and knocked on the office door of the Reform rabbi. The address had been supplied to them by Irwin Bender. They told the Rabbi they wanted to begin a program of study leading to conversion.

43

Alexandria, Virginia
1969

At 9:30 a.m., Captain James Ennis was being paged through a scratchy overhead loudspeaker as he walked through the busy halls of the Pentagon. He picked up one of the phones located on a nearby wall and identified himself. A voice answered on the other end, "There's a call for you, Captain Ennis."

"Who is it?"

"Dr. Miguel Garcia. Says it's personal and important."

"Get his number and give it to my secretary. Tell her to tell him I'll call him back as soon as I'm finished with what I'm doing here. Maybe in an hour."

"Yes, Sir."

After completing his assignment at the Electric Boat Company, a two-year posting during which he rose to Captain and Rickover to Admiral, Ennis was assigned to the Pentagon. He was now back to assessing top secret documents in Spanish, French and German. He had one year to go before reaching 60 years of age, and had promised Lucy he would then retire. Placed on the review list for Rear Admiral, he hoped he would make it. In any event, he was committed to retire in 1970 and spend his leisure days in Groton, which he had come to enjoy as much as Lucy. But he did have another plan in mind.

On the west side of the Thames River from Groton, was the U.S. Coast Guard Academy at New London: at Groton there was a college and the administrative offices of the Electric Boat Company. Surely, as a highly qualified retired Naval officer, he could find a position in one of the schools or even the Boat Company. He wouldn't have to sit home all day, getting in Lucy's way, and he would feel good about still being busy and useful.

He also planned to buy a 44-foot sailboat. He'd been looking at one for several months. It was something he had long wanted to do, but lacked the time to enjoy. The one he liked had a nice, roomy cabin with its own head. He and Lucy could settle comfortably there. There was even a smaller cabin for guests. The galley and salon were arranged well and designed so that they could be easily converted into sleeping accommodations for either Michael or Rachel.

He and Lucy could sail down the Thames into Long Island Sound and nearby Mystic Seaport, where there was a maritime museum. He could even sail further west to New York's Montauk Point or Block Island for long weekends. Lucy was healthy and full of energy. He wanted to spend these years with her without having to worry about being posted to a base far away from her. The boat would be their second home.

୨୭ ଈ

"Hello Mickey, it's Jimmy. Where are you?"

"I'm here at Langley. At CIA headquarters. I'm not far from you. Can we meet for lunch? I have something interesting to give you. I guarantee you'll thank me for it."

"Sure. Where do we meet?"

"You know King Street in Alexandria?"

"Yes, I do."

"Meet you at a restaurant there in two hours."

"Great. What's the name of the restaurant?"

"You can't miss it, Jimmy. It's called Lucy's, like our Lucy."

"I know it, Mickey. See you there in two hours."

Lucy's was a popular place. King Street was the heart of Alexandria's tourist section, called Old Town, and Lucy's had its fill of diners, tourists and locals. Ennis spotted Mickey immediately. A little thicker, a little greyer, but still Mickey Garcia. He rose from his chair and gave Jimmy his usual Latino hug. The two men sat down and filled one another in on the time since they'd last been together.

"I've been in Europe," Mickey explained, "on the front lines of the Cold War. Got back three months ago. Didn't call you because I had so much work to do, and no one was supposed to know I'm here. Great work you did on the atomic sub. You deserved your promotion. Now you're back to languages. You're due for another promotion, to Rear Admiral. The word is, and I didn't tell you, that you'll make it. Congratulations Jimmy."

"Mickey, you never fail to amaze me. How are you able to acquire all this information?"

Mickey ignored the question. "Aren't you going to ask me why I called and told you I have something for you?"

"I figured you'd tell me when you were ready and eager to hit me with one of your usual dramatic flourishes. I only hope that you're not thinking of sending me off to the other side of the world on one of your wild schemes, because I won't go."

Mickey laughed. "That's why I love you, Jimmy. I can't keep secrets from you. Let's order and eat. Then I'll get to business. And I'm not sending you off on a wild one. At least, not today."

Halfway through a Chef's Salad, Mickey reached into his jacket pocket and pulled out a white business envelope. He didn't hand it to Jimmy, but furtively slid half of it under his plate, keeping his hand on it, as he spoke.

"You know, Jimmy, I have over a dozen people working for me in my section. As far as I know, I'm the only person at the CIA who does this. What is it I do? Before I make the important final decision to hire someone, I give them a task. Has nothing to do with the job, you understand. It's mostly detective work, locating long-lost stolen automobiles, dredging up old newspaper articles about people, drawing a detailed profile of some high-ranking Russian officer, or locating lost people. I want to see how they work. How they go about their tasks." Mickey paused. Jimmy thought it was for Mickey's usual dramatic effect.

"Finding lost people. Ah, yes. I thought of you and our conversation at Rocky's restaurant all those years ago back in New York. After any meeting or conversation, I always make notes. I went all the way back and found the notes of that day in 1942, and the other talks we had, about how you tried to figure out who your people were before and after they came to Newport."

Mickey wiped some salad dressing from his lips, took a sip of his cold white wine. He looked at Jimmy and knew that he had him wondering what he was going to say next. Mickey Garcia always enjoyed keeping people off balance. It was an essential part of his profession and knowing he was successful at it always gave him a stab of pleasure.

He finally pulled the envelope from under the plate. All the while he was talking, he noticed Jimmy's eyes fastened on it. He opened the unsealed flap and pulled out a neatly typed sheet of paper.

"I'll read the problem I set for one of my candidates to solve. By the way, Jimmy, this guy gets an A-plus for his efforts. He did an excellent job. Of course, I hired him."

"Locate the grave of Solomon Ennis, a soldier, 19 years of age who served with the 21st Continental, Massachusetts, under Col. John Tyler. Ennis fought at the Battle of Long Island, August 27-30, 1776. He may have been killed on Long Island or during the evacuation from New York to Pennsylvania, at Valley Forge. Ennis' original family name was Henriques and he was most probably a Jew."

"So here, Jimmy, is his report. I'm sure you'll like it." Mickey removed another sheet of paper from the envelope and handed it over with a toothy smile and a flourish.

Ennis took the paper and began reading.

To Dr. Miguel Garcia:

Of what significance, if any, does the fact that a man is a Jew have to do with his burial? I consulted a Rabbi of the Jewish faith who assured me that if it were known the deceased was a Jew, every effort would be made to inter him in a cemetery set aside for Jews.

Knowing this, I located at least two Jewish burial grounds which were in existence at the time of the Revolutionary War. One was in Philadelphia, the other in New York. There may have been others.

I didn't have to go further than New York, where a synagogue, Shearith Israel by name, maintains the oldest Jewish cemetery in America. It was the only Jewish one in New York at the time in question.'

Checking in at the synagogue, which still exists, I learned that our Mr. Ennis was wounded at the battle of Harlem Heights and died of his wounds in the Village of Newark in New Jersey about two or three days later. His original family name was verified to be Henriques. Solomon changed it to Ennis and moved to Boston to avoid arrest by English soldiers who were looking to detain him for anti-royal activities.

He was not formally buried until 1816, when it was verified that he was Jewish. As he was dying, he'd requested a Jewish burial. The synagogue has an old stitching, which I saw, evidently sewn by Ennis' wife, which she placed into his clothes. It states that Ennis is a Jew and he should be buried accordingly.

There is a three-page report, very detailed, by a doctor named Witherspoon of Newark, New Jersey. It was he who treated Ennis as he was dying.

The synagogue will make the report and the stitching available for inspection to bona-fide members of the family, or scholars.

"It's yours, Jimmy," Mickey said softly and with tenderness in his voice. "Now you know about your background, which I think you may have suspected for a long time." He handed his friend the envelope with the other paper. Jimmy was silent for a long time. Then he thanked Mickey, who had found in a few days or weeks, what he had been searching for, for decades.

44

Congregation Shearith Israel
New York City
1969

"Hello, my name is Captain James Ennis. I would like to speak with the person in charge of your cemeteries." Jim was speaking into his telephone.

"One moment, sir. Are you planning to bury a relative?"

"No, it's a personal matter, concerning someone who is already buried in one of your cemeteries."

"Please hold, sir. I'll see if Mr. Rath is in."

"Good morning, Captain Ennis. I'm Morris Rath. How can I help you?"

"Well, it's a little complicated. Can I meet with you to discuss the matter?"

"Sure. I'm free after 2 p.m. Do you know where we are?"

"I do. But I'm calling you from Washington. Can we do this tomorrow at your convenience?"

"Yes, you can come any time after 11."

"Thank you. See you tomorrow."

James Ennis paid the cab driver at the corner of Central Park West and 70th Street. It was 11:30 in the morning and New Yorkers were experiencing what they call Indian Summer, an unusual 85-degree day for late October. Central Park West was nervous with automobile traffic, but West 70th Street was alternately calm. Before him stood the 1897, neo-classic building that belonged to the Jewish congregation *Shearith Israel*, the Remnant of Israel. Popularly known as the Spanish and Portuguese Synagogue because its founding congregants were of those origins, it was founded in 1654 and is America's first Jewish Congregation.

Ennis entered through the office door and met with Morris Rath, a 70-year-old retired real estate developer, a congregant and volunteer worker for the synagogue. He was trim, white-haired, and stood less than five feet, ten inches. He was not a descendant of Spanish and Portuguese Jews. As were most of the current congregants, Rath descended from Ashkenazic, or Central European Jews. Most of the descendants of the original founders had intermarried with non-Jews, or with the Ashkenazic newcomers of Europe.

After introductions, Ennis told him about the report Mickey Garcia's agent had prepared, and said, "I'm a descendant of Solomon Ennis. I understand he is buried in your cemetery here in Manhattan. Although I'm not Jewish, I would like to see his grave. Is that possible?"

"It is. Can you tell me how you are descended?"

"My family name was once Henriques. Solomon changed his name in 1775. As a member of the Sons of Liberty, he was being hunted by the British. He moved from Newport to Boston and changed his name to Ennis. It was there he married a lady, Miriam Mendoza, who he had been courting in Newport. They had a son with the same name as mine, James. It's all here in the report." He turned over a photocopy of Mickey's report to Rath, who took time to read it carefully.

"I haven't seen this report, but yes, the man who prepared it was here a few months ago. He said he was doing research and interviewed me. I showed him what we had on Solomon Ennis. I expected that sooner or later, someone would show up in connection with this burial. Wait a moment, I'll be right back."

Rath returned in a few minutes with a small cardboard box. He lifted the cover and drew out the stitching Miriam Ennis had sewn almost 200 years earlier. Then he gave Ennis Doctor Alexander Witherspoon's three-page document.

Jim silently read the tragic story of his ancestor. He now felt a closer kinship with this dead soldier. It was solid, no longer hazy or questionable as it had always been. Holding Miriam's stitching, he felt he was holding her hand. Dr. Witherspoon's detailed report was the final positive link over the centuries, to his ancestor Solomon Henriques.

"I would like to visit the grave, Mr. Rath."

"That's possible. When would you like to go? I'll open the gate for you."

"I'll call you again to let you know," Ennis said, as he reluctantly handed back the stitching and the doctor's hand-written biography.

Rath noted Ennis' hesitation and remarked to himself, *I understand.*

ݠ ݡ

"Michael, it's dad. I'm here in New York. Can we meet for dinner tonight? I'm at the Sheraton Russel on Park Avenue and 46th Street. If you can make it, I'll look for you at seven at the bar. I have something interesting to show you." Knowing his son was probably busy in court, he left a message on Michael's answering machine.

Michael was the elder of the Ennis' two children. He had graduated from Columbia University and New York University Law School. He was working in a law office that specialized in international law. Picking up the message and preparing to meet his father, he was unaware that the search for Solomon Henriques was coming to an end.

Walking into the bar of the Sheraton Hotel, he saw his father at a corner table. He wasn't dressed in his uniform, with the peaked cap adorned with the gold leaves of a high-ranking naval officer – what they called 'scrambled eggs.' He was proud of his father, who had served his country so well and always looked so fine in his uniform.

Ennis rose from his seat and embraced his son. They had not seen each other for several months. During dinner, he showed his son Mickey Garcia's report and told Michael that he had seen and held Miriam's stitching and read Dr. Witherspoon's report... and how emotional it was for him.

"It was like holding history in my hands. It was unbelievable. I'm arranging for all of us, you, Mom and Rachel, to visit the grave."

"Of course, Dad. But we'll have to wait. I have a trial coming up and I need to prepare for it."

"How much time do you need?"

"Let's say two weeks to prepare, and then try."

"Okay. Let's do it in three weeks."

Returning to Washington, James knew he would think of little else for the coming weeks.

👁 👁

The phone rang at the Ennis home in Virginia. "Dad, it's Michael. Before we go to the grave site next week, I want you to know a few things."

"Sure. What's up?"

"I've been seeing a rabbi and I've been taking instruction in Judaism. Dad, are you there?"

"Yes, I am."

"How do you feel about it?"

"You're an adult. If that's what you want, that's what I want for you. I'm sure your mother agrees with me. Is it to learn more about the religion or to convert?"

"Yes. To convert. I've been thinking about this for a while. The Ennis family was once Jewish. It makes sense."

"It's a big move."

"Yes, Dad, it is. There's something else I have to tell you."

"Sounds like a bombshell, Michael."

"Maybe it is."

"Well, go on. I've been through some tough spots in my life. I can handle most anything."

"I've decided to change my name to Henriques."

"Well! That's something I didn't expect." There was a long pause. "You know, Michael, knowing what we now know about Solomon, if I were your age, I might consider doing the same thing. He changed his to survive and fight for his beliefs, not because he was ashamed or unhappy with it. I've been thinking of it as a courageous thing for him to do. Imagine a boy of 19. At that age, you were just entering college. Solomon had already crossed an ocean to start a new life in a strange place and he was on his way to being married at 18 and then at 19 becoming a father and a soldier in Washington's army.

"Maybe you're right. Someone should go back to Henriques. Carry on the name. Be proud of it once more. You can be both an Ennis and an Henriques. They're honest names. I've had the feeling for a long time that Solomon has never rested easy, knowing there are loose ends hanging among his descendants."

"I'm glad you feel that way, Dad. I've arranged to appear in court the same day we visit Solomon's grave. I want you to be there, mom and Rachel, too. I'm going to be Michael Ennis Henriques."

James arranged for Morris Rath to meet the family at the old cemetery at Chatham Square. The Ennis family arrived early and stood in front of the gate leading to the cemetery, which was surrounded by old tenements.

"I read about this cemetery," Michael offered. "This neighborhood was once all rural country north of New York City." He had to raise his voice, as lots of heavy and noisy traffic passed by. They were in Chinatown, where some of the writings on the doors and walls were incomprehensible Asian pictographs. Horns honked, trucks rattled and made loud jaw-jarring thuds as they descended into potholes in the roadway. Street vendors pushed their wares across sidewalks and there was the unmistakable, mouth-watering odor of Chinese cooking in the air.

Before Michael could finish, Morris Rath pulled up in a grey sedan, his driver gliding to a halt alongside a nearby bus stop. The driver sat behind the wheel while his passenger carried on with the business of opening the cemetery gate. Parking was unavailable in this busy place and the driver had to be prepared to move if a fussy cop didn't like where he had stopped.

Rath greeted the Ennis family and opened the gate. They entered the cemetery through a stone archway secured by the iron gate. "Here it is," he said, as he walked toward a corner of the cemetery. "Solomon has been here since 1816. There are other heroes of the Revolutionary War buried here. The graveyard was once much larger. The city appropriated a large part of it, through Eminent Domain, for road improvements and housing. By good fortune, Solomon's grave was not touched.

"Our synagogue has three cemeteries in Manhattan. They are all National Monuments. This is the largest of the three and the oldest Jewish cemetery in the United States. The other two, like this one, were cut down when the city needed space for roads and other improvements. One is in Greenwich Village, on East 11th Street. The other is on West 21st Street. That one has the grave of a Cardozo who died in the Revolutionary War; he's an ancestor of Supreme Court Justice Benjamin Nathan Cardozo. Altogether, there are 22 heroes of that war in the three graveyards. Solomon Ennis is one of them. Each Memorial Day, we honor them with a visit to say prayers over their graves and leave flowers by the tombstones."

Rachel had a camera and took pictures of the grave site. Jim bent into a crouch in front of Solomon's grave and ran his hand over the fading marble tombstone. The stone was time-worn from weather and the acids lurking in New York City's air and rainfalls. He asked Morris Rath if he could return to do a rubbing of the stone. Rath assured him it could be arranged. After a few minutes more of looking at other graves and remarking that many of the names were Spanish, they started to walk to the gate to leave.

"It's traditional to place a small stone or a pebble on the tombstone to signify that someone has visited the grave site and remembered the deceased. You might want to do that," Rath suggested.

"Of course," Lucy said, as she bent down to pick up five small stones, handing one to Michael, Jimmy, Rachel, and Morris and keeping one for herself. They all placed stones atop Solomon's headstone.

As they passed the gate, Rath said, "I'd like you to come back to my office. There are some things for us to discuss."

"We have a commitment in court in an hour. We can be there after lunch, say 3:30?" Michael asked.

"Sure. I'll expect you then."

Jim pulled Rath aside as he headed toward his waiting car. "Mr. Rath, my family would like to make this gift to the synagogue." He handed an envelope to Rath, who opened it and looked at the check inside.

"Thank you, Captain Ennis. On behalf of the congregation, I thank you and your family for your generosity. I'll look for all of you this afternoon."

ဏ ၜ

It was a short walk from Chatham Square to the nearby New York State Supreme Court building at Foley Square. The family climbed the wide steps into the large and impressive rotunda of the courthouse, which was constructed of marble and stone. There were murals and statuary throughout. They walked up another flight of the stairs to a court room which had a sign posted on the outside wall stating it was Trial Term Part III.

Posted inside a glass case on the wall was the day's court calendar. Michael read it and told his family he was number three on the docket and they should be out quickly. They walked inside and sat down on a long bench up front. After a few minutes, a uniformed Bailiff opened a door, striking it hard with his hand and shouting, "All rise, those having business before this Court, the Honorable Milton H. Fowler presiding."

The Judge appeared from a door behind his bench and climbed a few steps to his desk, which was raised above the spectators. He seemed young for a judge; perhaps a bit over 40, with dark, wavy hair, a smooth face, and large eyes. He looked out at his Court and with a warm smile said, "Please, everyone be seated."

When Michael's turn came, the Bailiff called out, "Docket number 3543MHF. Petition on behalf of Michael Ennis for a change of name. Michael Ennis, step forward, please."

Michael presented himself before the Judge.

"I see you didn't use an attorney, young man."

"No, your honor, I prepared the petition myself."

"That's an excellent job you did. What do you do?"

"I'm a lawyer, your Honor."

"So that explains it. What's your specialty?"

"I'm with a firm that practices international law, your Honor."

"Tell me, why do you want to change your name?"

Michael then spent the next few minutes explaining the story of Solomon Ennis nee Henriques. When he was finished, the Judge looked at him and said, "That's quite a story. I see the people who were sitting with you; they are your family?"

"Yes, your Honor."

"They support your decision?"

"Yes, sir, they all do."

"I'm pleased to grant your petition." Judge Fowler rapped his gavel and shouted, "Petition granted." He handed the petition to his law clerk and ordered her to enter it appropriately.

ာ ၜ

The family returned to *Shearith Israel*. Morris Rath was waiting for them. Another man was with him. He was introduced to the family as Philip Mayer, the synagogue's president. Mayer was holding the box that contained the Ennis material.

He addressed the family, saying, "First, I know Morris has thanked you for your gift to the synagogue. I want to also thank you personally. Also, Morris met with the Board of Directors last week. He felt that the stitching and Dr. Witherspoon's report really belong to you. Your ancestress stitched the plea that was placed in Solomon's clothing, and the doctor's report is an important document that links your heritage to the Henriques family. I'm happy to say that the Board unanimously decided to return these precious relics to you, as they are an important part of your family's history.

"However, we would ask you to grant us a short delay. We have arranged with one of the ladies in the congregation who does needlepoint as a hobby, to make an exact replica of Miriam Ennis' stitching. She assures us she can do this, even to duplicating the material Miriam used. Another of our members is a calligrapher: he creates those wonderful personal invitations made by hand for upscale society weddings and affairs. He tells me he is a first-class forger and has agreed to make an exact copy of Dr. Witherspoon's report.

"We do this because these things were part of the material Reverend Pinto used to consider Solomon's eligibility for burial in our cemetery, and so they are also an important part of our history as well. As soon as these two tasks are completed, the originals will be turned over to you. Before you leave, you will receive a letter signed by me, confirming what I have just said.

"And for now, Michael. Morris told me that in conversation with you, Captain Ennis, you indicated your son was taking instruction in Judaism so that he may undergo conversion. We would like him to have, with our compliments, our daily prayer book, the *Siddur*. We would welcome one of the Henriques family as a congregant upon his conversion, after having been away so long from the religion of his ancestors." Mayer turned the book over to Michael and shook his hand.

James and Michael stood up and shook the hands of both men, thanking them. James held back his tears: a Navy Captain is not supposed to cry. Lucy and Rachel cried for both their men, unashamedly wiping tears away with lacy cotton handkerchiefs.

As the family left the synagogue and hailed a cab, James Ennis said, more to himself than to Lucy, Rachel, and Michael, "Solomon, now you can rest in peace."

ℒ ℰ

Dr. Miguel Garcia

Mickey, you can never know how much the Ennis family appreciates your efforts in closing a great gap in its history. We will be forever grateful to you.

> *Lucy especially.*
> *All our love,*
> *Lucy and Jimmy*

45

The Yom Kippur War
October 15-17, 1973

The Israelis had won their war for independence in 1948. Little Israel had defeated the outsized Goliath, made up of many Arab states and hundreds of thousands of Arabs dedicated to the destruction of the Jews. As far as the Arab nations were concerned, the War was not over and would never be. No, not until they saw the final destruction of the Jewish state.

Two years after fighting in the War for Independence, Dani Henriques had earned his engineering degree. He began working with a company that performed engineering services for the builders who were now creating a modern Israel. Within ten years, Dani became a partner, leaving later to form his own company.

Dani was now a Captain in the reserves of the Israeli Defense Forces (IDF), successor to the Haganah. From the first days he set foot on Jewish soil, he had been called upon regularly to defend his new homeland. He was no different from other men in this new country. He spent several weeks each year on reserve duty and was often called out on local emergencies. As a Captain, the unit he led was a company of Combat Engineers.

In 1956, an indecisive war was fought over control of the Suez Canal. Egypt was preventing Israel, France, and England free access to its international waterways. The three nations attacked Egypt, to force it to open the Canal and the entrance to the Red Sea. As a result, free passage through the Canal and the Gulf of Aqaba was guaranteed to them by Agreement.

Dani spent five weeks in uniform, as his engineers constructed landing fields for the Air Force and roads for the trucks that backed the troops on the front with food, equipment, and medical supplies.

By 1967, Arab leaders led by Egypt's Gamal Abdel Nasser threatened to abrogate that Agreement, renewing the rattling of swords in Israel's direction. Frightful predictions were being made by the Arabs, such as, "We shall drive all the Jews into the sea." These threats were made daily over Arab radio stations throughout the Middle East, preparing their citizens for a new war. Israelis were facing another full-scale attack, which Egypt, Syria, Lebanon, and Jordon swore would destroy them forever. The Six Day War, as it came to be known by historians, ended in Israel's stunning victory. In less than a week, all the Sinai Peninsula to the East Bank of the Suez Canal, the Golan Heights and the West Bank fell into Israeli hands. The great prize, however, was the capture of the entire Holy City of Jerusalem, now completely in Jewish hands.

Israelis hunkered in along the East Bank of the Canal, fortifying their side, insuring free passage for its vessels. Located on this side of the Canal was an abandoned Egyptian experimental farm which contained Japanese equipment. When Israeli troops occupied the farm, they found Japanese writing along the walls and on the machinery. Mistakenly believing it to be Chinese writing, the soldiers soon began calling it the Chinese Farm. Israeli military maps designated it the same way. Six years later, the farm would be the site of one of the hardest fought and bloodiest battles in Israel's military history.

On October 6, 1973, during the solemn observance of Yom Kippur, one of Judaism's holiest days, synagogues were packed with congregants. It is a day of penance. The streets throughout Israel's cities were quiet. Shops were closed. The whole country was, in effect, shut down. During the day-long service, which included a fast, an urgent call of emergency was suddenly made from pulpits throughout the country: all regular army and reservists were to immediately proceed to their units – fully armed.

Without warning, Egyptian troops had swarmed across the Suez Canal to the East side, and Egyptian jets, artillery and rockets attacked undermanned Israeli fortifications along the Canal. They easily and quickly overwhelmed all its lightly defended positions. To the north, Syrian tanks were swiftly rolling towards the Golan Heights in alarmingly large numbers, threatening to regain that territory. Jordanians were exerting pressure on Jerusalem. All Israel was in a panic, including the country's leading politicians and military leaders.

Dani Henriques, with four other men, left their synagogue in Haifa, commandeering a taxi to drive them to a designated station where the men encountered much confusion. Dani and about 30 men, most of them still in civilian clothes and lacking weapons, which were allotted to them later, were sped on a bus bound to the Canal. Word among the soldiers was that the Egyptians were marching unopposed, eastward across the Sinai Peninsula after successfully crossing the Canal.

The Israeli Air Force, the pride of Israel's defense system, was of little use. They could not hold back the Egyptian army. They had been neutralized by the placement of highly sophisticated, Russian-built, anti-aircraft missiles, effectively grounding the jets.

After massive initial losses, Israel consolidated its forces, rolled back the Syrians and Jordanians, and began dealing with a determined Egyptian army. They were not easy to defeat. After many days of desperate fighting, the Israeli command developed a plan to cross the Canal on bridges built by the Combat Engineers.

Jewish soldiers assembled a strike force to push open a road from the Chinese Farm to the banks of Canal, which would allow engineers to move a bridge to be laid across the water. First, they had to clear the Farm of Egyptians who repeatedly repulsed the Israelis. The IDF counter-attacked, trying unsuccessfully to spearhead the movement toward the selected crossing area.

The first few counterattacks were unsuccessful as they were met by well-entrenched Egyptian infantry and their armored units. Finally, after several bloody battles including hand-to-hand combat that lasted three days, the Israelis were able to open a corridor to the Canal. But the battle took the lives of many Egyptians and Israelis. The IDF, now accompanied by tanks led by General Ariel Sharon and a unit of paratroopers fighting as infantry, pushed out of the Chinese Farm to the shores of the Canal. They began crossing over the bridges with tanks, infantry, and the Israeli Parachute Brigade. Making a wide sweep to outflank the main force of the Egyptian army, the Israelis cut off and trapped a significant part of the enemy's troops on the Canal's west side. It was but a short trip to Cairo from there.

The Air Force was able to assist by strafing and bombarding enemy positions, after the paratroopers assigned to destroy the Russian missiles were successful at their task. At the Golan Heights, scores of Syrian tanks were destroyed before they could reach their objective. Jordan was effectively neutralized at Jerusalem.

Days later, the defeated Arabs sued for peace. Israel won the War but at a terrible loss of men and equipment. The War had lasted almost three weeks and in its early stages, the fate of the country and its citizens was in great doubt.

Looking over at the now quiet and desolate battlefield at the Chinese Farm, military observers remarked that they had never seen such a wide scene of destruction and death. There were dead men and destroyed equipment as far as one could see. Egyptian and Israeli soldiers lay in each other's arms, dying together during hand-to-hand combat. One officer said, "It was the valley of death."

Among the many casualties was Captain Dani Henriques, who met his death with a comrade when a grenade exploded several feet behind them. At age 46, Dani had known war all his life, when all he wanted to be was an engineer building things, instead of destroying them. He never married. His only close relative was his father Chaim, who had come to Israel after finally giving up hope that this wife Hannah had somehow survived the death camps.

A letter informing the next of kin was taken personally by Dani's cousin, General Shimon Henriques, to Dr. Chaim Henriques at his Tel Aviv clinic at *Rehov Acharon*. After reading the letter, Dani's father excused himself from Shimon and his patients. Later, he would say that he didn't remember walking into his office. He locked the door, sat in one of the wooden chairs meant for his patients, his head bowed almost between his legs. He was all alone now. His whole family was gone, simply because they were Jews. He began to cry uncontrollably, the condolence letter in his hand falling to the floor.

46

The Henriques Family Bible
Amsterdam, Holland
1975

Jim Ennis was not pleased with himself, waiting so long to link up with his friend Aarnald Henriques. Over the years, he had received many letters and phone calls from Aarnald, asking him to come to Holland and personally make new entries into the family bible. He would be adding to the genealogical history of the Henriques family. Aarnald could have made the entries himself; he had all the necessary information which Jimmy had sent to him. But he felt Jimmy should do it, in his own hand, since it came after such a long search. Over the centuries, it had become traditional that whenever possible, entries in the book were made by the persons themselves.

Now Jimmy came to Amsterdam with Lucy, Michael and his wife Sylvia, and his sister Rachel. They were fascinated with this flat city of many canals; its cobblestone streets lined with gabled houses looking as if they were models for a child's picture book about kings and queens.

Despite a broad smile and a genuine greeting, Aarnald Henriques looked nothing like the man Ennis had first seen in the picture album at the Alhadeff Gift Shop in Gibraltar more than a quarter century ago. The change had little to do with aging. Two scars marred his lower lip, four spidery red scars ran from his lower left eyelid to the top of his cheekbone. The upper part of his right eyelid drooped. And a broken nose, which could have been fixed but never was, were the medals he was awarded for his courage and obstinate refusal to give information about his Underground comrades while in the hands of the savage German SS thugs.

Aarnald's home was comfortable, that of a sturdy, middle-class Dutch Burger, exuding the air of the owner's well-being. He occupied a three-story gabled house, built in the late 18th or early 19th Century. Today, the house was filled with Aarnald, Jr. and his family, and Aarnald Sr.'s wife and his friends, many of whom worked for the government in which Aarnald now had a role as an independent consultant. Ennis was introduced by Aarnald to everyone as, "The man who saved my life."

Bottles of Dutch gin and wine were lined up on a table next to plates of hors d'oeuvres, some of which were the tasty Indonesian Rijsstafel dishes. Older pre-war Dutch colonials had imported these Asian foods and came to enjoy them from the time when the Dutch were an East Indian colonial power. There was nasi goring, fried rice and lemper, rice rolls, among several other exotic dishes. And there was much camaraderie. Most of the guests, including adolescents, spoke good English, the result of historic necessity. Many Dutch, who are citizens of a small country, also speak the language of their close ally, Great Britain, located just across the English Channel.

Jimmy, as everyone was calling him five minutes after introductions, was asked to repeat the story of Aarnald's rescue more than half a dozen times, accompanied with approving pats on his back and offers of strong Bols gin, the national drink. It was Mijnheer Lucas Bols' 19th Century concoction and his contribution to Dutch pleasure: genever, they called it.

By six-thirty in the evening, the last of the guests had filtered out of the house. Two maids hired for the event were now clearing tables and sweeping up. Aarnald sipped some wine, only his second drink of this busy day. He sat beside Jimmy and draped an affectionate arm around his shoulders.

"Now, my friends, to some serious Henriques family business." Aarnald guided everyone to the room that was his office. Drawing a key from his pocket, Aarnald unlocked a door built into a wall and pulled out a large, thick, black leather-bound book. He placed it lovingly on a coffee table in front of a couch. It was the Henriques family bible. The entire Ennis family, Aarnald Jr., his wife and Mayra, Aarnald's wife, were either seated or stood before this book.

Before he opened the book, Aarnald offered an explanation.

"This book really starts in 1432, when the Jewish Henriques family, then living in Cordoba, were forcibly converted. Before that entry, the book explains how the family came to Spain and were given the honor to serve the royal family of Castile as overseers. That's when they took the name Henriques, which in Old Spanish means 'Lord of the House.' Before Henriques, they had a Hebrew name, *Ben Moshe*, Son of Moses. The history continues until 1493, when the three Henriques children escaped the Inquisition after their parents were murdered by that institution for practicing Judaism. They fled from Spain to Braganca in Portugal, with the help of a Christian man who worked for the family, and his sister. There, the three Henriques children returned to Judaism."

Aarnald paused. He took a small, dry cigar called *Schimmelpennick*, from a tin box on the table, offering them to his guests. Only Aarnald, Jr. took one. Father and son lit up. Then Aarnald opened the book to a page revealing an ornate and flowery handwriting, in Spanish, and in a dark black ink. The page was not faded, for despite its age, it was always in this closed book, stashed away from the fading action of damaging light and destructive acids accumulating in the air of the modern world. Paper manufactured during medieval and renaissance times contained no acids, as does modern paper, which causes it to turn yellow and deteriorate. Tiny bits of broken twigs were evident on the pages of the ancient hand-manufactured folios. They were created by pounding a mixture of minutely shredded rags and wood into a watery white pulp, which was then placed in sheeted frames and left in the sun to dry, becoming paper.

"You will notice the handwriting and the languages differ from page to page. Obviously, it's a result of the preference of the book's owner at the time who makes the entries. From 1452, the entries are in Spanish. After 1497, the Henriques family is once again forcibly converted, after having returned to Judaism. This time in Portugal, where they had sought refuge only five years earlier. Now, the entries are in both Portuguese and Spanish.

"In 1755, three members of the Henriques family who, although forcibly converted, secretly practiced their old faith, as they called it, escaped to Holland after a great earthquake in Lisbon, where they lived. The family returns once again to Judaism when they reach safety here in Amsterdam. Now the entries are in Spanish, Portuguese, and Ladino.

"A generation later, the family splits: some go to England and one to her colonies in America. Others remain here in the Netherlands. The family reminds us that the oldest son, Charles, stayed in Lisbon after the earthquake and they await him. It never happens. At least, we have no record of it.

Aarnald turned over a page and with a smile, pointed to an entry. "Here," he said while looking at Jimmy and his family, "is your ancestor Solomon, who went to America from London." Lucy, Michael, Sylvia, Rachel, and Jimmy moved closer, Jimmy gliding his hand over the entry, trying to feel Solomon's presence.

"From this point on, all the entries are generally in Ladino, French, Dutch or English, as they are the languages most of our ancestors used at the time. But you will sometimes also find Spanish, Portuguese and even Italian and German." Aarnald closed the book, leaving his left hand between the pages of his last entry.

"Now you must understand that in 1492, when Jews were given the choice to leave Spain or convert, most of the Henriques family left Spain for Portugal. Other went east, to the Ottoman Empire. They are also our kin but follow a much different history than our families." He swung the book open again.

"The reason they went to the Ottoman Empire was because the Sultan sent ships for them and made life easy for them once they came east, settling mostly in Istanbul, Izmir and Salonica. Later, they moved to the outer parts of the vast Ottoman Empire, to Bulgaria, Albania, and Rumania in cities like Sofia, Sarajevo, Monastir, and Dubrovnik. They kept the Ladino language alive while adapting an Eastern caste to their lives. Now you will see entries in Ladino and English from your cousins around the world, when they would come to Amsterdam or write to inform the possessor of this book to make entries on their behalf. Occasionally there is something in French or Italian or even Dutch. But that's rare.

These are family stories from South America, South Africa, Florence, Livorno and Rhodesia and The Congo."

Aarnald smiled. "There are even entries from Siam, Shanghai, Singapore and Hong Kong. It fills up the rest of the book, many, many more pages than the beginning entries that filled this book before 1755 and the Lisbon earthquake."

He opened the book again and carefully turned the pages forward. They showed movements to France and French North Africa, where Jimmy had met Avraham, his son Jacques and wife, Dora. Here were the entries of Aaron and Jaime, captives of the Barbary pirate; of Shimon Henriques, now living in Israel, with a description of the fight at Bir Hakim; and Dani Henriques, the Greek Partisan who lost most of his family in the Holocaust and later, his own life at the battle of the Chinese Farm during Israel's Yom Kippur War; and Chaim, Dani's father, now over ninety, living in Tel Aviv and still overseeing a renowned clinic specializing in treating traumas arising from the Holocaust.

It seemed as if all the Henriques around the world knew about this book and wanted their family stories inscribed in it. There were entries from a family that settled in Hamburg in the 1600s; Danish Henriques from Copenhagen and its West Indian colonies of St. Thomas and St. Croix; English Henriques in the Caribbean living in Jamaica, Barbados and Nevis. Some of the Dutch branch of the family also settled in the New World colonies of Curaçao, St. Eustatius and St. Martin.

The entries poured over the pages, Aarnald translating the Ladino, which he had studied to be able to read all the entries. Finally, they came to the last entries in the book, the pages following them blank, waiting for any new stories about this family. Aarnald gently moved the book in Jimmy's direction. Holding a pen, he said, "The next entries are about you, Jimmy, and then, Michael."

Jimmy Ennis entered the history of his family in America starting with Solomon, always putting the name Henriques in parentheses after that of Ennis. He made an entry for the Henriques of San Francisco, which Dorothy had asked him to include, as she couldn't attend the meeting. Michael was next, logging his return to

Judaism and his assumption of the Henriques name. A tear dropped from his eyes, leaving a small smear on the ink.

Aarnald took the book, looked at what had been written, and with a satisfied smile, said, "Yes. That brings us up to date."

It was now close to midnight. Before the maids completed their tasks, they brought in sandwiches, coffee, tea, soft drinks, and dessert; what Jimmy, while at sea, would call "the night lunch." As they sat enjoying the snacks, Aarnald said, "Jimmy, I spoke with Lucy before you came to Amsterdam. She tells me that Groton is a nice community, and you enjoy your retirement there. I've had an inquiry from what you Americans call a Think Tank; they would like me to join their organization. They have offices in Boston. I'd like to buy a house in Groton, if you have no objections. They tell me that I would only have to be in nearby Boston once every month or so, when they get together for round table meetings; most of my work can be done at home or over the phone. They tell me I could even install a telex for quick responses."

"Aarnald, I'd love to have you as a neighbor! But under one condition."

"And what is that Jimmy?"

"You don't tell anyone that I'm the man who saved your life."

47

A Conclusion

Jimmy Ennis stood at the helm of his forty-four-foot yacht, *Buenaventura*. He was dressed in white flannel trousers and white, red rubber soled sailing shoes. He wore a navy-blue cable knit sweater with a shawl color. A neon-yellow life jacket covered his torso. He topped it all off with a black Greek fisherman's cap.

He and Lucy were sailing east on Long Island Sound. They began their trip from their home at Groton, Connecticut, destination Newport, Rhode Island. The day was almost perfect for sailing. Jimmy noted some dark clouds aft of his yacht, near Block Island, but they were far away, and the wind was at their back, filling the *Buenaventura's* sails. The sun above them was pleasantly warm.

Lucy came out of the galley, one deck below, to the main deck. She carried a sandwich and an ice-cold bottle of ginger ale for her husband. She had recently cut her long hair short. It was no longer completely blonde but surrendering to outcroppings of grey. She wore a bright red sweater and dark blue slacks. She, too, wore a yellow life jacket.

Handing Jimmy his sandwich and drink, she kissed him on the cheek and said, "A penny for your thoughts, sweetheart."

After biting into the sandwich, Jimmy answered, "This is probably the same route our Solomon's ship took on its last leg to get to Newport. In those days there were only empty fields across the way." He waived toward Connecticut. The shoreline was filled with old and modern buildings, and Jimmy could see a red, white, and blue Amtrak train snaking its way between the structures on its way towards its final destination at Boston.

"But I sense that he was surely excited when he saw land, after a long voyage with only rough seas to look at for weeks."

"It's hard to imagine a youngster like him," Lucy added. "Barely 17, ready to start a new life in a new land. I look at our Michael. At that age he was just embarking on a long regimen of education: finishing high school, college and then law school."

"Yes, and Michael was dependent on his family to help carry him through the process. Solomon was here all alone, with no one to fall back on."

"Yes, Jimmy, but education wasn't as important then as it is now. What would Michael and Rachel be doing if they didn't have a college education?"

Nearing Newport, they could see the spit of land, the peninsula that guarded the narrow entry into Narragansett Bay. As they closed in on the port, they saw a harbor filled with the masts of sailing ships. These were not the traders of merchantmen that had filled the port two centuries earlier. These were pleasure boats. What emotions must have beaten in Solomon's breast as he saw those merchant ships lined up, waiting to be loaded or unloaded?

"This is where it started," Jimmy said to Lucy. "This is where the Henriques family began its life in America. What a long journey it's been. First Spain, then Portugal, Amsterdam, London and finally, Newport."

"You know," Lucy said thoughtfully, "The pity is that young Solomon never lived to enjoy a full life here."

"The life he gave up was so that others could do exactly that," his descendant replied.

48

Family Notes
1980

Through the efforts of Aarnald Henriques, Sr. and Rear Admiral James Ennis (USN ret.) who were close friends, a reunion of the Henriques family was held in Toronto, Canada. Over 300 members attended, from all over the world, many connecting with each other for the first time. Not all of them were Jews. The group was able to trace and acknowledge their ancestors with origins in Spain and Portugal. Michael Henriques proposed the establishment of a bi-annual newsletter to apprise the family of the activities of their relatives. Not only was it unanimously accepted, but it was also accompanied with strong applause.

Here are a few of the entries that have appeared since the newsletter, HENRIQUES NOTES began printing.

Lt. General Shimon Henriques, (Ret. Israeli Defense Forces), one of the heroes of the battle of Bir Hakim in World War II and a participant of the 1948 War for Israel independence, the Suez-Sinai Campaign 1956, the Six Day War 1967, and the Yom Kippur War 1973, has passed away. According to his wishes, he was buried on the Mount of Olives in Jerusalem.

Archbishop Pedro Henriques Villamil of Cordoba, Spain, has just written a book about his Jewish ancestors, the Henriques. It covers their arrival at Cordoba during the 13th Century and their forced conversion to Catholicism in the 1430s. Written in Spanish, its title is: *La familia Henriques en Cordoba: judios y cristianos.* (The Henriques Family in Cordoba: Jews and Christians.) At our last meeting, the Archbishop told us how proud he was of his Jewish ancestry.

Carlos Henriques de la Hoya has relocated from Buenos Aires, Argentina to Barcelona, Spain. He becomes Senior General Manager for *Navieras de Iberia,* an international shipping company. Although not Jewish, Carlos tells us that among his mother's effects he found a Jewish Star, candle sticks with Hebrew writing on them, and a *mezuzah.*

Dorothy Henriques of Omaha, Nebraska, announced the marriage of her daughter Victoria, to William Levy, also of Omaha. Dorothy, originally from San Francisco, teaches psychology at the University of Nebraska. Dorothy has authored a New York Times best seller based on letters written by members of her family and is working on a follow-up of her family's history. Through genealogical studies, Dorothy has found that she and Admiral James Ennis have the same ancestor in Portugal, who came to Amsterdam after the 1755 earthquake.

Prof. Emeritus Sir David Henriques, DSO, OBE, has just completed his 18th book, which will be published by Gast, Potter and Mills of New York, London and Toronto. The title of the book is *Captors and Captives.* Sir David was with the British forces that liberated the concentration camp at Bergen-Belsen in 1945.

Aarnald Henriques, Jr. has married Miss Bette Caceres of Curaçao, Dutch West Indies. The couple will live in Amsterdam where Aarnald Jr. maintains a security consulting company with his father, Aarnald Sr. Arnald Sr. has been a security consultant for the Dutch government since 1947. He maintains another home in Groton Connecticut, and is a Distinguished Fellow at Western World Issues, located in Boston.

Michael Ennis Henriques has been named senior partner in the New York law firm of Bailey, Suarez, and Shaw. The firm is one of the leading practitioners of International Law. Michael will have charge of international transportation.

Francesca Ponti Henriques of Florence, Italy has enlarged her clothing designing business by opening two new stores, one in Paris and the other in London.

Martin Henriques Shaw has joined the Canadian Broadcasting Company as one of CBC's leading journalists. He will be living in Ottawa.

Manuel Henriques Maldonado, who converted to Judaism in 1976, has completed all his requirements for his PhD in Jewish studies. He will take a position at the Semitic Studies Department of Arizona State University, where he will be teaching Crypto-Judaism. He has been teaching at Texas State University while studying for his PhD.

Consuela Henriques of Mexico City, one of Mexico's leading modern artists, is currently negotiating to present an exhibit of her works at New York's Museum of Modern Art.

Simon Ennis Henriques, son of Michael and Sylvia Henriques and grandson of Rear Admiral James and Lucy Ennis, has just been admitted to the United States Naval Academy at Annapolis, Maryland. His older brother, Philip Henriques, is studying for the rabbinate at the Reform Jewish Seminary at Cincinnati, Ohio.

Rear Admiral James Ennis, USN Ret., has been named Associate Dean of Groton College. He also consults at the US Coast Guard Academy, New London, Connecticut. He advises us that he has requested that upon his death, his gravestone will read: James Henriques Ennis.

AUTHORS NOTES AND ACKNOWLEDGEMENTS

This is a work of historic fiction. As I worked on this story, I often found myself going to the history books to verify dates and places, insuring credibility. If there are any errors, I apologize. Nevertheless, as fiction I had to change history purposely when it added to the drama. For example, parts of the story involving General Mark Clark are not true. That his mother was Jewish is a fact. Clark became a Christian during his second year at West Point. The essence of his meetings with French Gen. Giraud and the French military is correct, but not in the way depicted in the novel. Nor is the scene with the removal of the Jewish stars. That never happened, but I wanted the reader to believe it was so; that it might have happened. There are a few other twists of historical facts which I deemed necessary to advance the story's dramatic interest.

The purpose of the book is to shed light on a little-known fact of world history which has influenced us even to the present. I have had the privilege and opportunity to meet and work with descendants of Jews whose ancestors were forcibly converted to Christianity five and six centuries ago. That they continue to remember that their families practiced Judaism is, to me, astounding. They are called anusim, forced ones in Hebrew. As I have shown, they can be found everywhere. Their descendants have served in many governments in the Western world; they are Nobel Prize winners, authors, scientists, philosophers, artists, and I could go on.

For the last two decades I have been associated with the Society for Crypto-Judaic Studies (SCJS): first as a member and then on its Board. In that capacity, much of what appears in this book I learned from my studies of Crypto-Judaism and of the people who lived as anusim. Members of the Society, some of whom are anusim, filled me in on the culture and mores of their lives.

I am ever conscious that a writer always owes debts to those who have written on his subject before him. To all of you, I thank you for the insight gathered from your efforts:

My wife, Barbara Tasch Ezratty, for editing my manuscript as she has done for all my previous works. She has, indeed, acted as my personal Muse over the years, always urging me on.

To Richard Gottesman, who also over the years has undertaken the graphics task (beautifully, I might add) of putting my books together and creating appealing covers. Thank You Richard!

To the SCJS and its members, for its information, and the opportunity to meet with descendants of the Jews who were so cruelly torn away from their religion many centuries ago.

To Prof. Stanley Hordes who 20 years ago invited me to read a paper on the anusim of Puerto Rico at an SCJS convention in El Paso. From that time, we became friends and Stanley has patiently guided me through the maze of the history of the Spanish Court and its relationship to Jews and the Inquisition. He has taught me to understand what I considered to be some of the quirks of Crypto Jewish culture. Stanley is one of the original founders of the SCJS and an authority on the Crypto-Jews of America's Southwest.

To Cary Herz, lamentably deceased, who with her camera, roamed through the Christian graveyards of New Mexico and showed me her eye-popping photographs of tombstones bearing both a cross and a Star of David, dates of birth and death based on the Hebrew calendar and names of the deceased in Hebrew.

To Rabbi Stephen Leon, of B'nai Zion of El Paso and founder and director of the Anusim Center of El Paso, for his dedicated work at returning Crypto-Jews on both sides of the Rio Grande to their ancient heritage.

To Sonia Loya, living in the New Mexico mountain town of *Ruidoso*, for putting me in touch with men and women who were struggling to understand Judaism in the weekly services that she held in the part of her shop dedicated to a sanctuary. And for her personal journey to return to the faith of her ancestors.

To those of us at Temple Beth Shalom, San Juan, Puerto Rico who, with patience and wonderment answered the many questions about Judaism from the Puerto Ricans who at first gingerly attended our Friday night services and who we then helped along the road to their return to their ancient faith.

Finally, I thank my father, Joseph Ezratty, now deceased. A true Sephardi, and on both sides of his family, a descendant of Italian, Spanish and Portuguese Jews expelled from Spain and Sicily in 1492. He counts among his Portuguese ancestors several distinguished Rabbis who were judges and Cabbalists. As far back as I can remember he always discussed history with me and instilled a love and passion for it which has never cooled. He was conscious of his ancestors and passed that on to me.

As was my father, I, too, am a descendant on both sides of my family of those who left Spain in 1492. My father's presence is always with me when I read or write about the Sephardim. I like to think that I am as inspired as he was.

Harry A. Ezratty
Baltimore Maryland
2022